EVERY
BODY
SHINES

Sixteen Stories about Living
Fabulously Fat

EVERY BODY SHINES

Sixteen Stories about Living Fabulously Fat

Edited by
Cassandra Newbould

BLOOMSBURY YA
Bloomsbury Publishing Inc., part of Bloomsbury Publishing Plc
1385 Broadway, New York, NY 10018

BLOOMSBURY and the Diana logo are trademarks of Bloomsbury Publishing Plc

First published in the United States of America in May 2021 by Bloomsbury YA

Bloomsbury books may be purchased for business or promotional use. For information on bulk purchases
please contact Macmillan Corporate and Premium Sales Department at specialmarkets@macmillan.com

Library of Congress Cataloging-in-Publication Data
available upon request
ISBN 978-1-5476-0607-8 (hardcover) · ISBN 978-1-5476-0608-5 (e-book)

Book design by John Candell
Typeset by Westchester Publishing Services
Printed and bound in the U.S.A. by Berryville Graphics Inc., Berryville, Virginia
2 4 6 8 10 9 7 5 3 1

To find out more about our authors and books visit www.bloomsbury.com and sign up for our newsletters.

To those who still dance in the shadows,
may these stories light the way.
And to my family, I shine brighter with
you, always. —C. N.

CONTENTS

EVERY
BODY
SHINES

✦

Sixteen Stories about Living
Fabulously Fat

INTRODUCTION

Aubrey Gordon, creator of *Your Fat Friend*

My fat friendships came to me well into adulthood. I knew other fat kids in middle school and high school, but we didn't talk about our shared experiences of fatness. I didn't even dare name my body—to do so would've called too much attention to the ways it deviated from a thinner ideal that I was supposed to aspire to.

At that time, before I had the fat community I have now, I longed for someone to tell me that my body was just a body. It wasn't a measure of whether I could be liked or loved. It wasn't an indicator of whether I could be a good friend, a good sibling, a good daughter. It wasn't a reflection of my work ethic or my character. It was simply the shape of my skin. I longed to be understood. And for too long, I didn't know people who could see me as I wanted to be seen.

Fat friendships changed my life.

I was in my late twenties when I first met David, one of my closest fat friends. We were working for the same organization and on a work trip together. We had just arrived at a retreat center for several days of meetings. I looked out over the room, crestfallen and anxious. The comfiest, sturdiest chairs were filled with thin bodies, leaving only a few rickety, lightweight folding numbers. My breath caught in my chest, a windmill powered by gale force anxiety.

That's when David sidled up next to me. "I don't trust these chairs," he told me. "They're not made for fat kids." I laughed, looking out at our choices. As fat people, he and I were both used to spaces that weren't built to fit us, chairs that might give way beneath our abundant bodies. We had both watched, tense and uncertain about what to do, as the seats around us filled up.

"I think I saw a bench outside—want to move it inside?" he asked me. I did. And for the next three days, David and I sat together on what we came to call the Fat Kid Bench.

In years past, I would've been too embarrassed to ask for a chair that fit my body. I would've been too consumed with the idea that my body was at fault. But in that moment, having a new, fat friend made all the difference. Here was someone who *understood*. He wouldn't roll his eyes at my need for different accommodations, nor would he simply brush off my concern, telling me with false confidence that "I'm sure these chairs will be fine."

David understood. He, like me, had broken chairs before. He, like me, was acutely aware of the ways in which our bodies would be afterthoughts to the world around us. And, unlike many of my thinner friends, he was willing to talk about what it was like to be fat. He didn't recoil at the sound of the word, which meant we could talk about what it was like to live in bodies like ours. So we did. And we do.

Fat friendships—like my friendship with David—changed everything for me. With fat friends, for the first time, I could describe my body as fat (it is, by any measure) without someone else gasping and insisting, "Sweetie, no! You're not fat!" I could order a salad without someone else suggesting I must be trying to lose weight, or I could have an ice cream sundae without being met with judgmental stares. My fat friends understood that fat people do everything thin people do—we're just not always given the space to do it. With my fat friends, I can cook, eat, exercise, go swimming, go shopping—all with plenty of understanding and no judgment.

Whether or not you've got fat friends you can rely on, if you're like me, the stories in this collection will have you feeling understood, validated, seen, and celebrated. In Nafiza Azad's "Dupatta Diaries" and Chris Baron's "Food Is Love," you will learn about loving your family even when they don't always know how to love you back. Catherine Adel West's "Orion's Star" will teach you that you aren't just a star, you're a whole constellation, even if those around you struggle to connect your dots. You'll get ready for the prom, and get some much-needed support from friends and family, in Jennifer Yen's "A Perfect Fit" and Alex Gino's "Prom Queers." You'll see yourself as a fantasy or science fiction lead—maybe for the

first time—in stories from amanda lovelace, Hillary Monahan, and Sheena Boekweg. You'll find your strength, both
emotionally and physically, in Monique Gray Smith's "Filling the Net." In these sixteen stories you will watch fat
people take center stage in ways you may not have seen before.
You will see yourself reflected, and where you don't, you will
feel yourself growing in real time, expanding your world to
include experiences beyond your own.

Because like anyone else, fat or thin, you deserve the
world. And you deserve a world that knows that.

The world we live in has a lot of rules for fat people. We
aren't supposed to call ourselves fat. We are only supposed to
acknowledge our fatness as a short stop—a temporary set-
back on the road to thinness. We confuse and sometimes upset
people in our lives when we take joy in our bodies, and celebrate them as they are, whether or not that's where we want
them to be forever.

Telling stories like the ones in this collection—and stories like yours—is part of how we change the world around
us. It's also how we find each other, find solidarity and connec-
tion in a world that makes that harder than it needs to be.

So read on. Find each other. Find you. Be your most
glorious fat self, even when the people around you don't understand it. Read these stories. Tell your own. And yes, change
the world.

GUILT TRIP

Claire Kann

Mia pulled the last roller out of her hair. She twisted it back into shape with quick, careful movements. Using a hair pick, she fluffed her roots, giving her curly, heart-shaped afro more volume. She turned her head to the left and then to the right. The glitter she'd dusted on the tops of her cheeks caught the light.

Not bad. Mia smiled at her reflection. Not bad at all with twenty minutes to spare.

"Mia?" Her dad, Rudy, knocked on the open door. He was cute like that—respecting her space by giving fair warning before he walked in. She appreciated the effort and made a point to terrorize him a smidge bit less in return. Sometimes.

"Perfect timing. I just finished getting ready." She stood up, smiling brighter than the summer sun glaring through her open windows.

Her dress was *the* perfect shade of sparkling midnight blue. Squared, slightly puffy three-quarter-length sleeves. Fitted under her bust and flared at the bottom, optimized for twirling. Her sister, Maddie, had sewn four buttons down her centerline, pale turquoise and white—the same colors and spotted cloud pattern as on her bass.

Finding cute and trendy clothes in her size was always an uphill battle, followed by free-falling into a very special kind of hell only fat girls could understand. But for once, fate took her by the hand and led her to the winning dress with minimal bruising.

Still, deep in her heart, a nervous twitch of doubt showed up like clockwork. "What do you think? How do I look?"

"Oh. *Oh.*" Rudy covered his mouth with one of his hands. "When did you get so grown up?"

"Dad, that's not a compliment. *Come on.* Give me the goods."

"Sorry, sorry. Lost myself for a second there," he said, laughing. "What are the kids saying these days? Beautiful? Radiant? Luminous?"

"Goddess-tier?"

"Ares is holding Aphrodite back as we speak."

Mia spun in a preening circle. "Take my picture." She tossed him her phone, immediately posing after.

Rudy knew all her best angles, as expected of her newly promoted partner in crime. "I think that's good," he said, returning her phone.

"I checked the traffic. It's clearing up, so we should be good to leave now. I kind of want to get there a little early, you know? Get a feel for the room, get my bearings."

A few months ago, Mia's favorite band, Pumpkin Spice, had announced their summer tour with a twist: at each stop, a fan would perform a mini-set with them, any position for three whole songs. To enter the contest, fans had to submit a video of them playing or singing a Pumpkin Spice song live. Whichever submission received the most votes for their selected tour date would win.

Tonight would be the best night of Mia's life.

Rudy cleared his throat, gaze drifting toward the ground. His smile disappeared.

She knew that look—dreaded it with every fiber of her being. "Oh no. Oh no, no, no."

"About tonight."

"You can't do this to me."

"There's been—"

"I'm wearing my perfect dress on my perfect night. You are not allowed to finish that sentence!"

"I'm sorry, sweetie."

Mia didn't whine or cry. Made of equal parts steel and snark, she squared her shoulders and looked him in the eyes. "Dad, you *promised*. We don't break promises."

"We don't break promises *unless there's a good reason*. Why do you always leave that part off?"

"Because it's convenient for me, obviously." She couldn't make him suffer through a proper guilt trip if she acknowledged that "unless" clause.

"We're short-staffed. Frank knows how important tonight is. He wouldn't have called if he had any other choice."

"That's not an emergency. You're always short-staffed."

"But there could be. That's the entire purpose of a fire station—to be there in case of an emergency."

"What's more important? A fire that *might* happen or your daughter's first live performance? The scales should be tipping in a hereditary direction, *Dad*."

"Maddie's on her way. We've got it all worked out."

Mia muttered, "She wouldn't have to be on her way if she still lived here."

Maddie had agreed to marry a sentient pile of bad luck in a human skin suit, aka Michael. Ever since the engagement party, misfortune had settled around her family like white on rice. Weird accidents, hospitalizations, unexpected bills, failed tests, canceled plans, and mysterious work shifts that suddenly *only* her dad could fill—thank God Mia had won the contest before Michael popped the question and ruined everything. He was strictly forbidden from coming to her show. She'd only asked for two tickets to prove her point.

Rudy continued, "Maddie's going to record the show. We'll watch it together tomorrow."

But Mia *needed* her dad to be there. With her sister gone, moved out and living with Michael (Meyers the Thirteenth), she hadn't exactly been doing well. She was moody. Surly. Yell-y. Stomping past Maddie's old room during the day and crying in there at night.

The contest was suddenly a shining star worth holding on to.

And her dad had *understood*. He didn't laugh, didn't say she wasn't good enough yet. No, Rudy, the most amazing dad to ever dad, scheduled a Friday night off work to be the cameraman for her submission. It was his idea to shoot at sunset on a cliff in the hills. He thought the weather would be unreliable (which it was), so he packed a fan to create Beyoncé-style hair wind. He even chose her song and brought a portable battery for her amp and microphones to pick up the sound better.

While the rest of the submissions were full of people just sitting in front of the camera, showing off what they could do, her dad had single-handedly turned her one shot into a full production. And she'd won—almost ten thousand votes between Mia and second place.

Now he wouldn't even get to see what they'd worked so hard for.

"It won't be the same." Pouting wasn't her style, but disappointment weighed her down against her will.

"Please don't be sad, sweetie. I'm sorry. I promise I'll make it up to you."

"Unless there's a good reason not to."

Rudy sucked in a breath. "Walked right into that one, huh?" He crossed his arms and leaned against the wall. No one pulled off saddened amusement quite like he did. In this case, she figured he was sad because he had to cancel even though he genuinely wanted to be there and he was amused by how ruthless she was about it.

Mia would never admit it out loud, but she understood. It wasn't the first time he had to cancel on her because of work, and as long as he insisted on being gainfully employed, it wouldn't be the last. He was the kid who'd declared in kindergarten that he wanted to grow up to be a firefighter and *meant* it.

However. Mia was honor bound to lay a guilt trip as thick as she could manage on him about it per the Jackson Family Code of Ethics. If he thought he could let his guard down because Maddie was gone, he was gravely mistaken.

Mia couldn't have him getting lazy on her. She needed to keep him on his toes.

"You know what would make me feel better?"

Rudy sighed.

"I could drive myself."

"With what license? In whose car?"

"Questions like that will only matter if I get caught," Mia said. Fifteen was *not* too young to start driving. "Since Frank needs you so bad, tell him he has to come pick you up, and you can leave me the car."

"You don't know how to drive."

"I think it's fair to say that's debatable."

"Playing Mario Kart is not the same as taking driver's ed."

Mia pursed her lips. "It can't possibly be that hard. I feel like it's one of those things where confidence will get you ninety percent of the way there. And I got that in spades."

✦ ✦ ✦

Sitting on the couch in front of the living room window, Mia watched her dad drive away without her.

Rudy had a laugh like sunshine, bright and full of warm promise, and a face that could make anyone trust him—shaped like a U with a dimple in his chin. He was tall and gangly, all big hands and larger feet.

Mia wished she looked more like him. Her round cheeks and pointy chin, thick calves, and muscular thighs seemingly came from nowhere.

Old pictures showed her that she didn't inherit her mom's sharp cheekbones or delicate wrists. Videos drove it home that she missed out on a swan-like neck, sturdy shoulders, and svelte legs. Her mom had been a dancer, a defiant Black prima ballerina with grace and style to spare.

Mia never got a chance to meet her.

But they were both performers. Her mom had twirled around stages in pointe shoes. Mia learned how to dance with her bass. And just like her dad, she was devoted to her passions.

Mia's phone rang. She grabbed it—5:00 p.m. Still good on time. "Hello?"

Maddie said, "Hi, I love you, don't get mad."

"Oh my God." Her blood pressure spiked *immediately.*

"There was an accident on the freeway. I've been parked, actually parked, on the overpass for twenty minutes."

"Why did you take the freeway? It's five o'clock! What were you thinking!?"

Mia imagined Maddie in her car, windows down because she hated using the AC, hands strangling the steering wheel while she fought against all her road rage impulses. Neither of them looked like their parents, but they did resemble each other a little. They had the same nose, same shade of warm brown skin, same kinky hair, same unruly eyebrows, and gave the Super Mario Bros a run for their money. Maddie, tall and lanky like Luigi. Mia, short and stocky like Mario.

"I was thinking of my precious baby sister and how cute she's going to look onstage in her perfect dress with the buttons I made for her," Maddie said. "Clearly, I was beside myself with sisterly affections and not at all responsible for my bad decisions."

"That doesn't work on me."

"If an earthquake hits right now, there's a 99.99 percent chance I will die, plummeting to a crushing death, so per the Jackson Family Code of Ethics, you are legally not allowed to be mad at me."

Mia stared straight ahead at the wall. She herself might have been ruthless, but Maddie was brutal. How Rudy had survived raising both of them alone was a true mystery of the universe.

Maddie continued, "If your last words to me are in anger, you will regret it for the rest of your life. Do you really want that kind of suffering hanging over your head? You have to say you love me and I'm the greatest, most spectacular sister ever."

"I'm supposed to be at the venue at six," Mia said in a plaintive tone.

"And you will be because I have a plan. I called Michael."

"*Oh no.*"

"He just got off work, and he's closer to you than I am."

"Don't do this to me."

"He's on his way to come get you."

"Why do you hate me?"

"I gave him strict instructions to film everything and yell louder than everyone there."

"Screw you both! I'll just walk!"

"Mia! What part of 'I love you, and you're the greatest, most spectacular sister ever' was unclear?!"

ı ı ı

"Hey, Mia. It's Michael."

Mia sighed. "Yeah. I know. Caller ID is a thing." Still in the living room, she'd been waiting with her bass and packed bag, looking hopefully out the window like an adorable puppy waiting to be adopted, unaware that Cruella De Vil was about to show up because she wanted a new coat.

She had never felt so pathetic in all her life.

"Oh, sorry," he said. "I'm on my way, but please don't get mad, okay? There was an accident and—"

"NO." She hung up the phone.

✦ ✦ ✦

Mia had been looking forward to this day for weeks. She practiced her songs twice a day, at different speeds while blindfolded to challenge herself. She knew exactly what she wanted to say to the band, brought them all little gifts to say thank you for creating music that endlessly inspired her.

Come hell or high water, she would get to that venue.

According to the bus website, if Mia took two different buses and walked a mile, she would make it to the venue by 6:15 p.m. She emailed her contact to let them know she'd be late. They weren't exactly happy (neither was Mia) but said they would make it work. The opening act went on at 6:30 p.m., and the show itself started at 7:30 p.m. The Pumpkin Spice members needed at least twenty minutes with Mia to go over logistics for her feature.

Her perfect platform shoes were for show, not walking, so she changed into some tennis shoes, slung her bass onto her back, snuggled her cat goodbye, and marched out of the house.

Within minutes she began to sweat.

Her makeup had taken an *hour*. If she could see what the humidity was probably doing to her hair, she'd start crying.

The brown bus stop bench came into view at the same time as a familiar, and obnoxiously red, Jeep turned the corner onto her street.

"Mia!" Michael slowed down. "Where are you going?"

She ignored him.

He made a three-point turn to drive beside her as she walked. "Didn't Maddie tell you I was coming?"

"Go away."

"I got here as soon as I could."

"Good for you!"

"Come on, we're gonna be late."

"We're? There's no 'we're.' Leave me alone and take your bad luck with you."

"I don't have bad luck," he said. "Why would you say that?"

"Because you do!"

A car blared its horn as it sped past him. He drove closer to the curb and turned on his hazard lights.

"Mia, come on. Just get in the car. Maddie will kill me if I don't get you there on time and make a video."

"I'm already late."

"And you're making it worse. Why are you so stubborn?"

"Stop harassing me!"

The car tires screeched. Mia kept walking. Her stop was only a few feet away, bus scheduled to arrive in four minutes. She didn't want to talk to him. She didn't want anything to do with him. He ruined *everything*.

"Will you stop?" Michael grabbed her arm.

Mia spun around, pointing one threatening finger. "Don't do that."

"Sorry," he said immediately. "Very sorry."

Michael was two inches shorter than Maddie. Mia knew that because it was the first thing Maddie had told her about him after their first date. Other than that, he looked like Maddie's ideal type—lean yet muscular, big expressive eyes, a goofy smile, and a patchy beard that somehow worked on him. He must have come straight from work because he was still wearing a dress shirt, slacks, polished shoes, and a tie.

Mia started walking again, and he kept pace with her. "Why won't you let me give you a ride?"

"I don't need one. I'm taking the bus."

"I promised your sister—"

"My dad promised me and canceled. My sister promised him and canceled. And now, you promised her. Do you see the pattern yet?"

"Point taken. But I'm actually here. That should count for something."

"No, it doesn't because you're the reason they're not here. I don't need you." She sat down on the bench, holding her bass close to her front. "Go away."

Seven agonizing minutes later, the bus had yet to show up. If she lifted her arms, there'd probably be giant stains on her pits. Her bottom lip had developed a disgusting tremble. She kept biting it to keep it still.

And worst of all, Michael had sat silently next to her the entire time. "If we leave now, we can still make it."

Mia knew that. She *knew* that. But accepting help from Michael would be like making a deal with the patron saint of calamity. Sure, her prayers would get answered, but at what cost? "If I get in your car, you'll probably get a flat tire in the middle of an intersection, and no tow trucks will be available for an hour. Promise effectively broken."

"That's oddly specific." He shook his head. "It's unlikely to happen, whereas you will definitely miss your performance sitting here waiting for the bus."

She checked her phone. 5:40 p.m. The venue was a smooth twenty minutes away by car.

"I won't make a promise since you're sensitive about those," he said. "If I get a flat tire, I will call you an Uber to take you the rest of the way."

"You can call me an Uber now."

"You're out here slandering my good name with bad luck. At least give me a shot to clear it."

Mia's left leg began to bounce. She peered down the street one last time—nothing. Not a single rumble of exhaust to be heard. Out of time and officially out of options, Mia stood up quickly before she could change her mind. "Fine."

As soon as Michael started the car, the air kicked on, and Mia sighed in relief. She pointed all the vents at herself.

"Foot belt," he said.

Mia dug through her purse, searching for her makeup bag to touch up her face.

"See?" Michael asked as he drove. "Nice and safe. So far, so good."

"You're still bad luck," she said, and fixed her lipstick. Everything else seemed surprisingly okay. God bless Jackie Aina and her thirteen steps to immovable makeup glory.

"I'm—" he began, but then paused. "Is there a reason why you keep saying that?"

"For one, my bus didn't show up today."

Michael scoffed. "According to Maddie, Sacramento had crappy public transportation way before I moved here."

"Two: The pipe burst in the bathroom during your engagement announcement."

"Freak accident. Hardly my fault."

"Three: I got food poisoning from 'the new family' dinner."

"So did I. We both suffered from Maddie's cooking. Doesn't count."

"Four: My dad got hurt at work and had to be hospitalized for two days."

"There's no logical way you can pin that on me."

"Luck isn't logical," Mia said. "Five: My sister moved out on my birthday weekend."

"Oh. Well. Okay, I admit the timing on that one was *terrible*, but we didn't have a choice."

"*She* did have a choice. And she chose you." Maddie crossed her arms and stared out the window.

"Ah," he said. "I'm not trying to point fingers, but it sounds like you're actually mad at Maddie and not me. I'm just an easier target. It's cool. I don't mind being your punching bag. If I had a great sister like Maddie and someone asked her to marry them, I'd be upset too."

"This is the most important day of my life so far, and no one in my family is going to be there. I'm way past upset."

"Wow. Uh." He cleared his throat. "That didn't hurt. Nope. Not at all. I'm fine," he said, voice straining. "Yep. Totally fine."

"You're only proving my point." She rolled her eyes. "You don't even know how to give a proper guilt trip."

"I know, and I've been *practicing*. Maddie is so good at it. Half the time, I don't know what hit me."

"The best offense is a good defense. You have to stay ready with her."

"That's what I figured." He laughed. "Maddie loves you. A lot. Like, a scary amount. When she called me this afternoon, she was screaming at me in panic because she knew she wasn't going to get to you in time, and she knows you're mad at her. This was supposed to be her 'triumphant return to Mia's good graces.' Her words, not mine."

"I don't think she wants you to tell me that."

"You're probably right," he said. "But you're her sister, which means you're going to be my sister—"

"That's not what that means."

"That's what I'd like it to mean. I'm not trying to take her away from you," he said. "It's more like I was hoping she'd share her family with me because I don't have one."

"I know," Mia sank down in her seat, feeling like absolute trash. She knew about that too—he'd grown up in group homes. Plural as in more than one. He didn't know his parents at all.

Mia didn't know her mom because she'd died after giving birth to her, but the memory of her was everywhere. Her dad and Maddie made sure of it.

"You probably don't want to hear this, but meeting Maddie was the best night of my life. I went from thinking I didn't have a future to *knowing* I would the *second* she smiled at me."

Mia looked at him then. He kept his eyes forward, lips pressed into a firm line, both hands on the wheel.

"I love her. I love your dad, and I love you. You three are the most important people in my life, which is why I ran three red lights on the way to your house. I could've *died*."

"You can stop now," she whispered, turning her head to hide her reluctant smile. He really had been practicing.

✦ ✦ ✦

From up on the stage, the small club felt like it stretched on forever. The house lights had been dimmed, and the stage lights were hot on her face, but Mia could see the crowd. Her people, other devoted Pumpkinheads, overjoyed to be there, with their phones raised in the air to record the show and take pictures. She caught a few smiles, more thumbs-ups, and someone even shouted, "I voted for you!" making Mia's stomach jump with nerves.

She'd been instructed to stand to the left of the drum kit right next to the actual bassist, Lemon, who promised to let Mia do her thing as long as it sounded good. She squeezed Mia's shoulder. "Don't worry. I got your back," she said.

The opening chords of the first song blasted through the speakers, and instinct took over. Mia's hands moved into place on time, in time, without missing a single beat. She never used a pick, priding herself on her fingerstyle, created by cutting her teeth on the sickest funk and punk rock songs she could find. But too afraid to move forward, she hung in the back, still playing and hating herself.

She'd only ever played in her bedroom. Jumping on the bed, dancing in front of her mirror, and even hanging upside down, until her dad forced her to stop because that was too dangerous.

Mia wasn't shy—she'd never been shy. So why was she afraid to show everyone what she could *really* do?

When the chorus kicked in, Mia hunched against the deafening roar of the audience as they sang and screamed the lyrics even louder than before. She searched the crowd, frantic for a familiar face, one that looked a little bit like hers, but didn't find it.

Instead, there, on the left side, Michael stood alone, his camera held up high, watching her through the screen to make sure the video was perfect for her, for her family.

He wasn't her dad, and he wasn't Maddie, but he was someone there for her and her alone.

Like magic, the tension disappeared from Mia's shoulders, the doubt unraveled and left her mind. She took a confident step forward to the front of the stage and began to dance shimmying and swaying and twirling with the footwork to match. Closing her eyes, she smiled, feeling the music, trusting her body and her bass. Never missing a beat.

"Mia, Mia, Bo, Bia," the lead singer, Apple, sang and laughed as soon as the song ended. "What was *that?* Come *here*, cutie."

Mia made her way toward the center of the stage, performing breathing exercises to calm herself and get ready for the next song.

Apple threw her arm around Mia's shoulder. "So, you're obviously gunning for Lemon's job. Wasn't she amazing?" she asked the crowd. "*My God.*"

Mia laughed, shaking her head as the crowd cheered and started to chant her name. A bubbly joy began to spread inside her, giddy and unexpected. She'd suspected it before, but now she was sure: this was where she belonged—onstage, performing and entertaining.

"Don't be modest. I don't like it," Apple teased. "You're adorable, and I love this dress."

"Thank you," Mia said, and then, "Is it okay if I say something?"

"You're not going to sing, are you? I don't think I can handle the competition."

The crowd began to scream for Mia again.

"No, no, I promise I'm not." Her cheeks began to hurt from smiling so much. "I just want to say thank you to my almost-brother-in-law for driving me here today. Due to a series of unfortunate events, I was thissssss close to not making it tonight." Mia turned to the left. "Thanks for helping me get here, Michael. I still think you're bad luck, though."

She had to keep him on his toes.

SHATTER

Cassandra Newbould

The cargo van is bearing down on me again, and there's absolutely nothing I can do to stop it.

Believe me, I've tried.

I mean, you don't get hit six times in as many days without at least *trying* to stop the van from slamming into you, right? You duck. Dive. Run. You wave your arms and scream like a banshee. Nothing helps. So, here I am, again.

As I fly through the air this time, the thing I pay attention to is the all-encompassing silence. The sound a van makes when it hits a pedestrian is quieter than you'd assume. The world dissolves. Melts like crayons in the blazing Miami sun. Shuts out everything but you and the air. And your brain blanks, and there's overwhelming silence . . . for about half a second, until you slam into the concrete.

That's when all the noise and the pain come rushing back.

Broken flesh on pavement makes for a macabre dance. The asphalt finds a home within my skin, shredding it, and my dignity, as my dress flies over my head.

My luck being what it is, I don't even get the relief of unconsciousness this time. Every little infinitesimal moment goes by in slow motion.

Then I finally think of something else loud and clear: *I never showed the world my six-step! Rae's gonna kill me!* Everyone else gets their life flashing before their eyes. I'm stuck with the realization that maybe I'm just a coward. My older sis, Raegan, always tried to take me out to the clubs I've dreamed of going to. I turned her down. Every single time.

Now I'll never get a chance to show the world, or her, I can dance.

I mean, my body *did* just twist into some pretty sick moves as I flew through the air this time, but the middle of Collins Avenue isn't *quite* where I planned to make my b-girl debut.

"Somebody call 9-1-1!" A man leans down with a notebook in hand, pencil awfully close to my face. "Don't move! Do you hear me, honey? Help will be here soon."

I try to answer, but all I can do is cry. Then I hear Rae's screams, filling in where mine leave off.

"Easy, she's in shock," Notebook Man says in a shaky voice.

"What do we do?" another person asks.

At first they agree the safest choice is to leave me on the street until paramedics arrive. Minutes. Days. Years pass. Raindrops explode against my bare skin. I drift in and out of consciousness. My body shivers hard enough that my teeth chatter.

Traffic flows on. Engines purring as drivers peek to satisfy their morbid curiosity.

"We need to get her somewhere safe," Rae shrieks. "She needs to be off the road!"

"I . . . I don't know if that's—" Notebook Man tries to interject.

Rae doesn't wait to find out what he's insinuating. "Now!"

Is he more worried about my injuries or the fact that it will take all of them to lift me? I am not a skinny girl. But I'm tired. I won't let that be my last memory. *No fucking way.* Tears leak down my cheeks, and I wish I could swipe them away, but I can't move my arm.

Blood-soaked hands grasp my cold, wet limbs with a gentleness I've come not to expect from the Saturday late-morning brunch crowd.

"It's okay, sweetie, help will be here soon." Notebook Man cradles my head in his arms as they lift me into the air. They carry me to the sidewalk and I become the newest installation of Miami's modern street art. Gawking tourists hungry for a free show stand salivating at my demise.

I lie here, thoughts fluttering through my mind like the flash of a camera. Through all that noise, the loudest question circling my head over and over like a vulture is: *Why does this keep happening to me?*

"Why?" I scream to the sky.

One of the onlookers drops her umbrella. Another elbows her sharply and says something unrecognizable. My brain's melting.

Or maybe that's just more rain falling on my head.

Sirens fill the air. Voices fade in and out. The umbrellas move to reveal a few paramedics. The pain's too much to appreciate a guy in uniform. My sigh turns into a grunt when they take my vitals.

"Excuse me, miss, can you tell me what day it is?"

"Uhhh. Friday?"

"Do you know the date?

It takes longer than normal to form words and get them out. "Uh, no. But not because I have a concussion. There's no point knowing the exact date since I've lived this day about seven times now."

His face scrunches in confusion. "Okay, still . . . let me be the judge of that. Can you tell me what happened?"

I blink stupidly up at him. He *never* asks me this question. He asks *Rae*.

The world flexes around us. I see multiples of everyone. The EMT leans over me. His carbon copy reaches for my wrist to check my pulse at the same time he does. It's like we're stuck in a double-exposed photo. When I blink again, the world comes back into focus.

Now there's only one of him. But something's different. Even the tilt of his head has changed. I struggle to breathe. My pulse kicks into overdrive. "My sis and I were, uh . . ." *Can we get in trouble for skipping?* He's a paramedic, not a police officer, but there are officers here.

"Miss?"

Right. "Anyway, I parked over there." My arm tries to lift and point in the direction of my car. I can see it from here, but damned if my arm doesn't want to cooperate. *"Anyway,* the light changed and we went into the crosswalk. Rae was in front of me, trying to convince me I should have gone club-bing with her last night. I said, *'That's not happening.'* And as soon as the words left my lips this van came out of nowhere like it was headed straight for Rae."

I stop talking to the EMT and face my sister for a second as I remember a vital piece of information. I'm almost afraid to mention it, but I manage to blurt out, "You know what the weirdest part is? This time the guy in the van looked a lot like Adrian."

Rae ignores my mention of "this time." Instead, she mum-bles, *"Adrian?"*

A series of emotions flutter over her features before she opens her mouth wide. The sound that leaves Rae's throat next falls somewhere between a strangled cry and primal scream. Her grip is so tight on my wrist that I swear if it wasn't already broken there's a good chance it is now. Rae's face closes down.

Whatever she's going through, it looks like she's doing it solo, so I turn back to the EMT and finish my description. "The van was headed straight for Rae, so I pushed her out of the way. But then another car slammed into the van, and made it slam into me, and then BAM. There I go, flying into the air!" Laughter, on the verge of hysterical, escapes, as snot drips down my face. Or maybe it's more blood.

The paramedic's eyes leak sympathy until I'm drowning in it. *Why are you looking at me like that?* Isn't this time different? My arms clench tight, and the pain in my chest pulses in excruciating waves.

Voices build around us. As a few paramedics clear the area, I notice the guy they pulled out of the van. He leans against a wall while cops put him in handcuffs. I get a good look at his face and gasp . . . It *is* Rae's ex, Adrian! I wasn't hallucinating.

Seeing him triggers something in my brain. Memories of each accident loop hit me with the force of a punch. I remember everything.

Adrian in the van.

Rae always begging him to stay with her.

Pleading for forgiveness.

Me fading into the light.

In two seconds Adrian steals the fiber of who we are. Rae becomes a shell of her former self, and I am no more.

I want to vomit. For some reason he's after Rae and I'm the one suffering for it. I wish I could make myself invisible. The last thing I want is his attention. But when Adrian lifts his head, he only has eyes for one thing.

Rae.

And the rage that fills his features turns me cold. He's screaming Rae's name over and over, and words like "slut" and "die" fill the empty spaces between.

Another boy appears at Rae's side. I manage to get a proper look and recognize him immediately. He was driving the car that pushed the van into me.

Blood drips from a cut above his eye. He swipes it away and glances at me with pity before turning his attention to Rae.

We've been here before. I remember you.

When Adrian screams *"Cheating bitch!"* the boy turns.

Rae grabs his sleeve. "No, no, don't. Stay. Please."

Who is he? Why does she care so much?

I doubt this kid will listen to her. He hasn't yet. I try to remember every feature before he runs away. I zero in on a scar that's carved along the side of his cheek. Not something you see every day. But I recognize it. Although I'm certain we've never met, I do know him.

I get to know him a little bit more every time.

He pulls away from Rae with a hurried *"Sorry,"* and runs over to Adrian and punches him straight in the mouth.

Silence.

Rae blanches. Usually this is the moment Rae chases after Adrian. Telling him *she's* sorry (like she's the one at fault for his absolute dickery). I hate it.

I hold myself steady. My time is up. I've never made it past this.

Universe, why are you doing this to us? Why are we stuck?

The timing could just be coincidence, her giving up and my body giving out, right at the same moment. But I won't lie, seeing Adrian act like the victim tends to send me into a fury, which probably isn't the best for my current condition, and that's usually when I blink out, like watching my sister give over her power sends me straight into the light.

But she doesn't do it this time. Instead the world flexes

around us, bending and waving like blades of grass in the wind. Carbon copies of Rae fan out around us. Just like what happened with the paramedic. Some of them run to Adrian. Some hug the new guy. The majority of her clones turn to me, an apology written on their features clear as day.

I blink and the world snaps like a rubber band. All the copies disappear.

Rae straightens, a cold calculation leaking into her stare.

I swear she whispers *"I'm so sorry, Bri, it should have been me . . ."* before she takes off to pull the boys apart. She spits in Adrian's face and yells, "You tried to run me down?! You hit my sister?! You're such a fucking toolshed. We're done, Adrian. You'll never have power over me again. Take a good look, because this is the last time you'll ever see me. I hope you rot in jail."

With every word it's like a scale of armor attaches to her body until she shines. She fills with power. He fades and shrivels.

When Rae looks over her shoulder, searching for me, I try to nod. I'm so proud of her at this moment.

The police separate everyone, taking each boy in a different direction. Rae crumples, wrapping her arms around her knees. Tears slide down her cheeks.

"It should have been me . . ." What happened between Rae and Adrian last night that led to this? *Why didn't I go into the club with her? Why was I so afraid?*

She's been trying to get me to go out dancing with her for the past six months, and I've brushed her off every time. Now maybe I am dying, but *she* was supposed to? Something pulls at me to hold on to this loop and find out what's really going on.

I'm sorry, Rae. I want to be brave like you.

The truth is, I want to dance. I want to be free in my body. I want to be there for her when she needs me. I want to see Adrian get locked away so he can't hurt her again.

Please, please, I promise I'll take more chances, I'll—

Before I finish begging, the world shrinks and the silence builds. I know this part all too well. I try to hang on, but I'm slipping and there's nothing solid to grip. "Uh, I don't feel so good." I try to catch the paramedics' attention.

How can my . . . my . . . my chest hold a flying bird? It hurts. Why is it trying to break my ribs? Stupid bird. My toes. I—I can't-t-t-t f-f-f-feel my—my—my to—

The world continues to blur, faces fading. Everything's so heavy.

Is it too late to live?

This time I promise I'll get out of the car if you just let me live.

I swear.

✦ ✦ ✦

Everything's dark. *Am I dying?* Oh, wait . . .

When I open my eyes, I'm in my car in the parking lot of Club Warsaw and not bleeding out on Collins Avenue anymore. This is new. Different. Every time before this I'd die at the moment Adrian yelled at Rae and travel right back to the second before the van slammed into me.

My body tenses for impact, but no. The van isn't coming.

"Rae, am I dead?" My voice chokes as I wait for my sister to answer. There's no response. I'm alone. I think back to my last few seconds of the loop. Pride swelling in my chest when I remember Rae stuck up for herself . . . *did that change my path? Hers?* I need to find Rae. Now.

I raise my arm experimentally, expecting pain, but it moves easily. My heartbeat stutters. I push through the fear and check the rearview mirror.

I look tired. But not like I've just been hit by a van. There's not a scratch on me. My hair isn't dyed with blood. *What's going on?*

I try to remember everything. The car, the accident . . . I know I should be bleeding out, but I can't hold on to the details. An image of a blurred face sits on the edge of recognition, just out of reach. *Is it the person who hit me?*

Is this a do-over? Maybe the van hit me so hard it flung me into the past. Dunno, but I'm gonna go with it. Otherwise I might just break.

This particular moment in time and place isn't unfamiliar. I've spent the past three weekends before the accident waiting in my car, watching Rae go inside the club, while I work up the nerve to be a part of the world inside the massive, black double doors that lie beyond my fogged-up windshield.

Have I been given another chance to be a real b-girl and not stand on the sidelines, or wait in my car, as life passes me by? Or is this just my purgatory? An afterlife of looking at all the things I missed.

I can't believe I never even left my car. I was working up the nerve to ask Rae to take me out again, but then that stupid van hit me. She stopped asking me to come along last night. I mean tonight. At least I think tonight is last night. Either way, she stopped asking and she isn't here now.

I suppose I don't blame her.

From nowhere my sister's voice fills my mind. *"I'm so sorry, Bri, it should have been me . . ."*

I wish I knew what happened between Rae and Adrian last night. Why he tried to run her over. I do know one thing: tonight will be different. Tonight's the night I leave the parking lot and make it inside. If this is the moment my brain sent me back to live, then I'm done being scared. I want to live like Rae does for once. I want to help us both change our destiny.

A group of kids walk by, teasing one another, smiles bright and shining. The deep timbre of their laughter seeps in through the cracked window.

With one last inhale I unbuckle my seat belt. It's now or never.

I run a hand through my hair, twist it into a quick bun, adjust my shirt, and open the door. *This can't be real.* If I don't want to completely lose it, I need to at least pretend I'm alive. *Right?* I wish I knew how to act.

Inhale. Exhale. Wash, rinse, repeat. You can do this, you've got it. No one is looking.

They're all looking.

I tug at my belt loops, dragging the denim higher over my belly, waiting until the fabric settles onto the dip of my skin, right between the folds it calls home.

No one is looking.

They're all looking.

I walk to the double black doors, and the music is so loud the sound waves push against my hair, vibrating my shoulders. Tickling my neck. Working their way through my pores until they nestle inside me, growing stronger, heavier.

A man says, "ID," arm outstretched, eyes barely registering my presence.

"You—you can see me?" For some reason I thought I'd just ghost by him. That's what dead people tend to do, right?

His brows furrow, a question forming on his lips, so I say, "I mean, usually people treat me like I'm invisible . . . or whatever . . ." I trail off weakly. The dude wasn't paying attention to me before, but now he rolls his eyes.

"If you're looking for Club Goth you're in the wrong place. I'm sure they've got ghosts, and vamps, and whatever else might float your boat."

"Right. No, I think I'm where I should be," I mumble, and dig into my back pocket to pull out my faded rainbow wallet.

Inside the pockets lies my golden ticket, Rae's stolen, fake ID. My chance to experience her secret world. As I pass him the flimsy piece of plastic I stare at my shoes, his knees, his shoulder. Anywhere but his eyes.

"Five bucks at the door, no reentry." He hands the ID back and is already scanning beyond me for his next patron.

That was . . . easier than I thought. I ignore how he's flirting with the girls behind me and shove the ID back in my wallet. One more step and I'm through the doors.

I pay the entry fee to a short girl with a pixie haircut and nose ring and wait in the steamy air for my vision to adjust. Her eyes are lined in blue glitter, and she's wearing a pacifier on a cord that hangs around her neck. I don't realize I've leaned in for a closer look until she giggles. Quickly, I stop look.

The girl's upper lip curls when she takes my money. "Been here before?"

"Me?" I ask, certain she's talking to someone else. When she tilts her head, I answer in a whisper, "First time, but my sis, Rae, is here all the time."

Her eyes widen. "Rae's your sister? Why didn't you say so in the first place? Have fun, baby doll."

Before I can respond, she grabs my hand, stamps it, and drops something small and hard into my sweaty palm.

"What's—"

She stops my words with a shake of her head and lopsided grin. "You'll thank me later. Just remember to stay hydrated! And tell Rae I said what's up." Then she turns to the girls behind me and says in a voice not nearly as welcoming, "You know the drill. Five bucks. Each."

"But, Meg," one girl whines.

I wander off before Meg answers. Meg. She was so

welcoming, so . . . *What. Is. This?* Tiny and round, stamped with a heart, a pill sits innocently in my hand. I want to turn and give it back to her. Drugs aren't my thing.

The other girls surround Meg as they try to talk her into a three-for-one entry. Meg's voice is rising, and I don't want her to think I don't belong. I really don't want her to tell Rae I don't belong here.

The old me would drop the pill and keep walking, but tonight is all about experiencing something new, and if this isn't something new, I don't know what is.

Meg said I'd thank her. I suppose it can't be *that* bad, then. Before I lose my nerve, I swallow the pill. I wander over to the bar and ask for a water. The bartender hands me a glass without a word before turning back to his paying customers.

Swarms of people dance, a sea of souls. Maybe that's why no one notices the dead girl standing right in front of their faces.

Self-consciously, I reach down in an attempt to straighten my shirt. Maybe I should leave, maybe . . .

Something collides into me, and I land on the floor in a tangle of arms and legs.

A girl unravels herself, a sheepish grin playing across her face. "My bad." She reaches out to grab my hand. "Here, lemme help you up."

We sit, and I pull my knees to my chest, face burning.

Her short, dark hair lies casually across one vibrant green eye, and her full lips are pulled into a wide smile that fills her face. "Come on, there's a circle starting. Or are you planning on sitting this dance out?"

I close my eyes. *Deep breaths. You can do this.*

When I peek, she's still zeroing in on me. I dunno if I'm ready to dance in public. I've been practicing breaking for the past two years, and Rae swears I'm as good as her, but I think she's just being nice.

"Uh, I'll pass. Bass feels better down here anyway." I pat the floor next to me. "You can stay if you want?" I ask aloud, but inside all I keep thinking is: *Get a grip, Brianna Moran.* My face burns hotter. Why would anyone choose to stay down here with me? All I need to do is wake up and I'll be back in the never-ending loop of May 13, the day I die. *WAKE UP.*

Nope. Nothing.

The girl shrugs. "Why not?" She lets go of my hand, settling back on the floor, crossing her legs, head bobbing to the music.

The moment I lose contact with her, my grip on reality slips. Not knowing what else to do, I reach for her hand again. Calm envelops me as her fingertips touch mine.

"Do you mind if I hang onto your hand a lil longer? I know this sounds weird, but I sorta need it right now." I seriously sound like a fool. I'm grateful for how dark the club is because my face is pretty much an inferno.

"Don't worry, you'll come down soon. I've been there plenty of times." She winks at me, her smile growing into infinity.

"But . . . I . . . I mean, I'm . . . not really here?" I leave my words hanging without an end. It's not like I can finish that sentence without her committing me somewhere. To be fair, her thinking I'm only high is way more believable than me telling her *hey, by the way, I might be rolling, but I was just in an accident before that. I really should be in an ambulance dying . . . or maybe I'm already dead.*

The longer I'm here, the more the accident seems like a dream. I don't know what's real anymore.

The girl leans up against me, using my shoulder as support for hers, and rests her head against mine. "We are right where we belong. Whatever you're on, can you pass some over?"

"Sorry, it seems I've taken it all. I'm Bri. Nice to meet you."

"Sienna. I don't think I've seen you around here before."

"First time. Inside anyway. My sister comes here a lot, though."

Sienna giggles. "First time inside?"

"Ah, yeah. Usually I just hang out in the parking lot. I mean, I . . ." *Why am I admitting my loser status to a complete stranger? I doubt this is why I've been given a second chance. I mean, seriously, could I be any more—*

"It's all good. I get it." Sienna interrupts my train of thought. "Who's your sis?"

"Her name's Rae. Tall, big brown eyes, bleach blond. Acts like she owns the world."

"Oh *yeah*, she's . . . something. Wanna dance?" Her eyes narrow as she moves her head to the beat.

Dance? People don't ask fat girls to dance. But this is the moment I've been waiting for. The moment I prayed I'd get. I can't let that pass, right?

I open my mind to the beat. It winds its way around every single nerve and squeezes until I can't sit still. I don't just *want* to dance. I need to. And I realize I don't care who watches me at all.

"Yeah, I think I do." I stand and pull Sienna up with me. Her eyes shine in the strobe light as she backs deeper onto the dance floor. I'm transfixed, and it takes me a second to catch up, but then we flow like it was our destiny to be right here, right now. I don't care if I'm dead or alive—I just want to be in this moment forever.

The beat pulses, teasing me to move my body in ways I've only ever done in the privacy of my home. At first the freedom comes slowly, like raindrops exploding against my skin, until all of a sudden the sky pours down. I lift my face and fear washes away.

My arms are liquid as they weave around my body. I spin. My feet slide over the floor. Smooth. I'm melting glass. Bass propels me as I pop and lock and glide into a six-step. Contort my body into a baby freeze to airhook to chair. I almost fall, but catch myself at the last second, swinging my knee to the ground and lifting myself up to a standing position before finishing with a k-kick.

People scream, arms in the air, cheering me on. Sweat drips down my chest, my back, in my eyes. When I focus on Sienna, her mouth hangs open wide.

"Never seen a fat girl dance before?" I laugh so hard it

shakes my entire body until I almost can't breathe. Right now, I'm more alive than I've ever been.

Sienna laughs with me. And we start dancing again as the beat tells our feet where to go.

The energy on the floor builds and builds and builds. We are infinite. We could power the sun.

The time for thinking passed moments ago, and I don't care if I'm ever anywhere but here. It doesn't matter if I'm skinny or fat or scared or brave. This is where I belong. It's where I've always belonged.

Not knowing what else to do, I act on impulse, grabbing Sienna and pulling her close. "Thank you for asking me to dance." The words vibrate when they roll off my tongue.

"Welcome home." Her voice is a whisper that wraps around my heart.

Home.

We lace our fingers together, weaving in and out of the crowd, spinning and laughing.

"I know we just met, but I feel like I've known you forever." I bite my lip and keep talking. "I've never had a friend into"—I spread my arms wide, taking in the entire scene—"this kind of life before. Not really." The words are like poison as they pour from my mouth. *What will she think of me now?* My tongue burns with the admission. Shame has a flavor, one I hope to never taste again.

"I can be your friend. Everyone needs one sometimes, right?" Sienna's words are sincere, and she shrugs like it's nothing.

Maybe it's nothing to her, but to me, it's everything. I belong.

We find the beat again as it finds us. Sienna has the swag of a true Miami girl. The kind I've dreamed of being. The kind I'm now realizing I already am.

Before we get too far into the next song, a boy in a hoodie jumps in front of us, blocking our path. "Hey, Sea, nice moves. Who's this?"

His features hide in shadow, but his voice has the same lilt as Sienna's, only deeper.

"None ya business, Tino." Sienna turns to me and starts to pull. "Let's get out of here."

The boy grabs her arm. "Wait, Sea, you're not dipping. Mom would have my head if you just left me here."

"You're such a wuss. It's not my fault you snuck out." Sienna turns from her brother and looks at me. "You coming or what?"

"Seaaaa."

"Bro, chill. We'll stay a lil while longer, 'kay?"

Tino turns to me. "So, you Sea's new chick or what?"

Shaking my head at the thought, I laugh. "I'm no one's girl."

"I'm gonna go grab us a few waters. Be right back." Sienna takes off without a backward glance.

Tino nods at her retreating figure and turns to me. "Never seen you before."

"Nope. I've been out of town." A giggle escapes before I can stop it.

"You're a strange one."

"Says the guy wearing a hoodie in a hot club." I reach up and touch the edge of his hood, pushing it back ever so slightly. Tino stands still, but lets me reveal his face. There's no way I know this guy, but I stare, trying to remember where I've seen him before. Bright eyes like Sienna's look back at me, set in more masculine features marred only by a long scar that travels from the bottom of his right eye down the length of his cheek.

I whistle. "Man, that's a beauty."

"Whatever." Tino swipes my hand away and pulls his hood close, but before he can cover his face again, I reach out and stop him.

"Sorry, I was being serious. It really is beautiful. Your whole face, in fact. Don't hide." I continue to pull his hood away. That must be why I feel like I know him: he's enough like Sienna that he could be her twin.

Sienna sidles up, breaking the moment and taking in the scene between us as she passes around the water.

"Ah, Ti, you've come out to play. Nice to see you." She reaches out and rubs his head as she leans in and whispers something to him.

Tino digs in his pocket and discreetly hands her his cell. When she looks up her face pulls into a frown. "Oh, if it isn't Miss Thing herself," Sienna's voice growls as she peers over my head at someone behind us.

I turn toward the entrance. Like magic, ghosts breeze in. Rae!

She strides toward Meg, swinging her arm up into a high five. Alongside her, six feet and three inches of the biggest jerk I've ever met grabs Rae by the shoulder and pushes her past Meg.

It's Adrian. I'm surprised to see them together. She broke it off with him last month because he was too controlling. Looks like he hasn't gotten the hint. Or maybe she's giving him another chance. I hope not. He doesn't deserve it.

Rae shrugs out of Adrian's grasp, pushing him away and walking quickly ... from of him. Fulling hing's off. Suddenly my ears ring. My mouth goes numb. Images flash through my mind of the crash, him driving the van, him in hand-cuffs, screaming that he wished she'd die. They hit me hard and fast, drilling into the gaps in my memory. If that really does happen tomorrow, and it will, then something happens here, tonight, to make Adrian want to hurt Rae.

Is that why I'm here? Am I supposed to save her?

"I'm so sorry, Bri, it should have been me . . ."

I spin in a slow circle, searching for something that might be the catalyst for what happens next. Then I land on Tino. Except this time, I really see him. Especially the way his eyes soften, his face relaxes, at the sight of my sister. And when I follow his gaze, I see her light up, smile stretching wide as she sees him.

You'd have to be oblivious to not recognize the affection radiating between them, and if I see it, then . . . *Oh no, no, no, no, no.*

So does Adrian.

I need to warn her about tomorrow. "This can't be happening," I say over and over.

Sienna leans in, calmly whispering in my ear, "Relax, it's all good, you're in a safe space."

She thinks I'm having a bad reaction to the pill.

Am I? Is any of this real?

I can't take the chance it's not. I need to warn Rae and Tino. But what if I screw up? *Could I make us both wink out of existence? Will changing things tonight help me live tomorrow? Does it doom Rae to die if I change our path? Do I get to live?*

Or are my worries all for nothing because I am already dead?

I blink, the club swarming into focus again. Sienna stands by my side as I search for Rae. I see Tino rush across the dance floor, and he accidentally-on-purpose bumps into her. They look at each other like they're the only ones in the room before Adrian steps in between them and squares off.

Rae tries to de-escalate the situation. She mouths the word *please*, fingertips brushing Tino's wrist, before she screams, "I told you to leave me alone. I'm with Adrian."

Tino takes a step back, face falling. He says her name, but Rae ignores him, grabbing Adrian's hand instead.

Adrian laughs. I can't make out his words. Whatever he says, it's enough that Tino's shoulders sag and he takes off for the door.

I want to yell that Rae's lying. She's just trying to protect him. But I can't. Then Adrian will know too.

What do I do? What can I do? I'm a grain of sand, lost in a turbulent sea.

Sienna turns as if she's torn between us.

"Go on, I'll be okay here."

She looks down in defeat at the cell still in her hand. "Maybe I'll get your number another time?"

"Yeah, I'd like that."

The door shuts behind Sienna. I may never see her again. I almost run after her, but I'm pulled back to Rae and Adrian ⁙⁙⁙⁙⁙⁙⁙ ⁙⁙ ⁙⁙⁙ ⁙⁙⁙⁙ ⁙⁙⁙ ⁙⁙ ⁙⁙⁙ ⁙⁙⁙⁙⁙ floor. He's dragging her to the door.

I need to stop them. Then the door closes behind them. I'm too late. I'm always too late.

My ears ring. I try to take a deep breath. It gets stuck somewhere between my throat and my lungs.

The bird returns to my chest, beating its wings so hard against my breastbone that this time I'm certain it'll burst through. I try to hold on to this reality, not wanting to let go of the way I feel, of Sienna, or my need to find Rae. The universe isn't done with me yet. I scream as my world breaks apart, the shards ripping and tearing me to pieces.

✦ ✦ ✦

The sunlight is so bright I shield my eyes.

"Thanks for coming along, it'll only take a minute." Rae walks with her hands in her pockets.

I blink. *Where am I now?* "Sure. It's not like I had anything better to do."

"I just need you to know that whatever happens next is going to happen for a reason, so you can't lose it, okay? I need you to be a witness. I need you to get this other guy to be a witness. It'll all be over soon." Rae says that last part as if to herself.

"A witness? To what?" I don't like the sound of this.

A hard determination lights in her eyes. "You'll see."

"Maybe we should go home." I place a hand on her arm. She comes to a halt and finally looks at me. Her face is strained. Traces of glitter dust her cheeks.

My body remembers the bass, the humid club, eyes greener than my envy, and a smirk that sets my heart to pounding. It all hits me then. Today is the day. *The* day.

I die today. And I don't remember this part. At all.

"Look, Bri, I know we don't always get along. And I know you think I'm Mom's fave or whatever, but I need you to know that I can't do this without you and I'm really happy you said yes."

What did I say yes to? "Uh, yeah, about that. Could you repeat it one more time? Nerves, ya know?"

Rae punches my shoulder gently. "Ha. Like any of this is forgettable. All you've got to do is hand that envelope over to the guy who will be waiting at Jamrock. He's the witness I was talking about. I know you don't understand, but you two are my ticket to freedom. It will all make sense soon, promise. And make sure you're crying when it goes down. Adrian needs to believe that I'm dead or this won't work, got it?"

"Adrian? Dead?" My mouth hangs open as I try to process her words.

Rae tilts her head as she examines me. "Last night you promised you could do this. I can trust you, right?"

Can she? What did I promise?

"Bri!"

"Yeah, of course." I hope she can trust me. I wish I could remember.

"I owe you." Rae looks at her cell. "Okay, it's time."

As if on cue, rain starts to fall. Big warm drops, the kind that are guaranteed to soak you through. Typical Florida springtime. I let it wash over me, wishing it could wash away all my insecurities.

Rae pulls me along, grumbling about the rain. I barely notice where we are, what we're doing, as I try to remember what we talked about last night. Then Rae lets go of my shirt and yells to someone behind her, "Take your hands off me!"

Rae turns to the newcomer and says, "I can't believe you followed us."

Sienna. *Why is she here now?* My heart pounds as my body remembers last night. Of course. Meeting her must have changed the loop again. I smile shyly, but the only person Sienna has eyes for is Rae, and it seems like she's about two heartbeats away from pounding Rae into the ground.

She pushes Rae again, saying, "If you think Tino's gonna do some wack stunt like this and I'm just gonna sit back and let it happen, you're crazy."

"Sienna, it's the only way. He's not going to hurt me. He's not going to get in trouble. I swear." Rae's voice breaks.

"You don't know that!"

"Adrian will kill us before he lets me go. It's the only way."

"Maybe you should have thought about that before now!"

"I love Tino. We're just trying to get out of here. Please, Sienna. I need to do this."

It's then I really take in our surroundings. We're on the edge of a sidewalk. My body freezes as I recognize the street. Lights flash in front of my eyes. My tongue turns sour with the bile that crawls up my throat. This is where it happens.

I must look like I feel because both Rae and Sienna stop arguing to stare.

It's then that Sienna really notices me. "Who are you?"

She doesn't know who I am.

"Rae's sister," I say, as Rae says, "This is Bri."

"Yeah, whatever. Look, Rae—"

My heart drops with her dismissal. *This means last night didn't happen? And if it didn't happen, then what did?*

I take a step toward them. "Sienna, maybe we can just talk about it? I mean, she's obviously desperate or she wouldn't be doing this in the first place, right?" I wish I knew what "this" was, but I can't ask. Rae already doubts my loyalty.

"You seem chill, Bri, really. But I love my brother, and I can't let you do this, Rae. There has to be another way." Sienna loops an arm around Rae's waist, pulling her from the crosswalk.

Rae screams, fighting her way to freedom. At first I

don't think she'll make it. Then she turns, eyes pleading. "Help me."

I stand like a statue, torn between a promise I have no memory of and a girl who doesn't remember me.

The hope in Rae's eyes is replaced by a rage that most people never see. She yanks back, dragging Sienna into the street with her, one step at a time. They're screaming and pulling and punching, and if I don't do something fast they're going to beat the crap out of each other, and I still have no idea why.

I try to break them up, but Rae slips through Sienna's hold. The momentum sends her straight into me. I gasp at the impact and stumble as I try to overcorrect on the slippery surface. As I stumble to a stop in the crosswalk, I stand taller, happy to not have fallen in front of them.

I try to wave to let them know I'm okay. The rain is coming down so hard now that their faces blur.

Rae shrieks, "Adrian, no!"

And something hits me. I think I've swallowed my tongue, that the world has detonated, that maybe I never existed at all.

"Bri!" Rae and Sienna scream, their voices torn and tortured.

"I'm so sorry, Bri, it should have been me . . ." echoes all around me. It finally makes sense.

It was Rae's plan to get hit this entire time. She wanted a way to escape Adrian.

My whole life I've stooped in Rae's shadow. Unnoticed,

unwanted. As I fly through the air I feel two sets of eyes on me, and I know, bone deep, that they want me in this world. That they need me, like I need them.

I don't want to die. I want to be seen. I want to live. I deserve it. I always have. We all do.

The only problem is, it might be too late.

✦ ✦ ✦

Yellow light seeps between my eyelids. They flutter open beneath warm salt water.

A voice far away yells, "Clear!"

As the electric energy flows through my body, it's like years pass as I float through the space of my thoughts.

I need to get back to Rae and tell her we are more than we think. We deserve so much more. Like the universe hears me, everything rushes in at once.

And then, the world stops moving.

✦ ✦ ✦

I carefully open my eyes. Sunlight sneaks in through cracked blinds. Something tickles me. Makes me want to sneeze. I lift a bandaged hand to my face and feel tubes in my nose.

"Hey, don't touch those," Rae says gently.

I blink the fogginess away. Rae, Tino, and Sienna stand around what I'm guessing is a hospital bed. Rae and Tino hold hands. Adrian is nowhere in sight.

"Your sis is sort of a badass," Sienna says, tucking a strand of hair behind her ear.

I am? What did I do? I search Rae's features, trying and failing to figure out what's going on.

"Well, it's not every day you can say your sister saved your life, you know," Rae says. Her eyes glisten with unshed tears. We stare at each other, and in that moment it occurs to me that we might have a future again.

Rae mouths *I love you* to me before she turns back to Sienna and says smugly, "You thought *that* was badass? You should see her on the dance floor."

"Oh yeah?" Sienna looks down at me and says, "Looks like you're gonna have to get better now."

"Why's that?" I struggle with the words. My chest is on fire.

"Oh, I dunno, guess you'll have to heal up to find out." She winks before letting out a soft laugh.

I swear she recognizes me, but I can't ask. I'm afraid to move. For all I know, motion will throw me into another loop, and I'm not ready to let this one go just yet. So instead, I say, "Yeah, I'd like that."

Rae's free hand closes around mine, giving it a squeeze. Then the door opens and Mom and Dad rush in.

"Bri, we've been so worried about you . . ."

It's then I realize we've gone beyond the loop. It's truly a new day. We've got another chance to start over again.

I will not give up. When I wake, I'll be ready for whatever's going to come my way.

I close my eyes, my energy slipping, but I know that I'm falling into a regular sleep and let out a soft sigh. I had to die to realize I want to live, but I do want to live. More than anything. And now I can't wait to see what tomorrow brings.

The sound a van makes when it hits a pedestrian is quieter than you'd assume . . . But the impact? The force? Well . . . it's enough to shatter the world.

PROM QUEERS

Alex Gino

What if we went to prom?"

Sam looked at TJ dubiously. "We aren't exactly the prom-going type, you know."

Eighth grade prom was two weeks away, and black-and-purple signs had been up in the hallways of school for the last month, urging students to get their tickets.

"I know," said TJ. "That's why we'd go together. If the music is good, we dance. If the music is terrible, we hang by the snack table. I heard they're renting a laser machine. How bad could it be?"

"Lasers *are* cool."

Sam and TJ sat on the couch in TJ's basement, watching their favorite cartoon, *Peppermint Pirates and the Legions of Licorice*. They'd seen every episode at least five times, and could recite most of them, but it was comforting background entertainment, especially for important conversations.

"Wait, you don't mean like *together* together, do you?" asked Sam. People often assumed that they were a couple, and not just because they were the only out nonbinary kids at school. They were best friends, and cuddly ones at that. At the moment, TJ's head was in Sam's lap and Sam had just paused in stroking the hairline of TJ's tight fade. Sam's own thick dark blond hair was brushed forward and fell just short of their eyes.

"No!" said TJ with a jolt. "That's not our thing."

"I know that," said Sam with relief. "I just wanted to make sure you still felt the same way. I mean, you are demiromantic and all."

"Being demi just means I only get interested once I get to know a person, not that I get interested in every person I know. So, do you want to go to prom—*as friends*?"

"I'll think about it," said Sam.

"We'd get to dress up," said TJ.

"That's part of the problem. The second you get fancy, the clothes get gendered."

"True. But who said we had to wear clothes from all one gender? I'm thinking I can find a pinstripe suit jacket to go with my fuchsia blouse and those heels I got last month at Put a Sock in It." TJ was a fashion whiz. It was no surprise that they had figured out their outfit before even raising the idea with Sam.

"I'll think about it," Sam said again.

Sam and TJ held hands—Sam's thick pink fingers crossing with TJ's long, light brown, sparkly-nailed ones—and they watched *Peppermint Pirates* until it was time for Sam to go. Neither of them said anything else about the prom, but it was all Sam could think about on the walk home. Dancing in the gym with TJ did sound like fun. And they were right—there was no reason that either of them would have to wear clothing from all one gender. But TJ was slim and could get something fantastic to wear at just about any clothing store.

Sam was fat.

Plump, their mom would say. *Heavy-set*, their dad would say. *You have such a beautiful face*, their grandmother would say. But seeing as Sam was neither fruit nor furniture, they preferred to be called fat. And as for their face, it was fine, but ignoring their body was not. They were lucky enough to have been introduced to fat activism a few years ago, and they had learned to admire their large, nonbinary body in the mirror for taking them through the world, lumps and curves and changes and all.

Still, though, there was a difference between feeling good about your body and feeling good about the way clothing looked on your body. For Sam, most clothing looked, and felt, terrible. The few things that fit generally didn't match their gender. Most days, they wore a black T-shirt with some sort of picture or funny saying on it, and they were in a long-term relationship with elastic waistband jeans.

Sam let themself into their apartment, dropped their bag by the door, and switched into fuzzy slippers. On the way back out, they called, "Mom, I'm going up to see Jess!"

"Fine," called Mom from her computer. "But just a short

visit. Casserole's in the oven and we're having family dinner in fifteen."

"Okay," said Sam as they closed the apartment door behind them. They bounded up the flight of worn stone stairs and down the hallway. After their signature *knock-a-knock-a-knock-knock-knock*, they let themself in.

TJ may have been Sam's best friend, but Jess was a close second, even though she was an adult. Jess had a partner and a kid, but she and Sam both loved the original *Muppet Show* and M.C. Escher drawings, and the thread of conversation wove easily between them. They were family, even though they weren't related. And at that moment, she was the perfect person to talk to.

Jess was fat too, with a round belly and thick arms, and she said that was all the more reason to celebrate and decorate her body well. Her jet black hair was cut in a curly bob that framed her rosy white face, and even at home, she wore red lipstick. She said it made her feel special and prepared for whatever might happen. That day she wore a purple dress covered in manatees, along with hot pink leggings. Jess was a master of fashion. She was the first person to introduce Sam to the concept of body sovereignty, the idea that we each have the right to decide what we do with our bodies, and said she planned to live every day as the queen of hers.

Toddler Evie was on the floor, happily playing with a set of blocks. Mostly she was dropping them into a clear, fishbowl-shaped container with her stubby hands and then dumping them out again, but she took breaks to chew on a hard plastic bit now and then. Sam sat with Evie for a few minutes, taking turns dropping plastic pieces into the bowl, before hopping on the fluffy couch across from Jess.

"TJ invited me to prom."

"Is that a good thing or a bad thing?" Jess asked, which was exactly the reason Sam came to talk to her instead of Mom. Mom would be too busy getting excited to find out whether Sam even wanted to go.

"Good? I mean, I think it'll be fun."

"Cool."

"Yeah . . ." Sam trailed off into a hint for Jess to ask what the hesitation was.

"So," said Jess on cue. "What's the hesitation?"

"Well, it's just that dressing up means, you know, fancy clothes." Sam gestured down. They were wearing a black T-shirt with a molar standing on a boat below the words Tooth Ferry.

"Fancy clothes are fun!" said Jess.

"For you, maybe," said Sam. "Femme clothes are easy."

Jess laughed. "I wouldn't say *easy*, especially getting fabulous dresses in a 4X, but I get your point. What kind of clothing would make you feel fancy?"

Sam paused to think, but before they could form an answer, Jess's partner, Val, came home. They dropped their backpack on the table, kissed Jess lightly on the lips, and flopped onto the couch hard enough that Sam popped up a bit on the other end.

"Hey, Sam!" they said. "How's things?"

"Not too bad. How was work?"

"Worky. What have you two been talking about?"

"Fashion," said Jess.

"Ahhh." Val nodded. "Good times." They wore a dark vest over a white button-down shirt and red bow tie, and their hair was cut short, especially on the sides.

"We were just talking about nonbinary ways of getting a little fancy, my dapper sweetie."

Val framed their round, copper face with their hands in a series of poses, as though they were showing off for an imaginary camera.

"You would look charming in a vest and tie," said Val once they had finished preening. "We could even get you a cap. Maybe a newsie."

"Thanks," said Sam. "But that's a little . . ."

"Too butch?" asked Jess.

Sam nodded. They weren't entirely comfortable using the word "butch" themself, but Jess and Val tossed it around as easily as any other word.

"I mean . . ." Sam scratched the back of their neck. "Vests are cool, but all of it?" They vaguely gestured around their body with hands spread wide. "Too much."

"Is that so?" Val asked.

"For me, I mean," said Sam. "It looks great on you."

"Thanks." Val smiled, revealing dimples.

Jess's phone buzzed. "Your mom texted. She said that I should remind you that you are on a short visit and that you should be at the dinner table in two minutes."

"If it's eggplant rollatini, sneak your portion up here." Val grinned. They loved Sam's mom's rollatini. Sam thought it tasted like rolls of soggy rubber coated in oily bread paste and tomato sauce, and there was never enough cheese on it.

"If it's eggplant rollatini, she'll send some up. She always does."

✦ ✦ ✦

That weekend, Sam and TJ went to Buy. Sell. Repeat., TJ's favorite secondhand clothing shop. Sam had been there before, when TJ had dragged them along, but they had never gone with the intention of actually buying something. TJ, on the other hand, was there at least once a month, to check on what had shown up recently.

TJ waved at the person behind the counter, and strode confidently past the furniture and electronics to the back half of the store, where the clothing was. Sam followed.

"Looks like yellow's the color of the day," said TJ.

"I don't see a lot of yellow around." There was one yellow shirt hanging on the end of a long rack, but that hardly seemed to be enough to make it the color of the day.

TJ sighed. "No, I mean, anything with a yellow tag is automatically fifty percent off." They pointed at a sign on the wall with a wheel of colors and an arrow on the yellow wedge.

Sam looked around at the racks of clothing. There were signs that announced sections for Men, Women, and Children, but where was the section for Nonbinary People Whose Best Friend Has Convinced Them to Go to Prom?

"I'm gonna look at jackets," said TJ. "Want to come?"

Sam shook their head. They didn't want to wear a jacket to prom. Especially not if TJ was going to. Whatever TJ wore, they were going to look amazing in, and Sam didn't want to be compared with them.

When TJ dragged them to thrift stores, Sam mostly looked at accessories. Scarves, jewelry, things like that. Once, Sam had bought a black corduroy baseball cap, and had worn it nearly every day until they lost it two months later. When TJ was done fashion hunting, they would meet up in the games and toys section and see if there was anything decent.

Today, though, Sam was on a mission. A mission to find something fabulous for the prom. Maybe if TJ was looking for a suit, Sam would go for a dress. They found a round rack and started to hunt. The dresses weren't organized by size, but most of them were clearly too small. Out of the entire rack, Sam found three that looked like they might fit. Two were navy blue rectangles, the biggest difference between them being that one had white piping around the collar. The third was a satiny red that held some appeal until Sam noticed a large dark stain running down the front.

They half-heartedly looked through the skirts. Again, only a handful in an extra-large, and those were long and dark, like the people who had worn them were trying to avoid having bodies at all. Nothing exciting. Nothing for Sam.

They didn't even bother looking at the tops. Button-down shirts never closed at Sam's neck, or if they did, the rest of the shirt was way too long. And their bumps and curves meant gaps between the buttons, especially since their chest had been growing lately. Just the idea of air seeping in made their sternum feel cold. As for fancy tops without buttons, it was hard to find something without lace or bows or some other decoration meant to say, *please note: this fat person is a woman.*

TJ found Sam looking idly through the jewelry boxes. They wore a pinstripe jacket over their T-shirt, and with their angular face and slender limbs, they looked like Jack Skellington from *The Nightmare Before Christmas.*

"Look." They held up a matching pair of pants. "It's the whole suit! And it's even yellow-tag half price!"

"Wow," said Sam, and they meant it, though it came out sounding defeated. "That's really amazing."

"Did you find anything?"

"Do I look like I found anything?" Sam threw up their empty hands, with more force than they really meant.

"Harsh much?" TJ took off the jacket and headed to the front.

"Sorry, TJ," Sam said once TJ had paid and was heading for the door. "It's not your fault you found something great. I just wish it weren't so hard to find clothes as a fat kid."

"That does suck," said TJ. "You want to go to the mall?"

"NO!" Sam said, startling themself as much as TJ. "I mean, no. I just want to go home."

"Well, we still have time before prom. We can go to the mall next weekend. I'm sure we'll figure out something amazing."

"I hope so." Sam wasn't as certain.

✦ ✦ ✦

Over the next few days, Sam looked online and found some skirts in their size, including a beautiful piece that had the Milky Way galaxy printed across it. It was ninety dollars, though, which Mom and Dad both said was a lot of money to spend for clothing you couldn't try on first, even for prom. Sam thought it was worth at least that much for even a chance at a skirt that fit, especially for prom, but seeing as they only had fifteen bucks, the point was moot.

Tuesday afternoon, they were back up at Jess and Val's. Val was at work and Evie was napping, so it was just Jess, Sam, and the ideal time for a fashion consultation.

"Thrift shopping was a bust," Sam announced. "Well, for me, anyway. TJ found the suit of their dreams."

"Let me guess," said Jess. "Nothing in your size except a couple of dark boxy dresses, maybe one halfway decent number with a big stain on it, and some collared shirts with giant floral prints?"

"I didn't even get to the floral prints, but otherwise, exactly that. TJ said they'd go to the mall with me, but that's no good either. There's only the one store there that ever has stuff that fits me, and their stuff is all, well, too girly for me."

"Clothes from the mall aren't all that great anyway. I was just reading this article last week about 'fast fashion.' So many of those stores are filled with cheaply made clothes mimicking high fashion but that people only wear once or twice before they either fall apart or go out of vogue. And they're not the kinds of things that resell well, and no one wants to recycle them, so they're just piling up as waste."

"I just wish I could design my own style, you know? Something that fits my body *and* my gender *and* my personality *and* I like it. Is that too much to ask for?"

"Not if you're willing to do a little work."

"What do you mean?"

"Do you think everything I buy comes fitted to this beautiful body?" Jess gestured down at her curves.

"Oh, that's right!" Sam remembered that Jess sewed, and that before Evie was born, she used to always have her machine out, with pins and scraps of fabric all over the place.

"So, if you could wear anything fancy you wanted, what would it be?"

"Anything?" they asked.

Jess nodded.

"Well, I've always thought it would be fun to wear a tutu," Sam said shyly. "Not a pink one," they quickly added.

"Of course not a pink one," Jess agreed nonchalantly. "But what about something like a crinoline?"

"A what?"

"A crinoline. People used to wear them under their dresses to puff them out, but these days, they make their own fashion statement."

Jess typed into her phone and handed over a display of crinolines in various colors. Where a tutu is made up of layers of tulle that stick out from your waist, a crinoline is made of the same material but is the full length of a skirt.

"Ohhhh," said Sam. "I want a *crinoline*."

"What color?"

"Is it too much to say rainbow?"

"When it comes to fashion, especially *fat*shion, very little is too much. Give me a couple of days." Jess gave a grin that said her brain was already envisioning a project. "And make sure you have some black leggings and something to wear on top."

✦ ✦ ✦

Can you come over? TJ texted Sam on Sunday morning.

For a bit.

Jess had invited them to come up after lunch to show them her idea for a rainbow crinoline, but that was still a few hours away. Sam walked the five blocks to TJ's house, and TJ was at the door before Sam could ring the bell. They must have been watching them walk down the street from their bedroom window.

They greeted Sam with a giant hug. "So I was thinking about how we didn't find anything at Buy. Sell. Repeat. last week, and I got to wondering whether some other place would have more options. Another secondhand shop, or a thrift store."

"I really don't want to go shopping again." Just the thought of it made Sam feel weak.

"Don't worry. I did it for you." They let a smile shine on their face. "I went to six places, in fact."

"You did what?"

"Who knew how hard it was to find fashionable clothing in plus sizes?"

Sam pursed their lips. "*I* did," they said, but they followed up with a smile. If it was the thought that counted, TJ was worth a million.

"Oh, right. Sorry. Anyway, in the sixth store, I found your fashion Excalibur."

Sam tried not to let themself get excited. TJ wouldn't have bought something if it wasn't amazing, but it wouldn't matter how wondrous it was if it didn't fit.

"Now I know you said Jess was going to help you with some sort of skirt, so I was looking for something that might go with it, and then I found this!"

TJ held out a black silk vest with geometric designs woven throughout the front panels in thin silver fibers that sparkled against the dark fabric. "I remember you saying something about vests being cool. Any interest?"

"Oh, TJ, it's beautiful!" Sam took the vest and ran the smooth silk between their fingers. The tag said it was an XL. Still, they didn't dare breathe until they tried it on, and it fit fantastically. The two buttons at the waist even closed and lay flat. They looked in the mirror and grinned. They spun in a circle, imagining a crinoline below. They smiled again. Then they leaped on TJ with a surprise tacklehug that landed them both on the ground in giggles.

Sam thanked them again, and again, and one more time, between spinning around and looking at the vest in the mirror. It was really happening. They were going to prom! TJ put on their jacket and they danced in the room together to the *Peppermint Pirates* theme song before watching the episode about the day the pirates sailed onto Gumdrop Island and ate the king's son by mistake.

✦ ✦ ✦

After lunch, Sam *knock-a-knock-a-knock-knock-knock*ed on Jess's door and let themself in.

"Wow!" said Jess. "Look at you!"

"You like it?" Sam beamed. They were wearing their new vest over a plain black T-shirt, along with the black leggings Jess had recommended.

"I love it! Where'd you get it?"

Sam told Jess about TJ's shopping adventure.

"Wow," said Jess.

"Yeah," said Sam. "They're really dedicated to fashion."

"Sounds like they're really dedicated to you."

"I'd journey to a hundred thrift stores for TJ if I had to." Sam hoped there would never be a situation when they would be called on to do such a thing, but if the need was great enough, there was very little Sam wouldn't do for TJ.

"Have you thought about a button-down shirt to go with it?" Jess offered.

"Thought about and rejected," Sam said proudly.

"That's fair. Look at me, getting hung up on traditional clothing combinations. What you've got on now looks great." Jess paused. "Though the vest covers enough that you could probably wear it without the T-shirt."

"Jess, it's middle school."

"It's prom. Trust me, girls are going to be revealing more than that."

"I'm not a girl."

"Point, set, and match, my young gentlequeer."

Sam mimed removing a hat from their head and tipping it forward with an extensive flourish.

"Well, the vest is lovely. And since it's black, it leaves us full color freedom."

Jess's comment reminded Sam why they were there. "Where's the sewing machine?"

"Here's the thing," said Jess, with their hands as much as their voice. "Sewing tulle is a pain in the tuchus, as my grand mother would say. It gets caught, it pulls, and it's heck on needles. If I need to, I'll do it for you. But I think there's another way. Look at this."

Jess passed her phone over to Sam, open to a large femme with dark, thick curves and long, thin braids. They were standing in the sun wearing a gigantic smile and an amazing skirt. No, not a skirt exactly, or at least not a regular one. Strips of silver fabric were tied at one end to elastic around their waist, and left free to drape around their legs. They wore a pink pair of leggings underneath and a pink crop top.

"I was thinking we could do that, but with tulle." Jess reached behind the couch and pulled out a plastic bag full of bouncy fabric in bright colors. "I visited my friend Pearl. She's always sewing something fabulous for fat people. I asked her whether she had any scraps we could use, and this is what she gave me."

"Wow," said Sam. They didn't know what else to say.

"I made sure she didn't put any pink in." Jess grinned.

She dumped the pile of netted fabric onto the floor and

sat down to start sorting by color. Sam joined her and soon they had piles of tulle in every color of the rainbow, plus some fuchsia that had snuck in, with Sam's approval.

"This is okay. It's really the light pink I hate. Besides, it'll match TJ's shirt."

Once they were done sorting, Jess pulled out a roll of thick elastic and measured around Sam's waist.

"One of the beautiful things about D.I.Y. clothing is that it always fits!"

"D.I.Y.?" asked Sam.

"Do it yourself!"

"But you're helping. So should it be D.I.Y.W.A.F.? Do it yourself with a friend? Or maybe just DIYWAF?" Sam said it as a two-syllable word.

"I'll check in with the community."

"There's a community?"

"On the internet," said Jess, "everything's a community. And the D.I.Y.ers are all over."

Jess gave Sam a pair of scissors and showed them how to fold several layers of tulle over itself to make it easier to work with. They cut strips long enough to reach Sam's knees.

"Leave an inch at either end for me to connect it," Jess advised when Sam starting tying the tulle to the elastic. They started with red, then orange, and worked their way through the rainbow to violet. They tied on a fuchsia strip and began again at red. When they were done, they had a length of elastic with fluffy tulle hanging down in five rainbows, start to finish.

"This I can sew by hand," Jess said, and within minutes, she connected the ends of the elastic. She held it up and shook it out. "Go ahead. Try it on."

Sam stepped into the elastic and pulled up their creation. They turned to the mirror and gasped. They felt a smile forming on their face that they let grow until their cheeks hurt and they broke into a laugh.

"It's . . . it's . . . it's amazing!"

"It sure is." Jess gave a proud grin.

Sam twirled in a circle, then back in the other direction. "It's like being a rainbow and a cloud at the same time!" They fluffed out the strips of tulle around them. "Thank you! Thank you! Thank you!"

"You did a great job. And it goes so well with the vest."

"It does!"

"What are you going to wear on your feet?"

"My rhinestone sneakers." Sam grinned.

Jess shrugged. "I mean, sneakers are good for dancing in, I suppose."

"And rhinestones, Jess."

Jess held up her hands in surrender. "May the great Femme in the Sky forgive me. And rhinestones!"

"Can I go get them?"

"Well, I'm not about to."

Sam dashed downstairs and was back in moments with sparkling feet. They twirled for Jess and went back to admiring their new look in the mirror.

"Those shoes really do it. You look amazing."

"Thanks." Sam beamed, not just for the compliment, but because they believed it themself.

"So that's about it, unless you want any accessories. I'm always a fan of accessories."

"Like what?"

"Well, I know you said you didn't want a button-down shirt."

Sam wrinkled their nose at the idea.

"But that doesn't mean you can't wear a tie. Maybe even a bow tie. Or a bolo."

Sam tilted their head to the side. "Nah."

"Or maybe some jewelry. With short sleeves, a bracelet might be nice."

An idea struck Sam. "Well, there is something of yours I'd love to borrow, if that's okay."

"Sure! What's the finishing touch on this beauty?"

✦ ✦ ✦

The night of the prom, TJ's dad dropped them off in front of the school. TJ rocked their pinstripe suit, and had added a fuchsia pocket square to match the shirt that brought out the warmth of their brown skin. Along with a fresh fade, they wore a pair of glimmering stud earrings. They were also taller than usual in three-inch heels.

Sam knew that TJ would look amazing, but they were stunned to feel just as fabulous in their rainbow-cloud skirt, thrift store delight vest, rhinestone sneakers, and meticulously messy brushed-forward hair. And across their collarbone, they wore a necklace with a thick piece of purple-tinted mirror that said 𝓯𝓪𝓽 in bold, curvy letters.

Sam and TJ joined the trickle of students inside. Most of the girls wore dresses with their long hair down, and most of the boys wore ties and jackets with a touch of gel in their short hair. They were having fun, and had big smiles on their faces, but perhaps none so big as Sam's.

TJ opened the heavy door, and Sam followed them onto the gym-turned-dance-room floor, with laser images overhead vibrating to the music. Kids were dancing in pairs, in groups, and alone. More were gathered around the edges, chatting and occasionally stepping nervously to the beat.

"We Are All Beautiful" by Miss Chris started up, and Sam and TJ ran onto the dance floor, where lasers streaked across the foggy air. They danced until they were tired. Then they visited the snack table and went back to dance some more. They danced with each other. They danced with other kids. They even danced with a few of the teachers.

Sam couldn't imagine standing in the heels TJ was wearing, much less dancing the way TJ was, but that didn't matter. Sam didn't need to dress up like TJ. They didn't need to dress up like anyone but themselves.

DUPATTA DIARIES

Nafiza Azad

I look at the silver tureen containing the butter chicken, and my mouth waters. I can almost taste the naan dipped in the thick, orange, creamy sauce. There will be a bite to the gravy; I can see the fresh red and green chili halves. The chicken pieces will be moist and tender, infused with flavor. I swallow hard and look down at my plate. It is accessorized with wilting lettuce and cucumber slices that saw their peak sometime around nine this morning.

It would be so easy to ladle a bit of the butter chicken onto my plate. There's room for it and I am hungry. But I can feel my mother's glare. I know that if I dare to eat some of the butter chicken, I will be subjected to a lecture like no other once we get home. Butter chicken has too many calories, and I, having the audacity to be fat, don't have the right to eat it.

"Why aren't you eating the chicken, bubu? Don't you want

it?" my younger cousin asks with a perfect blend of concern and innocence in her voice. "You don't mind if I eat the last bit of it, do you?"

Of course I mind. I mind so much I might throw up the salad I am pretending to eat, but alas, my mother's gimlet eye won't let off even for a single second so all I can do is bare my teeth in a facsimile of a smile. "Please go ahead."

"Jamilah doesn't like greasy food," my mom says with a sweet smile. *What a liar. I love greasy food.*

"How very health conscious of her!" My cousin's contempt can no longer be hidden. She glances at me, furtively she thinks, and I can see the smirk deepening on her lips.

I don't understand why this cousin who I am not friends with and don't know very well insisted on accompanying my mother and me to shop for our outfits for my other cousin's wedding this weekend. My cousin's name is a slim and svelte Shahin while mine is a robust and plump Jamilah. If Amma had given me a slim name, would I have been thinner?

We emerge onto the street, where I squint in the bright sunlight, already missing the dim warmth of the restaurant. The boutiques selling Indian clothes are all located on this street, a long line of stores blaring the latest Bollywood songs and smelling, with varying intensities, of incense. Several of the stores have set out faceless mannequins wearing the newest styles of clothing on the sidewalk in front in an attempt to attract customers. I stop and stare at their plastic perfection for a moment. Adorned in shades of red, blue, and pink with their eyes caught in eternal blankness, they are what society expects from female bodies. In other words, they are (unattainable) goals. I glance at Shahin, who has stopped beside me, and see on her face the same longing I feel. Huh. She catches my glance and quickly turns her face away.

Interspersed between the clothing stores are the mithai shops that I am doing my best not to look at. The smell of the mithai, the bewitching aroma of roasted cardamom and condensed milk, does things to me that I can't talk about in polite company. I can see the orange jalebi, crisp and dripping syrup, sweet as sin, displayed in the windows. Right beside them are the mounds of gold motichoor ladoo with almond slices stuck on top. My favorite gulab jamun, a fried mixture of milk and dough rolled in coconut and dunked in sugar syrup, occupies its own place in the display. I swallow and make myself look away.

I have had gulab jamun only five times, and the last was when I skipped class just so I could buy some. I ate the sweets in a park near my house, hidden behind some trees so no one would see and tell my mother.

"Khala," my cousin calls to my mom in a soft, sweet voice, pulling me out of my trance, "can we get some mithai? I always eat something sweet after a meal!"

I hate her. I hope she falls into a crack in the sidewalk and is transported to a world where the only thing to eat is lettuce.

"Maybe later," my mom hedges, the smiling growing stiff on her mouth. "We need to get the outfits as soon as possible."

I drag my feet as I follow them into the largest clothing

store on the street. I am dazzled by the sparkling lehengas, the gharara shining with zardozi embroidery, the shalwar kameez in jeweled colors, gorgeous chiffons, silks, and satins. And the jewelry on the side is a feast for the eyes. Like any other sixteen-year-old girl with a healthy appetite for shining things, I am starstruck.

My mother and cousin are welcomed by the sales staff and immediately shown numerous outfits. The counter is full of potential lehengas and gharara that are worthy of gracing their bodies.

I, on the other hand, get looked up and down by the salesladies, who conclude their observations with clucking tongues and shaking heads.

"Why are you so fat, huh?" one of them says, sighing heavily. "How are we supposed to fit you into an outfit?"

A familiar feeling of humiliation envelops me. This is not the first time I have been in this store, and this is not the first time I have heard sentiments like this. The sting is still as sharp as the first time I heard these words, though.

"Don't say that, bahenji! Surely you can find something for Jamilah!" My mother appears right on cue.

"I don't know . . . ," a saleslady says reluctantly. It's as if Amma asked her to find a cure for cancer. "Let me see if there's anything in the back."

Moments like these, and there are many of them, I pretend I am someone else observing the situation. The body I am in is someone else's and I am renting it temporarily. I can feel people looking at me and judging every bulge, and so I judge me as well. I fold my arms around myself because the judgment is not kind.

A few minutes later, the saleslady reappears with a stack of outfits in her hands. She gestures us to the counter and then proceeds to show us the ugliest clothes in the history of womankind. Most of them are tents masquerading as garments, and I suspect there is the odd tablecloth in there. I like none of them and tell my mother as much.

"You should have one custom made," the saleslady says. "For twelve hundred dollars, you can get a beautiful outfit."

My mother's eyes widen, and I shake my head. We can't afford that. The highest we can go is three hundred dollars, and even that is stretching the budget.

"This blue one isn't too bad, Jamilah," my mom says, picking up a lehenga that I wouldn't be caught dead in.

"I don't like it," I tell her.

"Don't be unreasonable," she hisses to me.

I bite my lip but shake my head. I won't give in to this. Perhaps because I am fat, I am not allowed to have an opinion on the clothes I wear. Perhaps I am supposed to like something just because it fits. I won't, though. I can't.

"What's happening, khala?" Shahin reappears in the middle of the now-silent standoff I am having with my mother.

My mom appeals to Shahin. "Areh beta, can you convince your cousin to buy this lehenga? See, it is so pretty!"

My cousin looks at the outfit and wrinkles her nose expressively. "Maybe we should try other stores. Honestly, khala, this color doesn't match bubu at all."

I breathe in sharply, taken aback by the unexpected support. Amma gives in to my cousin, and the two spend the rest of our time in that shop choosing outfits for her. She has no spending limit and everything fits her so she gets three outfits—after trying them on and modeling for us, naturally.

I am envious, of course I am. What would I give to have a body like hers? To not be on a constant diet? To be able to look into a mirror? A lot. I would give a lot.

After dropping off the shopping bags full of Shahin's clothes in the car, we resume our search, store by store, all the way down the street. Either they have no clothes my size or they do and they are too ugly or too expensive. An hour later, we have come to the last shop on the street. I am the world's last dinosaur. And one that wants to wear an Indian outfit. I have no hope for this store either.

It is tiny and packed with clothes. My mom and Shahin immediately weave their way to the counter to talk to the boss, but my attention is caught by a glimmer of red stuck in the middle of a stack of white and gray unstitched fabric. Without realizing what I am doing, I lift up the top half of the stack of fabric and put it aside. The red belongs to a dupatta; the long red rectangular material is diaphanous with gold thread running through it. Flowers are embroidered in the same gold thread at both ends of the dupatta.

I pick it up and as it unfolds in waves down my body, am immediately hit by the desire to wrap it around myself. To own it.

I own other dupatta, of course. I wouldn't be a desi girl if

I didn't, but none of them have made me feel quite the way this one does. This world constantly judges me on how I look, but if I put this dupatta on, I feel like I could control who sees me and who doesn't. Perhaps it is ridiculous, but I feel like putting on this dupatta would be an act of reclamation of my body. Of both my inner and outer selves.

I turn to see my mother, my cousin, and the boss of the store staring at me with different looks in their eyes. My mother looks frustrated and angry, my cousin is contemptuous, and the boss looks pitying. At this moment, though, I don't give a damn about them.

"I'll have this," I announce to them.

"It's a good thing a dupatta fits everyone, isn't it?" Shahin says with a beam.

I refuse to dignify her question with a response.

My mother doesn't protest and pays for it silently.

We have run out of time, so we leave Main Street without successfully completing the shopping mission. Amma and I speak very little in the car, but Shahin fills my mom's little Mazda with her chatter, incessantly going on about her new outfits, her new house, and how much weight she has gained since she moved to Vancouver.

We drop her off and leave without stopping as we usually do for chai and cookies. The car is full of an ornery silence, and I can see the barbed glare my mother directs at me when she thinks I'm not looking. Her eyes prick holes in the self-esteem I don't have until I sigh and look at her.

"What is it, Amma?" I ask even though I know very well what has her angry.

"You don't have clothes to wear to the wedding," she says as if I don't know.

"I will just wear my Eid outfit. I've only worn that once," I say in a low voice. The Eid outfit makes me look like an orange cupcake, but I happen to like cupcakes so I don't really mind.

"No! Everyone's seen you wearing that. People will say we aren't treating you well. You should have bought that blue one I showed you." She keeps the majority of her attention on the road. "Ugly or not, at least something fit you."

I know better than to be hurt. I do. Her words hurt anyway.

"I just won't go, okay? You can tell everyone that I am sick," I mumble, looking outside, wishing she would drive faster. I can't be trapped in this small space with her much longer.

Amma's hands clench the steering wheel so tightly her knuckles go white. I put on my headphones and turn up the volume on my music.

✦ ✦ ✦

The evening after the trip is a quiet one. I spend it ensconced in my room, refusing all audiences. My youngest brother knocks at my door once, opens it, takes one look at my face, and beats a hasty retreat. My other three brothers bang in and out of the house, too busy with their lives to bother with me. My daadi is in Fiji at the moment, so I can't even depend on her for support.

I don't go for dinner—not that I am called. I am hungry,

but then again, I am always hungry. Hunger is a lifestyle for the fat and the not-famous. I lock my door and sit on the carpet in front of my bed staring into the distance without thinking about anything in particular. I have friends I could call; there are even some who would listen and sympathize. But talking to people would mean admitting my wretchedness. I am keenly aware of how pathetic I am. I don't need other people to know it too.

Finally, unable to stand my self-loathing, I get up and turn on the lights. I step on a plastic bag, and the crinkle reminds me of the dupatta. I pick up the bag and take it out. The red material is soft and shimmery in my hands. I wonder how I'll look with it on.

I squint at the single, veiled mirror in my room and wonder if I should take the risk, if I should pull down the cotton sheet I draped over it. I have a complicated relationship with mirrors.

I wrap the dupatta around my head, arranging the excess to drape my bosom. It's strange and not entirely believable, but I am immediately infused with a sense of hope. It's a little like being injected with a shot of sunshine.

Finally.

A clear voice sounds in my mind and I freeze. I look around but there's no one here.

Hello. Can you hear me?

Have I stepped into an Adele song?

Let's not be tragic here.

"Who is this?" I ask awkwardly, and immediately feel silly.

The dupatta.

You expect me to believe that a rectangular length of fabric has somehow developed consciousness and is conversing with me?

I will exist whether you believe in me or not. And honestly, it is too early in our relationship for me to have any expectations of you.

What are you? I mean, dupattas usually don't talk even when I put them on.

I don't suppose you believe in magic.

Generally, no, but now that I am confronted by a talking piece of material . . . do I have a choice? Have you always been like this?

Like what? Able to talk? I don't think so. I gained consciousness and immortality along the way, though I am not clear on the details. Several women have owned me for brief periods of time.

Aren't you new?

Do I look new?

Yes.

That would be the immortality.

Oh. What kind of women owned you in the past?

Beautiful women.

Now you are owned by the not-so-beautiful me.

Why do you think you're not beautiful?

Suddenly I don't want to be having this conversation. Especially with a piece of material.

Perhaps the better question is: What do you think beauty is?

What I don't look like.

And what do *you look like?*

I look at the veiled mirror with some misgivings. Still, no one else is here, so perhaps I can endure its scorn. I approach the mirror and with my eyes squeezed tightly shut, pull the cover off.

The veil on my head seems warmer or maybe it's only in my mind that it does. The dupatta doesn't speak, and with every continuing moment of silence, the absurdity of the situation deepens.

I open my eyes and am immediately confronted by my too-festive reflection. My flushed face is 70 percent cheeks, my eyes are red, and my mouth is trying to stop a grimace from conquering it. I blink, and when the reflection blinks back, I realize that the girl in the mirror is a stranger—I haven't really looked at myself, apart from glimpses during rushed morning routines and late-night showers, in a long time. I don't know the girl in the mirror. The face in my head doesn't resemble this girl at all.

So, do you have an answer yet? What do you look like?

Ugly comes to mind.

If you are ugly, then what is beautiful?

Someone with a thin face, a thin body, and clear skin. With small hips, a graceful walk, an elegant laugh. Someone who doesn't need to eat to survive.

I see. The women who owned me before you did not all meet the conditions you have for beauty, and yet, in my opinion, they were all beautiful. Even the ones who had round faces, full bodies, and skin marked by acne or life. Their hips were wide. They walked like they were trying to get places, and they laughed loudly and wildly. All of them had voracious appetites. They loved food.

I move away from the mirror, uncomfortable with my reflection, mulling over what the dupatta said.

What kind of food?

I said all that and you ask me about the food?

I shrug mentally. *I have priorities.*

ㆍ ㅣㅣㅆ ㅿㅣㅣㅣㅕㅛㅣㅣㅣㅣ ㅣㅣㅣㅣㅕㅣㅣㅣ ㅣㅣㅣㅕㅣ ㅣㅣㅣㅣㅣㅣ ㅓ ㅠㅣㅣㅕㅣㅕ ㅿㅣㅓㅑㅣㅁㅣ ㅿㅠㅓㅣㅓㅣ.

There's a knock on my door, and I freeze like a cat caught eating cream it is definitely not supposed to. I get off the bed and open the door a crack.

"Jamilah, beta?" My abba.

"Ji, Abba?" I reply, opening the door.

"I like your dupatta. Is it new? You look beautiful in it." My father's eyes are sincere, and suddenly, to my horror, there is a lump in my throat. I grip the edge of the dupatta tightly and look down.

"Khana nai khayega, beta?" He is probably the only one in this house who worries when I don't eat.

"I'm not hungry, Abba." This is another lie. But how can I tell him I don't want to see Amma?

"Well, if you get hungry later on, your amma prepared a plate for you. It's on the kitchen table."

"Wait, Abba. What did you have for dinner?" I ask before he can leave.

"Your amma made chicken biryani. It was quite delicious.

I wouldn't miss it if I were you." I can hear the smile in his voice. I have tasted biryani exactly two times. Both of those were when my mom wasn't around. I remember the explosion of spices on my tongue, the taste of the seasoned chicken, and the coolness of the yogurt that brought all the flavors together. My mouth waters.

Let's go and eat. I haven't had biryani in ages.

I'm not going to ask how a dupatta can eat. My suspension of disbelief can only take so much. At that moment, my stomach growls, sounding like a bear in the depths of the night. I cave to the hunger, and after making sure everyone else in the house has retreated to their rooms, sneak out of mine. To get to the kitchen, I have to walk across the living room. Thankfully, unlike other nights, there is no one in the living room watching TV.

I make it to the kitchen and flip the light switch. As my abba said, there's a covered plate on the table. I look at it suspiciously. Perhaps the biryani is a peace offering from my mother. My mouth waters again, and I move forward with single-minded determination. Food. FOOD. Ohmygod, actual-not-salad food.

I forget that even though the rest of me is in ragged sweatpants and an equally ragged hoodie, I'm still wearing the dupatta on my head.

With bated breath, I uncover the plate.

A salad: lettuce, olives, onions, and cucumbers, sprinkled with vinegar. This is my dinner. I should have known better than to expect something else.

Where's the biryani?

Propelled by rebellion, I look in the pots on the stove, in the oven, in the fridge for that biryani my abba said everyone else in the house ate. I see no sign of it.

"Jamilah? Are you here to eat?" Amma is behind me but I don't turn. I am several different kinds of hungry, angry, and hurt. I don't trust myself to speak to her.

"I left you a salad. There's also yogurt in the fridge," my mother says.

Ask her about the biryani.

Suddenly I'm done. I have reached the cliff's edge, and the lack of biryani—no, of actual food—has pushed me off it. Hysterical laughter bubbles up in me, but if I start laughing I will cry. I turn around and look at my mother. She flinches as if my gaze hurts and looks away.

"Would you love me if I was thin?" I whisper because I'm scared of her answer. "Does my body shame you? Do you want me to starve? Will that make you happy?"

She meets my eyes for a quick second but looks away again.

"I'm doing this for your own good, Jamilah. I don't expect you to understand or be grateful right now, but trust me, someday you will thank me," she says in a small, stiff voice. Ha. The universal excuse for all parents everywhere as they put their children through crap.

"When will that be, Amma?" I really want to know.

"When you walk in a store and the clothes fit for once," she replies, and I step back. I think it would hurt less if she just slapped me. I stare at her, and this time, there's nothing

I can do. I stupidly cry because years of conditioning won't let me hurt her back. I can't say the cruel words crowding on the tip of my tongue because I've been brought up to respect my elders.

So, I leave. I put on my shoes, open the door, and leave. It's late at night, and I'm sure my abba is going to have words with me when I return, but staying in the same space as my mother isn't something I can do at this moment.

I have been dieting ever since I turned thirteen. I don't remember the last time I ate enough to fill my stomach. It has gotten to the point that just eating makes me feel guilty. No matter how much weight I lose, it is never enough.

Where are we going?

At least I'm not entirely alone. *I don't really know.*

I walk down the street to the park, probably looking weird with a veil on my head along with the sweatpants and hoodie. It's cold; the night is blue, just like me. I sit down on a park bench, trying to make myself into as small a ball as possible. Which is of course a ridiculous attempt since no matter how hard an elephant tries, it will remain an elephant.

You are not an elephant.

"Thank you, but my mother thinks I am," I mutter out loud. No one's here to judge me.

I don't know if you want to hear this, but your mother is just treating you the way her mother treated her.

How do you know?

I'm magic, remember?

That doesn't make it hurt any less. She's old enough to know the weight of her actions.

She eats the same things she gives you. Have you ever seen her enjoy food?

Now that you mention it . . . She doesn't eat with us at dinnertime. She has breakfast pretty early . . . and I have no idea what she does for lunch. When she eats, it seems like a chore. It's actually pretty annoying to eat with her. I lean forward on the bench and stare into the dimly lit, landscaped park. *That still doesn't make what she said to me okay.*

Of course not. Everyone has some kind of pain within them. If you know where hers comes from, you can understand why she causes you yours.

Why do I have to understand?

You don't have to, but you still have to live with her.

The dupatta has a point. Plus, it is getting too cold to be outside, so I shuffle back home, my footsteps getting slower and heavier as I walk up the drive. The door is open, and there are shoes at the threshold that don't belong to anyone in my family. I can hear voices coming from the living room and sigh.

I am not in the mood to entertain visitors, so I turn to go up the stairs to my room. Unfortunately, my cousin, the thin and pretty Shahin, sees me and exclaims loudly, "Jamilah! There you are! Mom, look, Jamilah's here now!"

Now, that is one troubled child. Beware of her. She is desperately unhappy and to alleviate her misery, she hurts others.

I walk reluctantly into the living room and greet my cousin and my mother's younger sister, my thin and pretty Zaynah Khala. She and Shahin look so similar, they could be siblings.

The dupatta whistles loudly in my head. *Wow, this lady has issues.*

Zaynah Khala's perfect.

That's what she wants everyone to believe.

I look at my perfectly groomed aunt. It's ten o'clock at night, and she looks as fresh as a perfectly cooked roti. Her makeup is flawless, and she is dressed elegantly in a shalwar kameez.

"What brings you here so late, Zaynah?" My mom walks into the living room carrying two cups of tea and a saucer of cookies balanced on a tray.

"Oh, Shahin said you weren't able to find an outfit for Jamilah to wear to the wedding? I remembered that I have one of the outfits you used to wear before you got married. It's old but it's in excellent condition. Maybe Jamilah would be interested?" Zaynah Khala picks up a gift bag from the coffee table in front of her and opens it. I watch her pull out an outfit even more hideous than the one I rejected during the shopping trip. My mom actually wore this?

"Your mom was . . . slightly heavier when she was a teen," Zaynah Khala says delicately, swallowing a smile. I narrow my eyes and turn to my mom. Her face is carefully empty of emotion. She appears unaffected by her sister's words.

It's because hearing these kinds of things is nothing to her. She has heard worse from her sister and the people around her.

And all of a sudden, I get it. I get my mother. I don't forgive her. I might never forgive her, but I understand her.

I turn to my aunt and smile very insincerely. "I don't wear ugly clothes."

"But these aren't ugly! Your ammi loved this suit when she was younger. Besides"—she looks me up and down—"Shahin told me you couldn't find any clothes in your size."

This woman meets the conditions you stated earlier for a beautiful woman. Do you really think she is beautiful?

You can be a horrible person while being beautiful.

It all depends on how you define beauty.

Society . . .

Can go to hell. You are the one who decides what is beautiful.

"I don't recall giving you permission to talk about my body," I tell my aunt. "Though you are my elder and a guest in my house, I need you to know that I will not sit here and be humiliated by you."

"Zarmeena, tell your daughter that there's nothing wrong with these clothes. I only want the best for her," my aunt protests, looking upset. I ignore them all and stand by the door, ready to escape.

But then my mother speaks. "Though you might mean well, and I sincerely doubt that, what you're doing right now *is* offensive."

Zaynah Khala gets to her feet in a huff, pulling Shahin up with her. "Bubu, how can you say that? I was just trying to help."

"Your help sounds very much like mockery, Zaynah. We won't see you out." My mother pauses. "You can leave the outfit behind. I know how to throw away trash."

Well, that was refreshing. I didn't expect that from her. Did you?

No. She surprised me. My cousin and aunt stalk out of our house with their noses high in the air, letting the world know how offended they are. My mother and I are left with a pregnant silence that is broken by my grumbling stomach.

I can hear the dupatta giggling in my head.

"Come with me," my mother commands. She goes to the kitchen and tells me to sit at the table. I obey. It doesn't matter that we're in the middle of a tense fight. She remains my mother and her word is law. Ten minutes later, there is a plate of kimchi fried rice in front of me. On top is a fried egg with runny yolk. I stare at the plate and then at my mother.

As an olive branch, this is pretty sweet. Try a piece of kimchi; I want to know what it tastes like.

Wait. I look at my mother. She still won't look at me directly. I breathe in the fragrance of the food and grit my teeth. "Are you trying to reconcile? If so, I'm sorry, but this is not going to work."

You have to hold out for the gulab jamun. You can reconcile if she gives you some mithai.

I ignore the dupatta. "Ever since I was a kid, you have

been treating my body as an enemy I have to defeat. You have convinced me that I am ugly and not worth love or attention. You've let me go hungry because starving is better than eating after six. But you know what you've never done?" I can feel the tears, damnit. They won't let me be as cool as I want to be. My mother looks at me. "You've never told me I am beautiful. Not even once."

I get to my feet.

Take the food! The food didn't do you any wrong.

That's true. I pick up the hot plate.

"Amma, it's not going to be easy for me to move on from everything you have made me go through. I get it, okay? I get that you went through the same things, but that doesn't make it okay for you to treat me the same way."

My mother bows her head, and I feel like a horrible daughter, but the hurt in me refuses to give in.

"You *are* beautiful, Jamilah," she says without looking at me. As such, her words are not very convincing.

"I know you don't think that, Amma. And you know what? It's fine. Actually, it isn't, but I can no longer live thinking my body is an enemy. You've been teaching me to hate the girl in the mirror. But I'm done hating her. I want to give her a chance. Maybe she's not your idea of beautiful. Maybe she won't win any pageants, but she doesn't have to. Maybe she can define beauty in a way that suits her. Is beauty the only thing that matters? The girl in the mirror knows food. She'll be great to take out to dinner. She's funny and warm." My voice slips into a whisper. "Maybe someday you will learn to see beneath her plus-sized exterior and like her too." My mother doesn't look up or reply even though I wait for her to.

Finally, I leave the kitchen, sad but also determined. I'm not okay, not by a long shot, but I will be. Someday.

You can't rush relationships, Jamilah. Give her time. Wait for the gulab jamun. Can we eat now? I'm starving.

You are a dupatta.

Just spill some food on me.

No way. I don't waste food.

FOOD IS LOVE

Chris Baron

Food and I have a complicated history. It's delicious, it's dangerous. It brings people together. It tears them apart. "I have to get to work, Grandma." I suck in my belly, and I try to tuck in my blue polo shirt so I can button my pants.

"Already?" she says. "Wait, where are you working? Shouldn't you be in school?"

"Grandma, it's four now. School's over."

She lifts the carrots, sets them on the cutting board. "Josh, will you cut these? Now, tell me about college."

"Grandma, I'm not going to college. I am working. I want to be a chef like you."

She looks at me with wide, wet eyes and breathes deeply. "A chef? How wonderful."

This is the infinite time I've told her this. I grip the knife, pushing the point into the cutting board.

For my grandma, food is sacred and powerful, but she was always at war with it. Since I was a little kid sitting on the counter learning to crack eggs, she's always said that food brings people together. Food is love. She had me cook with her every Shabbat. I love the process, the parts coming together, the smell of oil and candles burning, peeling potatoes, crushing garlic, tasting everything. Then there's the baking and mixing and serving giant plates of food to everyone, and of course, eating. But even as we cooked a huge dinner for the family, she would tell me that I have to be careful not to eat too much.

One night, she would tell me to eat everything I can, then the next day, she would put me on some fad diet. One day, we are eating black-and-white cookies at Akin's Deli, and the next day, we're sawing grapefruit in half and eating it with a tiny spoon.

I can remember when it started. When I was a little kid, I'd take the train to Brooklyn. Grandma would meet me at the station on Avenue P and take me to get a lemon Italian ice and a warm, soft pretzel. One time, when we reached her street, we saw some of her friends sitting in lawn chairs in the sun. I was used to this. They gathered around me, squeezing my cheeks.

"He's looking healthy, Mae," one said.

Then out of nowhere, my grandmother said, "Well, he's going to get on a diet, and he's going to be so skinny this summer." Then she squeezed my shoulder and slid her hand around my waist where my love handle gently spilled over the elastic of my sweatpants. I looked at the pretzel, dying to eat it but hating it all at once. I threw it as hard as I could into the gutter.

I know she meant the best for me. She always has, but spending time with her always used to mean having to learn about some new diet or exercise plan, or stories of Grandpa and how skinny he was, while at the same time her filling me up with all my favorite foods. If food is love, then love must be really confusing.

"I have to work at the restaurant, and I can't be late, I just told . . ." But I stop, remembering that it's not her fault. Her memories are frayed strings. It's so annoying saying everything over and over. I've told her that I want to be a chef, just like she was. I've told her every day. It's only when she's cooking that she seems exactly like she was—crystal clear, powerful.

She points to the carrots.

"Sure thing," I say. I cut the carrots in thick ovals like she taught me.

"You do that very well."

"You taught me this, Grandma."

She smiles and pulls several challah loaves from the oven. I watch her in case she ruins the bread or burns herself . . . but they are perfect. The loaves steam in the afternoon light.

"All right, Joshy, have a little before tonight, and then we'll set the table together."

"Grandma, I have to go, like, now." I look at my watch out of habit; it's been broken forever.

She grabs my wrist with sudden strength. "On Shabbat?"

"Yes, Grandma, I have to work. I can only work on the weekends. It sucks, but . . ."

"Well, here, then. Eat this." She pulls apart a challah loaf, hands me a steaming hunk of the bread, and swipes it with butter. "This is for your soul, Joshy. Food is love."

"Grandma, I don't eat bread right now." The steam from the bread rises into my face.

She looks at me as if I told her some lost and impossible secret. "Don't what?"

"I don't eat bread. I'm watching my carbs." I put my hands on my belly, then reach the sides of my pants and pull them up. "Trying to shape up."

She looks at me astonished, like words are piling up, but then she stops and smiles from a faraway place. She spent half my childhood lecturing me about what I needed to do to get thin. But, since her mind is changing, she's a different person. She has joy in her cooking, and these afternoons are different. She doesn't remember her daily assaults on me. It's like the cruelest parts of her have withered and vanished. I miss some of those parts now—almost like the sweeter parts need some salt to make them more real.

"Nonsense." She shakes her head. "Cooking is not only about eating," and I watch her mouth and silently say the words with her, "Food is about love, and this bread is love, and you need it."

Even though my mother has told me over and over to just accept the things she says, this pushes me way too far. I take off my headphones, and I look her in the face. "How? How is food love?"

She looks up at me.

"How? How is food love when you shove too much into your body until even your insides grow? How is it love when I have never even kissed a girl because I am always the friend, not the boyfriend? How is food love when every day I wake up and say that I will eat healthy today, but by the end of the day, I've had at least one bag of Doritos? How is food love when every bite I take is eye-rolled and examined by my own grandmother? Food is not love. Food is food: it goes in, it comes out."

"Joshy, will you set the table?" She takes the silverware out of the drawer for the second time. Then she pauses and looks a bit confused.

But I can't stand it. "GRANDMA!" and this time I yell because I just gave my speech, but she can't remember anything and none of it matters, and I shouldn't yell at anyone— not now, not ever—but I can't help it. "You WANT me to have bread? Have you seen what I look like? I'm like this challah loaf, Grandma! I wish you would just remember something for more than a minute."

She turns back to her preparations, and I put the challah on the counter. I grab my backpack, and at that moment, my mom comes in the door, just in time for me to leave.

"Sorry, Josh," she says, hanging up her coat. She hands me a few bucks for the bus. I shove them in my pocket. "Did you eat?"

"I did," I lie.

"Joshy, it's Shabbat. Where are you going?" My grandma faces me with the power of her whole kitchen.

I look at my mom.

But Grandma reaches for my arm, and in a voice like her own from years ago, she says, "Josh, I know it wasn't always easy to be around me. I was wrong most of the time. Forgive me, but I promise you that food is good. Important. Each bite is a chance to start again." She puts a new chunk of challah into my hand. I feel its perfect weight, the freshness. I imagine olive oil and crushed garlic.

I eat every bite.

✦ ✦ ✦

Just when I finish topping off my salt and pepper shakers, refilling the last packets of sugar and sweetener alongside an equal number of puffy packages of granulated pure sugar and the brown paper-bag shapes of raw sugar . . . just when I fold my final pile of napkins for the next morning's shift . . . just when I top off the coffee beans in both the regular and decaf . . . just when I finish stocking the hot tea stash, lemon wedges, and the side plates . . . they bring a party of four into our station.

It's an older couple with two kids. One of the kids is small, maybe nine, pushing his head into his father's arm in some kind of overtired protest. The other kid walks behind; he looks like a young teenager, and he is huge. He looks even heavier than me. His long, stringy brown hair covers his rounded face.

My manager, Mark, smiles heartlessly in my direction. He hates last-minute customers, but it's good for business and I know it's going to be a long night. Billy is the last server on tonight, and I am the last buser, so it's up to us. I don't really mind, though—I'm here to make money. More tables means more people, and my family has needed the money since Grandma got sick.

The thing is, I've never been good in school and don't really have the grades to go to college next year. So when my guidance counselor told me to try working in a restaurant to see if I could "apply what I know," it made sense. I'm good at two things: eating and cooking. The Market restaurant even has an internship program for graduating seniors who want to become chefs, so if I can do well here, maybe I can become a cook, a chef, or something like that. But right now, we need money.

The party of four is settled in. I slice their bread, arrange it perfectly on the plate with extra slices and butter. I add a ramekin of olive oil. I pour them water, even though we are only supposed to do so on request. Anyone who eats this late wants water.

The parents smile and say, "Thank you," their accents thick—German or maybe Dutch?

I slide into the back of the house and stand over Billy, who's on his phone like always.

"What is it, my fine fatted friend? You all done?"

"Billy." I smile. "We have a four top."

"What? Now? What the hell?"

He texts some final thing, gets up, and tucks in his shirt.

"Well, get them some bread or something. Don't just stand there!"

"Already did it."

We look over from the side station and watch them read menus.

"Look at that kid, Josh. He's overstuffed just like you."

It's the first time I can ever remember him calling me Josh.

"Maybe," Billy mutters under his breath, "I should suggest a salad right away."

He saunters over to the table, and I hear him offer a few things: pasta, salads, and other dishes that are quick to prepare and eat. He tries to make them sound appetizing, but the concierge at their hotel must have given them a recommendation because almost simultaneously their fingers dance to a specific menu item and they smile at each other like they discovered something. In the late hours of the darkening restaurant, when the chefs are midway through cleaning the kitchen and even most of the bread is wrapped up and put away, one word cracks the restaurant like an earthquake. Cioppino.

Cioppino is the bane of late-night cooking. It is a magical crock stuffed with every kind of shellfish, from cockles to mussels, calamari rings, bay scallops, prawns, and finfish, all sautéed in fresh marinara sauce. In the center, nestled in a bed of linguine, there is a giant spread of Dungeness crab legs, succulent and invincible. It can't be rushed in its preparation or in its eating.

They all order it. Billy grunts, then I hear them say, "'Scuse me? No par-slay," and then emphatically, "Please, allergic." The mother pats the head of the young boy and says it again. "Allergic."

Billy nods and then enters the orders into the computer, slamming his fingers onto the screen. "Did you hear them?" He looks at me. "They have accents. You know that means no tip, right?"

I nod, but I don't know. I've only been working here for a few months. Mostly I just try to fit in, learning, plating, setting tables, and listening to managers and chefs talk about the ingredients. My favorite is watching the fisherman bring fresh fish to The Market, seeing the ahi sear on the mesquite grills. The Market is the right place for me to learn. One of the best chefs to learn from is Betto, the station chef. He has a feel for when the restaurant slows down, and his singing voice gets louder, fills the whole back of the house with *Phantom of the Opera* and other show tunes in the weirdest, most off-key tones possible. But no one cares. Betto always shows me little things, lets me linger at the line to show me how to add pinches of this or dashes of that in just the right measures. Sometimes he lets me taste what he's working on, a small bowl of chowder, a new kind of pesto. He'll even ask me what else it may need. When he sees the order for cioppino, he just sings louder and begins lining up the crocks.

I keep an eye on the table. I bring them more bread, more water, while the cioppino is being prepared. Billy sits in the break room, scrolling through his phone.

I try to finish the rest of the side work while the cioppino takes its time. I fill the last dishes in the side station, pile them at different angles into the tub, and watch the buttery swirls of leftover scampi sauce, parsley potatoes, blackened salmon skin, sourdough crust, and panko calamari crumbs mix into the bin. I make the bin as full as possible to get it in one trip. My muscles are spent from this five-hour shift, so I am slower than I want to be, but I manage to get to the kitchen. Betto is busy singing and cooking the cioppino.

"Joshua!" He calls me over.

I drop my bin of dishes on the racks. On the line, there are four shining silver pans for the cioppino. I smell red wine and basil, butter and garlic, all simmering in pans behind the counter.

"Try this. It's my new aioli." He hands me a small plate. It has a bed of greens, and in the center is the creamy dip and a few pieces of calamari, fried to golden perfection.

I hold up my hand. "No thanks," I say.

He looks at me. "What do you mean, *no thanks*? I made this for you!"

I hesitate for a moment. I think about my fight against carbs. I think about my grandma, how she would never eat something not kosher like this. But isn't this what I want to do with my life? So I dip it like he's taught me. Don't drown it. Dip it, let the aioli settle into the panko bread crumbs. If you don't let it settle, it's like eating two different things at once. You want it to combine. I wait the perfect amount of time, but just before I take a bite, I feel Billy looming over me.

"Dude, you DO NOT need to be eating that. Get a cucumber or something. You can't be a chef if YOU eat all the food. C'mon, did you finish the side station?"

I lower the calamari from my mouth, but then I catch Chef Betto's face, and he makes some gesture in Billy's direction, nods at me, and whispers, "Go on."

I hesitate, but then I taste it. It's perfect. I stand for a while, let the flavors mix on my tongue, watching the cioppino simmer in the pots, velvety red and steaming, Betto ⸺⸺⸺⸺⸺⸺⸺⸺⸺⸺⸺⸺⸺⸺⸺⸺⸺ ing it all in like he's painting a wild portrait.

"You see it, don't you?" He catches me staring. "Cioppino is the heart. This food, it changes you. When I worked on the fishing boats in San Francisco and we couldn't eat another bite of fish, we opened old cans of tomatoes, heated it up right on the deck. We threw everything in. Listen, Josh." He leans in closer. "It healed us. Food can heal."

I look at him silently, praying that he won't tell me that food is love.

"You have a girlfriend?"

"No." If food actually were love, I would have more girlfriends than I would know what to do with.

"Here, take this." He hands me a folded piece of lined, yellow paper, a recipe scribbled with blue ink. "When you have a girl, cook with her. Make cioppino with her. This is my special recipe. She won't be able to resist."

I shove the paper into my pocket.

I check the table and refill their waters. "Bread, please."

The younger boy looks up at me, his round smiling face beaming. Then I see Billy standing in the kitchen doorway waving to me.

We bring the four cioppinos to the table. Usually, Billy likes to show off and carry all his plates out himself, but the service for the cioppinos is more challenging—giant silver crocks with garlic bread, crab crackers, bibs, lemon wedges, and special forks with extra plates for shells. They seem excited when we set down the food. They tell us they have everything they need.

"I'm going to the back for a few. Josh, keep an eye on them."

For a while, the restaurant is so quiet. The mahogany tables shine beneath the lamps. There's nothing to do but wait. Then, their hands go up like the food made them suddenly come alive. First, it is the father, who wants a beer, and then when I return with the beer, it's more butter, then more cheese and more ice and more bread and then water. They never look away from each other. Mystified by the crab legs, the father holds a beer in one hand, a loop of calamari hovering in the other, as he wipes marinara from his chin. All of them laugh together, a sense of ease like they are exactly where they are supposed to be, not worrying about what they are eating, just enjoying it—all of them except for the younger son, who holds his napkin by his mouth and is coughing a bit, his head down, like he got in trouble. Still, it's their Shabbat— their peace together. It feels like seeing just a bit of what my grandmother talks about but from the outside.

Then, almost out of nowhere, I hear the father say something that sounds familiar, not the word but the tone. He's angry, and he is letting his family know. Before long they are all arguing with arms waving and plates clinking. Maybe because the restaurant is empty, the voices echo and fill the whole place. The father's hands go up, and I look for Billy or Mark, but no one is around, so I rush over and find that a water glass is tipped over, and this just makes things worse. I try to help and stay clear as the arguments fade in and out, until they summon me over again for the millionth time; there isn't even a polite hand raise, just waving and snapping, even a whistle. I hear one of them call out in a low creaky voice with a mouthful of food, "Water!"

I grab a pitcher, which had been long since cleaned and emptied, turn the corner from the side station, and make my way as fast as I can, but the situation has transformed. The younger son sits there, his head still down, his hands gripping the solid oak table like he might snap it in two. The mother pats him on the back, while he coughs louder and louder. The father says something, and she looks at him with piercing eyes, but the younger boy is coughing more now. The more he coughs, the stronger she pats him. His shoulders sway without control while he's coughing, and then she embraces him with supernatural strength. He coughs more deeply, and by now, the father is digging furiously through his wife's purse. That's when I see it, the texture in the stew, and smell the aroma of the spice—there is parsley everywhere in his cioppino.

"Allergy?" I say, and point to the cioppino.

"Allergy!" The mother looks at me, nods, tears in her eyes. I hear the voices coming from the kitchen. The father pulls an EpiPen from the purse, gets it ready, and presses it into his son's thigh while the mother and the older son hold the boy tight.

By the time Billy and Mark get there, the coughing has slowed down. Billy stays behind Mark, phone in his hand, asking if they should call 9-1-1. The father stands over the table, and shakes his head. The mother takes a red napkin and dips it in the almost empty water glass. She wipes his chin and quietly speaks to him, and even though I can't understand the language, I can feel what she is saying to him. It's the language of a mother speaking to her son, rocking him back and forth, rubbing his head gently, and whispering in his ear. He might have been awake, but he stayed perfectly still in his mother's arms.

The father looks up at us, whispers, "All-er-gee," then he holds up two fingers with chopped green parsley on them. "It's okay. He's okay." Then he looks at me, smiles, and shakes my hand.

All at once, Billy remembers, and I see him actually lose his balance.

"Billy, did you forget to ask for no parsley?"

"What? Oh. I was so pissed I . . ." He drops into a chair, and for the first time I can remember, he's at a loss for words.

Mark takes care of their bill, and they gather everything together. The father drops some cash on the tip tray, and slowly they exit, the little boy nestled weakly against his mother's shoulder. I help them to the door. It feels like time itself has abandoned the restaurant. They stop and look at the lobsters in the tank, then go out into the night. I suppose for them food really is love, every clove of garlic, every bay leaf or exotic spice. It's complicated too, with parsley and maybe peanuts and other food that betrays, but they don't let it stop them. Every moment is precious, and it all makes so much sense. I may never be skinny, but I love food, and I know food. One day, I will make it as a chef.

I think of my own grandma. Maybe something can be two things at the same time? Salty and sweet. Delicious and dangerous. Perspective feels like concrete sometimes, but then suddenly washes away into fine sand in an instant. My grandmother was always trying to protect me, even if she was cruel or wrong sometimes. Don't I owe it to her to try again? To always try?

I walk to the table and pick up the cash they left as a tip. As I go to clear the last plates of the evening, I notice that three of the cioppinos were eaten all the way through, and one almost completely untouched.

✦ ✦ ✦

The next morning, I stop by Avenue P, like every Saturday, and make my way to my grandmother's apartment, but today, in my heart, I know it will be different. It's not all up to her. I get to play my own part.

"Grandma, is there any challah left?"

"Sure, Joshy." She spreads butter and honey across a warm slice. "Now don't eat too much. Bread has so many calories."

I smile and take a huge bite right in front of her face.

"Tell me about school. Where are you going to go to college?"

I take a deep breath. "Grandma, I'm not going to college. I'm going to be a chef. Like you."

"Wonderful." She smiles, and I see a tear come down her cheek like she's remembering something that she thought she'd forgotten. "Yes, a chef."

"You know when you were little you were a little boy you loved to make the latkes with me for Hanukkah. We fried them all afternoon together. I think we ate more than we served."

"Those were my favorite, Grandma."

"Oh, and how you loved to make the Shabbat meal with me. You were such a good helper."

"Grandma, if it's all right, I'd like to try cooking something together, a new bite. I want to make something new with you."

"Oh, exciting! What is it?"

I pull the lined, yellow paper from my pocket and unfold it on the counter, and together we read Betto's blue scribbles line by line.

"What's this? Some sort of feast?"

"Sort of. It's cioppino, Grandma." I lay out the ingredients on her counter, and she picks them up one at a time, examining, reading, asking questions.

"I've never had this, Josh."

"I know, Grandma. I know. We're going to make our own version of this—a new version, a kosher version.

It's time for something new,

a new chance,

something for both of us."

CIOPPINO COOKED RIGHT

1 lb. skinless red snapper or halibut fillets, cut
    into 1 1/2-inch pieces
1 lb. large shrimp (16 to 20), shelled (tails and
    bottom segment of shells left intact)
    and deveined
3/4 lb. sea scallops, tough muscle removed from
    each side if necessary
broth from sea scallops (as much as you need)
3/4 lb. cockles, mussels, calamari
Dungeness crab (if available)
1/2 cup olive oil
1-1/2 cups chopped onion (1 large onion)
1 cup chopped green bell pepper (1 large green bell
    pepper)
3 cloves garlic, minced
1 teaspoon salt
1 28-ounce can of whole tomatoes
2 cups red wine
2 cups tomato juice
2 cups fish or shellfish stock

1 herb bouquet of bay leaf, parsley, and basil
    wrapped in a layer of cheesecloth and secured
    with kitchen string
salt and pepper to taste
1/2 cup minced parsley for garnish

love   hate

ORION'S STAR

Catherine Adel West

She cups my face in her hands. Soft, wrinkled brown flesh melds into my round cheeks.

Don't cry, Orion. Don't. Cry. You gotta be strong. Granny Gemma raised you. Momma did some too. Dad bailed. Granny was constant. She was always there, and now she needs you to be brave.

Be who she raised you to be.

"You know you're going to be okay. Everything already is," Granny says.

"Yeah. Got no choice but to be, right?"

"Nope. No choice at all!" she says, then chuckles.

Rain mercilessly pelts the glass window of the hospital room, marring the hulking Chi Town skyline. Trees and lights and people melt into a mass of dingy colors. A soap opera drones on the television, white noise in a small drab space. My lips try forming a smile, but my bottom one quivers, and tears spill down my cheeks anyway.

"Oh baby, my RiRi," she sighs, and wraps her arms around me. Her hugs used to be bone crushing, but the medicine or maybe just being in this room changed them. There's no strength to them now. She always keeps her green scarf wrapped on her head. "Don't listen to them doctors. God knows what's best. Everything in His divine order."

But what if what's best is to take you away from me? Is God looking for a way to make a sixteen-year-old Black girl's life any harder than it needs to be?

"Come on, now. Fix yo' face. Tell me about school, that big project you got going on. Something about life ten years from now."

"Where will we be in ten years, Granny?"

She rolls her eyes. "Same difference, RiRi. So tell me. Take me somewhere outside here."

I sit in the chair next to the window. My hips spill over the sides, and the edges of the plastic dig into my thighs as I unzip my bag. I sift through books and papers, a University of Southern California brochure covered with smiling and carefree faces and fully realized dreams.

Momma was right, I need to clean it out, but isn't a messy bag a sign of genius? And I'm gonna be a genius, a god, rather a goddess, of film! Rummaging around, I finally find my purple-and-black notebook. My notes. My hopes. My way out. Right now, it's Granny Gemma's escape outside this room. Away from the tests and doctors' false smiles and hopeless eyes.

"I know how I wanna do it, how it's gonna fit together, but Momma isn't gonna let me do this."

"You already talking bad 'fore you even started. What you think she ain't gonna let you do?"

"I wanna go to Cali to shoot this. Take a tour of USC. Maybe go see Dad. I talked to him a month ago. He said I could stay with him if I ever come out there."

"Oh." Granny Gemma's face puckers slightly.

"Granny, maybe he'll—"

"Maybe he will, but just . . . just . . . If you bring this up to her, you know you're gonna need something a little more set. I believe in you, Orion, but don't set yourself up, get your feelings hurt."

And I'm there again. On a porch step. In my favorite pair of jeans and Star Wars T-shirt. My head snapping up and down the street, looking for Dad because he said we were going to the movies. Another time he said we'd go to a basketball game with nice seats. The next time we were supposed to go to a circus with tigers and elephants and acrobats.

Momma told me he wouldn't come, and he didn't. But I would give him chance after chance; after I'd close small doors in my heart, he'd open them back up with a smile or a hug or talking to me like I was the only person in his orbit. It'd happen again. He'd make a promise. I'd believe. He'd break it. And I'd trudge back upstairs to the apartment. Feeling a little stupid, but mostly empty, hiding my tears and the light bruises on my thighs from sitting for hours on the front porch steps.

Finally, six years ago, Dad stopped promising things and

just left. For California. Why would his promises be any different now? If I made it out to Cali, would he let me stay with him? Were those just words like his other promises?

"I got this, Granny. I can probably use the film when I apply to USC next year. Everything's gonna be okay. Got no choice but to be, right?"

"Okay, then, movie girl, show me what you got!"

I read aloud all the scenes, the angles, motivations, dialogue. Granny's smile is bright, like the sun hidden behind the concrete gray skies outside. She's clapping so loud and laughing, not at me, but in her happiness maybe she sees my victory and by some extension hers too.

"So seems like being a big director and all is what you want to do," she says.

"Am I crazy?"

Granny chuckles. "You no more crazier than any other person walking around with a dream in they head."

"But I don't look—"

"Don't matter what you look like. Lots of people doing big things don't look like what anyone expects 'cause they the first! Just be careful in how you trying to get there is all."

I stare at the window again, not past it into the dreary day, but I look at it. I look at me. My skin, a reddish brown matching my father's. All the curves people say aren't pretty, but I still see beauty. I see success.

Am I crazy?

"I hear you. But if you want a dream you gotta risk something, right?"

"Yeah, but we Black, so we always risking more than most," Granny counsels. She looks out the window. Her eyes darting over the looming skyscrapers marred by cascading rain.

"I gotta do this. See where I can go with it," I say.

"Yeah. I heard some version of this from your momma."

I swallow hard and close my notebook and stuff it back in my bag.

"Okay, RiRi. Don't get all in your feelings. What you need me to do?"

✦ ✦ ✦

"You know Rene's gonna be here in like two-point-two seconds," Cassie teases.

Once I place the last of the bacon and milk in the refrigerator, I turn around. "Let Momma hear you call her by her first name, I'm gonna be down a baby sister."

"Well, you'd get more attention as an only child."

Head bowed as if in prayer, Cassie is performing a ritual even more sacred, texting her friends about plans for spring break. "How was Grandma?"

I shrug. "You go to the hospital and you can see for yourself, Cassiopeia."

"Really? You're just gonna whole-name me and get all self-righteous 'cause I don't go see Granny every day like you?"

"When was the last time you went?"

Cassie gazes harder into her phone. She returns my shrug. "It's hard to see her like that."

The light bulb flickers above, and a reckless vein of lightning slashes across the sky past the other stunted apartment buildings of our neighborhood.

"What do you want for dinner?"

Cassie shrugs again.

"So you're not talking to me now?"

"I'll go tomorrow, okay?" Cassie whispers. She lifts her head. Small ponds of water cause her amber-colored eyes to shimmer.

"I'll make sloppy joes. The way you like 'em. Mashed Doritos on top."

Rain comes again; loud drops splatter against our window. I turn on the stove and start prepping the ground beef.

"You bribing me with food?"

"There's no other way I know how to bribe, Sis. I don't have that Ryan Coogler *Black Panther* millionaire money . . . yet." I wink.

We laugh. The door slams. "Orion! Cassiopeia!" Momma plods through the living room, heavy with rain and whatever else she's collected throughout her day. Cassie looks down again at her phone, pretending again she's reading the most interesting text ever written.

"You starting dinner already?"

"Cassie was hungry."

Momma looks at me up and down. "Cassie wasn't the only one hungry." Her side-eye is the worst, and I don't have the energy to argue with her. I don't want to give her even more of a reason to say no to me going to California. I have a plan. More than that, I have an ache. One I don't speak of with her. One I keep embedded in sinew and muscle. And the remedy lies far from Chicago. My darkness soothed by aerial shots and fade-ins, editing software and storyboards. And maybe by the man with whom I share blood and dark skin and thick lips.

Momma could surprise me. She could say yes, but I think she takes a special kind of glee in telling me no, watching my hope evaporate like water on sunbaked sidewalks. And I try to believe she never wants to be this mean, but she's angry in ways I can't name. I somehow know I'm the reason for it—or maybe Dad is. Momma would never say, "I hate you, Orion," or "I hate you because you're part of him." But sometimes the way she is, I wish she'd just throw down and say this anyway. Maybe we'd both feel better having it all out in the open.

"You want me to make you a plate?"

Mom takes off her coat and hangs it up in the front closet. "No. I'm going to make a salad. I can make you one too."

Cassie looks up from her phone and rolls her eyes.

"Sure. Thanks."

"You want one, Cassie?" Mom asks.

"I'm good," Cassie answers.

Mom disappears into her bedroom in the back of the apartment. I put a hole in the bag of Doritos and let the air escape. Then I use my fist and pound it.

Cassie snickers. "You imagining that bag is Momma?"

I laugh a little too loud. "Shut up," I order, then stick my tongue out at her.

Momma returns to the kitchen in a blue T-shirt and black yoga pants. She sets down a stack of papers on the table, then goes to the refrigerator and grabs spinach, tomatoes, carrots, cucumbers, and low-fat balsamic dressing. No cheese. No croutons. No bacon bits.

The ground beef in my pan sizzles, turns from bright pink to perfect brown. I open two buns and add the meat, cheese, and a fine dusting of Doritos and put my creation in front of Cassie.

In my head I go over the best way a sixteen-year-old can convince their mother to let them go to California to visit their estranged father and work on a short film.

Start off gently, Orion. Ask Mom about herself.

"How was work?"

"Same as always. Too much to do and eight hours to figure it out. I gotta grade these term papers, but now that spring break's starting, I can at least breathe for a little bit."

"Yeah. That's cool."

"I just hope they didn't all use Wikipedia for everything," Momma continues. "I told them not to, that you can't trust that information."

I eat salad with Momma. Constant bites. I eat it as if this is the best salad in the world. As if I'd rather have this than the sloppy joes with Dorito dust I made for Cassie. Honestly, I'd rather eat nothing. My stomach hotly churning. My gaze searching for any twitch in Momma's sepia-saturated face, any movement giving me an advantage into reading her thoughts, figuring out a way to her heart, to a part of her I've never been able to reach.

"You're really liking that salad, huh?"

"Yeah. It's good. Really good."

Smiling, I munch on the food, but register no taste on my tongue. I form bits of conversation from a million different angles. None of them natural, an organic melding of words into sentences to make her smile or laugh or see *me*, but I gotta ask. Dreams start somewhere, even with a "No."

"So I got that project for English class. About where we see ourselves in ten years. It's due the end of April, I think."

"You *think*, Orion? What did I tell you about keeping track of your assignments?"

Danger! Danger!

"Umm, yeah, Momma, you did, but I just went to visit Granny today. The paper with the due date is in my notebook, though. I actually figured out how I wanna do it. It's a good idea. A short film! I can work on it this week with school out."

"Oh." The creases in her face lessen; her eyes widen from the black slits cutting me a few moments ago.

"There's just something, though, something I think that's gonna make it so good. So good."

Mom stops eating and looks at me, her right eyebrow slightly raised. "Okay," she says, letting the *a* in her "okay" linger. I know this "okay." She's waiting for my ask. Moms always know when you're about to ask for something they aren't gonna cosign on to.

"Where can a budding film genius such as myself go to really work on her craft?"

"Her room," counters Momma.

Cassie laughs out loud. Momma whips her head in her

direction, and she stops midchuckle, looks down at her plate of half-eaten food, and takes another bite.

"California," I whisper. The answer so soft I barely hear my own words come out of my mouth.

"Did you just say California?" she bellows.

I don't look up to meet her eyes. My head bobs up and down. I slump in my chair.

"So how you plan on even getting there?"

"The money I got saved up from math tutoring. Almost seven hundred dollars."

Momma scoffs. "Seven hundred dollars won't last you two days there!"

Dove gray–colored skies hang so heavy outside, it seems they might crash to the earth—something at this moment I pray for. I'd rather my destruction now than finish this conversation.

"I can buy a plane ticket with it."

"No, I'd have to buy the ticket!" She looks me up and down. "Or *tickets* with them hips."

Every *"you can't"* she's uttered. Every eye roll when I shared a dream, when I handed her bits of my soul for safe-keeping and she instead recklessly cast them about with loud laughter or smoldering contempt. All of it breaks a calcified wall I built between me and the things I've always wanted to do. My dreams. That wall I built because I believed I wasn't pretty enough or good enough or strong enough or enough-enough to do what I wanted. But I am. I'm a good person and deserve to have dreams and see them come true.

"Granny helped me get the ticket. You don't need to do anything." My voice is stronger. "I'll call Dad and see if I can stay with him."

"These ain't your little movies, Orion! He hasn't seen you in six years!"

"You don't gotta believe in me. Why start now? But can you at least see I wanna do something that'll last, something that's beautiful?"

"Hmph. Something beautiful. You know what? Fine. Go. And when he disappoints you, I hope you got enough money to get back because I'm not helping. You're going to learn a hard lesson by yourself. Just like I had to with him."

Momma leaves me in the kitchen. Her slammed bedroom door vibrates the floorboards of the apartment.

Cassie gets up from the table, takes her phone and leaves her food. She walks to the doorway of the living room, her back to me as she asks, "You really gonna try and stay with him for the week?"

"Yeah."

"When you leaving?"

"Flight's at nine p.m."

Cassie turns around. "So you got a flight leaving in, like, four hours? I know you didn't pack yet."

"I was hoping it was gonna go smoother, you know? With Momma."

"Rene was right. This ain't one of your movies. She wasn't gonna hug you, say, 'This is the best plan you ever had,'" Cassie mocks in a singsongy voice.

I walk to our room with Cassie's bed on the right and mine on the left. I empty out my book bag and stuff it with jeans and T-shirts and underwear. There's no real method. I pack what I might need and hope whatever I forget I can do without for a few days.

While I gather my things, Cassie slightly turns up her nose. She bites her full bottom lip hard and folds her arms. My sister's face is something close to light nausea with undercurrents of frustration.

"What, Cassie?"

"You too messy when you pack. Give it here," she orders. "How am I the youngest and I gotta teach you how to fold your clothes?"

Cassie dumps out the contents of my bag and starts rearranging them. "You call him?"

"Not yet."

"Well, you need to let him know he's gonna have an extra body for a week."

I grab my phone from my dresser while Cassie folds my T-shirts in thirds and rolls my jeans so I can have more room.

I call his number. It rings. Once. Twice.

"Hey, baby girl," a deep voice answers on the other end.

"Hey. Umm, I got a favor to ask."

✦ ✦ ✦

"So you feel different now you somewhere different?" asks Granny Gemma. Her voice sounds far away.

"Eh, still feel like me. For now. We'll see."

"Well, just remember 'you' are wonderful and you is always the best thing to be. No matter what."

Granny coughs. Hard. My chest tightens at the sound. Murmurs in the background rise and lower just as quickly.

"Your momma just up here making a fuss over nothing." Granny Gemma's voice, weaker, hits my ears again, and I let go of a breath. "You wanna talk to her?"

"I'm good."

Sighing hard, "Both of y'all just stubborn. Got that Taurus energy." Granny chuckles, then asks, "Your daddy there yet?"

"No, ma'am."

"Well . . . stop talking to me and look out for him. He'll be there."

"Love you."

"Love you too, RiRi."

I end the call and stare at my phone for a moment. Sweat dampens the collar of my black hoodie. It's not the 79-degree weather blowing in lazy westward gusts. It's worrying about Granny Gemma. It's waiting for Dad. Wondering if he'll show up. Or will this be like home? Will I wait on a porch with bruised flesh and nothing to show for it?

Does he remember my face? Will I remember his?

I make out the shape of palm trees against the cobalt-embedded horizon. Except in movies and on TV, I've never seen them. Taxis and Range Rovers, cars with Uber or Lyft stickers whiz by. A black pickup truck swerves and screeches to a stop in front of me. He looks a little different. He grew a mustache. His hair is cut lower too. He's still as tall and broad as a tree. His russet-tinged skin, the same shade as mine, is smooth. His smile is wide.

"Starliiight!!!" he booms from the curb, and scoops me up in his arms as if there isn't a chasm, as if he hasn't broken a million promises, as if me coming here is a forgiveness of all the carnage he left behind. But I hug him back because I can't get away from this need of wanting him, of needing him to be the person who would've come and picked me up off those steps, taken me somewhere, *anywhere*.

"Ready, Starlight?"

"Orion, okay? I'm not a kid."

His smile slightly fades as he takes my bag and tosses it into the back seat. My heart thumps, trying to break itself from my rib cage as we get into his truck. The seat belt struggles across the bounteous arc of my chest and stomach until I hear the life-affirming click, and Dad drives into the Los Angeles night.

"So how's everybody—your sister, Mom? I heard Gemma was sick so—"

"She's strong. We're all strong." I look at Dad, and his gaze remains straight, on the road in front of us. I fidget with the zipper of my hoodie. "She's following doctors' orders."

Dad and I are careful to avoid the land mines of faulty parenting and abandonment. We talk about people other than us, focus on their problems rather than our own, or we keep it light. A ten-minute phone call here. A birthday card there.

"Anyway, Cassie and me are off for spring break. She's

on the honor roll. Me too. Mom is teaching astronomy at Malcolm X."

"Malcolm X College?!" He chuckles. "You know I met your momma at an astronomy class. She was the smartest thing there."

A wistful smile crosses his face, and I wonder, *Does he hold all the good memories while Momma holds all the bad ones?*

"You know she wanted to be an astronaut. Was gonna join the air force. That's where you and your sister got your names from. She was obsessed with that stuff."

The highway winds slightly, and Dad's bass voice fills the truck with stories of the "good times." Leaving him to his imagination, I nod every few sentences so it appears I'm paying attention. Mainly, I stare past the windshield at the road, street names blurring by, and eventually a blue-and-white sign reads: Welcome to Inglewood. City of Champions.

Dad pulls into the parking lot of an apartment complex. The buildings are beige stucco with big windows and balconies with barbecue grills uncovered during mid-April. His apartment is bigger than I expected, with a bedroom right off the kitchen and a living room boasting a balcony past the glass doors looking onto houses across the street. Bright orange light floods the block and cascades over the dark gray wood floors.

"So I got it all planned, Starli—, Orion. Just growing up on me, huh?" He grins. "Since this is your first time in LA, we can do some cheesy tourist stuff. Go to Hollywood Boulevard.

Oh, and Venice Beach! You'd like that. Super artsy like you. Then we can—"

"Actually, I already got plans. That school project I told you about. The short film."

"Oh yeah, baby girl. But you can carve out some time for your daddy, can't you?"

I sit on an indigo-colored sofa. Black-and-white photographs of blues and jazz musicians hang on the opposite wall.

"Why is your face all scrunched up?" he asks.

If Momma, Granny Gemma, or Cassie were here, they'd tell Dad this face is my "Oh no you didn't" face. As in "Oh no you didn't ask me to make time for you when I haven't seen you in over six years!" But Dad doesn't know this face or me, so I try to find words, some concoction of sentences that won't make him angry because—and I don't wanna believe he'd do this, but what if I say the wrong thing and he kicks me out? After the plane ticket, I only have $225.00. Where would I go? What would I do? What is he capable of? And that's the thing: I don't know.

"I'm just . . . tired," I finally answer.

"Oh, okay, well, I'll take the couch. Maybe tomorrow I can make you chocolate chip pancakes. You loved those when you was little."

I grab my bag and head to his bedroom. "Sure. Good night."

"'Night, baby girl."

I'm empty of words at this point. I only have the energy to

have one horrible fight a day with a parent. Today, it was
Momma. Maybe Dad is tomorrow, but not before I get those
chocolate chip pancakes.

✦ ✦ ✦

It's nice to have something to focus on besides Dad's anxious
eyes following my every move.

"You like 'em?"

I nod and keep chewing the perfectly fluffy and sweet pancakes with chocolate chips in the shape of a smiley face.

"Since you got that film project, I got an idea. A good one.
Finish up your breakfast."

"I really should get—"

"Trust me," Dad says. "Meet me downstairs."

He gets up from the table, dumps his dishes in the sink,
and leaves.

Trust me.

Dad said to trust him as if it was something he deserved,
something he earned and didn't set fire to so many times my
memories of him are ash. But what are my choices? I dump
the rest of the smiley face pancakes in the trash, grab my
jacket, and put my camera in my pocket. Maybe I can film
something usable on this trip, wherever we're going.

The sunshine is bright, and I witness this simple neighborhood in a new way. The night cloaked the greenness of the palm
trees and the rough tan of the bark. It covered the mountains!
Even in the distance they loom, magnificent, ancient, earthly
things. I imagine all the angles in which to film them.

I climb in the truck. This time, the seat belt slides effort-lessly across me, and we drive. Dad's sly grin catches the corner of my eye. Rolling down the window, I gorge myself on all the new scenery. Even the Walgreens are masterpieces! I'm in love with a city I've known for less than a day.

We cruise down a street called Exposition Boulevard, and it slowly comes into view. My eyes take in the large buildings with simple arches and reddish-tan brick, the dark emerald tint of the grass, the towering, majestic trees flanking wind-ing cement or brick-paved pathways, the bright yellow and crimson flowers. USC!

"The University of Southern California! Yeah, I figured this is a place you'd want to see," Dad says, cockiness weav-ing its way through his words. "You mention this place all the time when we talk." He glances over at me. "I know that should be more."

I'm not trying to hash out his parental shortcomings right now. I just want to cross this street and start filming every-thing! Every brick and blade of grass!

In two years, I could be walking this campus. On my way to class. Laughing. The smell of the Pacific Ocean wafting under my nose. Is the ocean close enough for me to smell? I need to look at a map and figure this out so my imagination can line up with reality.

"You ready?" Dad snaps me out mid-daydream.

"So ready!"

✦ ✦ ✦

"How many people dress up like this?"

Elsa from *Frozen*. Superman. Batman. Iron Man. Captain Jack Sparrow. Darth Vader! All offering to take pictures for a few dollars.

"Well, it's Hollywood, baby girl. This is the best place to play dress up."

We linger in front of Grauman's Chinese Theatre, dwarfed by two fire-red pillars with dragons at the top of each and two lions guarding the entrance. I look down at the stars embedded in square blocks and imagine my name in one of them. I place my hands or feet into some of the handprints and footprints in the courtyard. Nothing fits, so I take pictures. So many pictures. If I don't, I won't believe when I'm back home I came here. With my father. That he promised to do things with me and kept his word. He's been . . . steady. And I'm scared. I'm scared of steady. I don't know what to do with it.

"Hey, Orion, let's take a picture!"

I walk over, and he puts his arm around my shoulder and takes a picture. I see how I smile wide and bright and how I crush him to me. How much we look alike. Eyes. Nose. Lips. Skin. In that picture, in that scene, we're father and daughter happy and inseparable. And I want so much for it to really be that way or maybe have a hope of it being that way.

Maybe one day. Maybe there is hope for us.

✦ ✦ ✦

"Dinner's ready!" Dad yells from the kitchen.

I'm not hungry. I'm way too deep into editing. Into molding

these digital bits of shimmering urban vistas, busy boule-vards and high-end shops, mountains and palm trees into a story of my future. The bedroom door creaks open. Dad pops his head in. "Come on, get something to eat. You been at this for three days now."

"It's not right yet. I just gotta do some more," I say, never taking my eyes from my screen.

"For the love of—" Dad walks over and closes my laptop. "I'm talking to you, Orion. We only got two more days. And I just wanna spend some more time with you before you leave."

"Are you serious?!" I snatch the laptop from him and open it again to make sure my work is still there . . . and it is. I hit the save button on my film-editing software and thank little baby Jesus Dad didn't ruin hours of my work.

"So I'm supposed to make time for you whenever *you* want?"

"I ain't trying to do all this during your visit, Orion. Come on, we can be nice. Can't we? We been doing good these past few days. I just wanna . . . well, not make up for time, but I wanna make it right. This is a start. Not everything, but a start. You gotta see I been trying."

"You've been trying for a few days. The last time I saw you was six years ago! What about that?"

Dad scoffs. "You sound like your mom. But I'm gonna tell you the same thing I told her. I can't grow something with no nourishment. I call you. You don't return my calls, unless you asking me for something. How do you think that feels?"

"It feels like that's what all parents have to do! Me and Cassie are *your* kids! We're always gonna need something! You weren't even doing any of the heavy lifting. You left that to Granny and Momma when you just decided to stop being a dad. Why? 'Cause it was too hard? We weren't what you wanted? Or maybe I wasn't what you wanted."

"How do you want me to answer that? What do you want me to do?!"

I stand up, my legs hitting the chair so hard it crashes to the ground. "Fight! For me! For Cassie! I just want . . . I—I needed you to fight, to hold on to me! Like I was worth something!"

Dad tries to hug me, but I push him away. My movements are so fast, I'm outside of his apartment and down the block in a few minutes. I walk past other apartment buildings and half-full parking lots.

There's no direction or purpose, but movement helps push my thoughts away. Ten years from now, is Dad part of the life I've built for myself? Behind a camera lens and stories, movie premieres and red carpets and golden statues? If I never became a director, like Momma never became an astronaut, would he be there for whatever I decided to make of my life? Or would he decide it's all too hard and leave again? Maybe I'm more like him than I thought. We yelled at each other, and I just got up and left. Like Dad.

I stop walking and turn around. I didn't make it too far

from the apartment; the burgundy awning of Dad's place is still in sight. I head back. At least *I* can finish what I started. As I enter the parking lot, Dad stands on the balcony, a deep sadness etched on his face. Did my words hurt him that much?

I trudge up the stairs and go to knock on the door, but he opens it and hugs me. Hard. "Baby girl, after you left, Cassie called. Your grandma is gone."

✦ ✦ ✦

Momma smokes on the moss green couch in her black suit and royal blue blouse. I haven't seen her smoke a cigarette since I was seven.

"You want me to fix you a plate?"

She shakes her head. "I'm not starting up again," she assures me, blowing smoke out the side of her mouth. "Need to relax is all."

On top of the long table, fried and baked chicken, spaghetti, potato salad, ham, collard greens, cakes, pies lie temptingly before me. I put whatever I want on my plate and walk to the floral high-back chair Granny Gemma sat in while she hummed an old Temptations song or something from Earth, Wind & Fire, or the Stylistics or any old-school R&B band she considered "her music." A yellow sweater is draped across the arm.

"She said to leave it," Momma said, gesturing to the sweater. "The . . . last time she . . . went back. Said she still wanted it to smell like her and not like the hospital. I just knew she'd be sitting here again. I didn't see her not coming back. Being here." Momma wipes away a tear before it has the chance to slide down her brown cheek. I inhale the soft, sunshine-saturated fabric. It still smells like vanilla and soap and cinnamon. Like Granny Gemma. Like all good things mixed together.

"I wish I was there," I say. Tears flow from my eyes, but I don't wipe them away. They soak my face. I wear my grief. Momma tries to erase hers.

"Well, you felt you had other things more important. Some times following your dreams, you leave people behind. It's a hard lesson."

"I—I just thought—"

Mr. Jackson from the third floor putters past me and shakes Mom's hand. "That was a lovely service."

"Thank you so much for coming," Momma says. Mr. Jackson takes his coat from the hook near the door, but he drops it. He tries to bend and get it. Cassie picks it up and hands it to him.

"Help Mr. Jackson upstairs, Cassie. Then go to the store and buy some trash bags. Forgot to get some."

"Okay, y'all be blessed now and I'm sorry for the loss of Ms. Gemma." He then shuffles to the door behind Cassie and closes it.

"That's the last of 'em," Momma says. She exhales the smoke at an angle, trying to make sure only a small amount floats in my direction. "You eating all of that?"

I start in on the spaghetti and take a bite of chicken.

Setting sunlight slices through the bay window of the living room. "Yes. It's really good," I say, my cheeks full. She *hates it* when I talk with my mouth full.

Momma scoffs and rolls her eyes. I finish my bites of food as she takes a greedy drag of her cigarette. "Have fun with your daddy while you was out there?"

The aroma of soap and vanilla and cinnamon still floats under my nose. "You gonna just make small talk?"

"Ma would want me to ask you about the trip. So I'm gonna do that, Orion, and what you can do is get the bass out of your voice and answer my question," counters Mom. Her tone carries a dark sharpness, warning me to tread carefully, think very, *very* hard about my next words.

I take another bite. Vibrant spices turn to bland ash on my tongue. "Umm, it was cool. I had fun. I mean, everything wasn't perfect—"

"Nothing ever is with him," she interrupts.

"Heh, nothing ever is with you either."

Mom's head quickly turns in my direction. She drops her cigarette into a partially drunk cup of orange juice.

I keep my voice low and even, as respectful as possible. "You wanna know what we did? Dad took me to USC and Hollywood. He made me pancakes and I worked on my film and then we had a fight, which was gonna happen 'cause . . . he wasn't trying to be a good person or a dad until now, but I mean, he's trying. And it might end bad between us, but we're both still here and he's trying with me like I try with you, Momma, but you're not easy. And I can't share things 'cause you're so busy shutting me down . . . and I don't know why."

"I . . . Okay, whatever you say, Orion," Mom replies. She walks to her room and closes the door.

✦ ✦ ✦

"Get up!" a voice orders from the blue-black space of my room. Cassie snores to my right. My eyes adjusting, I see Momma standing before me, tired and smaller than I recognize. She turns and leaves the door open. A slim strip of electric light marks the floor. I get out of bed and follow her into the living room.

Momma sits down on the couch, her hair wrapped underneath a blue-and-white scarf.

"Do you hate me?" I ask.

Her eyes go wide. Tilting her head, she answers, "Wha— . . . I . . . No! I don't hate you! You're part of me."

"Would you talk to yourself the way you talked to me if you did? Would you look at yourself like you hate what you see? When I *first* told you I wanted to be a director, you laughed at me. Did you laugh at yourself when you decided you wanted to see the stars?" A tear escapes from my eye. I quickly wipe it away. "Or before I left. The crack about me needing two seats."

Momma flinches. "You have dreams, Orion. And I get that, and we believe dreams are these immovable things, but they move. They shift and disappear, and then you gotta figure out what's next. I wanted to protect you from having to do that, from not knowing, because I . . . didn't recover. I hated myself for that. Sometimes I still do, but it's not you. It never was about you."

Mom stands up and walks to me. She grabs my hands and squeezes them. Her fingers are soft and warm.

"You hate Dad?"

Momma shakes her head. "I'm trying to learn not to, but he hurt me and you so many times. I don't know how I got so caught up in loving him that I lost myself. By the time I wanted to figure out who I was again, you were here, and Cassie was learning how to walk."

Momma is becoming this shape of a person, a puzzle I can piece together, the scenes of her life allowing me to create this movie of who she wanted to be versus who she became.

"When I saw Ma before she . . ." Mom's voice wavers, and she takes a deep breath. "Anyway, she couldn't stop talking about you and me and Cassie. About your film project and all you told her with the angles. She even tried to use some of the phrases." Momma chuckles light and sad. "Ma talked about where she saw everybody and what she wanted for everybody. I want that, Orion. That faith she had in all of us, but I need someone to show me how to find it."

I'm crying so hard, my body is shaking. Mom hugs me.

"Will you show me? Will you show me how to believe in you and me? In us?"

✦ ✦ ✦

Warm lemon-glazed rays of sun coat my skin as I enter Doheny Library. The maroon-and-ivory-checkered floor leads to long dark walnut tables. Bronze chandeliers mutely shine on the bookshelves flanking both aisles. My bag digs into my shoulders so much they lightly throb. I wish Cassie was here to repack it. Sitting down, I somehow still expect the chairs to be more comfortable, mold a little better to my body.

My eyes sprint past words in my textbook on film history. I pull out my purple-and-black notebook and find a rare blank page and jot down an idea I have for a paper due next week. And I smile again. I also panic because I have two midterms and a team presentation due at the same time.

Golden light fades. Cotton-candy-pink shadows dance across the table. I work and work and work until my phone buzzes with my weekly alarm. I pack up and leave. My feet glide past narrow bodies with smiling faces like the people on the USC brochure I once carried in my bag. Now, I'm one of them! A breeze caresses my full face. It isn't an ocean breeze. The closest beaches are probably Dockweiler and Santa Monica, over ten miles away.

I quicken my pace, heading east from campus. A tangerine-tinted sky now smothers the horizon. Perched on the edge of Exposition Boulevard is the black pickup truck, Dad scanning crowds for my face until he finds me.

"Starlight!" he shouts.

I jog toward him.

"Hey, baby girl."

I hug him. He returns it tightly and kisses my forehead.

"Hey, Daddy."

He opens the passenger-side door. I climb in, ready for our weekly outing. One he hasn't missed in almost two years.

"So I got an idea," he says, a slick smile crawling across his face. "You trust me?"

And with all my heart I finally answer, "Yes, yes, I do."

WEIGHTLESS

Sheena Boekweg

It takes a million credits to send one pound of weight off a planet.

Two hundred sixty-three million credits. That's how much I weigh.

That's the cost of enough air filters to serve a major city. A new high-rise building to bring the poorest people above the smog level. So many cases full of oxygen masks.

Fuel is expensive out here in this end of the star system. But I'm proud of that number. I had to work really, *really* hard to reach it. So many turns around the track. So many math equations measuring my food intake against my energy expenditures and minutes of cardio against the propulsion necessary to break me out through the atmosphere.

Acceleration times mass. Simple. It's a matter of calculations, and math is kinda my thing. No wonder I get so caught up in counting calories.

The metal scale is cold on my bare feet. I struggle to stand steady; I feel so light-headed from a lack of food that my hands tremble. There's a discussion from the testers in the back of the room. An argument I don't have a say in. No one else is talking. But I know all the Academy hopefuls are watching, wondering like I am if my top scores and giant brain will be enough to offset the cost of sending this fat body into space. I just know some of them, especially those who want to take my place, must wish that number I had to fight so hard to reach will disqualify me from the mission.

All I have is hope that I'm not too expensive. A hope that they'll see my brain as valuable enough to let me save this dying planet.

No matter how heavy the body carrying it is.

✦ ✦ ✦

Six of us line up at the top of a rickety bridge to the cabin of the ship. Six. A nice, safe, round number. The salty wind tugs my hair from its braid, but the molded plastic suit that hugs every bump and curve of my body is impervious to the wind.

Captain Avry crosses the bridge first with nimble steps. She's the same age as me, but her confidence makes her seem older. Zi follows right behind her, each of his steps shaking the bridge. He's the next biggest after me, but he's military, so they make an exception for muscles. Zi's young too, but his reputation is sharper than the blades he brought with him.

Funny how nobody even mentions how heavy the weapons loaded in the ship are. They weigh twice as much as

I do, but no one watches the weapons eat. Not like they do me.

Weapons. Military. Our mission to the planet Silosi is supposed to be a peaceful one. Scientific. Silosi's scientists have found a method to alter the particles of pollution that are drowning parts of my home planet and convert them into bricks, and we're on our method to figure out how. This is a science mission. A chance to see a miracle. A chance for millions of our people to live lives without tainted air in their lungs.

But Zi's mission is to take the answers by whatever means necessary if I can't figure them out in time.

I narrow my eyes at him. Zi's only here in case I fail.

SM47 crosses the bridge, each robotic step sure and even, and I have to hope they'll pilot us through the Phase just as smoothly. Finly and Croda go next. Of course the science crew boards last on a SCIENCE MISSION.

I glance down, far down the field where my moms and Vim are observing from the stands, but I can't tell which one of those insect-sized dots is them. They'll be okay. My selection for this mission will mean privileges for them—like better air quality after they move from the ratty housing with the substandard filters to the upper decks. Vim will be able to breathe without an oxygen mask. I can't even imagine my little brother's face without one. I should be proud, no matter what fears make me want to turn around off this bridge and never look back.

It's my turn.

Each step across the bridge feels heavy. As I pass

through the too-narrow door and down the aisleway, my body bumping into my crew, I carry apologies on my lips. I shove my body into a seat that wasn't made for my size, strap the ties to hold me into place like my fat butt isn't well and truly wedged into the chair. The mask covers my face, and I think of prime numbers, *2, 3, 5, 7, 11, 13, 17, 19, 23, 29, 31, 37, 41,* higher and higher until the countdown starts and the ship reaches an altitude above where I can compute.

✦ ✦ ✦

The ship has five levels: level one is the cockpit, two is mess, three is for sleeping, four is the lab, and five is for storage and sightseeing, because the bottom level features our one and only window. I slide down the ladder into level three, the sleeping pod, and find Zi there, watching me.

A shiver runs up my spine, and I look away at the pristine white cabin with tuck-in drawers and silver privacy curtains covering the bunks. I'm not tired yet. I just need to get my bearings on the ship where we'll live for the next nine days. I need to find a place I can close the curtain and not be watched all the time.

I step over the two-foot gap from the ladder to the landing, my grip tight on the metal railing. Then I scan the sleeping area for a bunk I can claim, trying to ignore the heat of Zi's stare. Why do I feel so visible all the time? I've earned my place here. I belong here.

"You lost?" Zi asks. His voice is steady and gentler than I expected from a cold-blooded killer.

I freeze. My crewmates rarely spoke to me during the testing before; we were all kept in small groups with those competing for our seats on the crew. But it's hard not to notice the best of each position, so I know their names and reputations and curious stares and not their voices. But maybe now that we're stuck together, I won't be so visibly present, and unwelcome like I was before with the math officer hopefuls. Maybe things will be different. I mean, obviously we aren't going to be friends, but friendly maybe? It's not like I can be on the outskirts of this group, when the spaceship is literally less than a thousand square feet, minus the amount of room the supplies subtract from the mess hall. I do a quick calculation of available space now that the ship is loaded: 784 square feet. Wow, we sure brought a lot of food.

Zi's eyebrows scrunch together, and I realize he asked me a question. One that a normal person might actually answer.

"No," I say quickly, my voice rough with disuse.

The corner of his lip lifts, like I've done something funny. He has a dimple on his left cheek. Why haven't I noticed that before?

"I'm just exploring," I add.

"Aren't we all?" His deep brown hair swoops in front of his pale eyes as he leans forward. There's a crease in his tan neck, like all that muscle of his is covered in a layer of padding, but he never acts self-conscious about it. Like he probably never even thinks about his weight, and why am I thinking about it right now? *WE'RE IN SPACE. MAYBE LOOK OUT A WINDOW, SARKA.*

"Okay, 'bye," I say, super eloquently and not at all awk-wardly. Then I climb back onto the ladder at the center of the room and leave the sleeping pod without even claiming a bunk.

Smooth like plasma.

✦ ✦ ✦

In the lab level just below the sleeping pods, Finly and Croda are checking that the plant samples we brought survived the launch. I kinda break into their conversation when I slide down the ladder, but neither of them looks my way.

"Amino levels?" Finly asks as she stands by glass cages lit by an artificial blue light.

"Adequate." Croda answers as he digs through a box. "How's the—"

"Alkaline? Suboptimal. Do you have—?"

Croda passes Finly spray oxygen without looking. Since the science team holds two positions on a standard crew, these two lab partners trained together and now it's almost like they're two halves of the same person, or their friend-ship is symbiotic or something. Finly's hair is dyed a green that looks warm against her dusky skin, and Croda, short and mousy-haired, looks like the tiny creature who takes shade beneath Finly's leaves. Our trainings before the testing intersected for a few classes, but I always kept to myself. It's easier that way.

The math officer training group hated me. There was one seat on the crew and twenty of us who wanted it. I don't know if it was just that I was better at math than they were, or if it was because they knew I could be easily distracted by making fun of my weight, or maybe I'm just an awkward human garbage can and they just liked kicking me over to see what spilled out, but they were a group full of outright jerks and jerks pretending to be nice people, and I wasn't about to open my net of friendship into more complex competitive drama I had no time for.

I keep to myself and no one gets hurt.

I continue down the ladder without saying anything, and neither of them seems to notice.

At the base of the ship, the lowest level, I find Captain Avry staring through port screens at the stars, leaning against metal boxes that store our food. My home planet, Bilj, seems as small as a grain of rice against the vastness of space. I've never seen such a clear vista. For a second all I can see are the lights and the dark, dancing together in a swirl of cosmos. It makes me feel weightless. Like when I cracked the Xensabar calculation when I was twelve, or the Filos mutation at seventeen. It was order and chaos and numbers and every beautiful thing I've ever wished for. It's enough now to make me forget I even have a body. It's enough.

When I pry my eyes away from the screen, Avry's eyes are glistening.

"We're too young for this," she says quietly.

I lean back, surprised. Avry Gi took top scores on every physical, and top five on the entire academic. She's gorgeous with her night-dark skin and tight curls, but she's so friendly to everyone that I forget how pretty she is. She doesn't seem like someone who could have vulnerabilities, and I would never guess that I'd be the one she let see them.

But how . . . how can I respond? It is not uncommon on Bilj for seventeen-year-olds to go to space. We've finished our schooling period, and the breeding period is still two decades away. Now is when we're supposed to take these kinds of risks. Now is exactly when we're supposed to earn our honoring. It's our duty to lift our families higher. She knows that. Winning captain's training lifted her family to the highest honor class.

In a nanosecond, the light shimmering in her eyes blinks away, and her perfect smile is back. She taps my arm. "I'm glad you are here," she says in the warm voice they must have taught in captain's training. "I know you can find how the Silosi tech saved their people."

The weight of that sits heavy on my shoulders. "Thanks," I say, and as she leaves, I get the distinct impression that an exam has just happened and I've flunked it.

Me and my big brain.

My shoulders hang heavily. Even the stars seem to dim, and though I can't see Bilj anymore, I still feel the crates of oxygen masks, and the filters, and the buildings they can't afford now because they sent me.

Nine days on a ship. And I just know that every day the entire crew is going to be asking the same question as everyone back home.

Am I worth the jet fuel it took to get me here?
The stars beyond the ship hold no answer.

✦ ✦ ✦

I'm starving, but I can't be the first one to eat.

I climb up the ladder toward the mess hall. With the artificial gravity it feels like I have to work extra hard just to move my arm. Going down was easy. Up is another story.

The lights flicker, and for an instant nothing pushes me down. The feeling should be comforting. I've thought about my weight so ad nauseam that being weightless should be a gift, and for a second it kind of is. The slight pain in my ankles lightens, my arm muscles get a rest, but my brain moves into overdrive, calculating how long it will take to run out of oxygen, how far off course we could be if the engines stopped even for a millisecond, and how absolutely alone we are.

I grip the bar, and shout at my brain to shut off. Math is supposed to be comforting.

When the weight returns I'm glad to have it back.

✦ ✦ ✦

The artificial gravity flickers again two days later. I'm in my pod, a notebook full of Dialosi calculations on my chest, hunting for a solution they are all depending on. A fully slurped tube of stew discarded next to my elbow shimmers in the light as it lifts, like some ghost on garbage duty is cleaning up.

The tube falls as gravity returns. Not at all disconcerting.

I slide my privacy curtain open. The other bunks are empty. Someone's shouting in the mess level above me. It sounds like Captain Avry, though our pilot, SM47, shouts back so quickly their voices garble together, like static on the ansible line.

Finly sprouts her head up the ladder. "What was that?" she asks.

I'm about to answer when a low humming stops and the lights and gravity flash off.

Silence.

And then more shouting. I begin counting, not prime numbers to comfort me, but the seconds since the engines turned off. We're going to be off course. I push off out of the sleeping pod, aiming through the dark toward the ladder at the center of the ship.

"Finly, you okay?" I ask as I count. I can't see her in the long shaft down.

Her voice comes from below. "We're working here! Croda, make sure the mice have air!"

I float toward the ladder. A light flickers two levels above me. A flashlight.

"Everybody stay where you are." Captain Avry's command echoes down the long tunnel. I reach through the darkness for the ladder, for something to hold on to. The captain is right. I should have stayed in my pod, but I keep counting, numbers spinning in my head. They are going to need me, they are going to need my math to know how far off course we are.

It's so dark. SM47's robotic swearing echoes throughout the ship.

The engines start to hum. Thirteen seconds off-line. The lights flicker on, bright and blinding as I calculate the speed we were traveling and the thirteen seconds navigation has missed. My eyes adjust enough to see the ladder is just an inch away from my left hand.

I'm still floating. I move to grab the bar, and the artificial gravity turns back on.

The force thrusts me down.

My fingers slip from the cold metal.

And I fall.

My head hits the metal railing that is supposed to protect us from slipping into the hole at the center of the ship. Lights behind my eyes flicker off, and all I have to hold on to is math.

Newton's formula for gravity is $F = G\frac{m_1 m_2}{r^2}$ *where F is the force of attraction between the two bodies. G is the universal gravitational constant, m sub 1 is the mass of the object . . .* My shoulder hits the edge of the landing between levels, then my head smacks against the floor. *Frex.* My hands jut out, but I can't grab anything. My feet tangle on the bars.

I crash. Fall. My brain calculates the distance between the centers of each object—my body and the next landing. I know to the decimal point the force that slams into me as I hit the next level down, figure the circumference of my turning, tabulate the instant I will crash into the bottom.

Open metal boxes rush forward. The metal looks sharp. I tense.

But when my body finally finds the impact, there is no math that can compute the level of pain that cuts from my shoulder through millions of nerve endings. I can understand every millimeter of pressure that slams my head into the floor.

Until darkness, blacker than the space outside the ship, swallows me.

And I lose the math for good.

✦ ✦ ✦

Beep.

Zi's hand presses against my arm. "Sarka. I want you to hold still."

Beep.

Black.

✦ ✦ ✦

Pain. Sharp between my shoulder blades. Then a pinprick in my neck.

Black.

✦ ✦ ✦

Croda's face sniffs close to mine. Cold air rushes into my mouth. Oxygen. The walls the bright white of our sleeping quarters. They've moved me. How did they move me? The air is cold and sweet, but why was I taking it?

Their mice need that.

Black.

✦ ✦ ✦

Shouting covers the beeping. The skin on my chest is cold and damp. There's tugging at my shoulder and the copper smell of blood. Mine. I bend my chin toward my chest and see something sharp and metal blooming beside my collarbone. It's mangled. Unrecognizable. My suit is ripped. My chest is bare. The round curve of my skin seems to glow in the flickering fluorescent lights.

Four members of the crew, everyone except our robot pilot, surround me, talking so fast I can't catch their words. They move quickly, expressions frazzled. All but Zi. His military training has kicked in, and he looks calm and steady. He looks me square in the eye and then back to his hands as they stitch a thread through pale skin.

ΙΝΙ ΤΗΑ

Five crew members. Six is lucky.

I don't remember why.

Black.

✦ ✦ ✦

When I wake again everything feels like it's floating, but it's not the glitching artificial gravity—it's the pain medication. I try to throw my hands out to catch me, but I can't move. My breaths come hard. Am I paralyzed? Dead? A bandage blocks the corner of my left eyebrow as my gaze shifts from side to side. I recognize the white plastic walls and the push-out drawers of my sleeping pod, but there's a prismatic shine over the air and tubes connected to ports on the wall.

"Help," I whisper, my voice dry and weak.

Zi's face hovers over me. "You're okay, Sarka," he says intently.

"I can't move!"

"That's just the medicine. To help your spine heal."

"Oh Frex." My spine?

"You're on your third treatment and healing well." He sighs, and the rush of breath sends a lock of my hair over my nose. "I'm so glad you woke up." He drops his shoulders, and a smile lightens his dark expression.

"I'm not dead?"

The corners of his eyes cut soft creases. "No."

"Was it close?"

Zi sits on the edge of my bunk. "Closer than I'd like."

I relive the fall, wincing when I remember the sharp pain in my shoulder. I try to bend my neck to look down and find I have a little range of movement, enough to see tubes have made a pincushion of my arm and I'm wearing a white cotton undershirt, my shoulders covered with a clean bandage. I wiggle my fingers and the toes I can see move but I can't feel. I can't feel much of anything below my heart, not even the weight of Zi sitting against my legs.

My mouth is dry, but there's something I need to say. "When you were stitching my shoulder, where was my shirt?"

"I had to cut it." His voice is quiet.

Frex. "Have you seen my boobs? Oh Frex. This is mortifying. But why am I thinking about that when I almost died, and why are all my thoughts so loud? Wait. Am I speaking out loud?" *HOW MUCH OF THAT DID I SAY OUT LOUD?* I sink back down on the pillow and force my mouth to close.

Zi scoots forward. "I've never heard you say that much. Must be a reaction to the medication."

"Answer my question."

The tips of his ears turn pink, but his expression is neutral and professional. "We saved your shoulder, so you should regain full mobility."

"Boobs, Zi. Boobs. Tell me the truth. Have you seen my boobs?"

His gaze shifts up.

FREX. "And my head? I don't think my head is supposed to feel quite so swimmy, and it's like the air is glowing in prisms. And why am I talking so much? I do not talk this much. I don't—"

He touches my hand. "The meds have this effect sometimes. You're healing. That is what's important. The zap is doing its job. You just might not have as many inhibitions while you're doused."

The shine over everything starts to sparkle. I close my eyes tight. "I feel like I'm untethered."

"That's a good word."

"Like usually, it feels like there's something sitting on my chest pressing down and telling me to shut up and to not say anything because why would anyone care what I have to say?"

"Your chest is fine."

"Oh Frex, why did I bring up my boobs again?"

Zi chuckles. "Sorry. It's not professional to laugh."

"Yeah, it's rude."

"I'm sorry."

He just sits there trying and failing not to laugh. Zi. I turn my head 12 degrees and take him in, his stark white uniform, his hands big enough to wrap around a Cilfi's throat. I've heard rumors of Zi's deadliness. He alone is the security team in charge of getting us home safe. That's a lot of trust our government put in him.

Maybe that's why it feels like I can trust him. He lifts a canteen to my lips, and I open my mouth. Cold recycled water seeps into my throat. His hands are gentle as he brushes my hair off my face. My head still hurts, but it's a distant pain. Like the pain is back home with my family and they're watching over it while I'm here. *Oh, I miss them.* I want my mom's arms to fall into and my momma's voice to sing to me. I want to help Vim with his math.

The math. "Am I going to be okay? Like, I couldn't remember prime numbers before and now I'm panicking that I can't remember—"

He squeezes my hand. "Breathe out."

I do. "—basic quadratics. Are they just out of my head? Like, what's the Pythagorean theorem, oh wait, it's $a^2+b^2=c^2$, so that's good, I don't know what I'd do if I lost that one, but how about Cylliandria's algorithm, $1c \times 1$—"

"Okay, *okay*. Stop. Breathe, Sarka. Let your brain rest."

I let the algorithm finish in my mind, and then I close my eyes. He's right. I need to let my brain rest in order for the medicine to heal any brain injuries. I'm nothing without my brain.

I drop my head back on the pillow. "I've never been good at that."

He gives a little smile. "I know."

I turn my head. Fifteen degrees this time. It's improving. "How do you know?"

The tips of his ears turn pink again. "I don't know. You're impressive. Your test scores. That calculation thing you solved when you were, what, ten?"

"Xensabar calculation, and I was twelve."

"So old."

"Ancient, really." I can't believe he noticed me.

He touches the bandage next to my eye, his fingers trailing over my skin. "It's hard to ignore hope. Especially when you think you might have lost it for good."

Warmth puddles in my stomach. "I'm your hope?"

"You're all our hope."

That doesn't add up. "But you're here because they don't believe in me. You're here to shoot everyone who stands in our way when I fail."

The fluorescent lights hit a spark of gold in his eyes. "You're my hope I won't have to."

I blink. "But you're Zi Visco. Number one in your class, ninety-seven percent accuracy on kill shots, battle hero, you hold the bench press record for nineteen-year-olds . . . oh no, I should stop talking."

His dimple cuts in again. "Now who's paying attention?"

I swallow hard. "I paid attention to everyone at the testing."

His gaze lowers. He licks his lips. "Would you believe me if I said I prefer this side of the job? Healing more than killing?"

"No." My cheeks warm. "I mean, I wouldn't have. Before I knew you."

I do know him. In a way.

He gives a sad smile. "We're all more than the stories they tell about us."

"So you didn't kill the Drilog without getting blood on your uniform? You weren't the only one of your company to survive the twelfth landing?"

He stands, his back rigid as he checks a machine connected to my tubes. "You should rest. No math."

I sigh and sink back into the pillow. "No promises."

He turns and glares at me with a weight that could turn our enemies into ice. "Sarka."

"Okay, I swear I will not do math . . . if I can help it."

He pauses by the door. "It's good to hear what goes on in your head," he says. "I hope when the medicine goes away you keep it up."

✦ ✦ ✦

"I'm sorry," I say a few hours later when Zi comes back to check my bandages. "I didn't mean to bring up the twelfth landing. I'd blame it on the medicine, but I don't know if it was that or if I just felt comfortable around you, but either way it was rude and you've been so kind to me, which is weird when you think about it because you are literally a killing machine. Who knew you could be so nice?"

"Well, I can see the new dose is working." He checks my bandages again. He smells like the strawberry-scented soap in the cleaning pod.

"I'm sorry. Am I talking too much? I get this way with my moms and my brother sometimes, but when I'm around strangers I just shut down and clam up. I don't know. I guess I feel more comfortable around you now. Did you take a shower since I last saw you?"

"I did. Figured it was probably time; I was beginning to smell."

"Why? When's the last time you showered?"

"Before you fell."

"Frex."

"It felt like bad luck to leave you before you woke up."

"How long was I out?" I ask.

"Three days."

"Three days? So we have—"

"No math, Sarka. Estimated fifty-two hours until landing."

Sparks. "And we're back on course?"

"SM47 is the best bot left in the fleet."

I blink. "That's good."

He was here with me the whole time? "Croda could have watched me. Finly. Even the captain has some medical training."

"I know." He shrugs a little. "Like I said, I'm superstitious." He holds up a silver tube. "You hungry?"

"Starving. " I swallow hard. "But somehow I feel full at the same time."

"The feeding system does that, but some more calories will help improve brain function."

"Strange to think calories can help."

His eyebrows furrow. "It's proven science. Sugar and fats help brains develop, help improve thought processes."

"No wonder I'm so smart," I say with humor I don't feel.

Sometimes you have to mock yourself in order to get the joke out of the way.

He doesn't smile. "Sarka, you are dangerously malnourished. I've seen the scans. All your caloric restricting has harmed your growth and brain function."

The doctors back home talked to me about this before. "I know. But every pound I weigh meant something was taken away from our people by the cost of sending me here."

"That doesn't make any sense."

"I've done the math."

"Well then, add this. They sent you here because you're the smartest of us, but missing those calories you needed harmed your brain function. You are harming an asset of our people by not eating."

"That's . . . I'm not being selfish. I'm trying to help people."

"Destroying yourself won't help anyone."

I turn away. "I take it back; you're rude."

He shrugs. "I've not trained to be nice to the person who is hurting an important member of my crew."

Is he right? I count the beeps of the monitors until I can let go of my anger. No, it isn't anger. It's self-protection. I press my lips together. "Maybe that's why I peaked at twelve."

"Maybe it is." His shoulders soften. "I have stew or ramca."

I glance at him and immediately start that familiar math. Stew has half the fat and no carbohydrates except the dinky potatoes, while ramca is rich and warm and heaven in a tube. But stew has protein and veggies, way fewer calories than my brother's favorite food. But maybe Zi is right. I've starved myself of anything good for far too long. "Ramca, please."

Zi's lips turn up at the corner. He opens the tube and holds it to my mouth. His index finger rests against my lips and smells like strawberries. I try to take it from him, but the medicine is still working and I can't lift my arms. So I take a slurp—peanutty and creamy. Just like Momma used to make back when I'd eat it. His gaze is warm and steady, but I can't meet his eyes as I eat. I'm trying not to look at him, trying to not let him know how hard it is to take in more calories than I should. How hard it is to have him watch me do it.

But I eat it all. And afterward he seems proud of me as he lifts the empty tube away. When his gaze breaks from mine, I go back to counting, but this time I'm counting the hours I've missed.

"Why that face?" Zi asks. "Are you in any pain?"

"No. Not really. It's just . . . three days? And everything is running fine without me. I'm just not really necessary here."

"No, of course not."

"Ow."

"What did I say?"

"Nothing. It's just an awful lot of money to put me on a ship where I'm not needed."

He sits on the side of my bed. "We're just your ride, Sarka. But it's worth every single half credit to get you to Silosi safely."

Tears well up in my eyes and my vision blurs.

Zi's eyes search my face. "Are you okay?"

"THAT WAS SO NICE."

"Shhh," he says, looking back over his shoulder.

"You are so nice and so good and you're like really handsome and I'm feeling all sorts of—"

He stands. "Okay, shhh. Sarka. People are sleeping."

"No, this is important. I want you to know something."

He hesitates. "Okay, but don't say anything you wouldn't want to say if you had full control of your inhibitions."

"I'm glad you saw my boobs."

"Oh Frex."

"They're spectacular."

"Sarka, this is not—"

"I'm not embarrassed."

"And you shouldn't be. This is just the medicine talking. And I'm a professional. I've been trained in this . . . sort. Of thing."

"I bet you have." I lift my arm a few inches and reach for his tattooed arm. His muscles are hard beneath a layer of softness.

He grabs my hands and holds them together, then places them back down at my sides. "I'll be back to check on you a little while later. Rest. No math. Okay, 'bye."

✦ ✦ ✦

Did the lights just flicker?

The tube sticking into my arm lifts, and my body is floating.

What is going on with our ship?

I know the crew's got it. Best thing I can do is stay put and rest like Zi said.

But I love this medicine. I don't know what's in it, but this is awesome. SO SPARKLINGLY AWESOME. And Zi is so nice, and he sat with me for three days? Wow. That's cute. That's, like, seriously cute and I handled this perfectly and maybe he's my boyfriend now. I've never had a boyfriend before, but he's a nice one. THIS IS THE BEST.

✦ ✦ ✦

Frex.

Frex Frex Frex.

This is the worst. This is mortifying. I am so . . . Oh NO. Can you die of embarrassment? Like, is it physically possible, because I'm feeling all the symptoms: racing heartbeat, pallid skin, a possible fever. I need medical attention BUT NOT BY ZI. My gods I might die.

✦ ✦ ✦

Croda visits me next, and by then the medicine has worn off to the point that I can feel pain whispering in my joints and I basically want never to speak again.

"Hi," he says hesitantly, his hair hanging over his dark eyes. "You doing okay?"

"Mmm hmmm," I say without opening my mouth.

He steps forward. "How's the pain?"

How do I communicate without using words? Numbers. "Two or three."

"Out of ten? That's good."

A little creature peeks out of his shirt pocket.

My jaw softens. "Is that?"

Croda's expression lights up. "Oh, this is Marbles." He picks up the small white-and-brown mouse and holds it gently in his palm. "Do you want to hold her?"

I nod a little, and he places her on top of the blanket. Her little feet skitter across my stomach and over my chest, tucking between the tubes and wires, her whiskers twitching as she sniffs me. I bend my head down 40 degrees and feel tiny cold breaths on the tip of my nose.

"She likes you," Croda says.

I smile. "How are all the mice doing with the gravity shifts?"

His shoulders droop. "We've lost four so far."

"I'm so sorry."

"It's okay. We gave them a proper send-off. Not many mice can say they were buried in space."

"I'm sorry, though."

Croda's nose twitches. "You're nicer than I expected you to be."

"Me?"

"You never said anything to me back in testing and school. You didn't really talk to anyone."

"You had Finly. And . . . I don't know, I thought everyone hated me."

"Why?" His eyes widen.

My throat feels tight. *Because I hate me.* I swallow hard. "No reason."

He picks up Marbles. "We're a little intimidated, I guess.

Stuck in our own dramas. But I don't know anyone who hates you."

"Zi might," I mutter.

Croda snorts. "Zi hates everyone; that doesn't count."

That's what I always thought. Before. Maybe I was just intimidated by his reputation.

Like they are by mine.

He perches Marbles up on his shoulder. "So I'm supposed to check your bandages for any sign of infection, and administer another dose."

"No!" *BE NORMAL, SARKA.* "I'm fine. I don't want any more medicine."

"Are you sure?"

"I want to keep my brain clear for as long as I can."

He nods like he understands and makes an expression that I would know in my sleep. He's doing math. "I'll give you three more hours, and I'll check back to see how you're managing. This is supposed to be your last dose, so I know there's a little bit of wiggle room." He checks the bandages. "Everything looks good here."

"Thank you. And thank you for bringing Marbles. Maybe you can bring her back again?"

He raises his eyebrows. "I get it. I'll note you're up for company."

✦ ✦ ✦

Finly comes up next, chats for a little while, and leaves a small potted plant in my bunk that brightens the whole space considerably. SM47 even visits, though their visit is short, a quick

scan and a shouted I'M GLAD YOU'RE FUNCTIONAL message that leaves me rattled.

When Captain Avry visits, I'm up to my neck in pain I'm
trying to ignore.

"What's going on with the ship?" I ask as soon as she pulls
the privacy curtain back.

"Well, hello to you too."

"Why is the artificial gravity malfunctioning? And why
is the power flickering?"

She glances over her shoulder. "We have it under
control."

"But why? I thought this was the best ship left in the
fleet."

"It is."

"Then how bad is our fleet?"

She ducks her head. "It's the best ship they left behind."

"What?"

"I'm surprised you haven't worked this out yet. Think
about it, Sarka. You're so smart. How can you be so obtuse?
The fleet took all the upper levels, the high-ranking citizens,
loaded them in their best ships, and left the planet."

My stomach drops. "But . . . we're going to save them.
We—"

"We're going to try to save those they left behind."

"And if we can't?"

"That's why they left. They don't think we can do this. If
they thought it was possible, they would have sent a crew with
more experience. Not us. First and second work years? We're

nothing but an empty promise made so no one fought back as they took the best ships and left us."

"But they were so kind, so hopeful. They spoke to us like this was a certainty."

"We're not! We're their excuse that they were trying to save the people they abandoned. We're the justification that let them leave millions of people with rotting air."

I close my eyes. I want to fight it, but I know it's the truth. I know it like it's the right answer to a math problem. "How did I miss it?"

Captain Avry shakes her curls. "I honestly don't know."

The pain stabs closer, through the last haze of the medication. And all of a sudden I understand. I missed it because my brain was full of other things. How much smarter would I be if I didn't waste so much thought on counting calories, or on hating myself, or on worrying about how my body looks? How many problems could I solve for others if I wasn't constantly thinking about myself?

I swallow hard. "I need another dose of medicine." I don't care if it makes me say embarrassing things. I don't care.

Millions of people need me. They need my brain. They need hope.

And I'm going to give it to them.

✦ ✦ ✦

Finly and Croda sit close to my pod with notebooks and pencils ready. SM47 has downloaded the last available scientific papers that came out of Silosi, and we're retracing their steps, finding the paths their studies were taking. Marbles is tucked into a small circle in the space between my chest and the curve of my stomach, like a soft and perfect nest to sleep in.

"I keep coming back to the math on trial 1298407d13," I say.

Croda flips through the files. "But that's about virology."

"But I wonder about that mass figure. They are computing to the smallest variables . . ." I can see glimpses of a new path toward something, but I can't find the destination.

"It might be cross-applicable." Finly tucks her head to one side. "But you'd have to account for the—"

"—effect of gravity and moisture," Croda finishes.

"SM47, enlarge 1298407d13," I say.

Numbers, like the most beautiful stars, cover the ceiling of our sleeping level. I turn my head 45 degrees to see past the pod above me. Improvement. These medication treatments are nearly done.

Croda and Finly lie down on the ground next to me.

"It's like the Dias principle!" I say softly.

Croda gasps. "Except for in inverse. Sarka, you're brilliant."

My blood pulses. "Make sure you account for the air pressure. It should be $3m +$—"

"Sarka," Zi says from across the room.

I turn my head and take him in. He sits the farthest from me, his uniform wrinkling with overuse but still spotless. "No math," I say grudgingly. His expression softens into a smile I can't return.

"We got you," Finly says quickly. She rolls onto her stomach and starts doing math. I close my eyes.

"It's not forever," Zi says. "Just one last treatment and you can do any math you want."

My throat feels tight. "But this is important." What if they get it wrong—what if I'm the only one who can help all those people? My moms, my brother.

"So are you," Zi says.

I smile at nothing. Zi pulls at his sleeves. Then our eyes meet again and my heart starts to race.

"Okay, can someone explain what's happening for the non–math geniuses on the ship?" Captain Avry asks.

I turn. "I think we just found the math the Silosi used to make their discovery."

"Croda, can you check this?" Finly hands over her notebook.

"It's just the first step," I say. "Once we understand the math of their discovery, we'll need to reverse engineer the tech."

"Or steal it."

I shake my head at Zi. "We can't steal it. Their people need that tech. We need to replicate it."

Finly's shoulders droop. "If this math is correct—"

"—and it is," Croda interrupts.

"—then we're still missing half the equation. The amount of mass that would be needed to transform air to matter is nearly half the planet!"

I look over her figures. "So they must use something that condenses mass. Like a black hole?"

"Like the Artivic?" Captain Avry says.

My eyes grow wide. Of course. "SM47, show all info on the Artivic L3."

A hologram of a small silver sphere shoots lightning like a sun flare.

I grin.

Zi stands. "That's against the galactic code."

Captain Avry shakes her head. "The Silosi have been using an illegal, planet-destroying weapon to change pollution into building materials."

"The tech itself isn't evil," Croda says.

"Hmmm. A planet destroyer could also be used to save one," Finly says.

"Hopefully two," I answer.

"You aren't serious," Captain Avry says. "We cannot bring an Artivic back."

"How are we going to get the Silosi to help us?" Croda says. "They have to keep this classified. They might try to kill us for even landing on their planet."

"I'd like to see them try," Zi says as he stands.

"Stop. Do you understand what we just did?" I ask. "We just figured out how to save our planet." I turn my head. "Yeah, it's impossible, but at least we're facing the right direction now."

"She's right," Zi says. "And we have two days until we land on Silosi to figure out a plan, and in three hours Sarka will be able to do math."

Finly grins and sits on the edge of my sleeping pod. "Basically our planet is as good as saved."

Croda smiles wide at me.

Captain Avry leans against her bunk, a smile playing on her lips. Zi sits tall, and when he meets my eye, his eyes are shining with hope.

Hope I feel with every inch of my body.

✦ ✦ ✦

By the time I can lift my hands, we've figured out the full equation the Silosi used.

By the time I can sit up, we've reverse engineered the tech, and now a holographic Arthur hovers in the center of the sleeping pods, where my crew is sleeping in shifts. I can't sleep. I've got to figure out how to remake a planet destroyer without breaking any galactic laws.

By the time my math restrictions are lifted, Zi removes the cords and tubes from my arm and chest. The lights are dimmed. Croda and Finly snore softly, and the only other sound is a rustling of papers as Captain Avry reads over our notes from her bunk.

Zi slides my feet from the bed to the smooth plastic floor and then takes both of my hands in his.

"Steady," he whispers. "Your legs are going to feel weak at first, but I've got you. I won't let you fall."

He tugs on my hands, and I try to stand. At first it's fine, but as I stand my knees buckle. I reach out, but Zi's already there. His strong arms wrap around my ribs, and for a moment I'm pressed against him, trusting him with all my weight.

I know he's strong enough to hold me steady. I glance at

him, but I can't meet his eye, so instead I lower my gaze to his neck, where a vein pulses, quick and fast as an engine.

As my legs remember how to stand, he loosens the hold and I carry myself. He doesn't move his arm.

"Are you scared?" I ask, speaking without thinking, even though I don't have any medicine in my system. "Your pulse is—"

"Zi Visco doesn't get scared," he says with an eyebrow raised. "I've stared down creatures and armies and certain death and kept an even pulse, but you, Sarka, *you* are terrifying."

I inhale sharply. "Why?"

"Because all they can do is kill me." He grips my hands. "You make me feel alive."

My eyes widen. *OH MY STARS, that was cute. That was so cute. And it was real. I'm nearly positive that that really happened, although it's been a long day, and I've been doing a lot of thinking, so maybe this is a math-induced hallucination? But he's still standing right there, and I can feel his arm on my back and I can smell the sweetness of his breath and his strawberry soap so it is real and it's really happening and oh no I should be talking by now.*

"How do you feel about that?" he asks.

"Um." I swallow hard. Do not say anything foolish. "Untethered?"

His eyes crinkle at the edges, and his dimple is deep enough to sink into. "That's a good word for it."

An alarm buzzes, and Croda and Finly squirm. Zi and I both let go of each other, and I'm standing on my own.

I'm standing.

I'm made of hope.

And now I can do math.

✦ ✦ ✦

I sleep.

I do math.

I eat.

I do math.

My crew helps as much as possible, but there's a moment when Croda can no longer follow the math I'm doing, and while Finly understands the concepts ahead of me, she really can't do much more than keep me fed, and ask the right questions as I bounce impossible questions off her.

I'm not on any medication, but I speak all my thoughts out loud, and my friends listen to every word. Every number. Every question. But as I get closer to the solution, my brain starts humming and I feel this buzz that makes my limbs feel light and I grow quiet. I'm no longer seeing the numbers. I'm no longer looking at the hologram that I'm designing with a twitch of quick fingers. I'm made of math now, and I'm the happiest I've ever been.

Everything clicks, and I stare until I realize there are no more questions.

All that's left is the solution.

I lean back.

She's done.

And now I look at her shining in silvery-blue light and I smile. The math is sound. The design is sleek, and safe, and what's most important is that it's replicable. I did it. I actually did it. We can deliver the plans to the Silosi like a thank-you, and then return home to make it ourselves.

Croda snores softly on the ground as he lies on Finly's lap while she leans against the side of a pod, her eyes closed and her mouth agape. Captain Avry is asleep in her pod, both of her arms folded against the edge of her bunk, her head hanging over the side.

Only Zi's awake.

"How long do we have?" I ask.

"Three hours to landing."

I grin. "Plenty of time. Any other world-saving problems you need me to solve?"

"Just one more." He reaches out, tucks his fingers around mine, and then pulls me toward his bunk. I lie down next to him, my head on his right arm, his left wrapped on my waist. The bunk isn't designed for two large bodies like ours. But as I rest next to him, I close my eyes.

If I can remake a planet destroyer, I can make the world fit me.

✦ ✦ ✦

When I cross the minuscule aisle to the launch seats, my body bumps past my crew, and I don't apologize. They grin back at me. Finly shakes my arm in celebration, Zi watches each of my steps like he wants to hold me up, and Captain Avry squeezes my fingers. I shove my body into a seat that wasn't made for my size, strap the ties to hold me in place like my hope for this mission isn't enough to keep me planted. I cover my face with the oxygen mask, and breathe deep.

As SM47 counts down to touchdown on Silosi, I think of prime numbers. I think of algorithms I love and I never want to forget again.

I don't think for one second about the number that I weigh.

Because it doesn't matter to the crew on this ship. Once we land, it won't matter to the Silosi. And it doesn't have to matter to me. It never has to. I'm more than my body. More, even, than my brain.

I'm weightless.

And I'm enough.

OUTSIDE PITCH

Kelly deVos

Okay.

Be the ball.

Cliché, right? But it helps me to think of things like that. It's forty-three feet from the mound to the home plate. The ball is seven ounces of cork covered by synthetic yellow leather. I've got a callus on the tip of my right thumb because I rub the red cotton stitching for luck before each pitch. It helps me to imagine myself as the ball, hurtling through space at seventy miles per hour, gliding through that pocket on the edge of the batter's strike zone, and smacking safely in the catcher's glove as I hear the magic word—*Strike*.

I can't help but smile watching the second batter from the Castille Colts retreat to the dugout. As I wait for the next batter to get set up on the plate, I wipe the ball on my jersey.

Like the ball, I'm on the roundish side of things. A couple

of years ago, when I first started as the relief pitcher for the JV team, there was some bullshit from the stands. Somebody shouted, "Why don't you go home and eat a muffin, fat ass?" A couple of dads hung back after the game to ask Coach why the fat girl got to play.

Yeah. I'm fat and I don't care what you think, or what Julie Lambert's dad thinks, or what the world thinks about it. Right now, all I really care about is pitching another perfect game. Because I'm one of the best high school girls' softball pitchers in the country and I'm leading the Tomponah Tigers to an undefeated season.

I scan the bleachers for anyone who might be the UCLA college scout. Don't think I'm that person, though—the small-town sports hero whose game is their only ticket out of a dreary, hopeless future.

I actually love Tomponah. I want to stay here forever. Yeah, it's a truck stop town in the middle of the hot-as-hell Arizona desert. Yeah, the biggest topic of conversation is the price of gas. And yeah, half the town works at the rest stop up on I-10.

But the people who live here are real and all call each other by name and at night it gets really cool and you can drive a couple of miles away from the Dina's Diner neon sign and see every star in the Milky Way.

Every. Single. One.

Plus, we've got the one and only Clown Motel. More on that later.

A tall girl swings into the air at my change-up pitch.

Strike. From the dugout, my team calls out to me. *Right to the glove, Hayley Jean.*

I wind up my fast pitch.

I strike out another batter. Her ponytail bobs up and down as she jogs back to her own dugout. Her coach pats her on the back as she enters.

One more strikeout and the game is over.

Again, I scan the rows of the cheering crowd. Still no one who looks like a scout. *It's okay.* Coach told me to be prepared for this. That scouts would show up now and then during our last few games. Or not.

My gaze lands on the one person who seems out of place. This. Guy.

The kid is in the first row of the bleachers, and he's easily the palest person I've ever seen in a state with 360 sunny days. He looks like he could be the son of the ghost of Edgar Allan Poe, with his long, black hair that maybe hasn't been washed in a while. He has a small box in one hand and a bouquet of flowers in the other.

Weird.

As I throw the last pitch of the game and it hits Margie's mitt with a satisfying smack, another thing hits me. My mom isn't at the game. Again.

She has a habit of not showing up, but I was hoping that she'd come today.

This game determines who goes to the semifinals.

What is even weirder is that a trio of city slicker people, all dressed in black jeans and tees, is headed toward the field.

They get closer, and I notice one of the guys is hoisting a camera over his shoulder.

I approach Margie where she's standing on home plate, removing her catcher's mask. She grabs a couple of bottles of water from the chest that Coach dropped near her feet and presses one into my hand as our teammates jump and cheer around us. Margie's parents miss a lot of games too, and we remain on the field together watching the rest of our team hit the bleachers to high-five smiling moms and dads.

Margie looks her head at the film crew. "Think they're with Channel One Sports?"

"Maybe," I say with a shrug. We're not exactly celebrities, but we've been on local cable a couple of times. Usually in the middle of the night when only my grandma and the night clerk at the motel are watching.

But the crew migrates toward the bleachers instead of coming to film our little celebration. They're searching for someone in the stands.

After we finish packing up our gear and loading the bases and water cooler onto Coach's cart, the crew enters the field, kicking up a thin cloud of dust. The emo guy from the bleachers is a few paces ahead of them. They're coming straight for me and Margie.

The guy gives me a little smile and a wave. Like he expects me to recognize him. "Hello," he says. "We've reached the winter of our discontent."

"Dude, what?" Margie asks, almost dropping her bat bag.

There's something about this guy that's just sort of wrong. Like he's in the wrong place at the wrong time. Like he was on his way to Coachella and got off on the wrong freeway exit. But he's wrong in an oddly right way. Like the rabbit that comes out of the magician's hat. Or the toy in the cereal box.

"Is that . . . um . . . Shakespeare?" I ask.

His smile widens. "More like classic cinema."

Before I can make much sense of what's happening, a woman in her thirties with her dark hair up in a neat ponytail steps out from behind Emo Guy. "Hayley Jean Rollins?"

"Yeah, hi," I say.

The woman holds out her hand for me to shake. "I'm Natalie Baker, an assistant producer for *Ferret Out.*"

✦ ✦ ✦

Natalie offers me a ride to the diner in her generic white rental, but I find myself hesitating in the parking lot. People stare at me as they get into their own cars or collect their bikes from the park's rack. Emo Guy is hustled into another vehicle by someone from the crew. Natalie smiles at me.

We've been going over the same information for the last ten minutes.

"So you work for the TV show *Ferret Out*? And you guys run around finding people who are pretending to be someone else on the internet?" I ask, the loose gravel crunching under my Cons as I shift from foot to foot. My stomach flutters, nausea building within me.

She shakes her head. "Believe it or not, it usually works

the other way around. The person who's posing as someone else is the one who contacts the show."

Is she saying what I think she's saying? The asphalt is like jelly underneath my feet. I wish the parking lot would swallow me up. "You're saying *my mom* contacted the show?"

Mom set this whole thing up.

"And then she took off? And left me to deal with it?" That last part was supposed to be my inside voice, but I must have said it out loud.

Natalie nods along. "Yep. Oftentimes the person who reaches out to us wants to come clean. Or make amends. And it's pretty common for the subject to get cold feet and not show up for filming."

Oh. Great.

So what now?

Like she knows what I'm thinking, Natalie says, "We usually wait around for a day or so. Most of the time, the subject shows up and we can get started."

I force myself to take a gulp of water from my bottle.

"Okay. Wait. You are seriously telling me that Mom, my mom, has been going on the internet and posing as some teenager?" I ask again.

She opens the driver's-side door and lets out a frustrated sigh. "Not some teenager. You. Dina was impersonating you."

My heart falls into my stomach. I load my gear into the backseat and get in the car.

We make the short drive to Dina's Diner, the place my

mom opened with the last little bit of her divorce money. "Your mom was some kind of beauty queen back in the day?" Natalie asks.

We cruise up Main Street. "Yeah. She was Miss Grand Canyon State. And . . . homecoming queen too. Back in high school." My face heats up as I ask, "Uh. So. That guy? The one who looks like a roadie for the White Stripes? Is that who she was DMing?"

"Oh, you'll get to meet Jett," Natalie says with a smile.

She steers between a bunch of big rigs as we pull into the large truck stop lot. The diner is usually pretty busy on Fridays after school. The truck drivers who like to move with the light are getting ready to end their shifts. The ones who drive all night long grab some pie before getting going. Even outside, the air is thick with the aroma of grilling hamburgers and baking rhubarb pies.

Okay. So, I *am* trying to use softball to get to college. Since you don't get rich flipping patty melts at the truck stop, paying for tuition isn't in the family budget. And I need a good education because I have ideas. Ideas about shipping Grandma's pies all over the country, maybe even all over the world. Maybe even have Dina's Diner franchises.

Someday.

Today, I make my way toward the diner with Natalie trailing behind me. The cameraman, whose name I learn is Steve, is already in the parking lot, positioning a camera on a stand and focusing it at the diner's neon sign. But it isn't dark yet so the sign is the dull, daytime version of itself.

"What are you doing?" I ask, coming to stand alongside him.

"B-roll," he says.

When I continue to stare at him, Natalie elaborates.

"We get a bunch of shots that can be used as filler. Or establishment shots. The producers like to have options in the editing room," she says. She points at the diner sign, an old piece of neon that depicts a pink waitress on roller skates. "Steve will get a time-elapsed shot of the sun setting behind your sign."

At least they know what they're doing.

Inside the diner, it's even busier than the parking lot would suggest. Every booth is crammed with truckers, and all the stools at the counter are taken by TV people. There are even a couple of production assistants, dressed in what seems to be the *Ferret Out* uniform of black jeans and black tees, milling around the diner door, next to the old, out-of-service phone booth. I leave Natalie out there and head to the kitchen.

Caesar's behind the grill, sweaty and overwhelmed by a long row of waiting orders. I hustle into the back room, stow my gear, and quickly change into my uniform. I'm tying the strings on my pink apron when I almost run into Grandma, who's carrying a coffeepot in each hand and pushing her way through the kitchen doors.

"Oh thank the Lord," she says. "Billy's runnin' late." Billy is the busboy and he's always late. But there's a limited labor pool in a small town. "Table five needs ketchup. Folks at nine need refills on tea and Coke. Table seven has some of those damn TV people, and they want lemon for their water and honey for their tea. I told 'em I'm not sure on the honey—"

"Grandma! Mom's missing," I say, staring at the deep wrinkles that line her face.

On the other side of the kitchen, Caesar plates out a patty melt and fries. There are at least six meals under the heat lamp waiting to go.

"Missin' as in you saw her get sucked up into a spaceship? Or missin' in the sense that she ain't here?" Grandma asks.

Not here. *Again.* That part remains unspoken between us.

A lump gets stuck in my throat. "Should we call the sheriff?"

Grandma sets the coffeepots down on the stainless-steel kitchen counter behind her. She tucks a strand of her blue-gray hair behind her ear. It's kind of a lost cause, though, because the knot at the base of her neck is a frazzled mess. "You know dang well what he's gonna say."

Your momma will come back when she gets damn good and ready.

Grandma squeezes my arm. "Let's get through our shift and figure out what to do next."

"What about the TV people?" I ask.

"I reckon either your momma will show up. Or she won't. The TV people will stay. Or they won't," she says. She puts the coffeepots in the huge steel sink and goes over to the soup tureens and ladles out two bowls of potato chowder.

Real zen, Grandma.

With a sigh, I grab a round serving tray and load it up

with a few plates. I swipe a bottle of ketchup from the rack of condiments on my way out the kitchen doors.

The next half hour is a blur with me dropping plates at almost every table and the regulars calling out my name for refills and me searching through all the old packets of mayo and mustard that we keep in a jar for something that resembles honey. Finally, things calm down and there's only one order up on the rack.

It's a portobello burger that's been fried so long it looks more like a hockey puck, with a heap of cooked spinach even Popeye would refuse to eat plopped next to it. God only knows how long those veggie patties have been in the freezer. Mom bought them off some handsome restaurant supply guy once, and nobody ever ordered them.

"This looks . . . interesting," I say to Caesar.

His white apron is covered with grease, and he wipes sweat off his forehead with the sleeve of his T-shirt. He's in no mood for banter. "What does this look like?" he says with a wave of his thick hand around the wide, utilitarian kitchen, "A Salad and Go? This is a truck stop diner. I do two things: burgers and chili. And if . . ."

I grab the plate and hustle out the kitchen doors before he can finish the rest of his rant. Grandma took the order, and it's for the seat at the far end of the counter, nearest the jukebox.

Of course it's him.

I place the veggie burger on the counter in front of Goth Guy.

He has the sad little bundle of flowers resting next to his silverware on the diner's glossy wood counter. He's reading *Slaughterhouse-Five*, and up close he's even paler and bonier and more emo.

He's like the kind of guy who would unironically wear a beret.

"I'm Jett Jones," he says, looking up from his book.

Jett? Who names their kid *Jett*?

But his eyes are the same shade of brown as the counter-tops, and I stare into them for a second longer than I should.

Mom could have catfished anyone on earth, but this guy, a skinny, Kurt Vonnegut–reading, My Chemical Romance T-shirt–wearing, portobello mushroom–eating vegan is who she chose to reach out to.

"I'm Hayley Jean." I turn around and reach for the iced tea pitcher. "But I suppose you know that already," I say as I refill his glass. I force myself to concentrate on the ice cubes as they float to the surface of the glass.

Jett pokes the burnt top bun of the veggie burger.

I pick at my apron. "You know, out of all the people in here, you look like you need a real hamburger the most. Are you at all concerned with, like, anemia, or iron deficiencies, or whatever?"

The boy unrolls his silverware bundle. "Protein is thirty percent of the calories in spinach." He dolefully moves the green lump around with his fork. "Assuming this actually is spinach."

Jett still has the little box of chocolates, which are even

sadder and more smooshed than before. Was he disappointed when he saw the real me? Had he seen my mother? Would he prefer her starry-eyed-beauty-queen, conventional good looks to my regular-truck-stop-girl big body and pumped-up pitcher's arm?

He sets down his fork. "The producers have been interviewing the diner regulars for the last twenty minutes. No one here seems especially concerned about your mother."

Sigh. He did seem pretty interested in Mom. "She's taken off before."

"Where did she go?" Jett asks.

I should tell him to mind his own business or go back to Phoenix or go sit on a cactus. Instead, I find myself saying, "She's hit the road a few times. Once . . . um . . . she went to Vegas for a long weekend. Another time she met this artist and they spent a few weeks at some commune in New Mexico. And . . . ah . . . this one time she hooked up with a traveling roller derby. When I won Rookie of the Year, she was gone. When they named me captain of the Tigers, she was gone . . ."

Jett nods. "So, it bothers you that your mother misses these important things?"

I tuck my hands in my apron pockets. "I didn't say they were important things. I was just answering your question. Mom's taken off before."

"Why do you think she disappears like that?" he asks.

"Why does anybody do anything?" I snap.

His eyes widen a bit. This weird situation. The fact that Mom is gone again. None of this is Jett's fault.

"Look, I'm sorry you got dragged into all of this," I say, fishing a cloth from my pocket and making a show of wiping the counter next to his seat.

He's actually about to shove that gross veggie burger in his mouth. "I didn't get dragged into anything. I knew what was going to happen before I came here," he says. His voice is surprisingly deep and mellow. "The show had to brief both me and my parents about what your mom did. I came anyway because I wanted to meet you. The real you."

And for a split second, I stand there holding the iced tea pitcher in the air and wondering what he's interested in about the real me.

Jett puts the burger down and rests his bony elbow on the counter. "You know, out of all the people in here, you look like you need a friend the most."

✦ ✦ ✦

When we close at midnight, we have precisely one slice of pie left in the rotating case.

A slim, gelatinous piece of Key Lime.

Caesar is more pissed than I've ever seen him. After working fourteen hours straight, he's hunched over with an aching back and is cursing Mom out in Spanish under his breath. She was supposed to relieve him at three. He tosses his apron in the laundry hamper and leaves without even saying goodbye to Grandma, which is unusual for him.

Grandma's exhausted too, so I volunteer to prep tomorrow's pies.

She reluctantly leaves, yawning as she locks the diner's front door. Lucky for her, she has a double-wide right behind the diner.

Mom and I live in the trailer next door. Or just I do, until she decides to come back.

But okay. Time to focus on pie.

Making the perfect pie is an art form. And rule number one, the secret to the best pie crust, is *keep it cool*. We use ice-cold water and chilled butter for Grandma's famous pie.

I'm busy cutting the butter into the flour mixture when I hear a tapping sound coming from the diner's front door. I grab the tire iron that Caesar stashed next to the wall phone just in case and peek out the double door with one eye.

It's annoying that I immediately recognize the gaunt silhouette outlined by the fluorescent light spilling over from the truck stop gas pumps.

Jett Jones.

God. He's skinny and I'm fat. Like, if we stood next to each other we'd look like the number ten. But . . . I'm pretty sure the guy didn't drive all the way from Phoenix with a film crew in tow to murder me at a truck stop, so I dig my keys out of my apron pocket and open the front door a crack.

Jett's got his hands in his pockets. "Can I come in for a second?"

I hesitate.

"Please?" he says. "I don't know how much time we have. I had to sneak away from the *Ferret Out* crew. They want to film all our conversations and capture some big scene. I guess they need to *ferret out* some kind of confrontation."

Stepping aside, I hold the door open and make room for him to pass. "Okay, but I've got a tire iron and the best arm in the state of Arizona."

"Right," he says. It gets kind of chilly at night around here. Jett's wearing a baggy gray-and-black-striped sweater that he might have borrowed from Jack Skellington.

I motion for him to follow me into the kitchen. "And if you stay, you gotta work."

"Cool."

In the kitchen, I get him started rolling out the dough into what are supposed to be neat rounds. His crusts are shaped more like home plates.

I pull a couple of containers of Grandma's pie filling from the cooler. "So, who are you exactly?"

He leans against the steel counter. "Well, I am *exactly* Jett Jones. And yeah, my parents are weirdos who idolize Tony Hawk and The Cure and basically assigned me this emo identity at birth. I was born in San Francisco, but we moved to Phoenix when I was a baby. Assuming I survive high school, I'm gonna study film. Maybe at Arizona State. Maybe somewhere else. Wherever I can go and not have to take out a billion dollars in student loans."

My face heats up. "Is that why you went along with this? To see a real film crew in action?"

Jett drops the rolling pin. "I've produced three student films. Last summer, I did an internship at Lionsgate. My dad is a grip. I've seen a *ton* of real film crews in action."

I can feel my face scrunch up in confusion, but I make myself concentrate on the vat of custard pie filling. "Well. Then why did you—"

"Do you watch a lot of movies?" Jett asks.

"Um . . ." Truthfully . . .

"I know. I know. You're always playing softball," he says.

This is bananas. The way he's talking to me like we've had a hundred conversations before. And it was Mom who stuck me with this. Again. She was always taking off and leaving me to pick up the pieces. "You spent months talking to a middle-aged woman who works at a truck stop. How is it that you're not totally pissed by all of this? How are you not—" *As angry as I am?* I don't finish that thought because I turn away from my pie-making assembly line long enough to catch a glimpse of the small lopsided half smile on Jett's long, oval face. He's staring at me with his wide brown eyes in a way I don't think anyone ever has before.

It's a look that makes my insides melt the same way Grandma's pies do.

He smiles wider. "My mom used to make me watch all these old nineties romances, and there's this thing called the Meet Cute," he says, resuming his truly horrible crust rolling. "It's where the hero and heroine meet for the first time. One of my favorites is from this movie *Reality Bites*. I don't suppose you've seen it?"

"Nope," I say as my stomach flutters. He's rolled a crust into the shape of Bert's head from *Sesame Street*. I'm going to have to redo all of that.

But somehow, I'm not mad.

"Okay, in the movie," Jett says, the smile on his face widening into a half moon, "there's this cool girl named Lelaina, and she pulls up next to this guy, Michael, at a traffic light. They're strangers, and he's such an obnoxious yuppie that she flicks her cigarette into his car. Then Michael is so distracted by the cigarette that he crashes his car into Lelaina's. And they meet. By accident."

I stop working too. "This Michael guy goes out with Lelaina after she throws a cigarette at him?"

Jett shrugs. "He has to. It's fate. Anyway, I came because I think that this"—he waves his hands in a wide gesture—"is our Meet Cute."

"So our lives are a movie?" I ask, trying to sound casual, even as my heart sputters along.

This guy is basically saying we are fated to fall in love.

"Maybe," he answers with a smile that sends another wave of shocks through me. "Anyway, I can't be mad. So many people go through life and nothing interesting ever happens to them. They don't take any chances. They don't answer when opportunity knocks. What if this is the start of something really great? My question is, what are we going to have to overcome to get our happy ending?"

It's quiet in the kitchen for a second.

I'm ten seconds away from telling this perfect stranger that my whole life seems like an obstacle that needs to be overcome.

"Oh!" he says, reaching into the front pocket of his sweater. "I forgot to give you this."

He places the small box of chocolates on the counter. The container is all smashed up now, but I can see that it's a box of Cella's Chocolate Covered Cherries. "These have seen better days," Jett comments, looking embarrassed for the first time. "You . . . I guess, I mean, Dina told me they're your favorite."

Cella's *are* my favorite.

I smile in spite of myself. "My grandma always says that the best things in life aren't free but some of them might be plenty cheap. These cherries are the best. And only three bucks a box."

Jett's about to say something when there's a sharp rap at the door. He peeks out the kitchen door. "Crap. It's Natalie, the producer."

"Doesn't anyone understand the meaning of CLOSED?" I ask.

"Let me out the back," Jett says. "I'll make sure she follows me to the Clown Motel."

I lead him around to the back door that opens up to the lot where all the big rigs park. We pass the storage racks filled with hamburger buns and extra jars of mayo. "What room did they put you in?" I ask as I unlock the door.

"The Eric," he says grimly.

All the rooms at the Clown Motel are named after famous clowns and decorated with clown art. Some of them are way creepier than others. "Ugh. The Eric is the worst."

Jett nods. "You're telling me. I mean, how famous is Eric the Clown, anyway? He was only in that one episode of

Seinfeld. And whoever did that mural of George Costanza seriously needs to consider some talk therapy."

I hold the door open for him. "Well, there really aren't that many famous clowns when you get right down to it."

He hesitates for a moment, his face unsure and awkward. "I knew it wasn't the real you. I found this clip of you on some high school sports show. You looked like you wanted to pelt the interviewer with softballs. Someone that fierce doesn't spend their nights chatting with weirdos on Instagram. But I just knew that the real you was someone extraordinary."

My face is probably redder than the ketchup we pour on the burgers.

"What's your favorite color?" I blurt out.

"Blue," he says as he steps onto the asphalt. "Yours is gray."

And I silently curse my mother.

Because he's right.

✦ ✦ ✦

Saturday morning practice is brutal.

I had to stay up until two last night making pies, but I lay in bed even later, listening to the music of people coming and going from the gas station. My mind racing along like a car on the interstate.

My game is off. Like really, really off.

And Jett Jones is in the stands cheering every crappy ball I throw. Or, like, trying to cheer. He claps at the wrong times and at the wrong things. Like someone who watches sports movies and not actual sports.

After practice, Coach drops a heavy hand on my shoulder. "You're gonna be ready on Tuesday, right, Hayley Jean? We're counting on you."

"I know. I'll be ready to rock." I paste my most reassuring smile on my face.

"You gotta filter out the noise," he says.

I stay busy packing up my bat bag. "Yep. Got it."

"Good."

Margie waits for Coach to leave the dugout and then says, We're driving over to the lake tonight. Is there any point in asking if you want to come?"

"Can't," I say with a frown. "With Mom gone, I have to cover her shifts."

She hesitates. "We're taking off from my place at dark. Come if something changes."

Which just leaves Jett Jones.

I've never really had a boyfriend or anyone except Mom or Grandma waiting for me in the stands, so this is uncharted territory. The stands have mostly cleared by the time I make my way over.

"Great job," he says with a smile. "I can totally see how you pitch so many all-hitters."

"I brutally, brutally sucked," I say. My voice shakes a little.

"Well, you looked good to me," he says.

"Well, you seem to know as much about softball as I do about movies." But my insides warm a bit and I'm conscious that my shirt is stained with sweat. "The term is *no-hitter*. The idea is that the other team gets *no* hits."

"Right. Okay," he says. Jett's dressed in the same pair of black jeans but in a different black band T-shirt. He's got on a black hat with a Dolby logo on it.

"Where's the *Ferret Out* crew?" I ask.

Jett shrugs. "Packing up. They say if they can't find Dina in the next few hours they'll have to pull out."

"Oh." I fight off the disappointment. I wanted them all to go, right? Then things could get back to normal.

As if reading my thoughts, Jett says, "I'm staying until tomorrow. Let's do something tonight. Me and you."

Me and you.

Okay. Stay calm.

"Two problems. One. There's literally *nothing* to do in Tomponah. And two. I have to work at the diner," I say. It sounds appropriately casual. But my palms are getting sweaty and I lose the grip on my bat bag, dropping it on the yellowing grass next to me.

"There's always *something* to do," Jett says. "And I talked to your grandma this morning. She said the diner's usually slow on Saturday night. She can spare you."

That would leave Grandma and Billy working alone. "I don't know . . ."

"I'll be waiting for you in front of Eric at seven," he says. "Hopefully, I won't get stood up in front of a terrifying clown statue."

I watch him walk off toward the parking lot and get into one of the crappiest, most beat-up cars I have ever seen. Like, you could be in the demolition derby in that thing. It starts after three tries.

At that moment, my whole life plan is about to dissolve like Tang in a pitcher of water. The sheriff's office is right across from the sports field so I walk over there. The small, beige office is stuffy and overloaded with too much pine-scent air freshener. Sheriff Walker is a big burly man with red hair who's behind his small desk listening to the Diamondbacks' game on the radio. He grimaces when he sees me.

"Hayley Jean," he says, "you know that your momma will be back when—"

Mom and the sheriff used to date in high school.

I drop my bat bag and take a seat in the familiar, squeaky leather chair across from him. "Can't you at least fill out a missing person report?" I ask. "It's been twenty-four hours."

He hesitates and rubs his red beard. "I could. But you're still seventeen. If I start an official investigation, I have to do the whole thing by the book. I have to call Child Services. Your grandma would have to go to court. When your mom shows up again, as we all know she will, you could be looking at home visits from—"

"Forget it," I say. The chair makes a loud squeal when I push myself up.

I've got my hand on the door when the sheriff calls, "Hayley Jean? I'll call in a favor and see if I can track her credit cards. I'll give you a heads-up if I find anything."

He still has a soft spot for Mom.

"Thanks, Sheriff."

It's around three when I get to the diner, and it is pretty slow. There's a family of tourists in one booth and a couple of truckers drinking coffee at the counter. Billy is robotically wiping off a table while staring at his phone. I mostly refill coffees and ketchup bottles until about five.

Grandma makes a fresh pot of decaf. "Don't you have a date to get ready for?" she asks.

I'm about to tell her that I can't leave her to work all night by herself.

"Billy and me'll be fine," she says. "Worst case scenario is that folks have to wait a couple of minutes for their burgers."

"But—"

Grandma drops a check on the counter in front of a trucker finishing a patty melt. "But nothin'. Go on, girl. How many cute boys do you think are just gonna show up in Tomponah of their own volition?"

"You've gotten damn lucky if there's even one," the truck driver says with a snort.

Grandma's face is a little pale and gray. But she grins. "You know that's right. The universe has spoken. Go. Be a teenager for one night. And not a softball star or a restaurant mogul in the making. Be Hayley Jean."

But who is that exactly?

✦ ✦ ✦

I take slow steps to the trailer. I have only ever been on one date before, and I'm not even sure if that counted because it was basically, like, thirty of us walking to the middle school dance. After spending a few minutes rifling through my own

drab assortment of lip glosses, I end up in Mom's room. She's
the one who's really good at this stuff. She has every kind of
eye shadow and blush tossed haphazardly across her vanity.

Picking up a palette of earth tone shadows, I do my best
to make myself look like someone who didn't spend all afternoon cleaning an industrial coffee maker.

I'm not totally sure if it's a success.

I leave the trailer right at seven and make the five-minute
walk over to the Clown Motel. The sun is setting behind Jett
Jones as he paces around in front of the totally bizarre statue
of Eric the Clown. I've always thought that there was something odd about the Eric, but with Jett standing alongside the
statue, it's clear what the problem is. The clown's proportions
are all wrong. Its legs are too long, torso too short, and it has
stumpy little arms that would perfectly fit on a T-Rex.

Jett, on the other hand, looks . . . perfect.

He fluffs up the clown's rainbow wig and takes a picture
with his phone.

"Ah, thank God," he says when he sees me. "I wasn't sure
how much longer I'd be able to stay out here."

He smiles. "You look nice."

I think he might actually be wearing a bow tie.

We go around to the side of the motel. Since the film people cleared out, it's pretty quiet and empty. From here, you
can just see the lights of the Phoenix cityscape sparkle and
twinkle on the edge of the horizon line.

Jett has set up a picnic on one of the motel's quilts. He
better hope that Manny, the motel owner, doesn't find out.

Manny's really precious about his clown memorabilia. Jett's tied a sheet to the clothesline that the motel uses when their dryers break down, and he has his laptop hooked up to a small projector.

"This is really strange," he says as we sit on the blanket. "How do you make conversation with a stranger that you know everything about?"

I smirk at him. "You don't know everything about me."

"Try me," he says.

"Okay, what's my favorite song?" I ask.

Jett taps his laptop and the screen comes to life. A *Reality Bites* logo appears on the sheet. "'Immortals,' by Fall Out Boy."

That was true. Um. Okay. "Favorite food?"

"Chicken soft tacos with extra sour cream."

Right again.

Jett opens up his picnic basket and pulls out a bunch of stuff that looks like he must have gotten it at the gas station in front of the diner. He's got a selection of chips, a few of the quote-unquote *fresh* containers of fruit salad from the cooler, and some candy bars.

"Favorite book?"

He hesitates for a second. "*A Wrinkle in Time*," he says. "You haven't done a lot of reading since you became obsessed with softball."

I can feel my face flushing. "I'm not obsessed with softball." But I'm struck by the fact that Mom remembered my preoccupation with Mrs. Whatsit.

It's silent for a few minutes while the credits of the movie play. "What did you talk about with my mom?"

He holds a package of Red Vines out to me. "Mostly softball and movies."

"Like *Reality Bites*?" I ask.

"No. We never talked about this one." Jett stares at Winona Ryder on the screen. "This is *our* movie. The real us."

"Do you have any idea why my mom would do this? Why she would catfish you, and pretend to be me?"

He sighs and roots his hand right next to mine. His warmth radiates into my palm. "Well, you are pretty awesome."

I frown, unhappy both with that answer and also that I'm asking a complete stranger to explain my own life to me. "Seriously."

Jett's having trouble opening a bag of sour cream chips. "I am being serious. But look, you are a person who knows exactly who you are and what you want from life. And I think your mom wanted to experience that. If only temporarily."

"What do *you* want out of life?" I ask.

"To do something real," he answers without hesitation. "To be real. To say something of value. With my work and with my life."

I hope that what is happening between us could be real.

I reach over and take the bag of chips. When you eat as much gas station food as I do, you become an expert chip bag opener. "How did you get so wise? From movies?"

"Maybe," he says, taking a chip. "I've seen *The Notebook* a lot of times."

I laugh in spite of myself.

We watch the movie in silence for a little while. It's nice and dark now and Jett scoots over a little and I end up resting my head on his shoulder and my lips are very very close to his neck and I could tilt my head up a little and . . .

A car cruises into the motel parking lot, kicking up a ton of dust.

Jett breaks out into a coughing fit as the Tomponah police cruiser comes to an abrupt stop behind our clown-patterned blanket.

Sheriff Walker leans out of the driver's-side window. "Hayley Jean, we've got a problem."

My first thought is that he's found Mom. Somewhere she shouldn't be.

A siren breaks the silence of the night, and I can see red and blue flashing lights coming from the east side of town.

But there's something more ominous in the tough expression on his face. "It's your grandma. She collapsed at the diner. The call just came over the radio. Rural/Metro is on the way, and I've requested an air evac unit and it should be here soon. But we should get over there."

The news is like a line drive right to my gut.

This is all my fault.

I should have sent Grandma home and stayed at the diner. I should have stuck to softball and pies.

"I have to go," I say, getting up and brushing the dust off my jeans.

I should have told Jett Jones to get lost.

He stands up too. "Wait. I'll come with you."

I steal a last glance at his handsome face. "No. You need to go home. Back to where you belong. This isn't a love story. It's a freak show."

He steps back. Almost like I've slapped him.

Without waiting for a response, I hustle over to the sheriff's car and get into the passenger's seat.

I don't look back. Even though I want to.

✦ ✦ ✦

It's Tuesday.

Grandma's okay.

As far as heart attacks go, apparently hers was pretty mild. She'll be in a rehab facility for another week or so. But it's close to Tomponah and the sheriff said he'll drive me over there every day after school.

Mom still hasn't come home.

But today, right now, I have to focus on the game.

Coach says that the game is a way of life—we have to play this game as if our lives depend on it.

I throw another pitch using every muscle I've got and then wait for the call.

Strike!

I pitched a perfect game.

We're going to the state championships next week, and Coach has set up some meetings with a bunch of college scouts. I should be thrilled. Instead, I find myself scanning the bleachers for Jett Jones. We're in Phoenix and only a few miles away from his school, and part of me kind of hoped he'd show up here. That's what happens in the movies, right?

Sigh.

We high-five the other team and then each other. The field is clear, and the bleachers are emptying out, and we're headed to the bus. There's one person left in the stands. A woman with perfectly coiffed blond hair, sexy leather pants, and a cashmere sweater.

It's Mom.

I pack up my gear, and I'm about to walk right past her and go to the bus with everyone else when Coach stops me. "Hayley Jean," he says. "You gotta go with the pitch. Coaches always say that. The outside pitch is the toughest because it makes the batter think that they have to adjust their stance to move to the ball. But they don't. They just have to wait for the ball to travel to where it needs to be for them to hit it."

Um. O-kay.

He points at my mom. "Softball is a game. But life is an even bigger game. It's one that you have to play with some heart."

He gives Mom a wave and a *Hiya, Dina* and walks to the bus.

"Where the hell have you been?" I demand, putting my hands on my hips. "You've been gone for four days. Grandma is in the hospital."

"I know," Mom says. Somehow, with everything going on, she's managed to keep her perfect pink lipstick perfectly applied. "Bill Walker told me."

I roll my eyes. "We've had to let *Billy* cook at the diner. Have you ever eaten anything made by Billy? He's never met a food he doesn't like to burn. We're going to be lucky if every tourist on the interstate doesn't one-star us on Yelp."

Mom sighs. "*I know.* Caesar screamed at me for almost an hour when I got to the diner."

"Where have you been?" I ask again.

Mom's hands flop by her sides. "Does it really matter?"

"You sent a film crew to my softball game and then disappeared," I say. "Grandma had a heart attack. If you were in the rainforest searching for a cure for cancer or marooned on a desert island while all this was going on, I'd feel a lot better."

Mom ignores all of this. "You met Jett, then?"

"Yes," I say, dropping my bat bag in frustration. "Why did *you* meet him?"

"You need someone," Mom says. "And you're never going to press pause on the plan for world domination long enough to make a friend or go on a date. You have to take a chance in life sometimes, Hayley Jean."

Her oversize bag rests near her feet with a bunch of Mardi Gras purple beads and gold masks poking out. I spot a few mini bottles of Jack Daniels.

"I think you're taking enough chances for the both of us,"

I say, and grab my stuff. If Coach won't let me on the bus, I'll walk back to the diner.

Mom gets up. "Don't you understand how I got this way? I was exactly like you when I was young."

I point to my body and then to her to illustrate the differences in our size and shapes. "You were *never* like me. All your life, you've been told you're beautiful. You were Miss Tiny Tomponah and Miss Grand Canyon State. They still have your prom queen picture hanging up over at the Lions Club Hall. Then you got out into the world and you figured out that every high school has a prom queen. That every town has pretty girls. What if this thing that makes you special isn't enough? What do you do?"

Mom presses her lips into a thin line. "Are you talking about me? Or yourself? Because every town has elite athletes too."

Hot blood chugs through my veins, and my face flushes in anger. "Oh. Well. Maybe I should go on the internet and impersonate someone half my age to prove to myself that I'm some kind of zany, fascinating, devil-may-care kind of person."

I'm expecting Mom to get mad or yell back, but she deflates like a balloon, sinks down onto the bleachers, and dabs tears out of the corners of her eyes. "I don't mean be like me. When I was your age, I was always worried about the future. Always looking forward to something. You know what happens when you do that, Hayley Jean? You end up with all these memories. Of times that were supposed to be good but weren't because you weren't paying any attention to them when they were happening. I mean be like *you*. Just think what you really need."

I'm about to tell Mom that she has no idea what I really need.

But then I remember that she told Jett everything I liked and got all the details right.

"What happened with the boy?" she asks.

"I was a jerk to him and he left." It hits me right then that what I did is exactly what my mom would have done.

"What am I going to do?" I ask.

I'm kind of surprised when she answers.

"You need a grand romantic gesture," she says.

"Like what?" I ask.

"I have an idea."

✦ ✦ ✦

Sandy Koufax once said, "I became a good pitcher when I stopped trying to make them miss the ball and started trying to make them hit it." I didn't understand that until I met Jett. And then I wanted to throw my very best pitch and dare the batter to return it.

We spend the next forty-five minutes looking for a Walmart. And then searching for a boom box in the Walmart. Finding an old-school radio is tough. Mom uses her phone to play a clip of this old movie called *Say Anything* and shows me the plan.

"I've never heard of this," I tell her. "You think Jett knows about this movie?"

"Film buffs watch Cameron Crowe," she says.

"And so, I'm supposed to stand there holding a radio over my head?" I ask. "That's, like, romantic?"

"Yep," Mom says with a nod.

The only thing that they have at Walmart is this Bluetooth speaker that has been designed to *look* like a boom box. Mom says this will have to do. We spend another half hour trying to get it to connect to my phone and some more time after that searching for Peter Gabriel music on Spotify.

Mom has Jett's address, and I save all my snarky remarks about that fact for a later day. We drive through the suburbs and into what is clearly a pretty nice part of town. The large McMansions are flanked by cobblestone paths and lit by charming garden lights.

Our old green Camry shudders to a stop in front of a wide, ranch-style house.

Between the fancy neighborhood and my own nerves, I'm a heartbeat away from completely chickening out.

Mom dabs my face with some powder and lip gloss and then says, "Okay, go." She shoos me out of the car.

I have to force my legs to move, step-by-step, up the path to Jett's house. It takes a couple of tries, but I get the song playing and Peter Gabriel is singing and my arms are so tired from throwing softballs that I wonder why I agreed to this plan and . . .

Nothing happens.

I'm most of the way through the song when the porch light finally pops on. A woman in a bathrobe peeks her head out the door. "Jett," she calls out. "This one is for you."

And then what? The song is almost over. Like, should I start it again? Should I have some speech prepared?

The door opens and Jett walks out. He's in a white undershirt and a pair of sweats.

He makes his way slowly across the perfectly trimmed front lawn of his house.

The first song of my exercise mix has started to play and nothing could be less grand or romantic than that.

Jett's laughing as he stands next to me. "You're pulling a Lloyd Dobler, eh? I'm impressed," he says.

Mom was right. He got the reference.

"I was kind of hoping that you might come to my game," I say, frantically pressing buttons to stop the techno mix.

He takes the radio from me and turns it off. "I thought about going but . . ."

"I am such a jerk," I say.

"Well, there's that," he says. That half-moon smile makes another appearance.

"I watched the rest of *Reality Bites*. You know, Troy totally misquotes *Richard III* with that winters-of-our-discontent thing. And Michael is a jerk, and he and Lelaina don't even end up together," I say.

"Yeah, but like you said, this isn't a movie."

He leans down, and his lips are inches from mine. It's the smell of mint toothpaste and fabric softener and evergreen bar soap.

"But that doesn't mean there can't be a happy ending," I whisper.

Is that another cliché?

Jett Jones came at me like an outside pitch.

I don't know exactly what will happen in the future. Who will win the game.

And that feels just about right.

FILLING THE NET

Monique Gray Smith

Trapped. Imprisoned. For three days, I was wedged into a car with my mom, our cat, Freda, and all our belongings as we drove across the country. Well, maybe I'm exaggerating. It wasn't across the country, only three provinces, but still.

Staring out the window, I struggled to believe that only six months ago everything had been normal. When Dad was still alive, I could go for food with my friends and hang out, I had lots to post on Insta, and I was goalie on the best hockey team in our league. We were heading into the upcoming season as defending league champions.

And then it wasn't normal. "It's just the stomach flu," he had said. Weeks later, a diagnosis of stomach cancer. And within two months, he was gone. Dead, or passed over, or expired, or whatever way people said it, it didn't matter. My dad was gone. Never to come back.

And now we were moving miles away from the only home I'd ever known, my friends, my team, and all my family. Away from Dad.

We had been eating breakfast when Mom made her announcement. "I've been offered a job on Vancouver Island— Sooke, to be exact. It's a fast-growing small town on the ocean and there's a new medical clinic opening. They'd like me to come and be the director and still see patients as well. It's the best of both worlds for me."

"That's nice." I was only half listening. Drake's voice was in the air pod tucked in my ear and keeping me company as my mom rambled on.

"I've been offered a—"

I cut her off. "Yeah, yeah, I got all that, good for you, Mom. A little ego boost."

She blurted, "I said yes."

My hands flew up. "Whoa, whoa, whoa." I took one air pod out, shook my head, and looked directly at my mom. "What?" But before she could say anything, I continued. "You didn't say you've accepted a job in Sooke. That's not what I heard, right? 'Cuz that'd be crazy talking. I know we've had a rough go of it, Mom, but moving, that's—let me say it again. Craaaaazy talk."

"Yes, Jacqueline, that is exactly what I said. We're moving to Vancouver Island. To Sooke. At the end of the summer."

Mom reached for my hand, but I pulled away. I escaped to my room, where I kicked the door shut. The whole house shook.

I knew Mom felt bad because she didn't yell at me.

I only came out when I knew she'd left for work and went

back into my room when I knew she'd be coming home. I tucked Freda under my arm and took dinner to my room: chips 'n' dip, Diet Pepsi, pepperoni sticks, licorice, and an apple for good measure. No way was I ready to see her. Not yet.

The next morning, breakfast was silent except for the sounds of our spoons in the cereal bowls. When I was done, I gathered my bowl and stood to leave.

"Wait, my girl, sit for a minute."

I hovered.

"Please."

I sat, but my dirty bowl remained in my hand.

Mom's eyes were focused on her coffee cup, her thumb running up and down the handle. "I miss him. I miss him so bad I can hardly breathe. I have no appetite. I'm exhausted and yet I can't sleep. Everywhere I turn, there he is, but then I remember." Mom swallowed. She used the back of her hand to wipe away the tears sliding down her cheeks. "But then I remember, he isn't." She paused for a moment, tipped her head slightly, and looked at me. "When I got the call, about the job in Sooke, I could breathe. For the first time since Dad died, air actually filled my lungs. I have to listen to that, take it as a sign."

"You and your goddamn—" My voice broke off. I wanted to deliver an f-bomb, but knew that would be taking it too far. "You and your goddamn signs." I stood and the chair fell over. "I'm not moving, I'll live with Kookum or Auntie Teresa, I don't flippin' care, but I'm not moving. And especially not to Sooke."

I had googled it the night before, and there was No Way. The town's website said: "Where the rainforest meets the sea." What does that mean? And besides, I'm a prairie girl. What would I do in the rainforest or by the sea? And if that wasn't bad enough, the town and outlying population were a whopping 12,769. I didn't want to be 12,770!

But now here I was, a month later, in the car with Mom, driving across three provinces, to "our new home, a fresh start." Or at least that's what she had told everyone. I knew I was going to hate it. And I did. I was the only new kid in all of grade 10. I stood out, but I wasn't invited in. The school was full of small-town cliques. None of which seemed to have room for a fat girl with brown skin. I was quiet in class, pretty much invisible, and spent lunch in the library.

I had been at school for two weeks and not made any friends. I was lonely and homesick. Homesick for my friends, Kookum, my family, and for hockey. I decided to change my route home and headed to the arena. I craved the smell of the ice, the brisk air on my cheeks, and the sound of skates on the ice.

I stopped at the concession and ordered a snack. Hot dogs and hot chocolate always tasted better in the arena. As I waited for them to be ready, I noticed the sign. Hockey Registration Extended, Peewee and Bantam Players Needed. Register Online.

"Your two hots are ready," the woman behind the concession stand called to me. I put the website in my phone, collected my food, and went to find a seat inside. I watched as the players came on the ice. They looked about my age.

They were pretty decent, and I liked the practice the coach was running. It reminded me of the drills my dad used to put us through. But, no offense, they were in desperate need of a goalie.

Sitting in the stands, the smell of the ice, the sticks hitting the pucks, the whoosh of skates, the banter between players drifting over the boards: it all reminded me of him. Dad. I felt the sting behind my eyes and she *felt* the blur; as tears filled them. "Always remember you were born to be a shining star." Those were the last words my dad said to me before he died. Just three months ago.

From as soon as I could walk I had been my dad's shadow. He stayed home with me while my mom went to work. As a doctor, she made more money than he could as a teacher. But secretly, I knew he loved being home. He took care of us by cooking all healthy, playing with me, and keeping the house tidy. Well, to be honest, he wasn't great at the house-tidying part.

The only place I couldn't go with him was the rink. His games were too late at night. But first thing the next morning, he'd give me a play-by-play, sliding in his wool socks around our kitchen floor. The same kitchen floor where he taught me to move from side to side and to anticipate where the puck might go. The kitchen floor where I learned to play goalie.

Finally, when I was five, he took me to the rink to register to play hockey.

"We don't have a girls' team," the man at the table told my dad.

"That's fantastic news," Dad said, "'cuz we don't want the

girls' team." He turned to the woman also sitting at the table. "No offense."

She shrugged her shoulders and went back to scrolling on her phone.

"Jacqui here is gonna play with the boys."

"No matter if it's a boys' or girls' team, I don't think we have a jersey big enough for your lil sumo wrestler there." The man winked at me. He looked back at my dad. "Maybe you should have her ease off the fry bread all you people eat."

Dad put his hands on the table and leaned forward, his voice much deeper as he said, "I'm sure you will find a jersey for my daughter, who will play goal by the way. Her name is Jacqueline Cardinal. Remember it. She's going to be one of the best goalies this rink has ever seen. Now. Hand me one of those registration forms."

The woman reached across and handed Dad a form.

"Appreciate that," Dad responded as he took the form. The man glared at her. She gave him a fake smile and went back to her phone. Dad tipped his Toronto Maple Leafs cap, put his arm around me, and led me out of the rink.

Tears spilled from my eyes. Dad bent down, put his hand under my chin, and raised my head to look at him. "Now listen here, my girl. Don't let anything get into your heart or your head. You are beautiful, smart, kind, and funny. You hear me?"

I nodded and forced a smile.

"Now there she is, my star goalie. Just you wait and see."

And I believed him. I believed I would be a star goalie.

That's the kind of influence my dad had on me, and not just me but everyone he met. He had this amazing ability to help people believe in themselves.

My other love was hockey, especially being a goalie. I was pretty agile in the net, even though I hadn't lost my baby fat—well, if I ever had, it came back and found me as plain old fat. It didn't matter how much cardio I did, how much protein I ate, or how few carbs, nothing much changed. I was always larger than my friends, and definitely larger than my teammates. But when you're good at something and that makes you important or valuable, sometimes people forget you're fat.

Sometimes, even I forgot I'm fat. But that sometimes doesn't last for long.

✦ ✦ ✦

That night, after my stop at the Sooke rink, I kept thinking about the Registration Extended notice. Mom was always telling me to pay attention to the signs. Usually I blew her off, but maybe this time stopping in at the rink and seeing the notice was a sign? I never thought I'd play again after Dad, but . . . ?

At three a.m. I still hadn't slept. I turned on my laptop and went to the Sooke Minor Hockey page. I wasn't sure how open they'd be to a girl playing—it had taken a lot of convincing back in Regina. I decided to register as Jac Cardinal, and sent it in. I'd figure out the league fees later.

I woke to Mom saying, "Com'n, my girl, you got to get a move on or you're going to be late for school."

I rolled over and turned my phone on. There was an email from Sooke Minor Hockey informing me I'd been put on the Bantam C1 team and practice was this Friday at 6:30 a.m.

✦ ✦ ✦

Friday morning, I was up before my alarm. I chowed down on a banana with peanut butter and a glass of milk and headed out the door. I grabbed my equipment bag from the back deck and, as I hauled it to the rink, was grateful Dad had bought me a bag with wheels. The arena was open, I could hear the Zamboni cleaning the ice, but there was no one in sight. *Perfect.* I ducked into the women's washroom, into the handicap stall. I needed someplace big enough for me and all my equipment. Even with the extra room, it was still awkward. I had to shinny my jersey on—it was tight with all my protective equipment underneath—and the final effect was you couldn't even tell I had breasts. Fully suited up, I reached for my bag and headed for the door. I caught a glimpse of myself in the mirror. I fixed my hair under the helmet so it looked like I had a mullet. I looked at myself a moment longer. "You got this."

I peeked out the door to be sure no one would see me, and in my sock feet I hustled across the foyer, through the rink doors, and found a place near the bench to hide my bag. I pulled out my skates. I slid my left foot in, moved my toes around, pulled the sock tight, did up the laces, and tapped my foot three times. *Mind, body, spirit.* Same routine for the right foot. Just like Dad had taught me. I stood and stepped onto the ice. In the whoosh of my skates, I transformed. It was like all the extra padding I wore as a goalie not only protected me from the puck, but also the mean words. *Fatty, fry bread with legs, net filler, lardo.*

I did a few laps around the rink while the rest of the players made their way onto the ice.

Practice began with some conditioning, I held my own and was proud of that. Then we moved to shots on goal from the blue line. The other goalie went first, and then it was my turn.

"Let's see what the new guy's got, besides being able to fill the net. Seriously, Coach, where'd you find him? McDonald's?" That was Chad. He was one of the popular boys at school. Decent at hockey, but obviously not good enough to be on the rep team.

I was used to comments. My dad always said the comments said more about the person saying them than they did about me. I knew I had to prove myself, and that's what I was going to do.

I took my place between the pipes, slid from side to side, tapped each pipe with my stick, just like my dad had taught me, and then squared up in the middle of the net. I skated out a foot and stopped the first shot from the blue line, then the next and the next. I lost track of how many shots I'd stopped, was focused on the next one and was looking to the left blue line when someone let a wicked shot go from the opposite boards.

The shot hit me where the face shield and helmet come together and down I went. Facedown on the ice. As I lifted my head, stars swirled. Dad said I was born to be a star, but I don't think these were the stars he was referring to. Next thing I knew, Coach was kneeling beside me. "Jac, can you hear me?" I nodded. Chad's voice filled the rink. "Hey, Coach, you should wait for the crane. Like they do for beached whales." The team laughed.

Coach blew his whistle hard. "That's it! We're done for today."

A resounding "Whaaaaat?" from the players.

"You heard me. If you aren't going to be respectful to your teammates, then I don't want you on my ice. Go. Each of you. And only come back on Wednesday if you are ready to be a team player. Otherwise, I'm more than happy to help you find another team."

No one moved.

He raised his voice. "Go. Get off the ice." I heard moans and muttering of complaints as my teammates headed to the locker room. Coach put his hand on my back. "How you doing, Jac?"

I nodded my head and made my voice as deep as it could go. "I'm okay." I pushed myself up onto my knees and stood. I blinked a couple of times. "I'm okay, Coach. We really should practice."

Coach replied, "No. Look at me, Jac." I looked at him. "Don't listen to them. And don't listen to negative talk in your own head. Hockey is like life. Not only do you have to train your body to function well, but you also have to train your mind. That's obviously something most of our team has not yet learned." He turned my body so I could see the net. "What do you see?"

"The net."

"Yes, and what else?"

"I don't know. Ice. Pucks."

"Yes, pucks. Where are the pucks?"

I pointed with my stick. "Over there, and over there, and back there."

"Are there any in the net?"

I shook my head.

"Exactly."

I looked at him, raised my eyebrows.

"I think they took about fifty shots on you, and not a single one got past."

I scanned all the pucks and the net again. "Oh."

"Yes, oh! I don't know where you came from, Jac Cardinal, but I'm sure happy they put you on my team."

✦ ✦ ✦

Other than that brief conversation with Coach, I never said a word at practice. I arrived early and was on the ice before anyone. It wasn't until the end of the fourth practice that my secret was revealed.

I had stayed on the ice and done extra stretching until I knew everyone was in the locker room and it was safe for me to sneak into the women's washroom to change. I had just gone in when I heard my mom in the hall.

"Hi, Coach, my name's Margo Cardinal. I'm Jacqueline's mom."

"Jacqueline?"

"Yes, your new goalie."

"Jac? Is a Jacqueline?"

The washroom door flew open. Coach walked over and stood in front of me. My stomach flipped, and flipped again.

"Take off your helmet."

I reached up, grabbed it by the jaw, and eased it off. My eyes remained on the floor.

"You're . . . you're a girl?"

I nodded.

He leaned against the sink. His thumb and forefinger rubbed his eyes. He was quiet for what felt like eternity. Finally, he turned to me. "Why didn't you tell me?"

"I was afraid you wouldn't let me play if you knew I was a girl. And besides, after the first practice, it was pretty clear what the guys thought of me. All their comments about being fat, about being a beached whale. I had to prove myself. You know, prove that I was a decent goalie."

"Well, you did. You're a damn good goalie, especially for your size. And for . . ." His voice trailed off.

"For being a girl."

"Yes, there's that now too."

"Well, guess I'll just get changed and leave."

"Now, don't go getting all dramatic on me. No one said you had to quit."

"Oh." I looked directly at him and shook my head. "I wasn't thinking about quitting. I just thought maybe you needed me outa here so you could sort out how you're going to handle this with the team."

"Me handle it with the team? Oh no—you're going to tell them."

My body flinched back. "Me?"

"Yes, you." His head moved up and down as he informed me, "'Cuz what am I supposed to say, 'Hey, guys, guess what? Our starting goalie is a girl'?"

I shrugged. "Sounds good to me." My head swerved so I could look at him. "Wait. Did you say *starting* goalie?"

"Yes." I saw the sides of his mouth rise slightly.

I raised my fist in the air. "Yeah!"

This time, both Coach and I smiled.

"Okay, I'll tell them next practice." I told him

"Well, this is gonna be interesting." Coach stood. "You teenagers never cease to surprise me."

"Thanks, Coach, you know, for the nod in the net."

"You earned it. Now I'm gonna get outa here so you can change." When he reached the door, he turned. "Next practice, I'll organize for the girls' change room to be open."

"Thanks, Coach. For everything."

As he walked out, I heard him mumble, "Don't be thanking me just yet."

I didn't care. I was already fist pumping the air and singing, "Starting goalie, starting goalie, I'm the starting goalie."

✦ ✦ ✦

The next morning at breakfast, Mom announced, "I paid your registration fees."

"Thanks," I mumbled. I was still pissed at her for showing up at practice. I had no idea how she found out and didn't care enough to ask.

"I know Dad always used to work out with you. I'm not any good at shooting pucks."

"True story."

Mom smiled. "But I am good at yoga. Maybe we could do yoga a couple mornings a week."

At the top of my eye roll, I responded. "Yoga is for hippies. But hey, you moved us out here to Hippie Central, so why should I be surprised you think I might wanna do yoga with you?"

Mom sat back in her chair. "I read in *Sports Illustrated* that professional hockey and baseball players have taken up yoga."

"Really, Mom? When have you ever read *Sports Illustrated*?"

Mom took a long sip of her coffee, and did her best to try to stop the flood of tears forming in her eyes. She cleared her throat. "When I was cleaning out your dad's bedside table, I found a pile of his *Sports Illustrated*s and spent an afternoon reading them. It helped me feel close to him, if only for an afternoon."

Silence swirled around us.

"Look, my girl, all we have is each other. We've got to help each other through this."

I felt like a moron. Why was I always mean to her? "Okay, Mom, but not mornings. Before bed. Isn't there some kind of special"—I used my fingers for quotation marks—"go-to-sleep yoga?"

"Yes, there is." The tears had fallen out of Mom's eyes and

were sliding down her cheeks. She wiped them with her sleeve. "I'd like that."

I stood, kissed her on her cheek. The salt of her tears burned my lips. "'Kay, I gotta go or I'm gonna be late for chem."

"Love you, beauty."

"Love you too, Mom."

✦ ✦ ✦

At the beginning of practice, Coach called us together on the ice. "Gentlemen, gentlemen, listen up." Coach looked at me. "Sorry. And ladies."

"What?" Chad scoffed. "No chicks here, Coach."

"First of all, you're on my ice," Coach said, "and you'll be respectful. 'Ladies' is the term. And yes, we have one with us. Our new starting goalie, Jac."

The guys looked at one another. I removed my helmet and my hair fell onto my jersey.

Chad noticed first. "Holy f—" He stopped midsentence. "Not only are you a porker, but you're also a chick. *And* an Indian." Chad's head fell back. "And I actually thought we had a chance this season."

The other goalie, Sam, spoke up. "Hey, you can't say that anymore."

"What? Chick? Porker? Or Indian?"

Sam skated over in front of Chad. "All of it."

"You shouldn't be fightin' with me, dude, you should be fightin' with her. 'Cuz *you* just had a *girl*"—Chad pointed at me—"replace you between the pipes." Chad cackled, and other teammates began to laugh.

"You don't get it, do you, Chad? I don't care if she's a girl, because she's the best goalie I've ever seen, probably the best in our league." Sam glanced at me, and my head dropped. "If she makes our team better, I'm okay with giving up starting position, but you—you wouldn't know anything about team, would you? It's always about Chad."

Chad dropped his gloves and was about to take a swing at Sam when Coach skated between them. "All right, all right. That's enough. Everyone on the line."

A resounding "Ugh."

"Way to go, Chad. Now we gotta do conditioning," said one of the guys whose name I didn't know yet.

"Hey, don't blame me, blame what's-her-name." Chad jabbed his stick in my direction. "If it wasn't for Fatso, we'd be having practice as usual." He turned to me. "You should just go back to the kitchen where you belong."

"Chad. Another word from you and you're sitting for the first five games."

"That's almost half the season," Chad whined.

"Exactly. Choose wisely."

We did conditioning drills for over an hour, and I was spent.

"Okay, last one," yelled Coach. "Push-up challenge."

We had this one back home. Coach would count off push-ups, and the last one to keep going was the winner. I usually did pretty good, but I'd never won.

Coach started, and at ten push-ups some of the players

began to collapse. A few more at twenty, twenty-five, and then there were three of us left. Charlie, Chad, and me. At forty, Charlie fell to the ice and some of the team began chanting, "Chad, Chad, Chad."

I knew it was probably in my best interest to let him win, and for a moment I considered it. But I knew if my dad were watching, he'd be disappointed. I was raised to be a competitor, to do my best. To make myself, my family, and my ancestors proud. My arms were on fire and trembling. My eyes focused on my fingers. Up, Down. Repeat.

Finally, at fifty-nine, Chad fell to his stomach. I pushed up and back down. Sixty. I could've done a few more, but thought I better not make matters worse by rubbing it in. Although I wanted to.

"Well, I'll be . . ." Coach's voice trailed off for a moment before he announced, "The winner of today's push-up challenge is Jac."

Sam clapped, but stopped when he realized he was the only one.

Coach continued, "That's it for today. Next practice"— he looked at Chad—"I expect everyone will come prepared to be a team player."

✦ ✦ ✦

The first time I actually talked to Sam, besides on the ice, was in the library. I was looking for the new Eden Robinson book, *Trickster Drift*, and he had a collection of graphic novels tucked under his arm.

"Um, hi, Jac," he said. "Don't usually run into too many of my teammates in here."

"Nope, bet you don't." I smiled at him, my tone matching his subtle sarcasm.

He smiled back, and the outside corners of his eyes lifted. It was then I noticed how friendly his eyes were. They were milk-chocolate brown with green and gold flecks. My stomach flipped.

Sam shifted his books to the other arm and said, "I was thinking about going to get some food after school. Um, would you, um, like to come with me?"

My stomach flipped again. I could feel a warmth creep up my neck and across my face. My tongue stuck to the roof of my mouth. I nodded and managed to squeak out, "Sure."

We met up out front of school, and after a few awkward moments, we both relaxed and started laughing.

We spent time hanging out at the ocean, went for walks, read to each other, and went for food. Sometimes we'd take the bus to Victoria to see a movie or visit Munro's Books. Sam preferred to draw more than play goal, so he was quite okay with me replacing him as the starting goalie.

✦ ✦ ✦

We won the round robin and qualified for the semifinals against Cowichan Valley. The game was set for Saturday.

At the end of our last practice, Sam asked me if he could borrow my mask.

"Sure, but why?"

"You'll see," was all he said as he put my mask in his equipment bag and left the rink.

✦ ✦ ✦

On game day, as usual, I came into the change room once the guys were dressed.

"Hey, everyone, listen up." Instead of Coach, it was Sam. The room quieted down. "I know you all know there's no way we'd ever have gotten this far with me in net."

Laughter filled the change room. "Truth." "Say it, brother."

Sam held up his hand. "So I wanted to do something for Jac, to thank her." He turned to me and handed me a cloth bag. "I painted this for you."

I opened the bag and peeked inside. It was my helmet, but when I pulled it out I realized it was not just my old helmet. Sam had painted it so it looked like an eagle was staring at you. I had never seen anything quite like it.

Chad was the first one to speak. "Whoa, bro, that's sick!"

Sam's face turned pink. "Thanks."

"Put it on," Chad added, and then started to bang his stick on the floor and chant, "Put it on! Put it on! Put it on!"

The whole team chimed in, and I stood and slipped the helmet on.

I looked in the mirror. An eagle's face stared back at me, my eyes where the eagle's would've been. Just as Chad had said, it was sick! I turned and hugged Sam. "Thank you."

"Um, uh, you're welcome." He let go. "Now all of you go

out there and win us this game." The change room exploded with cheers.

The rink was pretty much full. Our making it to the semi-finals was a big deal in little ol' Sooke. As I skated toward the net, I saw Mom sitting in her usual spot, four rows up over my left shoulder. She pointed to my mask and gave two thumbs-up and then put her hand on her heart. I gave her a nod of my head, but inside my mask, I was smiling.

I think Dad would have been happy knowing we were doing okay finding our way in a world without him.

I took a squirt of water, offered my usual prayer to the ancestors: "Thank you for the gift of playing in this game. Please watch over me and everyone on the ice, keep us safe and healthy." I turned around in the net—time to play. From the moment the puck dropped until the last whistle, I could hear my breath echoing in my mask. Every sound was heightened, my peripheral vision expanded, and my ability to anticipate where the puck was going to go amplified. Not a single shot got past me. Or the other goalie.

At the end of three periods, we were tied 0–0. After the five-minute overtime, still no score. Shoot-out. Three players from each team were chosen to take penalty shots on opposing goalies.

I stopped the shots of the first two players, but so had the other goalie. If I stopped this next shot, Chad would have our last shot, and a chance for us to win.

As I skated into the net, I saw their captain at center ice. He was tiny and fast with a wicked wrist shot. He came flying down the ice right at me. I met his eyes and matched each move. When he let the shot go, my left arm sprang out. *Smack.* The sound of the puck in my glove filled the silent arena, immediately followed by cheers. I dropped the puck at the side of the net and glanced up at Mom. She was jumping up and down, clapping and wearing a smile that reminded me of who she was before Dad died. I touched my heart with my glove and then pointed to her.

I skated back to the bench, high-fiv'n the guys. Chad stepped onto the ice, I called to him. He turned and I waved him back with my hand. "Listen, I watched this goalie and when someone dekes a bit to the left, he cheats and begins to cut across the ice, thinking there's going to be another deke to the right. He leaves about half a foot open on the left side of the net. It's yours for the taking."

Chad put his mouth guard back in and skated to center ice. The arena was silent. Our whole team was leaning over the boards. Every second felt like a minute.

Chad skated flawlessly down the ice. At the blue line he took an extra step to the left, dropped his shoulder and head, and then motioned as if he was going to go the opposite way. Just as I'd described, the goalie cheated a bit and began to slide to the right, leaving a portion of the net open. I was whispering, "Shoot, Chad, shoot." Chad's stick slid along the ice as he sent a wrist shot flying toward the net.

Ping!

The puck flew off the post, hit the goalie in the shoulder, and ricocheted into the net.

Chad's arms flew up into the air, and our team leaped onto the ice and toward him. We circled around Chad, jumping up and down, everyone hugging one another and cheering loudly.

✦ ✦ ✦

In the change room, after Coach's speech, Chad came over to me. "Thanks for the tip, you know, about the goalie."

I nodded.

"Uh, you're pretty good for . . ." His voice trailed off.

I looked away, bracing myself for one of his nasty comments.

"Truth is, Jac, you're a freak'n sick goalie and we could've never done this without you." He gave me a hard smack on the shoulder and turned back to celebrating with the rest of the team.

It didn't even bother me that the next week we lost in the Island Finals. We had won in so many ways. While Chad and I would never be friends—don't kid yourself, this is Sooke, not Hollywood—we had become teammates. For that, and so much more, I was grateful.

A PERFECT FIT

Jennifer Yen

In a world of tens, I'm just a too. Too tall, too fat, too smart, too shy. Nothing about me is right—especially if you ask my family. At five foot even, Mama still wears the same size zero clothes from her twenties, while I've expanded into the *dreaded* double digits. Baba towers over her at five foot five, but I can still make out the growing bald spot at the top of his head.

As if that wasn't enough, Mama's the center of attention no matter where we go. She makes friends out of strangers in a matter of seconds. Meanwhile, I'm lucky if people don't forget I'm in the room. I did manage to inherit Baba's brains, but I would trade some of those for an ounce of coordination. There's nothing worse than getting hit in the face with a ball in PE . . . except when it happens in front of the guy you have a huge crush on.

At least it got Stephen's attention. He didn't even know I existed before.

Some days, I wonder if I was secretly switched at birth. Sure, I have tall uncles on Baba's side, and Mama's shown me pictures of her "fat phase," but at the end of the day, I'm the ugly duckling that never matured into the swan everyone expected.

"Elodie. Elodie!"

My head snaps toward Aunt May standing behind the register. She crosses her arms over her chest.

"What did I just say to you?"

"Um . . ." I search my mind, but come up empty. "I don't know."

The glare she shoots me is sharper than any knife, and I wince involuntarily.

"I asked if you had finished moving all the clothes to the sale rack."

It's more of a statement than a question, given the pile of clothes still draped over my left arm. I duck my head and move toward the circular rack we emptied out earlier.

Five years ago, Aunt May opened The Perfect Fit, a clothing store in Houston's Chinatown that caters to petite girls and women. The idea came from her own frustrations about never being able to buy clothes off the rack. She orders the clothes from suppliers in China and Taiwan, and Mama does the custom alterations.

At the beginning of this year, one of her salespeople left to go to college. With business slower than usual, Aunt May asked me to fill in until she could afford to hire someone new. The last thing I wanted to do was give up my weekends, but Mama reminded me we're family. So, here I am, working for free and surrounded by constant reminders of my too-tall, too-big imperfection.

I make two more trips to transfer all the sale items to the rack. It's mostly clothes that didn't sell last season, so I do my best to organize them in a way that will catch the eye.

"Are you done?" Aunt May asks.

I nod.

"Good. Then watch the register for me," she replies. "I'm going to check on our custom orders from last week."

She slips past the makeshift curtain that leads to our back room. I suppress a groan and drag myself behind the counter just as the bell on our front door tinkles.

"Welcome to The Perfect Fit, where— Cindy!" I round the counter and throw my arms around my cousin and best friend. "What are you doing here?"

"I just finished up a shoot nearby, so I figured I'd come visit," Cindy replies with a toothy grin. "Sorry we haven't hung out in a while, El. Between college and the job, I've been super busy."

I sweep my eyes over her heart-shaped face, delicate features, and willowy frame. Cindy is Aunt May's only child, and the pride and joy of the entire family. While puberty brought me awkwardness and thirty pounds, it gifted her with flawless skin and long legs. Between that and the grace she learned from years of dance, it's no surprise she got scouted by a modeling agency the summer before junior year.

"It's okay. I've been stuck here every weekend anyway."

Cindy glances around the store. "Have you sold anything today?"

"Nope. I don't think I'm very good at this."

"Maybe you just need more practice. Here. Pretend I'm a real customer."

She pretends to step into the shop again, gesturing at me when I don't immediately play along.

"Welcome to The Perfect Fit, where your dream is only a needle and thread away," I say, giving my best sales pitch. "We have a sale going on right now. Up to forty percent off select clothing."

I point in the direction of the rack I just filled, and Cindy heads toward it. I follow close behind as she flips through a few hangers before shifting her attention to the dress section of our shop. She quickly pulls out a baby blue halter dress in a floral print.

"What do you think?"

"It's nice, but you're going to need a strapless bra for that," I answer automatically.

"Ugh . . . that's a no, then."

Cindy puts it back and pulls out a pale yellow A-line gown with lace detailing.

"What about this one?"

"That's not a good color for you. It'll wash you out."

She grins. "This is exactly why I like shopping here. You always give me an honest opinion."

"And here I thought it was because you get everything for free."

We burst out laughing at the same time. Our giggles travel to the back of the shop, and both Mama and Aunt May pop their heads through the curtain a second later.

"*Bǎobèi*! Why didn't you tell me you were coming?"

"I didn't know we'd finish the shoot so early," Cindy answers, giving her mom a hug.

"You look tired. You've been working too hard," Mama chides. "Have you eaten anything today?"

"Not yet. Can Elodie take her lunch early so we can go get something to eat, Mom?"

If it was anyone else asking—including me—Aunt May would say no. But this is Cindy, and she always gets what she wants.

"Of course." Aunt May turns to me. "Just don't be late getting back. Miss Le is coming by for another fitting this afternoon."

I bite back a groan. Miss Le has come by for at least half a dozen fittings since she bought her wedding reception dress from us two months ago. Every time she stops in, I have to listen to Mama complain about her all night.

"I promise I'll be on time."

"Make sure you two pick something healthy too," Aunt May instructs, pinching me on the cheek. "You're starting to look like a dumpling, Elodie."

Cindy gasps. "Mom!"

"What? I'm just watching out for her. Better to hear it from your family than a stranger."

I'd rather not hear it at all, but Aunt May is the most

outspoken of everyone in the family. Even Mama isn't immune to her criticisms, and she's only younger by two years.

"You have been eating too much junk food," Mama chimes in. "All that salt isn't good for you."

I glance down at the floor. No matter how many times I hear their remarks, it doesn't get easier. Before the two of them can launch into a lecture, Cindy loops an arm through mine and drags me toward the door.

"Come on, El. There's a new Korean place across the street that's supposed to be really good."

"Remember, pick something healthy," Aunt May calls out.

Cindy waits for the door to shut behind us before turning to me with a wink.

"Did I mention this is a Korean fried chicken place?"

✦ ✦ ✦

The following Saturday, the shop is buzzing with activity. With prom only three weeks away, we're suddenly flooded with students coming in for gowns. Aunt May is helping up front, but we're overwhelmed, so she calls Cindy in to help. I've just roomed a customer with her picks when I hear a distressed cry nearby.

"Why won't this go up?"

I stick my head out of the room and immediately regret it. Not only do I know the girl standing in front of the three-way mirror, but she's with the last person I wanted to see. I glance around frantically, hoping someone else is free, but no such luck.

Steeling myself, I approach the duo. "Is there something I can help you with?"

Alice recognizes me first and bares her perfectly white teeth in a fake smile.

"Elodie! I didn't know you worked here."

"I think there's something wrong with the dress," Michelle pipes up. "I can't get it to zip."

I lean down to take a closer look. "It looks fine to me. Why don't I grab the next size up?"

Michelle stares at me like I just said her dog died. She shakes her head.

"No. There's no way. I'm a size four."

"Some of our brands do run small," I explain. "Maybe that's why it doesn't fit."

"But I tried this dress on just a few days ago," she insists. "It totally fit! Maybe it's just water weight."

"Or maybe you're just fat," Alice quips.

Her words are for Michelle, but her eyes are on me. I made the mistake of not letting her cheat off me in biology freshman year, and she's made my life a living hell ever since. Resisting the urge to throttle Alice, I grab the bigger size for Michelle to try on. As expected, it fits like a glove, but that only makes her more upset.

I slip away while Michelle weighs her options. Ultimately, she brings the size six to the register. As I'm ringing her up, Alice tips her head to one side.

"Do you get an employee discount?"

"No, I don't."

Alice twirls a strand of her chestnut hair. "Oh well. There's nothing here in your size anyway. Plus, it's not like you're going to prom, right?"

Anything I say will only confirm her suspicions, so I grit my teeth and finish the sale. I don't relax until they've disappeared out the front door.

Cindy appears at my elbow. "Everything okay?"

"Yeah, I guess."

Cindy looks ready to say something else, but Aunt May beckons her from across the store. A few seconds later, Mama asks me to help pin her customer. We stay busy for the rest of the day, and by the time we lock the doors, I've managed to shove Alice to the back of my mind.

While Aunt May and Mama go over all the orders we took today, Cindy and I plop onto the couch we keep by the fitting rooms.

"So, what does your dress look like?"

I frown. "What dress?"

"The one you're wearing to prom."

I laugh. "I'm not. Going to prom, that is."

"What?" Cindy twists around to face me. "Of course you're going to prom. You have to."

"No, I don't."

"*Yes*, you do."

"With who?" I ask, unable to keep the sadness out of my voice. "I don't have a date."

"What about that Stephen guy?"

I let out a strangled laugh. "Right. Like *that's* going to happen."

"Maybe he's just waiting for the right moment to ask you," Cindy replies gamely.

"Or . . . he's already going with someone who doesn't trip on air."

"Whatever. Even if he is, you still have a date." She points at herself. "Me."

"I don't recall agreeing to this."

"Too bad. You're going, so you might as well start looking for a dress now."

I sweep my arm across the store. "In case you haven't noticed, I can't fit into anything we sell."

"Then we'll shop somewhere else," she says, undeterred. "Either way, we'll find you that perfect dress."

I start to protest, but she gives me the Lin Face. The same one that Aunt May uses when she's super pissed about something. I cross my arms over my chest.

"Fine, but if I don't find a dress, I get to stay home."

"But—"

"No buts. Just because you'd look good in a garbage bag doesn't mean I will."

Cindy pouts, but I don't budge. Finally, she relents.

"Deal. We'll start tomorrow."

"Wait . . . what?!"

✦ ✦ ✦

"I can't believe we still haven't found your dress!"

I can, but I keep that to myself as Cindy and I traipse to the last department store on our list. We've spent the last four hours trying on what feels like every dress in the Galleria. We stop by a boba tea kiosk and grab a couple of milk teas to go. After swallowing a mouthful of the chewy balls, I peer over at her.

"I told you it wasn't going to be easy."

"Okay, but I didn't realize how *hard* it was going to be to find decent-looking dresses." Cindy shakes her head. "It's not like you're huge. You're only a size twelve!"

"Yeah, but we both know fashion is designed for people of a certain size. They assume everyone who's heavier is shaped the same. The larger you are, the fewer choices you have."

We walk into Markstrom's and head up the escalator to the third floor. As soon as we reach the formalwear section, we divide and conquer. She takes the left side, and I take the right. Once we've picked a few to try, we head to the fitting rooms.

"Are you sure you don't want me to help you?" Cindy asks as I step in.

"No, I'm fine. Thanks."

She frowns. "I guess I'll wait outside then."

I shut the door to the room and lean against it. As much as I adore her, the thought of her seeing me in my underwear is terrifying. It's hard enough for me to look at my body without cringing. The last thing I need is an audience.

I pluck the first dress off the hanger, a navy blue mermaid gown Cindy picked out. It's a gorgeous dress, with intricate beading all the way down to the hem. I step into the dress and zip the back before taking a deep breath.

"You've got to be kidding me."

My head snaps up at the sound of Alice's voice, but I'm still alone. When I turn to the mirror, however, I find her sneering at me.

"You can't seriously think you can pull that off. Nobody wants to see your rolls, Elodie."

I've never stripped anything off so fast in my life. It's a few minutes before I can summon the courage to look in the mirror.

She's gone.

"It's just your imagination," I say aloud. "She's not there."

Cindy's voice floats through the air. "Elodie? Is everything okay?"

"Yup!" I say brightly. "Just not a fan of the first one, so I'm going to try something else."

"Okay, then."

I reach for one of my picks, a black lace sheath dress that ends just above the knees. Knowing Cindy's probably getting antsy, I open the door and step out.

"What do you think?"

She makes a face. "I . . . don't love it. It bunches weird at the hips, and it doesn't give you any shape."

She pushes me back into the fitting room and stands behind me, gathering the material at my waist.

"See? That's much better."

I peek at my reflection with one eye, and then both. She's right. I heave a sigh.

"Okay. On to the next one."

This time, I choose another one of Cindy's picks, a V-neck,

plum-colored dress with white lace detail on top. There's a leg slit up the right side that ends at midthigh, something that makes me pause.

"It's too revealing, Elodie."

I stumble back against the wall of the fitting room. Aunt May is frowning at me from inside the mirror. She tsks.

"Only girls with smaller chests should wear that. Yours is too big. Your mom shouldn't have let you eat so much chicken. It's all those hormones they inject into them nowadays."

The choked sound that leaves my throat brings Cindy to the other side of the door.

"Elodie? Elodie, let me in!"

I reach over and unlock it. Cindy barges in and glances around.

"What happened? I heard a crash."

"I—I tripped," I stammer, cheeks flushed. "Sorry. I didn't mean to worry you."

"Oh." No longer worried, Cindy looks me up and down. "That's a nice dress. There's no gap at the top either, which is good."

At the mention of my top, I cover it with one hand while shoving her out with the other.

"I don't like it."

"Wait. Why don't you—" Cindy yelps in surprise as I slam the door in her face.

"Sorry! I'm going to change now."

I thumb through the rest of the dresses we chose. Too short. Too long. Not a good color. Itchy material. I'm just about to call it a day when I spot the last one hanging on the hook. A burgundy-to-blush ombré ball gown with a sweetheart neckline and tulle skirt, it looks like something right out of a fairy tale.

I remove it from its hanger and step carefully into it. Once I tug it into place, it's clear I won't be able to secure it on my own. I poke my head out of the room.

"Cindy? I need your help."

She steps inside and gasps immediately. "Elodie! I think this is the one!"

Warmth spreads through my chest. I spin around, silently praying it'll zip all the way. I don't exhale until I feel Cindy pat me on the back. Heart pounding, I squeeze my eyes shut and turn toward the mirror. Counting to three, I open them, and I smile so wide my cheeks hurt.

"I love it," I whisper. "It's beautiful."

"And you look beautiful in it," Cindy adds. "It's super flattering."

For a split second, I imagine Stephen spinning me around the dance floor. I tense instinctively, waiting for Alice or Aunt May to make an appearance, but only joy stares back at me.

"Oh, we should take a picture!" Cindy exclaims. "This is a momentous occasion, after all."

She pulls out her phone and starts snapping away. I don't even mind when she makes me twirl around several times.

Okay, Elodie. Don't get too excited. Make sure you like everything.

I take a closer look at the gown, examining the stitching and counting the layers of tulle. No matter how hard I try, I find no faults.

That is, until I reach the price tag.

"Five hundred ninety-five dollars?!" I moan. "I can't afford this!"

Against her protests, I make Cindy unzip me, and I change back into my clothes. I stare wistfully at my dream dress one last time, bidding a silent goodbye to prom before I drag her out of the store. We walk to the parking garage in silence and climb into my car. Once Cindy's buckled in, I find my way onto the road.

"What if I got my mom to order something similar from her supplier?" she asks once we're on the freeway.

"It's too late for that. It takes six to eight weeks for things to arrive," I explain forlornly. "And that's assuming nothing gets stuck in customs."

"Maybe you can find something online," Cindy suggests.

"Yeah, but if it doesn't fit, I won't have time to exchange it."

She slouches in her seat. To be honest, I'm pretty disappointed too. Despite my complaining, I was finally coming around to the idea of going. We spend the rest of the trip back to The Perfect Fit in silence. Once I pull into the spot reserved for the shop, Cindy twists to look at me.

"Don't give up just yet. I'm going to see if I can find anything on my favorite websites."

I try to ignore the sinking feeling in my stomach. I've spent enough time watching Aunt May buying inventory to know that kind of dress isn't easy to find. We part ways after one final hug, and I step into the shop.

Mama looks up from the shirts she's folding. "How did it go?"

I make a noncommittal sound. "We found a dress, but . . ."

"But what?"

"It's too expensive. I can't afford it."

She sighs. "My offer still stands, Elodie. There's nothing wrong with wearing an altered gown from the shop."

Mama's heart is in the right place, but walking into prom wearing a dress that was pieced together from two smaller ones isn't my idea of a grand entrance. Not to mention, her idea of something flattering involves covering up all my "problem areas."

"Thanks, Mama, but I'll pass."

I trudge over to the couch and sink into it. She sits down next to me.

"Do you have a picture of it?"

I pull up the ones that Cindy texted me. Mama's brows furrow as she zooms in and out of each one.

"It's . . . nice."

Nice? Just . . . nice? It's the most glorious thing I've ever laid eyes on!

"You don't like it?" I ask instead.

"Well, it's a ball gown. Ball gowns look best on girls who are . . ."

In a flash, I'm eight years old again. I'm shopping for a birthday dress with Mama. In the window of a children's

clothing store, a pale pink dress with puffy sleeves and a ballerina skirt catches my eye. When I point at it, Mama shakes
her head.

"That's not for girls like you. Let's find you a different
dress."

Not for girls like me.

Right.

I blink back the tears that have gathered in the corners of
my eyes. Mama puts a hand on my arm.

"Elodie, I only meant that . . ."

I shrug her off. "It doesn't matter anyway. It's too expensive,
remember?"

She starts to say something more, but only silence fills
the space between us. I keep my eyes pinned on my lap until
she stands and walks toward the back room, leaving me alone.

It's only then that I allow the tears to flow.

✦ ✦ ✦

Despite Mama's words, I spend the next week unable to forget the memory of how I felt in The Dress. I catch myself smiling in class as I imagine walking into prom with my head
held high. In my dreams, the airy tulle layers flutter around
me as I dance the night away.

I even go so far as to hover near the prom ticket table at
lunchtime, but I chicken out at the last minute. As I spin
around to leave, I notice Stephen staring intently at me from
across the cafeteria. Heat floods my cheeks as I rush out the
door.

For her part, Cindy keeps her promise and sends me pictures of dresses she finds almost every day. While many of them resemble The Dress, none of them tug at my heartstrings. By the time Friday rolls around, she's admitted defeat.

"You know what you should do," Cindy says while we're at dinner. "Go back and try it on again. It's the only way to know for sure if you still love it."

I pause midchew. "You really think I might not feel the same?"

"You never know," she replies. "You tried on so many dresses that day. Maybe you only loved it because it was the one that fit the best."

My chopsticks hover over a piece of nigiri. I didn't think of that.

"We can stop by the mall after this if you want," Cindy offers. "It's still early."

I pat my bulging stomach. "I don't know if I should after eating all this food."

"Well, you're going to eat before prom too, so you might as well make sure the dress will still fit."

With that settled, we finish our meal before making our way to the Galleria. As we enter the brightly lit Markstrom's, my stomach starts to churn. By the time we get off the escalator on the third floor, my heart is pounding.

What if I don't feel the same? What do I do then?

There's a moment of panic when Cindy forgets where she found the dress, but we soon spot it on the back wall. Dress in hand, I change in the fitting room, letting her in once I'm sufficiently covered. I suck my stomach in while she guides the zipper up, breathing a sigh of relief when it fits like before.

"So?" Cindy tips her head to the side. "Do you still love it?"

I meet the eye of the glowing girl in front of me. Just like before, birds start to sing and choirs of angels descend from the heavens. It's everything I remember and more.

But then, I hear it.

A whisper in the back of my mind, growing louder with every passing second.

Not for girls like you.

Not for girls like you.

Not for girls like you.

The light fades from my eyes as doubts fill my mind. Instead of layers of luxurious tulle, I see my wide hips. My waist bulges above the skirt like a stuffed sausage. And the strapless sweetheart neckline? Highlights my flabby arms and thick shoulders. I jerk my head away from the mirror.

"Elodie?"

"The dress is amazing," I whisper, "but it's not for me."

"What do you mean, not for you?"

"I'm too fat to wear this."

"You are not!" Cindy forces me to meet her eye. "Is this about what my mom said the other day? Because she doesn't know what she's talking about. Your face is fine."

I shake my head. She twists me around so I have to look in the mirror once more.

"You look amazing," she insists. "Just like a Disney princess."

I peer at my reflection, but no amount of staring brings back the girl who felt beautiful in this dress. Cindy must sense this, because she lets out a long sigh and unzips me without being asked. I don't bother asking her to leave while I get undressed. She might as well see the true me.

We leave The Dress behind, and the whispers follow me all the way home. And in my room, in front of the full-length mirror, as I count every pucker, crease, and roll on my body, pressure builds in my chest. When it becomes too much, I sink onto the edge of my bed and put my head in my hands.

"Why are you sad?"

I pry my eyes open slowly and discover eight-year-old me watching curiously from inside the mirror.

I groan. "What is this? Some twisted version of *A Christmas Carol*?"

She shrugs. "I don't know. You're the one who brought me here."

Ah. I forgot how sassy eight-year-old me was.

"You still haven't answered my question," she says.

I roll my eyes at Younger Me. "Shouldn't you be able to guess? You're in my head."

She rolls her eyes, crossing her arms over her chest.

Add "annoying" to that list. "Fine. I'm sad because I found the perfect dress for prom, but I'm too fat to wear it."

"So it doesn't fit?"

"No," I answer softly.

"Then why don't you just get a bigger size?"

"Because I . . ." I pause. "Well, technically, I don't need a bigger size. The one I tried on fits fine."

"Then why did you say it didn't fit?"

"It doesn't. I mean, it does, but it doesn't."

"That doesn't make any sense," Younger Me says. "It either fits or it doesn't."

"I feel fat in it," I amend.

"So then buy the bigger size. It'll be looser and you won't feel fat."

"That's not how—" I let out a frustrated sound. "Look, you don't know this yet, but girls like us can't wear certain things."

"Says who?"

"Says everyone," I mumble.

"Like who?"

"Like . . . Alice. And Aunt May."

"Alice is a troll, and Aunt May told you to eat more when she thought you were too skinny."

Imaginary or not, Younger Me has a point. When I was on the community swim team in middle school, I lost a ton of weight competing nearly every week. Aunt May practically shoveled food down my throat every chance she got.

"Okay, but Mama also said those dresses aren't for girls like us."

"Just because she's an adult doesn't mean she's always right, you know."

My mouth falls open. It's such a simple observation, but it shifts my world on its axis.

Who knew I was so smart?

I glance back at the mirror, but she's gone. Even though it feels a bit ridiculous, I say it out loud anyway. "Thank you."

✦ ✦ ✦

I promise myself I'll try the dress on one last time. Unfortunately, between end-of-semester exams and putting in extra shifts to help out at the shop, I don't have time to go back until the weekend before prom. Thankfully, Cindy comes to the rescue, stopping by Markstrom's and putting it on hold for me.

"How about I come with you to the mall?"

I freeze, my hand on the knob of the front door I intended to lock. It's Saturday afternoon, and we're closing up shop for the day. I'm already on edge after spotting Stephen walking past with his friends around lunchtime. When he glanced through the window, I ducked behind the counter so fast I scared a customer who was trying to check out.

Mama walks over to me. "Cindy told me you still haven't found a dress. Maybe I can help you find one."

I'm careful to keep my face blank. Fun is not how I would describe shopping for clothes with Mama. You'd think by the way she gripes about my fashion choices that I belong on some trashy reality show. I might be prepared for my imaginary foes, but dealing with Mama is far scarier.

"It's okay. I can go by myself. I'm just going to take a quick look," I say. "There might not be anything left at this point."

"Oh."

I don't expect the hurt that flashes across her features.

The words slip out before I can stop them. "But if you really want to come, you can."

"Great," she answers, brightening instantly. "Let me finish up in the back and we can go."

Twenty minutes later, I'm leading Mama toward the formalwear section. Reluctantly, I head for the customer service counter and give them my name. As I wait for someone to retrieve my hold, Mama cocks her head toward me.

"I thought you were just looking."

I rub the back of my neck. "Well, I am, but . . ."

I'm saved from answering when the saleswoman returns with my dress in hand. She ushers me over to the fitting room and hangs it up on the hook. Mama's eyes narrow when she takes a look at the gown, but she says nothing as the saleswoman smiles at me.

"My name is Leslie. Let me know if you need anything else."

"Thank you," I answer sheepishly.

Mama grabs a seat in the room across the way while I change. It takes a while to get the dress on, since I'm determined to zip it myself. After twisting and stretching for several minutes, I'm finally ready. With the memories of my last two visits still fresh in my mind, I brace myself before raising my eyes to the glass. Nonetheless, I stiffen when my eyes connect with hazel ones.

"I thought the other dress was bad, but this is way worse," Alice jeers. "You're not even going to make it through the door in that thing."

For a second, I accept the insult as usual. Then, I square my shoulders and stare Mirror Alice square in the eye.

"Not only will I make it in, but I'm going to have a great time. I can't say the same for you, though, since you'll be too busy trying to make other people miserable to have fun."

Mirror Alice lets out a startled squeak, her mouth opening and closing soundlessly. I squeeze my eyes shut and count to ten. When I open them again, she's gone. I heave a sigh of relief.

I take a moment now to really look at myself in the dress. Without the specters of my mind hovering over my shoulder, I finally notice details on the gown I missed before.

At the waist, there's a beaded belt that draws the eye. There are sequins and beads tucked between the layers of tulle in the skirt. As I twist from side to side, the skirt sparkles like diamonds, bringing with it some of the joy I felt the first time I laid eyes on it.

As I smooth my hands over the skirt, I hear Aunt May's unmistakable grunt of disapproval. I swallow a groan as I watch her pinch the bridge of her nose in the mirror.

"That does nothing for you, Elodie. You need something with sleeves and a corseted top, not something that shows so much of . . . everything."

My hands fist at my sides as she gestures up and down my body. Her scrutiny has always made me feel exposed, and it takes everything in me not to break eye contact. I draw myself up to my full height and raise my chin.

"I already tried dresses like that, Aunt May, and I didn't

like them. They're uncomfortable and hot. And so what if people see me? It's not like they don't know what I look like already. At least this way, I'll be wearing something I love."

"Don't you want to look thinner, though?" she asks. "Stephen will be there. Don't you want to look your best for him?"

"I doubt a dress will make him forget the fact I took a ball to the face, Aunt May," I say matter-of-factly. "Besides, aren't you the one who's always saying the best thing a woman can wear is confidence?"

"Yes, but . . . I was talking about . . . that isn't . . ."

With every word she sputters, Aunt May fades a little more, until there's nothing left of her anymore. I'm alone with my reflection, something that no longer intimidates me like before. If I squint just a little, I can make out the girl who will proudly wear this to prom.

Assuming, of course, I can make it past the final boss—Mama.

To be honest, I'm surprised she hasn't tried to barge into the fitting room already. Usually, she can't wait to offer her opinion on my outfits. Summoning up all the courage I have, I open the door and step slowly out of the room. Mama glances up from whatever she was looking at on her phone, and I try not to fidget as she looks me over.

"Is this the dress you showed me?"

I nod. She makes a twirling motion with her hands, and I do a little spin. A grin spreads across my face as I come to a stop, but it wavers when her words echo through my mind.

Not for girls like you.

Her mouth opens. Before she can speak, words spill out of my own like a waterfall.

"I know you said ball gowns aren't for girls like me, but I really love it, Mama. I feel so good in it." I hesitate, but press on. "Actually, it makes me feel beautiful. Plus, it's really well made, and it's comfortable too. Look at the beading . . . I think it's done by hand. And there's the ombré. The staining is really high quality . . ."

She puts a hand up. "Stop, stop, Elodie."

I fall silent. Mama stands and steps behind me. She reaches into the back of the dress and pulls out the tag, and my heart sinks.

"Mama, I promise I'll figure out how to pay you back."

She's silent as she unzips the dress and steps in front of me with an impassive expression.

"Go get changed."

I hold it together until I'm alone in the dressing room, then choke back tears as I put my clothes back on. Taking a steadying breath, I step out of the dressing room.

"Ready?" Mama asks.

I don't trust my voice, so I manage a small nod. I start to walk out of the fitting area, but she stops me and presses something familiar into my arms.

It's my dress.

"I have a coupon," Mama tells me. "It'll expire soon, so I might as well use it."

I follow numbly as she heads for the sales counter to pay for it. Once it's wrapped, I carry it to the car.

At home, I lay the dress onto my bed before turning to her. Though I'm terrified to break the spell, I make myself utter the words.

"You said ball gowns aren't for girls like me."

There's a long pause before she sits down on my bed with a sigh. "Yes, I did."

"Then why did you buy it for me?"

"Because I haven't seen you that happy in a long time," Mama says softly. "And it made me realize I was wrong to say that to you."

I sit down beside her, and she inhales deeply.

"I've always wanted the best for you, Elodie, and that's why I point out things you could improve on."

"Like my weight?"

"Yes, like your weight. I didn't want you to look back and ask why I wasn't harder on you. But our conversation the other day showed me how hurtful my comments can be." She takes both of my hands in hers. "You *are* beautiful. I'm sorry if I made you feel like you weren't."

I squeeze her fingers. "Thank you, Mama."

She leaves my room and shuts the door. I don't know how long I stare at the dress that night, but I fall asleep with a smile on my face.

✦ ✦ ✦

"Stop moving around, El, unless you want me to start all over again."

I go perfectly still in my chair, my back to the bathroom mirror, as Cindy puts the final touches on my makeup. She surprised me with a salon date to get our hair done earlier, and now we're back at my house to finish getting ready.

"Okay, done," she finally announces. "But you can't look just yet."

Cindy leads me into the bedroom, where I take off my T-shirt and jeans while she grabs the dress off the hanger. She holds it up for me to step into, and then zips me up, all the while making sure I can't sneak a peek at myself. After giving my hair a quick adjustment, she steps back to admire her handiwork. We hear a knock on the door, and Mama sticks her head in a second later.

"Can I come in?"

I wave her inside. Her eyes go wide as she steps closer. The butterflies in my stomach settle when Mama pulls me into a hug.

"Oh, Elodie. You look so pretty," she whispers in my ear.

I flush at her praise as she pulls away. Unable to contain my excitement any longer, I turn around and raise my eyes to the mirror. My eight-year-old self stares back at me with a smile.

"Perfect."

"We should get going," Cindy says, interrupting my thoughts. "Or else we'll miss our dinner reservation."

In the end, we still cut it close, because Mama insists on taking what feels like a million photos of us before letting us leave. I manage to make it all the way through our meal without getting anything on my dream dress. Soon, we're standing outside the hotel ballroom where prom is being held.

Cindy cocks her head. "Ready?"

I take a deep breath and nod. She leads the way through the garden arch decorated with artificial roses and fairy lights. As I go to follow her, I hear someone call out.

"Elodie!"

Stephen is walking toward me. I try not to stare at how handsome he looks in the navy suit he's wearing. I glance around in search of his date, but it's just the two of us in the hallway.

"Um . . . hi, Stephen."

He stops a few steps away and sweeps his gaze over me. I resist the urge to fidget with my belt. For a moment, I'm filled with doubt again, sure he's spotted the one imperfection I didn't manage to hide. Then, Stephen tugs at the collar of his shirt. His brown eyes don't quite meet mine as he clears his throat.

"So . . . are you here with someone?"

"Yes."

His shoulders droop. "Oh."

"I mean, not a 'date' date," I clarify quickly. "I'm here with my cousin Cindy."

"*Oh.*"

A smile spreads across his face, and an unexpected warmth spreads through my chest. Just then, Cindy pops back out of the doorway. She freezes when she sees Stephen and rushes back inside before I can say anything.

"What about you?" I force myself to ask. "Are you here with a date?"

He shrugs. "Nah. Just came with some friends."

We fall silent after that. I'm debating whether I should head inside when I hear a familiar melody floating through the air.

"I love this song," I say aloud.

"Yeah, it's pretty good," Stephen agrees.

"Then . . . do you maybe want to dance?"

I don't know if it's The Dress that makes me utter the words, but it doesn't matter. What matters is Stephen's brilliant answering smile.

"I'd love to."

He offers me his arm, and I take it. As he escorts me through the floral arch, he turns to me.

"By the way, you look beautiful."

For the first time in forever, I believe it too.

LIAR, LIAR, PANTS ON FIRE

Rebecca Sky

The pen shakes in my hand. "Maxie, sweetie, you can do this," I tell myself in my best Australian accent—I *almost* sound like my mom. I set the pen down and sigh, hugging myself and wishing the kangaroo stuffy she gave me was in my arms. I'd give anything to push its belly and listen to the recording of her actual voice, with subtle hints of her wild accent buried beneath the years of living in America, telling me she loves me and is proud of me. But wishing is useless, because my stuffy, the only thing I had left of her, is gone.

It happened in my best friend Billy's tree house—we'd snuck there to avoid the Bible study at my place only to find ants all over our old Popsicle wrappers. Instead of relocating them like I suggested, Billy pulled out a magnifying glass. I knew what he was going to do and didn't hesitate: I pounced on him. It wasn't our first brawler, and it wouldn't be the last.

Even though I outweighed him by thirty pounds then, he was wiry and more coordinated, and that made for a fair fight.

We were a tangle of limbs as I fought to keep his magnifying glass out of the sun, and we sounded like the church raccoons fighting over trash thanks to Billy's shrieking (he sure can be loud when someone bites him). I'd just taken an elbow to the chin when I picked up the first whiff of smoke. Everything happened fast after that. Billy's dad dragged me out, and I reached for my kangaroo, only managing to knock it over and start it playing Mom's message. He pulled us a safe distance back, though I wanted to run into the fire and rescue my stuffy. I wanted it so bad my entire body shook. But we just stood in the yard, Billy crying in his mother's arms, his dad resting protective hands on my shoulders, and we listened to wood crackle and pop, and the recording of my mom's voice warp into a low, monstrous screech as the fire consumed it all.

As the heat dried my tears, something sparked in me too, and at only twelve I knew what I wanted to be. I couldn't control cancer, but if I became a firefighter, I could control fire . . .

"Were you attempting an accent?" Billy asks, dragging me from the memory.

"What? No." I totally forgot he was here.

"Surrre you werrren't," he says, drawing out his words as he relaxes back into the couch.

I sigh and stare down at the application in front of me. A local animal rescue is partnering with my fire department for a contest to send volunteers to the front lines of the Australian wildfires. It's my chance to put my skills to use and help the land that gave me my mother. I flip the page and the parental consent and liability waiver form falls out.

Billy picks it up and looks it over. "You actually convinced Preacher to sign this?"

"It was surprisingly easy. I told him I want to enter a contest through my fire station to go help in Australia and I need his permission. He mumbled something about Ecclesiastes, and signed the form without looking up from his sermon prep."

Billy grins. "That's my girl, the old ask-him-things-he'd-normally-say-no-to-while-he's-too-busy-working-to-listen move."

I crinkle my nose—he knows I hate it when he calls me his girl. "I'm my own girl," I say, returning to the form.

Not even a second passes before Billy groans. "How many questions are there? It's taking forever. I want to go shoot hoops."

My pen hovers over the last empty box: BMI.

"One more," I say. "Can you google a BMI chart for me?" The words taste bitter on my lips. I hate that BMI is even a part of this. On the charity's Facebook page someone said that administrators won't look at applicants with BMIs over "healthy"—"for liability reasons." BMI doesn't reflect health, and even if it did, why would the charity discriminate against unhealthy people? They have just as much right to volunteer their time as anyone else. I'd be tempted to make a formal complaint if I wasn't worried about it costing me a shot at the contest.

"But why?"

I shrug. "It's on the form."

He sits up and punches in the search, then hands me his phone. I scan up to my height and across to my weight and land on the number. My heart sinks when I see it.

Healthy on the BMI chart is 19–24.

Mine's 33.

"Why that matters?" he asks.

"Apparently they won't take anyone over 24," I tell him, handing him back his phone.

He glances at me, then the screen, frowns. "Just put in 23. It's bullshit that's even one of the questions."

"My dad would nonviolently murder me if I lied, not to mention the firefighter code of ethics says—"

"Not this again." He groans. "I'm pretty sure there's nothing about supporting body discrimination in their code."

"No," I say. "But—"

"No buts." He gives a mischievous grin, and I know it's taking all his willpower to not make a butt joke. "You've been a volunteer firefighter for over a year," he says. "You've proven you can do anything people with lower BMIs can." He reaches up and flicks his wrists like he's sinking his jump shot.

"Lying just feels wrong." I picture Dad, standing behind his pulpit, a look of disappointment on his face.

"They won't know you're lying."

"If I get in, they'll see I'm fat."

"Yeah, but you'll blow them out of the water. You're strong and smart and—"

"Yes," I say with a grin. "But I'm also fat."

"Since when has that stopped you from doing anything?" He's acting nonchalant, but deep down I know he wants this for me as much as I do and if my acceptance came down to a number, he'd be the first at my side fighting the policy.

"I'm not ashamed of my weight, but I *don't* like that it might keep me from this opportunity. So my option is what?"

Billy rolls his eyes and grabs his glass of lemonade off the table. "This isn't going to be another of those 'don't burn the ants' lectures, is it?"

"If you're lucky."

He takes a big swig, smiling through the glass. "Lie if it gets you to Australia." He dries his face with the back of his sleeve, leaving a slobbery stain.

I raise an eyebrow, and he gives me his cheeky grin before trying to wipe it on me. I swat him, fighting back a smile. "Ugh, you're disgusting." But maybe he's right. I press my pen to the paper, watching the ink pool at the tip and tiny tendrils begin to spread. Maybe a little white lie in this situation wouldn't be so bad. *So why is my stomach flipping?* I'm about to pull away when Billy takes the pen from me and writes in "23."

✦　✦　✦

We've been parked for five minutes, and my hands still clutch the wheel—I can't seem to bring myself to let go. Billy gets out and circles the church van to the driver's side.

He opens the door, and even though he's tall he has to stretch around my stomach to unbuckle my seat belt. "You've wanted to go to Australia for as long as I've known you. You got in the contest. This is your chance."

I want this so bad, but I'm worried they'll take one look at my fat body and withdraw my spot.

He starts prying my fingers from the wheel. "You're going to crush it."

His faith in me is enough to get me to drag my eyes from the reporters crowding the animal rescue foundation. When I look at Billy, his tough-love scowl makes me smile. "Normally I'm the one taking care of you."

"I know," he says, sounding annoyed. He slips off his coat, and I laugh when I realize he's still wearing his pajamas—red lumberjack flannels that look ridiculous on his long frame: the sleeves are too short, and the legs end high on his calves.

"Seems I've dropped the ball on that," I say, exiting the van and nodding to his outfit.

He grins and waves me toward the line of contestants at the door. As we near, a muscular guy with long blond spikes approaches and gives Billy a once-over, smirking at what he's wearing. Then his eyes dart to me, pausing on my thick thighs and stomach before he crinkles his face. He turns back to Billy. "Contestants are supposed to check in at reception before media interviews."

I'm the one in active gear and sneakers, and he thinks the pajama-wearing guy next to me is here to compete? It's almost enough to make me turn back for the van.

Billy must sense my desire to run as he slips his arm around me. "I'm not a contestant, bro," he says, enunciating *bro*. "I'm just here supporting Maxie, who's going to kick the other contestants' asses."

"Good luck with that," the guy says, not bothering to make eye contact with me. Billy pushes us past him, keeping his arm on me, and I let him, liking it a bit, even. He maneuvers us around a crowd circling a fit girl with curly red hair. "It's my dream to be a vet," she tells the reporter and his camera. "I've been volunteering at the local shelter and training for a 10K. Basically I'm ready for whatever they'll throw at us. I'm here to win this."

I suck in a breath and try to blend into Billy as we slip past, avoiding the cameras. My urge to hide might have something to do with that *bro* perpetuating my feeling it's wrong being here—having lied on the application and all. I'm also a little nervous that my dad will catch me on the news and rescind his permission before I even have a chance to compete. Every time I've asked him to take me to Australia he's said he's too busy. I can't handle another no right now.

Billy drops his arm, making me feel strangely cold, and pushes into the reception room.

A beautiful Black woman with a name tag that reads Michelle/Michy welcomes us with a smile. She looks about a size bigger than me, and seeing a fat person working this event instantly puts me at ease.

"What can I do for you?"

"Hi, uh, I'm Maxie Cooper." As I wait for her reply, I can't help replaying the way the bro looked at my body and assumed it was Billy, not me, here for the competition. "Just hoping you still want me." The words come out before I can stop myself.

"Did you get our confirmation email?" she says.

"I did, but I—"

Billy leans into the counter. "She doesn't know if you still want her now that you see she's fat."

Michelle sucks in a breath, her eyes firing daggers at him, but then he smiles, and she realizes his words aren't meant as an attack. Her face softens. She motions to her body. "As you can tell we don't care too much about that around here."

Billy snorts. "Funny way of showing it."

"Excuse me?" she says, clearly getting annoyed.

I grab his arm before he says something else. "On Facebook," I explain, "someone posted that you'd only consider those with BMIs in the healthy range." I fight the urge to air-quote "healthy."

"I'm sorry you saw that," she says. "I had Frank delete the comment. Pierce, one of our regular volunteers, thought he was being helpful." She rolls her eyes. "I'm not his favorite person because I told him if he wanted to come to Australia, he had to compete like the rest of you. That post was likely a personal attack." She whistles. "Lord help me if he wins."

"Oh," I say, "'cause the application asks for our BMIs, and—"

"What?" She grabs a paper off a stack and reads over the page. "Frank! Get out here, now!"

An older man with pink cheeks and scruffy hair hidden

under a bright red ball cap that reads Make America Care About Animals Again pushes out of the attached office. "What's with the racket? The news could hear ya." He has a full Australian accent, and my heart flutters at the sound. He pauses when he sees us, frowns at Billy's outfit, then tips his hat, not realizing behind him Michelle is rolling the application into a baton.

"G'day—"

She smacks him over the head, knocking the hat off.

"Crikey! What was that for?"

"What was that for?!" She whacks him a second time.

He bends down for his hat, holding up one hand in defense. "What're you going on about?"

Billy chuckles, and I elbow him in the side.

When Frank's upright, she shoves the application in his face. "Look!" She points to the BMI question. "You promised you'd remove this."

His face drops, and he holds the hat to his chest. "Right, I did." His words are slow and careful. "I've been so flat-out, I reckon I didn't get to double-checking Pierce deleted it."

"You reckon?" She smacks him again. "I have to do everything myself!"

He pulls her into a hug and kisses her cheek. "Michy, darling." She resists at first, then relaxes into him. "You know I'd be lost without ya."

"I know," she says.

Frank turns back to us. "I hope it didn't put you off applying."

"Almost, but my friend told me to enter anyway." I nudge Billy.

"Good on ya, mate," Frank tells him.

Billy smiles and nudges me back; a look of curiosity twinkles in Michelle's eyes.

She searches the applications, and when she finds mine she scans the form, stopping on the BMI question. She chuckles while reading my answer.

I can't help but laugh too, and the anxiety that's been bubbling up in me is suddenly gone.

✦ ✦ ✦

Frank directs us to the group of contestants gathered in the lot, then makes his way over to the reporters. "G'day, welcome." The cameras zoom in. "As you've seen on the tele, Australia's lost over a billion animals to the fires, and as an Aussie, it's not something I can ignore. We here at Animal Wildlife Rescue will be going down under to help with the recovery and care of injured and orphaned animals from the fire front lines. My wife . . . come 'ere, darling"—he waves her over and proudly puts his arm around her shoulders— "Michelle will be helping on the admin side of things, and one of these volunteers"—he motions to the group of us by the cars, and the cameras pan over—"one of these lucky young folk will be coming along for the experience."

Everyone waves like they rehearsed it, and before I can join, Billy grabs my hand and waves it for me. I yank away.

"We're thankful to KWRZ news for televising this

contest," Frank continues, drawing the cameras back, "and send in those cash donations, would ya? Your generosity lets us help in situations like these."

The contestants applaud, and this time Billy lets me do it on my own as he's too busy mimicking the robotic way the girl with the curly red hair claps. I elbow Billy in the side, but he doesn't stop.

"You're not even supposed to be here."

"Maxine Cooper, am I embarrassing you?"

"Always."

"That's my girl."

"I'm not your girl." One of the contestants catches my eye. "I'm not his girl."

"But you like me, right—I'm endearing?" He's doing the robotic clap over my head now.

I cross my arms and glare. "Can you annoy me from over where the moms are standing?"

Billy grudgingly trudges to them. Seeing the parents group makes my heart sink. But even if he wanted to, Dad doesn't have the free time to be here and support me—the church keeps him busy.

Frank approaches the contestants and organizes us into two lines. The red-haired girl is in front of me, and I try my best to ignore Billy's clapping from across the lot.

"The person behind you is your partner," Frank says.

The red-haired girl turns around. "Hey." She looks me up and down. "I'm Amber."

I'm glad Billy isn't here to make some joke about the

unoriginality of a redhead named Amber. "Maxie. Nice to meet you."

She opens her mouth to say something, but Frank speaks first. "For round one, each team will get thirty minutes. First, you'll sew a pouch for an orphaned joey. Once your pouch is done, head to the animal station and feed a bottle to a joey coddled in your pouch." He points behind the group of moms (and Billy) to ten long tables with sewing machines and fabric, and behind them a large enclosure full of cages. "In Brissio we'll be working with joeys, but today we'll be caring for raccoon babies."

My heart races at the thought. We have a family of raccoons living behind the church house, and Dad wouldn't let me go out at night alone for years 'cause he thought they were dangerous. It's probably a good thing he's not here, then.

"Once you've successfully completed the challenge," Frank continues, "you and your teammate must recage your joey and return to your table. We'll score you on the tasks, and the top teams will move on to the next round."

"Do you know how to sew?" Amber asks, less in a friendly manner and more how I'd imagine a police officer interrogating somebody would.

"No, but I'm a quick learner."

She clenches her jaw and shifts on her feet.

"How hard can a pouch be?" I add, hoping to calm her a bit.

"How hard can a—? Nope." She searches the crowd, her gaze landing on Frank. "Excuse me, I need a new partner." She waves, trying to get his attention.

"You don't need another partner. I—"

"No offense," she says, "but I can't have anyone holding me back."

"Holding you back?" I say it a little louder than I should, but my fear of not being wanted here is quickly morphing into anger. I catch Billy's eye, and he looks like he's ready to come over and rescue me, but I can stand up for myself. "How do I know *you* won't hold *me* back? And I need this too. Partners or not, if you come between me—"

She steps into my personal space. "Are you threatening me?"

"If I was, you'd know."

"Ladies!" Frank shouts, his Australian accent making it even more stern. It's then I remember the camera crew and wish I didn't kick Billy into the moms' group, because I could use something tall to hide behind. "I trust you'll settle this and assume your positions for the contest," Frank says.

The blond-spikes bro shakes his head as if I've somehow further disappointed him, and Amber gives me one last glare before mouthing, *Don't make me regret this.* She faces Frank and the cameras with a big fake smile. "Everything's good."

"Glad to hear it," he says, waving us to the tables. A couple of the groups have already taken their seats and are reading over the instructions, waiting for the contest to start.

Amber sits in front of the sewing machine as Frank blows an air horn starting our thirty minutes.

"We need to cut the fabric," Amber yells.

I grab the cotton and spread it out, finding the pattern tucked inside. I lay it on, and Amber huffs out of her seat. "It needs to be cut on the fold." She nudges me out of the way and takes over.

The cameras follow Frank and Michelle as they circle the tables.

Michelle stops by us, sees me standing watching Amber cut. "You'll be judged on teamwork," she says.

Amber glances up, frustrated by the revelation. "Can you make sure the machine's ready, then?" she asks me.

Michelle nonchalantly points to the button on the side. I smile my thanks and flick it on. With Michelle watching, Amber's more teamwork oriented; she even lets me sew the first section, though as soon as Michelle leaves, she promptly unpicks it as I "didn't do a French seam right," whatever that is. Other teams are already done and moving on, but Amber insists on not rushing the pouch.

I read back over the instructions, noticing a disclaimer on the bottom that loose threads need to be clipped, so I do that as Amber finishes up on the outer part, then I slide them together how the pattern shows. She smiles, the first niceness she's offered, and takes the pouch, rushing to the raccoons.

I run after, hugging myself to keep the girls from swinging, and slide into the enclosure, struggling to catch my breath. We only have seven minutes left, so if our raccoon is hungry, we might make the clock. A volunteer points to a cage, and Amber holds open the pouch, motioning for me to grab the raccoon. Beside us another group is struggling to get their animal in. The girl's arms are cut and bleeding. *So nice of Amber to give me this job.*

Dad's voice fills my head, warning me to avoid this, but another distant voice is in there, telling me she's proud.

I won't let Mom down.

I take a deep breath, open the cage, and reach in, letting the raccoon smell my hand before cupping its little bottom and encouraging it out. It lets me pick it up and doesn't struggle too much. Amber holds open the pouch, and I tuck its little legs in my hand and guide it in first try. Amber's eyes are wide like I'm some sort of raccoon whisperer, and I don't blame her—I'm just as surprised. I hold the little critter-burrito tight to my chest and walk briskly but carefully to the chairs (the faster I move, the more my rolls bounce, and last thing I want is a jiggly love handle startling it).

"Five minutes," Frank calls out.

Amber rushes to the bottles.

The partners still sewing stop and head with half-finished projects to the enclosure. Blond-spikes and his teammate are putting their raccoon back in the cage. Amber offers the bottle to ours, and he takes it right away, sucking down the warm milk.

When he finishes, we put him back with the pouch still on, then head to our table and wait. We're the fourth group finished when the horn blows.

As Frank and Michelle tally the points, Amber paces.

"We did good," I tell her, but what I really want to say is: *chill already.*

Michelle brings a handful of pouches to the front. "The top three teams will be moving to the next round."

Amber kicks the ground and glares at me. "Great, just great."

Then Michelle holds up our pouch. "This team was the only one to put in the French seams and make sure there were no loose threads. This was an important step—we don't want the babies getting their nails caught on strings. Though this team didn't finish in the top three, because of their attention to detail, we're allowing them to continue to the next round."

Amber collapses into the chair with a big exhale. "You're welcome," she tells me.

I fight the urge to roll my eyes as Michelle announces the other three teams to move on. Blond-spikes and his partner high-five, so I'm assuming they're in.

I'm about to follow Amber's lead and take a seat, when Blond-spikes saunters over. "I'd say congrats, but we both know you shouldn't be here," he says.

"Uh, no, we both don't know that."

He snorts. "There's no way you told the truth on your application. I'm going to talk to Frank and see that you're removed."

I'm about to get into my second fight today, but then the familiarity of how he says "Frank" makes things click. This must be the guy Michelle was talking about. "I'm guessing you're Pierce?"

"Yes," he says, confused.

"I talked to Frank and Michelle"—I put the emphasis on "Michelle"—"and they assured me the BMI question wasn't supposed to be on the application. That is what you're referring to, isn't it?"

He shifts his stance and crosses his arms. "I, uh—"

"I guess you'll just have to lose the old-fashioned way." I whip around and am about to storm off when red-flannel arms yank me into a hug. "My little raccoon wrangler. Look at you kicking ass." Normally his hugs are like hugging a brother, but something about this one makes me want to lean in closer until it's only me and Billy and everyone else disappears. Billy stiffens behind me when he catches Pierce's scowl and realizes he walked into the middle of something. He leans in, his whispered breath warm against my ear, sending a shiver down my neck. "Does my girl need me to punch a bro?"

"No, and I'm not your girl," I say with a smile, "This one, I got."

✦ ✦ ✦

I reach for an ax, just as Amber's hand wraps around the handle. "That's mine," she says.

There are three unclaimed behind her, and this ax is closest to me.

"Take one of those." I nod to the others and refuse to let go.

"Uh, mates?" Frank takes off his hat and stands between us and the camera. He lowers his voice so the reporters don't hear. "Your arguing could impede donor generosity. No donations, no money for flights."

"Fine," Amber says, letting go and grabbing the one behind her.

"Right, good," Frank says, stepping back to address those of us left. "Now, do yous remember what the fire chief just told you?"

Pierce raises his hand, and Frank's shoulders droop. "Yes, Pierce," he says with a sigh.

"Put on the fire gear, work as a team to put out the fire, demolish the burn house, then race back to the office and grab the kangaroo trophy." Pierce sneers at me as if he's already holding the trophy above his head in victory. He doesn't know about my volunteer firefighter training and that the very fire chief who is overseeing this contest is the one who taught me everything—I'm ready to wipe that smirk off his face.

Frank guides the camera crew over to the moms (and Billy) behind a chain-link fence a safe distance back from our next challenge—a rundown barn on the edge of the charity's property that we're about to demolish. Billy climbs the fence and shouts, "That's my girl!" I bite my lip to keep from replying that I'm not, 'cause I'm not sure I fully believe that anymore.

As if on cue, there's a deep *whoosh* as two firefighters set the barn ablaze and a wall of flames flashes up. Even from this distance the heat hits me with a smack—suddenly I'm twelve again, watching my tree house burn and feeling like I'm losing Mom all over. My heart races; my palms begin to sweat. *You can do this,* I remind myself. *You've faced many fires since that day, and you're still here.* When Amber's phone rings, I nearly jump out of my skin.

She slips it from her pocket and walks a few feet away. "Hello? . . . No," Amber says, sounding dismayed. She's trying to be quiet, but I can hear everything. "I haven't got an update on Nan. Last the doctors said, it was smoke inhalation, and they have her in the ICU . . . No, she's at Royal Brisbane Women's Hospital . . ."

My heart sinks. She has a family member in Australia, injured from the fires. It makes sense now how uptight she is about winning this.

". . . I have to go; one more competition and then . . . This is my only chance." Amber turns quickly and catches me eavesdropping. "Now you know," she says, shoving the phone back in her coat.

"I—I'm sorry." I offer a sympathetic smile. "I get it, though. My mom was Australian."

"Was?"

"She died when I was little."

I can tell she wants to say something, but Frank has the air horn raised, so she gets in line.

My fingers tighten on the ax handle. "Maxie, sweetie, you can do this," I whisper in my best Australian accent as the air horn blows.

I rush to the gear, kick off my sneakers, and step into the fire pants and boots, pulling them up and securing the suspenders over my shoulders. The face mask goes on next, then the jacket. I'm bigger than the other contestants, but I'm fast at getting into fire gear—my fire chief made me do it non-stop until my dress-time was under a minute. They don't have packs for us, so I put my helmet and my gloves on and head to the hose curled up in a pile beside other supplies. Behind me the other contestants are still struggling with their gear.

A hose is a two-person job. I get into position and wait for one of the others. Amber's struggling with the mask, so I yell instructions to her. She glares at first, but then listens, and soon her gear is on and she and Pierce are racing down the hill to me.

"Grab the back of the hose," I tell her, and she does. "Brace yourself." I pull the lever, and water rockets out. My hands vibrate, and my entire body flexes. I pin the hose with my elbow and direct the surge, turning the nozzle to make a wider fog-stream to cover more wall.

"You've got this, Maxie," a familiar voice says. It's Matt, one of the firefighters from my station, who is over-seeing us.

Beside us, Pierce reaches for the other hose and, before anyone can join him, yanks the nozzle's handle back—water rockets up, and he trips onto his butt and drops it.

"Grab that!" I shout. But he takes too long and the hose snakes everywhere. The rest of the contenders make it to the barn and try to help. It trips two of them and smacks another in the head. The crowd gasps. The firefighters rush over. They've got it handled, so I keep ours pointed on the barn, sweeping the water side to side. "Moving forward," I yell to Amber. "Watch your step," I warn.

We take slow cautious steps, keeping control of our hose as behind us the firefighters manage to shut the other one off and begin tending to the injured contestants.

Pierce approaches, waving for me to hand him our hose. "This is about group participation, and I need a turn."

"You had your chance," Amber tells him.

He huffs and storms off.

"Forward," I say, letting Amber know we're moving again. As far as I know she hasn't had any experience controlling a hose, but she's doing a great job. In no time, the fire is out. I shut off the water, and we high-five. In the distance Billy gets the moms to chant my name; it's nice having someone here for me, even if it isn't my dad.

The ground is wet and slippery, and all that's left of the barn is a heavy soggy-wood roof held up by four support posts and a few charred boards. Amber and I recoil the hose as Pierce and the other two remaining contestants go under the roof and start chopping at one of the supports.

"Pierce, stop!" I call, but he ignores me and continues hacking the beam. I search for the firefighters, hoping he'll listen to them, but they're halfway up the hill, pushing the stretcher carrying the guy who took a hose to the head, and the two others limping beside. Frank and Michelle are heading to that crew, so it's just me.

"Pierce!" I scream. "It's going to fall on you. We need to take the roof off fir—"

There's a loud crack. The roof begins to tip like a tree going down. "Run!"

The three contestants drop their axes and sprint for the exit. Pierce slips, struggling to his knees in the mud. Before he can regain footing, the roof collapses with a giant yawn—smacking the backs of the two guys running and burying Pierce in the rubble.

The crowd gasps. A woman yells out Pierce's name.

Amber and I rush to help the two guys, all the while repeating, "Pierce, talk to me. Are you okay?"

A muffled "Help" comes back. Amber tries to lift the roof, but it doesn't budge. I grab a solid piece of wood beside her and pull up. Every muscle strains, my legs shake, but I manage to raise it a few inches. "Grab my ax and slip it under." Amber does, and I ignore my screaming joints and use the ax for leverage to push the roof higher. "Can you see him?"

"Yes!" An arm stretches out of the gap, and Amber grabs it and pulls. I grunt in exertion as Pierce wiggles his way from the rubble with Amber's help. Soon he's free and Frank's beside us, checking Pierce and shouting orders to the volunteers. I drop the ax, flopping to the ground to catch my breath and give my achy body a break.

Amber looks at me, then up the hill toward the office—there's a spark in her eyes. She hurries to take off her gear, and I know what she's about to do. My heart's speeding and my entire body aches, but I push off the ground and head for the kangaroo trophy. My steps are slower than I'd like. I'm used to running in gear—my fire chief makes us do laps in it—but still it's grueling in my current state. I'm counting on my head start to beat Amber.

The crowd gasps. Half of them watch me, the other half still engrossed by the hot mess at the barn.

The kangaroo's in sight. Amber's loud footsteps tell me she's catching up—then suddenly a memory of that droop of her shoulders and the vulnerable way she talked about her nan on that call comes rushing in—reminding me of how I was, waiting at the hospital for news of my mom.

She needs this more than I do.

The kangaroo's only a yard away, but next thing I know I'm falling to the ground and turning to watch Amber rush past.

But she doesn't.

She screeches to a stop beside me. "Oh hell no! You fell on purpose."

"Just grab it," I say.

"I'm not taking a pity win!"

Frank approaches, supporting a limping and dejected Pierce. "You two'll be the death of me. One of yous take the damn trophy already."

The cameras watch as instead of reaching for the kangaroo, Amber reaches down for me. "It belongs to Maxie."

"Well, I'm not taking it," I say.

Michelle smirks and whispers something to Frank.

"No," he says. "We told 'em—"

She whispers something else.

Frank throws up his free arm, hands Pierce off to her, and heads for the trophy. He smashes it. Over and over, in a fit of temper, until it breaks in two. Then he does the unexpected—he hands the base to Amber and the kangaroo to me. "You both win. You both can come."

"What!" I gasp out a laugh, and no time passes before Billy pulls me to my feet and into a hug. He hugs Amber next, and she smiles so big it changes her whole face. She almost looks nice.

The fire chief comes over, "Congrats, Maxie, I knew you'd win. Great job on the burn site. You saved that boy's life."

"Thanks, Chief, I just did as you taught—"

Someone clears their throat. "Maxie?" a familiar voice calls. I turn to see Dad's stern face, and behind him, the cameras. "I saw you on the news."

My heart beats faster. The chief pats my shoulder and turns to Dad. "One heck of a kid you have here," he says.

"I'm very proud of her," Dad replies, then smiles, and I almost collapse a second time.

The chief gets pulled into another conversation, and Billy hangs back, letting me and Dad talk. "You did good today, kiddo," he says. "Your mom would be so proud. But . . . if you're going to Australia, so am I."

"What?"

"Oh dang, we can do that?" Billy says. "Who's gonna pay my way?"

I want to ask about Dad's church obligations, all the times he's said no to us going to Mom's homeland, but instead, I cry and smile and cling to the kangaroo as Dad pulls me into his arms.

Frank leans over to us. "You'll have to pay your own way, sir."

Michelle nudges him and continues waving at the cameras. "Of course he will, love."

Dad's phone rings, and he gives me an apologetic look before letting go of our hug to answer and slip out of the crowd. Likely pastor duties beckoning. Billy takes the opening and grabs my hand, lacing his fingers through mine. We've never held hands like this before, but it feels normal, as if we've done it an uncountable number of times. His eyes lock on the trophy. "That's my girl," he says with his stupidly adorable grin.

I try to keep my face serious, but I crack into a smile. "I'm my own girl."

"Maxine Cooper." He sighs my name, and leans in, giving me a gentle kiss on my forehead. My heart's racing, and I don't know if it's from exerting myself or from Billy. He keeps his lips there, moving them against my skin as he says, "One day you'll understand that you have always been and will always be my girl."

I smile, and push a little closer into him, savoring this strange new feeling growing between us. "Fine," I say in a breathy exhale, not yet ready for his lips to leave. "We can share me."

"Agreed," he says, his warm lips tickling my skin.

Dad returns, and he pauses when he sees how intimately

Billy and I are standing. Billy laughs and wraps his arms around my dad, dragging him into our hug. I look down at the gold kangaroo trophy and know deep in my heart, Mom's here too. In this moment, in their arms, everything is perfect.

LETTERS TO CHARLIE BROWN

Francina Simone

A Regular Wednesday, August 29

Dear ~~Charlie~~ Boy-who-will-henceforth-be-known-as—C. Brown
(in case one day I become very famous and die and these
letters are included in my autobiography),

I'm Genie Raspberry, a sophomore at Dr. Phillips Magnet
School. This is all you really need to know about me. This and
that I picked you because, like you, I have no place in this
world.

In Spanish class today, Mrs. Fiddle instructed us to write
a letter (en español) to a person (*"Fine, Genie. Yes, they can
be fictional,"* she said when I asked), asking them questions
about themselves. You may have noticed this letter isn't in
Spanish, but that's because I'm almost sure you don't know
how to speak or read Spanish, so writing it that way would

be pointless. I tried to explain this to Mrs. Fiddle, but she said, and I quote, *"I am not in the mood for your philosophical musings today, Genie. Just write the letter."* I'm thinking about contacting the school board about her lack of enthusiasm for my education. But I digress.

Anyway, the question I wanted to ask you, C. Brown, is this: Why do you always insist on kicking the football? I am not trying to discourage you from athletic activities, believe me; my mother stresses how I could gain—or *lose*—with the ᴀᴅᴅɪᴛɪᴏɴ ᴏf ꜱᴏᴍᴇ ᴀᴛʜʟᴇᴛɪᴄ ᴀᴄᴛɪᴠᴀᴛɪᴏɴ in my life. But—it seems to me—if you know you're just going to fall and land flat on your back, then why continue making a fool of yourself? Maybe you don't know you look like a complete clown? In that case you're delusional and far beyond my help.

Mrs. Fiddle is looking over my shoulder and asking why I'm not doing the assignment correctly. *"Because,"* I say, *"the recipient knows little Spanish and might have enough trouble with the level of diction currently present."* When I ask her what the Spanish word for "delusional" is, she moves on, with a sigh and her loose hippie hair, to peer over Becky Russo's shoulder.

Look, I have accepted that Mrs. Fiddle is an American-born white woman from North Dakota, but I am *again* having serious doubts about her ability to teach Spanish adequately if she once again suggests I ask you simple questions like "Eres tus amigos simpático?" or "Tenes trabajador?" I know that your friends are, a few aside, generally agreeable, but— you're in the third grade: Why would I ask about your job?! Has she never heard of child labor laws?

You know what, C. Brown? Despite Mrs. Fiddle putting an English-to-Spanish dictionary on my desk, and demanding I write to someone who understands Spanish, I am going to help *you*. Because I think your bouts of low self-esteem and failure streaks are much more important than this assignment she's not even collecting. (Can you believe that? What is the point of doing an assignment she won't even collect? She's just announced that, and already I see Teddy Johnson dropping his pencil on the table and resuming his natural I'm-not-on-my-phone-but-I'm-totally-on-my-phone position.) But I digress! (For the second time now, I'm counting.)

You see, you're constantly letting other people bully you. Why kick the football when ~~Lucy~~ Lacy is just going to snatch it away? I've got some ideas for you, but I'm afraid right now, I am out of time and lunch is around the corner.

Sincerely,

Genie Raspberry

✦ ✦ ✦

The Skies Are Alive, Tuesday, September 4

Dear C. Brown,

I know I said I'd get to your bully problem—and technically I want to remind you this assignment wasn't collected, so all of this henceforth is out of the kindness of my own morally just heart—but something's come up. And I'm not saying your problems are less important than my successes, but we're going to talk about something that happened to me recently.

I want to start by saying, I hate the way spit hangs from my lip after I've thrown up. Sometimes I feel like my mind is doing cartwheels down a steep hill and I can't keep up with the swirling green and blue and ache and pain in my wrist and feet because my body is telling me to slow down, to focus on the blue sky or the green itchy grass one at a time.

But I can't.

And so I'm destined to vomit all over myself as soon as I tumble into the anthill at the bottom of the hill. I come out bruised, itchy, and covered in tiny volcanoes that bleed when I scratch them. I scratch and try to remember the exhilaration I felt when I watched the vibrant colors swirl by me. How I wanted to live in one color fully but also in the other at the same time. How I want to smell the dirt and the air all at once, but it is nearly impossible.

An ongoing, vomit-inducing cartwheel, C. Brown.

That is what my life is like right now.

I want to do so many things better than anyone else. I want to play my flute with such precise emotion that the last note, because it is the last one, quivers with sadness. I want to present my literature report on *The Scarlet Letter* with dramatics that transport my fellow peers back to the days when women wore their sins and men didn't because injustice was justice. I want to be the best dressed because I have an eye for colors that fit perfectly together like a man and a woman. I want Seth (you don't need to know his *real* name)—who has had a growth spurt since last year and is growing a mustache—to look at me the way a man lusts for a woman. I want Love, C. Brown.

Love.

And that is what love is like. Going so fast you can't take everything in and it makes you sick, but at the same time you are so full of it all, you might burst into tiny pieces of yourself and die. To live anymore after that moment would be like a life without Christmas. A life without those multicolored lights that you watch blink for hours on end because, even though you haven't had your hot chocolate yet, you are warm and you know Christmas means all of it: everything.

Love is like this and I know that now.

School has been canceled the rest of the week because there was a hurricane. Hurricane Bob, but it should have been called Hurricane Aphrodite because, after all, it was a hurricane of love.

There was no cable, no power, but our phones still worked. My mother paced around the house calling our relatives, and I made sure Fito—the deaf cat that seems to live in our bushes—had not been carried away by Aphrodite's love and into the arms of death. And then my phone rang. Seth, the most accomplished sax player ever, was on the other end.

"How is your family?" I said because it was polite and I didn't want him to think I am *That Girl*, the one who only thinks about herself and refuses to believe other people have families, especially during times of crisis.

And he said everyone was fine except for his dog, Tofu, who seemed to be having a nervous breakdown. After making all the right inquiries about Tofu and telling him that my family and I were all right—including Fito (who may as well be family, because if you're a deaf cat and you don't have family, then what else do you have in this giant cat-eating silent world?)—he said the nicest thing, C. Brown.

He said, *"Genie, I'm really glad you're not dead."*

"Thanks, Seth. I feel the same about you," I said, because I wanted him to know that he makes me feel good, but not that I have been cyberstalking him for a month now.

"In times of crisis like this, we think about people. You know, the people we want to be with. And I thought about you," he said, and parts of me tingled and I had to simmit up before I exploded.

"I thought about you too." I opened a window. The breeze after a hurricane is like flowers blooming; it only happens a certain time of year.

"Good. Great."

I started to feel like I was doing cartwheels and the wet wind was carrying me down faster and faster and all the while I could smell the dirt . . . the flowers . . . the rain—and it filled me up so much I wanted to close my eyes, spin, and laugh forever.

"How about we go out, then?" he said. I burst into little laughing mes flying in the wind getting caught in my green-and-blue curtains.

I said yes. My cheeks burned, aching for me to smile just a little less. His mom told him to help with the debris in the yard. I hung up thinking how one day he would have to choose between my happiness and his mother's, and he would choose me because his mother is a little crazy with her big orange hair and purple lipstick that only looks normal on the dead.

So you see, C., for three days now I have been a taken woman. I fit perfectly in the world because I am a girl and Seth is this boy that I fit perfectly with, and I am cartwheeling down a steep hill that never ends.

Sincerely,

A Cartwheel

P.S. Learn from my success, C. I assure you, it's far better than looking up at the world after falling flat on your back.

✦ ✦ ✦

A Troubling Tuesday, September 25

Dear C. Brown,

Something happened to me. I sit in the front of the school bus because it is the first seat available on the bus. I am not trying to make any other statement about what type of person I am, besides the type of person who hates spending long periods of time getting on and off this yellow tube of death.

Anyway, that is what I do every school day. I wake up at an ungodly hour, put on the clothes I meant to lay out the night before, brush my teeth, untwist my hair, and proceed to wait on the side of the road for a bus that rarely shows up on time except when I'm late.

Today just so happened to be a day that I was on time,

and Chantel—my best friend—was there putting on eyeliner. This is not the important event, but you have to understand the routine before I get to the point.

The bus pulls up, and there are two girls sticking their heads out my usual window seat, and one says, *"Oh, I'm so cool. I'm sitting in the front seat, so I must be cool."* And then the other one laughs and says, *"Yeah, because we think we're better than everyone else!"* I looked at Chantel and noted that it made no sense to me why those two girls had an abundance of energy when it's seven o'clock in the morning and their destination is school. Now, I *knew* that they were *really* talking about me because they have been ever since I started riding the bus. But I didn't care. Really.

Chantel had a look in her eye—it was the way Fito stared at me after I'd forced one of those worm pills in his mouth—and right then I knew Chantel wasn't going to let it go. When we got on the bus, we sat in the third seat from the front—what I still consider prime enter-and-exit seating—and I pulled out my granola bar and started chowing down.

Chantel was ridged.

I knew those girls (especially the one whose wig has a bad hairline) were trying to offend me, because they had spent the last month whispering about me every time I got on the bus. The girl with the cheap wig once said, *"She always has that same nappy hair and ugly hair scarf"* and *"Ew, is she wearing a thong?"*

I have no proof that she was talking about me, but I can only assume because I was in fact wearing said garment.

I had wanted to know what it felt like to wear something so tiny. How they knew I was wearing one is still a mystery.

But this time the girls laughed, looking back at me and Chantel, calling us bothered. I pretended like I didn't hear them.

All of a sudden, Chantel stood up on the moving bus and said, *"Shut the hell up, you ratchet bitch."* At first, I wasn't sure they understood her.

They stared at her as if she were some rabid animal that had just spit in their eyes.

"You shut the hell up," one of the girls said.

"Why don't you do us all a favor and fuck off? All you do is talk about me and my friend. What? Are you that jealous? You that bothered with your own life that you have to try and be in ours?"

"Fuck you," Wig Girl said.

"No. Fuck you, you stupid bitch," Chantel said right back.

Everyone on the bus, including me, was silent. The bus driver turned up the radio as if all teen problems could be solved by Hits that aren't really Hits. Chantel threw out her arms, daring the other girls to say something.

They didn't.

They turned around in their seats and talked to each other, saying things like *"Whatever"* and *"Don't even go down to her level."*

A rush of pride and awe filled me as Chantel sat back down and stared as if waiting for them to turn around again so she could ninja-jump over the chairs and unleash the beast inside.

The more I watched her stare at them, the more I realized I had said nothing. I hadn't stood up next to her. I hadn't added in a *Ratchet bitch!* or a *Say I won't!* I kept replaying the scene over and over in my head, thinking of all the things I could have said. All the things I should have said. After all, it was me they were really making fun of. Chantel was standing up for *me*. Not us.

At that moment I realized two things: Chantel Davis is going to be my best friend for life, and I am a coward. Maybe you and I aren't that diff... .. .l. .fl. . all, C. Drown.

Sincerely,

A Coward

✦ ✦ ✦

A True-Blue Friday, October 12

Dear C. Brown,

I'm back with a dark day that tops the darkest day of my life (I will not mention the picture day "blowout" here, as this letter can only contain one horribly scarring event).

First, I will tell you that I am sitting at my corner desk in my room with the blinds closed. The lights are off, and only the glow of day behind the blinds lights up my blue-and-aquatic-green wall decor. I wish it were dark outside too, reflecting the current state of my soul.

I am listening to Moonlight Sonata. Beethoven. The only version I have is one played by Chantel; she's a really good pianist, but there's one part in the piece where she forgets what she's playing, so there is a pause, and in that pause I forget that I am depressed—until she starts again.

I'm shocked, C. Brown. Shocked. There was no foreboding sign that today was going to be the worst day of my life—on the contrary, it was a beautiful day. The sun shone bright; marching band practice was delayed because Mr. Kaminski forgot the keys to the sousaphones' storage room at home.

I had decided it was the perfect opportunity for Seth and me to explore the wonders of each other's mouths. Ever since he got his braces removed it's like kissing a new person; I get a brand-new set of butterflies when our lips touch, and when I close my eyes it's as if I will erupt and die. The cartwheel of love!

This particular day he told me that he would rather sit on the bench we all call the Mall—because if you sit there you have the perfect view of everyone leaving school and no one can resist the temptation to people watch. I'll admit, the rejection of mouth-to-mouth resuscitation left me feeling worried. What if he had already gotten tired of me? Maybe because my teeth are already perfect, kissing them, as he had for months now, was not as exciting to him as it had once been? I bottled up my worries and stuffed them deep down because he seemed, my worries aside, happy and I didn't want to ruin the mood.

So, there I sat on the bench with him and—as one naturally does when sitting on the Mall—I watched my fellow students flee to their cars. While I was telling Seth that I wished I had a car to flee to, the most beautiful girl I've ever known walked by: Olivia James. I immediately looked for her flaws as I always do. They must have been there somewhere on her brown poreless skin, too much eyeliner, or the way her purple headband, holding back her moisturized-to-perfection curls, hardly matched her flowy white A-line dress. But what did I know? I've never been good with makeup or fashion.

So, I felt myself sinking into ugliness. How was I, a sensible girl, supposed to compete with *that*?

The answer came to me as if God spoke directly from the ⸱ᴵᵧ "*Oᵉᵤⁱᵉ*," ʰᵉ ˢᵃⁱᵈ, "*ᵧₒᵤ ₕₐᵥₑ Tₒₒₜₕ!*"

And then it hit me. I *am* beautiful. I might not be as toned as Olivia; she's a curvy girl but somehow her thickness is like being fat on purpose. Mine looks like I accidentally woke up with an extra ten pounds on each side. But! I have what every girl wishes she could have: a perfect boyfriend with new perfect teeth. I smiled and sat up straight on the sturdy wooden bench. I fluffed my hair; my natural curls a tad kinkier than Olivia's still accentuated my beautiful jawline. A feature Seth, after all, loved.

Seth would cheer me up. We were best friends—what more could I ask for? I turned to him and said, "*Do you wish I was as gorgeous as girls like her?*" I was slightly annoyed that he knew which girl I was talking about without me pointing, but he must have been admiring me and seen me looking.

He watched Olivia and said, "*No, because then you wouldn't want to be with me.*" I smiled, getting ready to smother him with a public display of affection, when I realized just exactly what he had said.

He *had* said, "*No.*" But it wasn't a *No, because you are beautiful as you are*, or *No, because that would be downgrade*.

I am a no because *I* am the downgrade, and he can't get the better version.

C. Brown, do you understand what this means? Seth is only with me because he does not believe he can be with someone beautiful. Just then, Olivia, with her purple headband that I'm not quite sure matched with her white A-line dress, looked at me and smiled. Her smile nearly broke my heart. It was so beautiful. Perhaps she thought she was doing ugly me a favor by gracing me with one thing beautiful in my life. Without returning her smile I stood up and ran to the girls' bathroom.

I didn't come out all practice.

So here I am in the dark, and do you know what I've learned? The truth hurts, C. Brown. Did you know ~~Peppermint~~ Candy Cane Patty once met the Little ~~Red-Haired~~ Pink-Headed Girl? Yes, C. Brown, the one you always go on and on about. After she met her, she said, "*I have a big nose, and my split ends have split ends, and I'll always be funny-looking . . . She's so pretty . . . She just sort of sparkles . . . I'll never sparkle . . . I'm a mud fence . . . I'm a plain Jane.*" C. Brown, the world is full of Little Pink-Headed Girls and Candy Cane Pattys. Olivia James is a Little Pink-Headed Girl.

And I am a Candy Cane Patty.

Sincerely,

A Nobody

✦ ✦ ✦

A Cursed Friday, November 16

Dear C.,

I am sitting in the nurse's office today writing you this letter. I know I am supposed to be lying down, but I'm too upset.

Sometimes I look at my hands, wiggle my ten digits, and I don't recognize them. It's like they (the hands) are magically suspended in the air, pretending they are like other hands; attached to someone else's arms. I feel like I am those unrecognizable hands, floating among my peers, pretending I am like them; full of happiness and math formulas. But I am not anymore.

Or maybe I never was.

You probably never noticed, but Chantel transferred in the middle of the semester to a school closer to her home. My best friend is gone and—I don't think I'm taking it as well as I had hoped.

I stole something today, C.

Sunglasses.

Beautiful, red framed with dark black lenses that reflect not only the sun but the whole world, sunglasses. They bend slightly inward, giving my eyes ultraprotection, and they make me look like a nineteen-twenties Hollywood producer. When I wear them I want to say, "*C., baby! Let's me and you do lunch!*" in my Hollywood voice. But alas, C., I cannot.

They are *tainted*.

It all started last week in the library. Our teacher said

since the world is full of fake news, she was set on us learning the *old school* way of finding and citing sources. I was at a computer looking up literary criticism books for my paper on Nathaniel Hawthorne's *The Scarlet Letter* when I saw them. They were just sitting there saying, "Hello."

I ignored their salutation and continued my search. I picked up a tiny pencil and an index card and wrote down: *vol. 2 (so red), vol. 45 (big like Hollywood), vol. 47 (they look expensive).* I exited out of my browser (it's rude to leave browsers open when you're not using them), I put the tiny pencil back in the pencil holder (after all, what if someone else needs a pencil?), I put my index cards in my book bag, and—you won't believe it, C.—I slid the glasses right into my book bag along with the index cards.

I looked around and saw the librarian at her desk watching a girl from my class make copies. But I knew someone had to have seen me. They must have seen me grab the red frames the way townspeople saw the red letter *A* on Hester Prynne's chest.

I walked over to the reference books (honestly, why do they make us use these ancient things?), and I knew, at that moment, that the owner of these spectacular frames could see them; she was looking straight through the triple-woven fabric, for added support, right into my book bag—and me. She must have seen me for what I really am.

A thief.

And worse, she would undoubtedly tell everyone.

No more than thirty minutes ago I sat in English, and I kept seeing my reflection in the bathroom mirror where I tried them on. They fit so perfectly on my heart-shaped face. How would I ever be able to wear them in public?

As soon as they touch my face, the girl—whose eyes will no doubt be squinting and full of cataracts—will see me and say, *Hey you! Give me back my sunglasses!* and I will have no choice but to confess to my crimes; I will have to pay for her laser eye surgery to correct her surly-by-now, glowing orbs; and I will be forced to wear an obligatory red letter *T* on my chest.

Sitting in English, I was so haunted by what people would think about that giant letter *T* that I nearly missed every other sentence in my presentation. I said the *A* stood for her shame, and I ranted about how she deserved it; she should have been more careful because now everyone knows! Then I cried because she was tricked, tricked by the allure that we are all subject to. *"We are all sinners!"* I shouted in class, and Mrs. McKinley stopped me before my presentation was over and told me to go to the nurse's office.

Who am I, C.? Who have I become? People will say, *First, she's stealing glasses; now failing presentations; next, she'll be waiting for band practice with Diana McIntosh, who uses her mellophone as a means to smoke her drugs.*

What will my mother think?

Sincerely,

A Thief

P.S. Only thing worse than being a thief is everyone knowing you're a thief.

✦ ✦ ✦

Just Another Thursday, February 14

Dear C.,

I know it has been a few months since I last wrote you, but I ask you to forgive my absence in the event that my life has turned upside down. Now that marching band season is over, symphonic band has taken my attention. I was challenged for my first-chair flute solo by Hannah Zimmer— whose tongue is so heavy I fear she might spit on me when she is trying to play the staccato notes—and though I knew the solo well I had been busy with other matters.

Seth has left me, and, I fear, for another woman, an *older* woman. A senior.

I have been betrayed.

He was my confidant. I am the only person who truly understands his soul, or at least I thought I was until this short and obviously unbalanced brunette cut her way into our relationship. Though I have no real evidence beyond Facebook that she is a home wrecker to say the least, I exacted revenge and pity upon her by turning her name into the counselors' office—in the box that reads: People I Know Who Hurt Themselves.

It felt good to help her and Seth see that she has severe psychological issues. I haven't told Chantel about this turn of events because I'm afraid she'll tell me a truth I feel looming over me. Even though that girl's name belongs in the box, my heart was not in the right place. But how could it be when it has been stolen and broken into a million little pieces?

But these are not the sole reasons my life has taken a turn for the worse. I recently found out that my family (and maybe Fito, but that is undecided as my dad is allergic) is moving again.

My mom assures me that I will still go to the same school, but living in our current lower-middle-class suburb is distressing to her because we are no longer poor and she wants a better home where all the rich people live. I know I should be happy, but I love where I live, I like being normal—my mother was happier when we were not cool.

Anyway, we drove by the new house today on the way home from band practice, and she pointed out a little pond by it as if I've wanted nothing more in my life than to be a fish. In a way, I wish I were a fish, a salmon to be exact; I wish I knew what it was like to venture out in life but always have one place that you recall when you tell childhood stories, the place you go every year for Christmas or have all your birthday parties and store your memories.

I've only ever lived in the same house for five years now. I started middle school in my old house. I finally had a bicycle and a neighborhood I could call my own. I had friends whose parents didn't seem sketchy because they didn't move from apartment complex to apartment complex like transient people on the run from life because re-signing a lease was notifying life that you had finally decided to settle in and live.

I think the day we moved to this house is the day we decided to start living. We got a street cat that no longer yawls in the bush next to my window and sea monkeys that swam in a little plastic tank on the windowsill in my shower. I used to wash my face and watch them grow from tiny specs into little brine shrimp, eat off the dead ones before them, and then die.

But one day my mother started writing and selling books and she stopped living with us. She's here, of course, but she's also far away in some world the rest of us can only visit if we pay $24.99 at the local bookstore. This Christmas she barely stopped working long enough to open presents.

I've already started packing—I've got boxes everywhere actually, and when I took my shower this evening, you'll never guess it, but the sea monkeys were motionless at the bottom of the tank slowly being covered in green-black algae.

We're not going to finish the lease on this house, and I can't help but feel like all the traditions we started to build are going to die like the sea monkeys in the bottom of that tank. I know I sound like a child, but when all you have is family because the only friend you made after not having friends for a very long time has left you alone in a sea as vast and wide as Dr. Phillips Magnet School, you start to feel small. Very small indeed.

But there I was, earlier today after band practice, in a much bigger house far away from everything I know, looking at my new home with wooden floors and a pond.

C. Brown, is it so much to ask to be a salmon? Is it too much to ask for a small place in the world to call my own?

Sincerely,

A Fish

P.S. At least now that I live farther from school, I don't have to take the bus—but my brother is a horrible driver so we'll see how that goes.

✦ ✦ ✦

A Blue Wednesday, February 27

Dear C.,

I went home (to the new house) early from school today. I told my mother that I was ill, but the truth is, I can't face the world. Seth and his mental-health-cautionary-tale girlfriend are everywhere (yes, they are officially dating), my mother still doesn't understand why I refuse to unpack my room, and I fear that when everyone at school looks at me, they see that Genie Raspberry, the girl with straight As and an outstanding ear for pitch, has cracked.

Today is the third time this week I had to hurry to the bathroom so I could cry my eyes out for no reason.

No, that is a lie. There is a reason. It is because when I look at myself, I see all the things I am not and all the things I will never be. I will never be the prettiest girl in school, I will never be the smartest student in class, I'll never have a doorframe that marks my growth and memories in one house, and because I haven't practiced for a week now I won't be the best flute player in the symphonic (not best) band.

If I'm not any of those things, then why get out of bed?

I am in the cartwheel, and I am seeing the colors, and none of them are mine. I am at the preverbal bottom of the hill, I have officially landed in the ant pile, and I am covered in little itchy volcanoes. I get it, C. When you're lying flat on your back things aren't so bad because at least you've stopped spinning.

Sincerely,

Who Cares

✦ ✦ ✦

An Odd Friday, April 26

Dear C. Brown,

I haven't written in a while. When you realize you are a mediocre nobody it's hard to pick up the pen. But the oddest thing happened to me today. Olivia James invited me to be a part of a school club she's starting.

Do you remember her? The prettiest girl in school, the one who everyone is always watching, and yet she walks like she hasn't a clue anyone is ever watching her at all. You know, the girl we all wish we could be if only we just had a little bit of the sparkle she has.

That Olivia James.

It was a normal Friday afternoon; I have taken to eating my lunch alone as you know there is a Chantel-sized hole in the space beside me. Just as I was taking tiny bites into my tuna sandwich to really appreciate the artisan bread my mother is so fond of, Olivia sat beside me. She said, in her very cool and level voice, *"Hey."* And well, I didn't know what to say because I hadn't said much to anyone over the past few months, so I just nodded.

"I'm starting a club—it's for girls. Like you and me." You

have to understand, when Olivia James graces you with her poreless smooth brown skin and dark lashes, it's hard to understand what she means when she says "you and me." *"Black girls?"* I said, because other than that what could we possibly have in common?

"Fearless girls. Beautiful girls. Girls who have something to say but aren't always given the space to say it. You're pretty awesome, so I thought I'd extend the invite." I don't think I've ever told you, but Olivia James has a magical laugh. The kind that makes me want to not only be like her—but be *with* her.

I am slightly ashamed to say, while she thinks of me as the verbose type, I uttered not a single word while she sat next to me and started to unpack her own lunch. But for the first time in my life I felt seen.

As I pen this letter now, thinking about how deep brown her eyes were as she took all of me in, I'm starting to wonder if I've been looking at the world through a faulty pair of eyes. But which me is real, C.? The one I think I am or the one Olivia seems to see?

Sincerely,

A Somebody

✦ ✦ ✦

A Musically Inspired Wednesday, May 8

Dear C. Brown,

I would like to cordially invite you to the spring concert. I know you cannot come, but I learned that it is rude to talk about events that you are attending without inviting the person you are talking about them to. Therefore, you are invited.

I am not the best flute player I thought I was in the beginning of the year. That title goes to Hannah Zimmer and her stupid squirrel fingers—they really are the quickest things I've ever seen in my life. If you're wondering, I didn't mess up on the sixteenth notes that climb higher than any I've ever played—no, I played those beautifully—I messed up on the whole notes.

Mr. Kaminski said I was in too much of a hurry. But I am at least second chair, so if she just so happens to break her fingers while dodging out of the way of a speeding vehicle, I will take her place. And sad to say, given the dangers of our school parking lot, it is a likely event.

I'm surprised at myself because I am calmer about it than I thought I would be. As I sat in class watching Hannah Zimmer's fingers move like one of our many cracked-out campus squirrels, I felt okay.

Do you know why?

Perspective, C. Perspective.

Remember the spelling bee, C.? The one you lost when you were so close to winning because you couldn't spell "beagle"? I was embarrassed for you even though you didn't need me to be. You turned a funny shade of green, and the look in your eye was the look of a boy who had just humiliated himself in front of the entire nation—well, because you had. You stayed in bed for days, and I understood that, because that was the way I felt when I saw Hannah Zimmer's name on the solo sheet Mr. Kaminski put up.

I wanted to erase myself from the world because not only did I know I didn't get the solo, but everyone also knew that I didn't get it because my name wasn't on the list; they knew, and I knew, that I wasn't good enough.

So there you lay, and believe me I was (metaphorically) lying there next to you, us both deep in shame and humiliation, and ~~Linus~~ Sinus, like all best friends do, came to check up on you, and you told him, *"I'm just going to lie here for the rest of my life."* Sinus said something that really made it all click; it wasn't just about the spelling bee

I understood why every time ~~Lucy~~ Lacy pulled the ball, sending you flying until you landed flat on your back, you always got up and tried again the next day. Do you remember the rest of the movie, C.? Sinus said, *"Well, I can understand how you feel,"* and I rolled my eyes because how could he possibly know? How can anyone know the crushing defeat of being singled out as *not good enough* so repeatedly it only takes a gentle blow to finally knock you out?

But he said, *"You worked hard for the spelling bee, and I suppose you feel you let everyone down. You made a fool out of yourself and everything."* You peeked out from underneath your bedsheets, and so did I because he was so right. *"But did you notice something, C.?"* he said.

"What's that?" you said.

"The world didn't come to an end."

I took a moment to think about how my world had come to an end. I was eating lunch all alone but then Olivia came to sit next to me. Now I'm in a club and I've made new friends. Yes—some of the girls are self-proclaimed witches and one tried to *smudge* me of my bad energies. But they listened to me about the thing that happened with Seth and they cared.

Things happen in life, C. Lots of things, but we must always have perspective! While life may have its downs, the ups are just around the corner if only we rise to meet them. If we are always lying down—then the ups will start to feel like downs too.

Looking back on things, I can admit that I don't know as much about life as I thought I did. But I've realized that getting up and trying is how I'll figure out the rest. I've got some boxes to unpack so—until next time, C.

Yours truly,

Genie Raspberry

love spells &
lavender lattes

amanda lovelace

*dedicated to the starbucks cup
in s8e4 of* game of thrones

the wood holds equal parts wonder & terror.

one never knows when they are going to encounter a unicorn teaching its young how to drink water, or a winged demon in the trees preying on a small goblin below.

for some people, the risk is too high, so they don't ever dare venture in.

as for me? i was practically raised in this wood. like so many others, i'm one of those poor orphans whose mother didn't have enough silver to take care of the both of us.

when i was just shy of six years old, she took me into the wood & told me we were going to play hide-&-seek. i had to close my eyes, spin in circles as i counted all the way up to one hundred, & then search for her hiding spot. like the obedient little girl i was, i didn't even peek until i got to twenty & forgot which number came next.

when i opened my eyes, she was long gone.

it's clear to me now that she had never intended to be found.

i wandered aimlessly for months before someone—a wolf named grey, who i consider to be my father & only family, even if we aren't able to live together as one—finally happened upon me. apparently, i'd survived by eating whatever wildflowers i could gather. mother always did say that's what the kind faeries ate. the food i would later eat at the orphanage was never quite as good.

this morning, the bright yellow light of dawn shines down through the green canopy, erasing all traces of the cold memory. i tilt my chin back to catch whatever rays i possibly can, closing my eyes & smiling in relief as i do so.

despite the warmth, the heaviness of an impending storm is in the air.

i skip down the overgrown trail, running my hands along the worn bark of the trees as i pass by. they know my hands so well they practically lean into my touch.

the trick is not to show any fear; fear is what turns this place against you. i've walked this path for all seventeen years of my life & i've yet to die, so why be afraid now?

truthfully, i'm much more afraid that my boss will have me murdered if i'm late to work—which i very well may be.

a light drizzle begins to fall, tickling my nose.

i take that as my cue, picking up my skirts as i transform my skip into a quick sprint.

a finch flies overhead, calling down to me, "aren't you going to be late, rosemary?"

"only if you keep distracting me!" i gasp between haggard breaths.

seconds later, the mouth of the wood comes into view, revealing the defunct-tavern-turned-café called *the teacup*. it's my third home, apart from the orphanage &, of course, the wood. soon i will be a girl of eighteen years & therefore too old to reside in the orphanage, but the wood will always be here, as will, hopefully, *the teacup*.

✦ ✦ ✦

through the now-torrential raindrops, i get the sense that the walkway has turned into a treacherous mudslide. i try my hardest to tread carefully, but nonetheless, my boots betray me & begin to slip.

i let out a bloodcurdling shriek, knowing i can do nothing to stop what's about to unfold.

just as my toes begin to point toward the sky, something—or *someone*, i soon realize—catches me by my hips & steadies me into place.

oh, thank goddess.

in a mixture of confusion & relief, i twist my neck to see the face of my savior.

warm & concerned brown eyes look down upon me. "are you all right, my lady?" my savior asks, holding on to me like i could break at any moment.

"quite," i say, but it comes out sounding a bit like a strangled cat.

despite my reassurance, his hands don't leave my waist, nor do his eyes leave mine. perhaps another girl might get butterflies from those long, thick lashes, but my stomach feels like it's going to drop out through my bottom & land straight into the mud below.

what a flattering first impression that *would be.*

after a few awkwardly quiet moments, i twist out of his arms, take a few steps back, & give him a curtsy of gratitude. now that we're separated, i can't help but notice his soft blue armor—a squire. the knight he serves can't be too far from here.

the squire smiles shyly in return, rubbing the back of his neck with vigor. his cheeks are slowly turning so scarlet i can bear to witness it no longer.

i clear my throat before speaking. "i hereby welcome you to *the teacup*," i proclaim as i open the door for him, gesturing inside. the hundred or so bells hanging from the doorknob jingle obnoxiously, announcing our entrance. agatha told me the old crone in the wood gifted them to her for the café. for protection from negative energy & spirits, or so she claimed.

he tilts his head curiously, drawing his eyebrows in. "is that not the job of a gentleman?"

"ah, i'm afraid to inform you that we don't do gender roles here," i explain with a bit too much attitude, stepping in just before he's able.

his surprised laughter rings in my ears as i walk to find my post in the back, never daring to look over my shoulder.

well, that was hellishly embarrassing, but there's much

work to do, i think to myself as i tie my apron on over my soaked dress.

the inside of *the teacup* is warm & toasty today. someone's taken the liberty of lighting the hearth in the middle of the room. the dozens of lanterns hanging from the ceiling have, too, been lit, i assume to combat the dreariness spilling in through the windowpanes. patrons fill the tree trunk tables—some reading tomes, some typing away on their laptops, some reading oracle cards, some playing games on their phones, & some watching the storm with coffee cup in hand.

unlike in some other lands, magic & technology coexist seamlessly here; we aren't too reliant on one or the other. it's difficult—& truthfully, even a bit disheartening—for me to try to imagine a world where it's anything different from this.

unfortunately, no one will be able to leave until the storm lets, which might not be until twilight. we'll need to have much fresh coffee on hand until then, as well as gather plenty of carrots for the horses outside in the stable.

before the café switched hands to agatha years ago, it served nothing but ale & steak. now it sells only enchanted teas & coffees as well as the occasional homemade pie. weary travelers used to complain about the change, but it wasn't long before they started to agree that our lavender lattes are a perfectly adequate replacement.

just as i begin emptying out all the old coffee, i can sense someone's eyes burrowing a hole into my back, right between my shoulder blades. i try to ignore it & keep working, humming a merry melody to myself.

they clear their throat.

i roll my eyes at the wall & keep humming.

they clear their throat louder.

"may i assist you in some way?" i throw over my shoulder, pouring fresh water into one of the machines.

"you're *late*, rosemary. that's *thrice* this week," catherine complains, as nasally as ever.

how does she always manage to bypass the bells?

when i turn to face her, her arms are folded tightly across her own apron. her nose is pointed up, making her appear as though she's twelve feet tall, which isn't hard to do, seeing as i'm so tragically short. considering my red hair, freckles, & a strong preference for the color green, she loves to call me a leprechaun—not just behind my back, but to my face too.

she thinks it's oh so endearing, but it makes me want to tug on that long blond braid of hers.

i slap my hand to my chest, feigning surprise. "oh, i didn't realize *you* were the boss of the place now! did agatha resign? was it just this morning? you must have forgotten to tell me."

she purses her thin lips into a line, making an unhappy *hmph* sound as she joins me behind the counter, holding her side in a pained manner as she does so. which means she's most likely wearing that damn corset contraption again.

we live in the same rundown orphanage with only a few coins to our names, yet you would never know it by the way she dresses. she has a habit of conning boys with rich families into buying her whatever she desires, & as soon as they oblige, she drops them like rotten apples. or so she likes to tell everyone, but i'm not totally convinced anyone wants to put up with her snobbish attitude.

the tension passes as catherine & i fall into our routine of readying the machines, preparing orders, & explaining to a handful of patrons that no, we absolutely will *not* send them off with cursed coffee for their list of enemies.

curses, as well as love spells, are highly forbidden in use at *the teacup*, as well as the entire land of feyhaven, & for good reason. generally speaking, we don't believe in messing with another person's free will; not only that, but that type of magic is so potent that it's nearly impossible to counteract.

however, that doesn't mean it isn't tempting to some.

as the storm slows, the tables begin to empty, & i'm finally able to take a much-needed breather.

i drape a tea towel over my shoulder & lean both elbows on the wood counter, quietly surveying the place for a moment.

in the process, i accidentally make eye contact with the squire for the first time since the incident. he's sharing a pair of earbuds with his oblivious knight. when he notices my gaze, he sends a goofy attempt at a wink in my direction, but he can't quite pull it off, so he ends up winking both eyes at the same exact time.

i bite back a chuckle.

"why is it *you* they're always eyeing?" catherine says from behind me.

i mentally brace myself for whatever nonsense she's about to spout, clenching my eyes shut. "excuse me?"

"that handsome squire over there has been staring at you this whole time. it just doesn't make any sense—why *you*? i always try so damn hard, whereas you—well, you—" she stops herself.

i turn my head slowly, glaring in her direction. "*what* do you mean by *that*?"

"i just mean that someone . . . well, as *plump* as you," she says, wrinkling her nose in disgust as she quickly eyes my silhouette up & down, "shouldn't be getting so much attention in the first place. to make it worse, you never so much as entertain their advances, even though you're incredibly lucky to be getting them in the first place. you should be taking every opportunity you're given, for there likely won't be many to come in the future."

ouch.

as confident as i am with myself, i must admit her words still sting a little.

i swing around to face her & unleash my wrath. "listen, catherine. i know the fact that i'm fat & content offends you down to your very core, especially since you invest a great deal into your own thinness"—i gesture to her corset & she's so shocked she looks as though she's swallowed a beetle—"& yet it still never seems to get you anywhere. why do you think none of those boys ever bother trying to marry you? not only are you childish & spiteful, but you never shut up!"

she looks around for eavesdroppers before she begins

whisper-shouting, "the nerve of you! how do you hope to ever attract a courter, let alone a husband? don't you want a fair chance out there once they send us packing from the orphanage, which is only a few months from now? your wretched *body positivity*," she sneers, putting angry air quotes around the phrase, "won't protect you on the streets!"

i've done the worst possible thing i can do to a girl like catherine: wound her ego. "i don't give a flying *cauldron*—" i screech.

i'm interrupted by the sound of a mug loudly hitting the counter. "s-sorry, my ladies, i don't mean to trouble either of you, but could i possibly get a refill on my brew?"

"of course," catherine & i both say in unison, turning to see the squire looking at us with a bewildered—& a very much frightened—look on his face.

how much of our squabble did this poor boy overhear?

plastering on a tight but nonetheless polite smile, i retrieve his cup & turn on my heel to make my way to the coffee-making station. before i'm able to take more than one step, catherine places a bony yet firm hand on my shoulder to stop me, snatching the cup away.

"don't worry, my *dearest* rosemary, i've got this all handled. why don't you stay here & *chat*?" she looks suggestively between me & the squire. "you were drinking the house specialty—a lavender latte—correct?" she asks him.

the squire nods, perhaps a little too enthusiastically.

i grumble something nasty under my breath as she sashays away.

perhaps if i try to look very busy wiping crumbs & coffee stains off the counter, the squire won't try to converse with me.

"what was that you said?" the squire asks, amusement in his voice, cupping his hand around his ear to hear me better.

"we both know very well what i said."

"it sounded quite like *witch*, except with a *b* in place of the *w*, but that can't have been it, can it? that would be, as they say, quite scandalous."

"oh, sir, of course not! how could you think i'd ever behave so improperly? i dare say i'm the finest lady in all feyhaven," i say, dramatically bringing the dirty rag to my chest as if it's a dainty handkerchief.

whatever he's about to say next is swiftly interrupted by the sound of catherine's magic sparking up at the coffee-making station. for a moment, the entire room fills with a bright pink light. a few of the patrons let out a yelp, & another few jump out of their seats.

i shout back to her, "everything all right back there, catherine?"

she shakes her palms out, her fingertips singed from the backfire. "oh, never better! apologies for the long wait—it will be ready in just another moment!"

i lean over the counter & say to the squire, "don't blame me if you grow a pig tail after drinking whatever she gives you."

he chuckles for a moment, but then his face becomes very serious. "wait—that can't actually happen, can it?"

teasingly, i shrug one shoulder as i step back to make way for catherine's approach.

"here you are—one lavender latte refill, with a few extra sprigs of lavender on top!" catherine announces, sliding the steaming mug over to the squire. she slouches & places her hands at her corseted waist, catching her breath as if she took a run through the wood & back. a proud smile grows on her face.

"for the record, if i *do* grow a pig tail, i'll at least be the most charming pig in all f.,l......," he says to me, pretending to "cheers" me just before bringing the mug to his lips.

catherine squirms impatiently where she stands, moving forward as if she's about to lunge over the counter at him.

she no longer looks proud.

is that . . . *panic* written all over her face?

i turn to stop her with my arm just before she's about to take the leap. "what in the world do you think you're doing?" i hiss.

"you, rosemary *i-don't-know-your-last-name-yet*, are the fairest maiden i have ever laid eyes on. i would go to war to defend your honor. i would write a thousand sonnets about that little piece of hazel in your eye—" the squire drones on, setting his mug down.

i turn my head slowly to him.

there are almost literal hearts in his eyes as he looks up at me.

she didn't.

"you didn't," i say to catherine, my voice eerily level &
calm.

except she isn't beside me anymore.

she's vanished.

✦ ✦ ✦

"where is it that you're taking me again, rosemary?" the
squire asks, following at my heels as i grab my cloak & pointed
hat from the back room. *"rosemary,"* he repeats dreamily.
"what an absolutely exquisite name. angelic, really."

i tie my long scarf around my neck four times as i reex-
plain the plan to him. "we have to go see the crone in the
wood. if we take your horse, it should only take a handful of
hours—that is, as long as we don't stop anywhere along the
way. she'll know how to fix this . . . this . . ." *love spell.*

maybe if i never utter the words aloud, it won't be true.

"so like, a date?" he says, gesturing excitedly with his
hands.

"no—*nothing like a bloody date!*" i scream.

through the open doorway, the café falls completely silent.
a few patrons stretch their necks over the counter, trying to
peek inside & see what the commotion is.

i poke my head out, grinning, i imagine, like a madwoman.
"terribly sorry about the noise! there's nothing to worry about!
we're just rehearsing some lines back here!"

lines for what, exactly?

goddess, you're a horrible liar.

i press my hands against his back & firmly usher him toward the back door. "we have to go. *now.*" before agatha notices. before his knight notices. before *anyone* notices us & tries to stop us from this undoubtedly doomed & dangerous quest.

we manage to sneak around the back of the café & into the stable to retrieve the squire's horse—named wanda, he tells me, with nothing but adoration in his voice—without anyone noticing. i've never ridden on horseback, though, so it takes me a few attempts to successfully sit atop the saddle. i slip & fall right on my bottom not once, but twice.

wanda does not speak as some horses do, but her irritable grunts tell me everything i need to know.

somehow, all three of us eventually make it out of the stable unscathed. as we ride, i cling to the squire's back for dear life, bunching his sleeves up in my palms.

the wood is completely silent except for the sound of hooves crunching the dry autumn leaves. it's almost meditative, but not nearly enough to calm my frayed nerves.

what if the crone can't *reverse the enchantment? what if the squire is infuriatingly enamored with me forever?*

stop. enough with the negative talk.

you don't want to manifest any of that into existence, do you?

it's not long before darkness begins to envelop us—winter's way of letting us know that she'll soon be here to stay.

like our own personal little lanterns, a group of will-o'-the-wisps light our way up the long, steep path to the crone's cottage. they have a habit of leading many a naive traveler astray; however, they can sense that i'm as much part of this wood as they are. a few of the smaller & more mischievous ones try to tie knots into my hair. lazily, i bat them away, giving up after a few minutes of their persistence. i have much bigger concerns right now.

"darling?" the squire inquires over his shoulder.

"don't *call* me that," i reply, exasperated.

"right. whatever it is that you desire." he pauses a moment before continuing. "i dare say, do you know how much longer it will take before we arrive? i'm starting to tire, & wanda probably can't take much more riding this evening."

of course he is. magic like this certainly takes its toll, & not just on the spell caster.

i look around, silently inspecting the horizon as well as the shadows made by the trees.

"i'm afraid we aren't making very good time. i'd say we still have a few more hours. we can stop & take a rest for the night, if that's what you would prefer."

he nods once, immediately guiding wanda off the trail & into the wood until we find a good & relatively comfortable spot.

while i prepare the fire—the old-fashioned way, as i'm tired as well, & exhaustion doesn't mix with magic—the squire bunches up his jacket & uses it as a pillow, watching me through half-closed eyes as i struggle to do the most mundane thing without magic. twice he insists upon helping me. i ignore him the first time & snap at him the second.

"stop! i'm not a silly little girl—i promise you i can handle this!" i shout, my voice echoing throughout the wood.

reader, i don't think i can handle this.

grudgingly, i request the squire's help after all. he bounces up immediately, thrilled that he can do this one little thing for me. together, we get the fire going within a few minutes.

"my gratitude to you, good sire," i say, yawning the words.

"of course. anything for you—anything at all," he ooo.

suppressing the urge to roll my eyes into the back of my head, i plop—very graciously, i'm sure—onto the rain-soft earth, as he does the same, snuggling back into his sleeping spot. my gloves come off & i point my palms toward the roaring blaze, relishing the rose-gold warmth i've been dreaming about all day.

while i truly loathe that there's still so much distance between us & the crone's cottage, i'm grateful for the time & space to clear my mind. here, in the wood, i'm always free to be still, even with the squire constantly making those awful heart-eyes at me.

it would be a very nice thing, i suppose, to be loved, though not like this.

never like this.

when—or *if*, i should say—i ever fall in love with somebody, i don't want it to be because of a mean-spirited love spell neither of us has any kind of say in. i want it to be honest-to-goddess *love.*

as kindhearted as the squire may be, i've never envisioned being some giggling accessory on a boy's arm.

ever since i was a little girl, i've always imagined waking up next to another girl. kissing her nose to wake her up at sunrise. cooking blueberry pancakes with her & making a mess. growing a garden full of lavender together. reading each other faerie tales until we fall asleep in each other's arms. not as *spinsters*, as they say in feyhaven, but as partners. as wives.

"i don't even know your name," i wonder aloud.

the squire doesn't bother opening his eyes before answering. "hmm?"

"what's your name? it's not actually 'the squire,' or so i should hope," i clarify.

he props himself up onto one of his elbows to see my face better. "oh. nobody ever really cares enough to ask me that. well, rosemary, my name is stevyn, proud squire to douglas the fearsome—"

"nice to meet you, stevyn—*just* stevyn."

i need you to know that you matter outside of your duties to others, i want to tell him but can't find the energy to.

stevyn grins sleepily, putting his head back down. "nice to be met by you, fairest rosemary."

i sigh, fluffing up my scarf to use as a pillow before i lie down on my side. "if everything goes according to plan, we could be best friends in the making, stevyn."

only snoring in response.

✦ ✦ ✦

i startle awake to a loud, unidentifiable noise & am met by the chill in the air as well as the burned-out fire. after a few moments of silence, i try to convince myself i imagined the sound & turn onto my other side to resume my slumber.

that's when the demon-like snarling begins.

"stevyn? stevyn, are you there?" i whisper through the darkness.

"rosemary, stay where you are & don't you dare move," he responds, a tremble in his voice.

what on earth?

rubbing my two palms together with nearly enough vigor to revive the kindling, i call on the light of the stars & moon to bless me. since i've had the chance to rest a bit, my magic has recharged a little since the stress & exhaustion caused by our quest, though, apparently, not to completion. my hands cast only the dimmest light—barely enough to see my own two feet.

i curse silently to myself before reaching deep into my dress pockets to find my phone. i activate the flashlight it provides, ignoring the fifty-three missed calls as i do so.

there are text messages too, but there's no time for me to read them. my eyes have but a quick moment to take in flashes of words & phrases.

so sorry—

regret—

no one deserves—

my temper—
i will fix this—
i swear.

to my profound horror, i find stevyn up on his tippy toes, his back pressed up against a nearby tree, looking positively pale & petrified. a paw belonging to a very large wolf presses squarely in the middle of his chest. the light from my phone catches the corner of the creature's eye, & it twists its neck to look for the source—*me*.

all the blood in my body suddenly rushes to my ears, causing my entire world to go topsy-turvy for a moment.

is this how i die? mangled & magicless?

i have no one else to thank for this except you, catherine.

"rosemary?!" the wolf growls, jaw agape with surprise. his paw falls from stevyn's chest, and stevyn crumples onto the ground in a messy heap.

"grey?!" i run & jump at the wolf, who catches me in his familiar embrace.

"oh, i haven't seen you in so long, my child! look how mighty you've grown—why, you're practically a woman now!"

i choke back tears, croaking something nonsensical in reply, which makes us both dissolve into crying laughter.

as it was told to me, when my mother left me in the wood all those years ago, grey was the one who found me just as i was about to be torn limb from limb by a group of hungry, battle-ax-wielding ogres. he had no idea who i was, let alone where i came from, & yet he risked his life to protect me.

if it weren't for his kindness, i truly don't know if i'd be anything but a pile of bones right now.

"i've missed you so incredibly much," i whimper, letting my tears & snot coat his fur.

grey & i both go stone-still when we hear the sharp sound of a sword being unsheathed behind us.

"unhand rosemary, you ferocious beast, you! you'll have to kill me before you lay a single paw on her!" stevyn says shakily, pressing the sword threateningly into grey's back. grey's eyes go so wide i can see the whites of them.

breaking away from grey, i vigorously wipe the tears from my face with the heels of my palms. i loathe letting people see me cry, lest they come to the conclusion that i have emotions. "oh, calm down & put that thing away, stevyn. this is my father, grey. grey, this is my . . . friend, i guess you could say, stevyn."

grey smiles sheepishly at stevyn as if to say, *did you get eaten, though?*

"did you say *father*? am i having some kind of fever dream, rosemary, dear?"

"no—you're perfectly wide awake, so you have no excuse. get used to my life or immediately see yourself out of it," i dare him, putting my hands on my hips.

stevyn considers my ultimatum for a long moment before craning his neck up to grey, gulping loudly before he addresses him. "i suppose i'll have to ask you for permission to marry your daughter, won't i?"

grey turns toward me with a knitted brow. "who is this again?"

i lower myself back down onto the ground, beside the firepit, gesturing to the open spot next to me. "that's a very long story. perhaps you should have a seat."

while we catch up, stevyn pretends to sleep, keeping one eye open at all times.

in any other situation, the protectiveness might be endearing, but alas . . .

eventually, the sun starts to rise, its rays glittering off the layer of frost covering the forest floor, welcoming me back into my reality.

i don't want to leave grey's side now that i've found him again, but i know i have to.

if i were the villainous sort, then i could just come back & roam these woods. i could run & hide from stevyn for the rest of my life & hope the spell eventually wore off over time, knowing full well that it can't. i could, but i won't. that's simply not me.

as grey hugs me goodbye, he assures me, "you don't need me to tell you this, little one, but everything is going to be all right."

"but how do you know?"

"if anything is clear to me after having seen you now, it's that you don't need anyone to hold your hand while you save yourself, as well as this strange fellow here. do you know how many people would be terrified to venture into these woods, let alone come face-to-face with the crone herself? but you— you're willing to risk it all to do the honorable thing. you are exactly the person i raised you to be. the next time i see you again, it will be with a girl you love who loves you back without any spells, or any other conditions."

"you say that with such confidence." i reply, a little surprised but ultimately unafraid.

"well, you're a daughter of mine, after all. i have always known exactly who you are & what you deserve." he beams, fangs & all, just like the proud father he is.

i sigh, feeling the weight of boulders lift from my shoulders. "good, because i am who i am, regardless of how ready the rest of the world may be."

"oh, i know that too," he laughs. "now, i need to get back to mildred & the pups, & i believe you have a crone to find."

i wave him off, watching him as he goes. i stand staring at the same spot long after.

eventually, stevyn begins to stir himself awake.

"it's about time, sunshine. ready to finish our hopeless mission?" i ask, the mock cheer evident in my voice.

for all i know, the crone will curse us the second we show up on her doorstep.

would that be better or worse?

in a half-asleep daze, stevyn begins gathering our things & readying wanda for the remainder of the quest. "are you sure we have to go, rosemary? don't you want to be in love forever? would that be so dreadful?"

in some ways, he's correct. it would be easier. safer, at least for me. however, it would not be right—not for me, & not for him. both of us deserve a fair chance at true happiness.

"yes," i say. "it would."

✦ ✦ ✦

"clearly you jest," is all the crone has to say after we finish telling our story, still hovering in the doorway of her small stone cottage.

she's younger than i thought she would be, but then i remember that she's taken many forms over the years— sometimes not even of the human variety. there were rumors recently that she'd transformed herself into a dragonfly. beneath the hood of her deep purple cloak, she appears to be a middle-aged, raven-haired beauty.

"i assure you, madam, that we do not," i say, trying not to sound too disappointed by her reaction to our plight.

the truth is that i could collapse where i stand. if she refuses us—which she has every right to do, seeing as how we're perfect strangers to her & she likely has more impor- tant things to attend to—there is no other feasible solution.

from behind, stevyn gently pulls the sleeve of my cloak, trying to get me to turn back around. "well, rosemary, if she doesn't want to help, perhaps we should just go. no hard feelings, crone. my parents have a lovely place for us on the coast of—"

the crone holds up her gloved hand to stop him. "oh, shut up, you foolish, foolish boy. you're in no state of mind to be making any kind of decisions. come in, children, & have a seat." she moves aside & gestures us into her home, albeit grudgingly.

she has us sit at her old, wobbly kitchen table while she brews us all some tea.

there's very little light in this cramped space of hers, &

the majority of it is coming from the hearth, where a large black cauldron sits.

the room is so wonderfully cluttered that my eye doesn't know where to look first—the dried herbs & flowers hanging from the spiderwebbed rafters, the shiny crystals on the windowsills, or the spell bottles that line just about every flat surface. it is a very magical yet intimidating place i would be delighted to wander for hours, if i were permitted.

while stevyn & i wait, i take out my phone to check it, only to find that the battery has died, then were texts from someone, weren't there? everything with grey happened so quickly, i can scarcely remember what they said.

the crone shuffles over to us, placing steaming mugs of tea in front of stevyn & me. the three of us sip anxiously for a minute before the crone breaks the silence. she can scarcely look at either of us as she says, "the unfortunate news is that there's little i can do to help you two out of this predicament you have found yourselves in."

"but—" i begin, all too aware that i'm about to sound like a petulant child who hasn't gotten her way.

"you must know that the only person who can break a curse or a love spell is the one who performed it in the first place. without this catherine girl here, it simply cannot be done. i make sure the village elders ingrain that into you from the time you're born—it saves everyone, myself included, the headache."

"you're . . . the most powerful woman in the world. surely you know some kind of loophole."

"well, child, that certainly makes me blush," she replies
drily, "but as skilled at magic as i may be, no amount of herbs
or tonics can ever change the laws of the universe."

i feel myself deflate.

"i am truly sorry, i am. if there were a way around it, then
i would have found it by now. i have been the crone quite some
time, after all."

nodding solemnly, i look down at my hands, both
wrapped around the little bit of warmth the mug still provides. even stevyn—still drunk on his infatuation for
me—knows better than to say anything that could upset me
further.

instead, he reaches & places his hand over mine, giving
it a friendly, reassuring squeeze. it is a small piece of comfort
in all of this.

i suppose that's it, then. i did what i could.

i have gone & failed us both.

the crone rises from her seat & begins tidying up the table.
"you two are welcome to stay the night, if you so wish. it is a
long way back into the village, after all, & you came all this
way . . ." *for nothing,* she means to say but doesn't.

"oh, we don't mean to impose on you at all," i say half-
heartedly. *please let us stay, for i'm not ready to face the
world just yet.*

"it is the least i—"

before the crone can finish her sentence, three frantic
knocks sound from the front door.

stevyn & i nearly jump out of our skin, but the crone, for

some mysterious reason, looks calm & collected, nodding to herself knowingly as she moves to open it.

this woman contains wisdom i could never hope to understand.

when the door opens to reveal who's standing on the other side, it's as though my mind simply cannot register it. it's the same as looking through your window to see a full-grown daisy standing strong & tall through a snowstorm—it's that unfathomable.

catherine bursts into the cottage like a wild animal & charges straight for the crone, grabbing her by her forearms as she falls onto both of her knees. "please—*please*, you must help me at once. i've done something terrible—*so terrible*—& i don't know how to fix it," she begs, her eyes as wide as tea saucers as she looks desperately up at the crone.

"girl . . . ," the crone begins.

"she just made me so *mad*—the things she *said* about me—i only wanted to get *back* at her—i only wanted to teach her a *lesson*"—catherine pauses to weep loudly—"but i went too far—i saw that right away—i let my rage blind me to what i know is right—"

the crone lowers herself onto the ground with catherine, taking her face in her hands, as a tender yet firm mother would. "shhhhh. we can make this right. you have gone & messed with things you should not be messing with, though, & to reverse it will demand great sacrifice from you. it won't be pretty, but it is what must be done—you already know that, don't you?"

catherine's gaze moves beyond the crone & finds mine, then stevyn's, her expression going from shock to guilt to stubborn resolve. "i'll do anything."

for a moment, i'm flooded with sorrow for what i know catherine will have to endure to counteract her spell.

sorrow, but not forgiveness.

BREATHE YOU IN

Hillary Monahan

The little mermaid wasn't so little anymore.

Young, yes; just turned seventeen after the equinox. But little, no. She was fat for the winter months, as oceanborne ought to be before the snows come. The gray-white horizon and screeching westerly wind promised brutal winter, and so she'd prepared, feasting, all so her already large body would be that much larger to insulate herself against the punishing elements. She was a pile of curves and pale flesh, her cheeks round, her hips wide. Even her tail was thick and padded, from the S curve of her rump all the way to the tips of her fins.

It was this last of the warmer autumn days that saw her basking upon her favorite rock—a boulder nine feet long and at least as wide, with enough flat surface for her and two companions. In that instance, said companions took the form of two black-skinned seal cows as pleasantly plump as she, one to each side of her, their bellies exposed to the sun, flippers lazily flapping while they snoozed. She draped her arms across them, smiling whenever one snored in its sleep, and outright giggling when the snores came point and counterpoint to one another.

Seals were loud. Smelly and loud, but she loved them anyway.

She tilted her head back, luxuriating in the warm rays on her face, her tail slapping against the boulder side with rhythmic, satisfying *thwacks*. Waist-length black hair rained over the rock, inky like squid leavings, the curls housing an army of tiny, shell-clad crustaceans scuttling through the mess. Her fingers toyed with the fringes of her halter top—a makeshift thing, salvaged from one of the many wrecks that riddled the sandbar. Once, it had been a flag billowing proud above a mast. Now, it struggled to contain her body, failing most noticeably around the gentle roll of her midsection.

It needed replacing now that she'd gained. She'd have to scavenge the wrecks for new finery. It wasn't a chore—she hungered for the human world and all it offered —but it was a risk. Her father's lectures were etched upon her brain, his booming voice condemning *and* demanding.

Stay away.

Stay home.

You can't. You can't . . .

It's why she had struck out on her own in the spring, forging her own path, finding other oceanborne who chose to leave over abiding his heavy hand. It wasn't so much that she and her father had differing opinions on landwalkers, but how his disagreement manifested. Shouting. Punishing words. Threats. Diminishing her to suit his arbitrary rules. Never once did he recognize her as a capable young woman. When she pointed out that she'd been sneaking off to devour every human everything she could get her hands on and he'd never clued in a single time, he forbade her from making contact anyway.

"You're forever my little mermaid," he'd said. "You stay with me."

It never occurred to him that little mermaids grew up to be big mermaids, and she had blossomed.

Thinking of her father soured her mood. She frowned, shifting upon her rock, grunting her irritation. One of the seals echoed her. Solidarity, maybe, but far more likely annoyance that its midday nap had been disturbed. The little mermaid stroked her fingers along the cow's back, skimming the soft, smooth fur, marveling at how it trapped the warmth of sunshine so efficiently. It was a soothing gesture—as soothing, perhaps, as the knowledge that while her father would never understand her, others did. Others even loved her for all the things he called "flaws."

She'd have been content to sprawl for hours, but a high-pitched squealing from the northern beach drew her attention. She rolled onto her stomach and squinted against the sun. A figure walked along the shore. A human, certainly, she could tell by the shape and gait. Dark haired, tanned skin against a white shirt, but distance masked the finer details.

Her hearts quickened inside her chest, her blood rushing through her veins and singing in her ears. Part of the allure of that particular basking rock was its proximity to human-kind without being vulgarly exposed. A line of white cliffs separated the beach from the closest port town, and yet a few trails existed, connecting the beach to town. Sometimes, she had opportunity to observe the landwalkers, and, if she so chose, to interact.

It was rare that she dared it; humans had their stories of oceanborne, but for the safety of all who lived in the water, that's how they had to remain. As stories. Fables. Myths and legends better suited to books and salty sailors' tales than anything else. Should she reveal herself, it'd only be under prime conditions: unobserved by anyone else, so only he would know her.

Whether or not those conditions were in place was yet to be determined.

She slid into the water, soundless despite her girth. The seals watched with interest but were too lazy to follow. Her body skimmed the ocean floor, her heavy tail lashing and pro-pelling her through the shoving tide. She wanted to see the human. To know it, and maybe for it to know her.

If.

If.

Twenty yards from the beach, she crested the waves. Her hair danced around her, tendrils splayed wide on the ocean top, writhing like tentacles. The second lens over her eyes, the one that protected her when she swam, slid away, allowing her to see the newcomer. A male, if the styling of blue pants and black boots was any indication. Handsome, with a square jaw and shadow along his lower face. An aquiline nose, thick arches of brows above brown eyes.

He blew into a long tube between his lips. The shrill squeal sounded again. Her gaze dropped to the instrument. He probably thought he was making music, or maybe human standards of music were poor. In either case, it was an unpleasant noise that caused more pain than pleasure.

The man continued his walk, never once spotting her bobbing on the current like a fleshy buoy. His steps were slow, measured, his boots pressing indentations into the sand. The tide quickly lapped them away, like it wanted no trace of him marring its coast. She approved of such discretion, if for no other reason than it suited her purposes.

As he moved, so did she, keeping low, ever suffering that awful "music" just so she could admire him. He wasn't a thin man, nor was he fat—more solid all over, with bulging biceps, thick thighs, and a hint of a belly. He was athletic, the muscle tone said, but also knew leisure. A man of means then, perhaps. The boots did look rather new.

They continued along together, one aware, one not, until at last he seemed to realize how far he'd ventured from the cliffs behind. He glanced over his shoulder and, with little fanfare, pivoted to make his way back, to retrace his erased steps and return to the town. The knowledge that in ten minutes, fifteen at the most, he'd be gone probably forever sent a fresh rush of adrenaline through her body.

To have him? To hold him?

Hers, even if just for a short while?

Just a taste of him?

She didn't know his language any more than he knew hers, but the noises she made from her watery hiding place were soft and inviting—a coo and a trill laced with a giggle. She wanted to evoke friendliness so he wouldn't startle. It took a few vocalizations for him to clue in to exactly where the sound was coming from, but when he turned to look for her, and then spotted her bobbing on the water, there was a much warranted gasp.

Don't fear me, please, she willed, wanting nothing more than for him to be as curious about her as she was about him. Slowly, so as to not scare him away, she crept nearer to shore, keeping her tones musical.

Unlike whatever noises he'd made with that instrument.

His eyes were already wide with shock, but seeing the prism play of blue, green, and purple across her scales when she hefted herself onto the beach, they grew twice as large. He said something beneath his breath, something quiet and low with a deep, lovely rumble of a voice, before crouching to peer at her.

She smiled, close-lipped, else he see her second row of teeth.

He continued to babble. She coaxed him near, perching on her coiled tail so her upper side—the part that looked most like him—was the part nearest him. The way he extended his hand to her face, knuckles offered first, almost like he wanted her to smell it, was off-putting. It was a maneuver she used on new seals so they recognized her as a friend. Her smile faltered, but only for a second. She ignored his gesture, instead capturing his hand, her fingers gently gliding over his. A thin sheen of her slime coat glistened on his skin.

He gasped at the contact. She didn't know if it was how warm he was versus how warm she *wasn't*, or if it was the webbing between her fingers or the rubbery texture of her skin. Another murmur, a shake of his head. His brow furrowed into so many lines it looked like a map. She clearly confused him, and on an obscene level, she was delighted. Innocence in such a strapping, hulking body was . . .

Well?

Cute.

He swallowed hard, his Adam's apple bobbing as he gently, slowly, grasped her much-smaller hand in his own. He turned her wrist to examine her, his finger tracing over the spidery, red veins there, and the talon-like curve of her black nails. He traced shapes in her slime coat. He skimmed over her webbing. He was so enthralled with her, his pipe slid from his lap and splashed in the water below. She hoped the tide gobbled it up. Later, after they'd made pleasantries, maybe she could claim it and see if it could make a pleasant song in lieu of that screeching he'd tried to pass off as music.

He shuffled closer. He hesitated for a moment, reaching for her face again. It was a less demeaning gesture the second time, his palm open, like he might cup her cheek. When she encouraged him with a nod, he delved his hand into the roiling mass of her hair. His thick fingers found a ripe curl, pulling it from her shoulder to determine its length. It dripped ocean water onto his pants, and he smiled, revealing straight white teeth. She smiled back, again close-lipped. There was a chuckle; he'd found a tiny crab nesting among the tangled black, and he plucked it free, watching its legs wave in anger. He flicked it off to splash into the water some feet away.

He spoke again. She shook her head to show him she didn't understand. For a moment, irritation twisted his features. It was so boringly, typically male; it never occurred to him that he ought to know her tongue, not the other way around. At least he was quick to collect himself, and for it, she rewarded him with gentle touches. Her pointer finger swept across his cheekbone. It skimmed down that long, fine nose and over his lips. He had nice ones, plump and pink, and she grazed them, leaving a thin crust of salt in her wake.

He never saw her kiss coming. One second she was perusing the planes of his face, the next she was leaning in, pressing her mouth to his. It was brazen of her, but she wanted him near, in her grasp. She wanted to show him who the oceanborne *truly* were. With her, he could experience the freedom of the seas like never before.

She wanted to show him a whole new world, even if only for a little while.

She pulled back to peer at him from beneath her lashes. He seemed stunned. He touched his lips like she'd branded him. She trilled at him, cocking her head to the side so her hair fell around her face veiled. She willed color into her cheeks, pumping her blood to change her hue to mimic a human flush. They liked that, though she wasn't entirely sure why. It seemed to do the trick, though; he hesitated only a moment before reaching for her again. Unlike before, this was no shy, stranger's touch: his hands settled on her hips, where skin turned to scale. His body collided into hers, her soft chest mashing against his hard one.

It was a passionate kiss, meant to steal her breath.

But it was her breath that would sustain him.

Their lips nestled together. His hands coursed over her, exploring swelling curves and hidden crevices. He deepened the kiss, his eyes closing on a moan. She never stopped watching him or the pleasure knitting itself across his face. Her arms wrapped around him, one across his shoulders, one across his lower back. When her grip was good, when she knew she had him anchored, she tensed all the thick muscle in her tail.

He construed it as ardor.

She knew it as preparedness.

She heaved back, pulling both of them into the sea.

He yelped at first contact with the cold water. He panicked more when he realized that she was far, far stronger than he and he couldn't escape. She cooed, offering oxygen and comfort, but he wasn't ready to receive either. His ragged scream was trapped by her mouth as he thrashed within her arms. Her fingers traced over his shoulder, over the smooth, drenched fabric of his shirt. It was a nice shirt, better than the dilapidated flag she wore. Perhaps, if she was lucky, she'd be able to wear it when their swim was done.

Deeper, deeper they dived, her tail pumping hard and fast as she dragged them from the safety of the beach and into the sprawling depths. There was a drop-off not twenty-five feet from shore, the wall jutting, craggy rocks and hidden caves. She rushed past it, into the deeper dwellings. It was a harsh place of stone and rusty ocean junk from wrecks long lost to landwalker memory, but there was beauty there too. Coral had formed over the emaciated carcasses of industry, life springing from abandoned human garbage. Fish, sea anemones, eels—they all thrived despite the intrusion into their watery domain.

He'd have appreciated it if he'd *just stop panicking.* She frowned against his mouth. His eyes were wide, his cheeks ballooned and flushed. He held his breath still. At this rate, he'd pass out and then what? She'd have to force air into him so he wouldn't drown—an unpleasant, risky prospect she'd prefer to avoid. No, he had to breathe. They'd come too far to squander it all now.

What came next wasn't kind, but it was necessary. Her hand slid along the back of his neck to fist in his hair. She yanked, hard enough he startled, not so hard she'd tear his scalp. It was meant to shock him into a gasp, and in that, it succeeded beautifully. He inhaled, albeit not of his own volition, but finally, he breathed her in, his lungs accepting the oxygen her lungs offered.

Understanding was swift and merciful.

He stopped writhing to suckle at the free air. His muscles remained stiff, but he no longer jerked within her grasp. He clung to her, squinting against the salt water. A few blinks, a long stare at her face, and he finally dared to look around him, to see the bounty of the ocean floor. It was dark, but glimmers of sunlight pierced the ocean depths too, granting him peeks at scuttling lobsters and bobbing jellyfish no bigger than his thumb. He pointed at one, and she gently pulled his hand away so he wouldn't get stung.

She'd seen that particular species paralyze a dolphin with its venom. She wasn't going to do all this work to bring the human home only for a pink, brainless blob to steal him from her.

She began to swim, to show him more of her world. She'd travel a short distance and stop so he could explore another reef, another species, another place human eyes had never before seen. He clutched onto her, and when she offered him a reprieve—surfacing a mile away from land so he could get cold, fresh air into his lungs—he wiped at his red-rimmed eyes and tilted his head back to laugh at the sun, the last of his reservations gone.

She squealed when he squeezed her waist and babbled excitedly. She didn't understand his words, but she didn't have to either—his body language told her what she needed to know. The tension had eased. Strain no longer distorted his face. He was soft and pliant and happy.

He was perfect.

He gestured back at land. She nodded, and before she

could kiss him, he kissed her, eager to go wherever she led. And where she led was back toward the shore, past the secret places she'd shown him with their finned, fanged, be-clawed citizens. She propelled them toward the drop-off with its angry cliffs and hidden recesses. Once reached, she again surfaced so he could breathe, again delighting in his delight, before bringing him down for one last, glorious dunk.

Their arms were wrapped around one another. Her hair danced around them, catching his neck, catching on the current and twisting like wild vines. Their lips sealed in an airtight lock. She spun them as she sank them to the bottom of the ocean floor, until the tips of her fins could feel the tickle of sand below. She opened her eyes. His were closed, but there were creases beside them as if he was smiling. So handsome, so pure.

She spun them, and spun them, until his back was to the crags of the drop-off.

Until his back was to the cave she called home.

Until the fat, black tentacles burst from the cave.

It was by design that he never saw it coming. A long, sucker-covered appendage wrapped around his neck and jerked, until there was an efficient snap. There was no jolt—no time for fear or pain. There was only death, and the little mermaid pulled away, allowing the human's head to loll forward. Allowing his body to go limp in her arms.

The tentacle around his neck was joined by two around his waist and ankles.

"What have you brought me, darling?" asked the low, rasping voice.

The mermaid relinquished her hold on the body, rushing forward only to be swallowed by a swarm of tentacles herself. She whirled in the grip, her arms encircling the neck of a woman twice her size, whose green skin, glowing yellow eyes, and palm-sized fangs made her the most glorious creature in all the seven seas.

"Presents," the mermaid whispered, nuzzling in close. The billowing gills on the sea witch's neck tickled her nose, and she giggled, burying her face in her shoulder. The sea witch chuckled her approval, pulling both mermaid and landwalker into the depths of the cave, careful to harm neither prize in the presence of sharp, angry coral.

She laid the dead man on the floor, pinning him so the gases in his body wouldn't float him to the ceiling.

"And did you do as I taught you?"

The mermaid beamed. "He was happy. So happy."

The sea witch trilled her approval; fear tainted the meat, made it tough and sour. The only way to enjoy landwalkers was to tenderize them, to be sure they went to their deaths with surging pleasure, not surging terror. All the mermaid's kisses, all her reassurances and soft touches were for the opportunity at yet another perfect meal.

And she had delivered.

And so, she devoured.

Later, when she reclaimed her rock by the shore, her faithful seal cows still basking in the last rays of dwindling daylight, she released her hair from beneath the collar of her new white shirt and pulled her pipe from the chest pocket. The first note was shrill, yes, but with practice, she knew she'd play a pretty, pretty song sooner rather than later.

UNPLEASANT SURPRISES

Linda Camacho

Why can't I come over?"

"You just can't." Tara's voice sounded strained over the line. I'd been back a whole day, and she was just now getting around to returning my call. She was the only person I'd let interrupt my billionth rewatch of *28 Days Later.*

"But why not?"

"It's a surpri— It's . . . a reveal."

My lip curled a little. "You said surprise."

"No, I said *reveal.* Reveal."

"A reveal of?"

"Of something you haven't seen. Except you have seen it before. It's just in a new way."

"Like the chimps." In the movie, the zombie virus infestation began with an infected chimp biting a scientist. It didn't turn out well for anyone.

"Chimps?"

"In *28 Days Later*? I've never been able to look at chimps the same way. Bottom line, change is death."

"Oh my God, Dee. My news isn't going to demolish the UK, so it's safe to say we'll be fine. Change can be good. You'll see. Anyway, can you believe we're going to be in high school?"

I could, actually, since it was long overdue, but I wasn't going to let Tara distract me. "Yeah, it's a treat. So how about I come over for a few minutes? Ten minutes, tops. My mom'll wait in the car."

"I'm *tired*, Dee. I'll see you Monday."

"Wait—Monday? What about tomorrow?"

"There's church and a zillion things to do to get ready for school. Mom's going to take me shopping, and you hate that."

"I'll suck it up," I said. "We basically live in Lane Bryant, so at least you won't drag me around the entire mall. We can ditch your mom and grab lunch at the food court."

"That does sound tempting. But—"

"And then later we can rewatch *White Chicks*."

"I don't know . . ."

What was the big deal? Didn't she want to see me? "Come on. It's our last day of freedom."

"Can't. I have way too much to do."

The teenage girl's dad turned into a zombie and went after her. I looked away when they took him down. Tara hated that part. "I haven't seen you in forever."

Tara snorted, "Yeah, like I was the one who ditched her best friend to spend the summer in Puerto Rico."

"With *family*. It was hardly a vacation." I winced as a zombie took a chunk out of some guy. Blood gushed. "Let me make it up to you. On Monday, let's meet after our last class and come back here. You can stay for dinner and say hi to Mom and Liv. I'll have her make empanadas."

Tara laughed. "Sounds like a plan."

After we hung up, I couldn't focus on the zombies ravaging England. Why didn't Tara want me to come over? If she was hiding something, she'd only be able to hide it for so long. Did she get a new haircut, chop it all off? That's something Tara would do, make a production out of something boring.

A haircut made sense.

✦ ✦ ✦

No matter what Tara's hair looked like, I'd tell her she looked awesome. My hair was annoyingly flat this morning, so I'd pulled it into a ponytail, styling my side bangs just so. My pink streaks had faded over the summer, so I'd refreshed with a bright blue this time. Between that and my crimson tart lip stain, I was feeling as fierce as a final girl in a horror film. One that doesn't need rescuing, thank you very much.

Coville High was a quick drive away from my house, but on a bus that made a bunch of stops, it became more like twenty minutes. Tara's stop was fifth after mine, so I had a good ten minutes before I saw her.

In the meantime, I tried to imagine how life would be different in high school. Going from middle school where there were a few hundred kids to high school where there were a few *thousand* was freaking me out. I was a little nervous about the schedule and the classes, the upperclassmen and the teachers— Hell, I was nervous about getting lost inside the insanely huge building. School was kids' stuff before, but this was the real deal. We were entering the land of driving and fake IDs.

It was the big leagues, but as long as I had Tara with me, I was fine. I turned toward the window and saw a spider on the other side of the pane, quivering against the wind as it tried to stay on the glass. I hoped it made it.

The bus squealed into Tara's stop, and I peeked out the window, looking for her trademark pink hoodie. Rain or shine, she loved that thing. She owned, like, five of them.

My stomach dropped.

If I'd been one of those typical fat kids you see on TV, I'd have been drinking a ginormous milkshake and would have spewed it all over the back of Benny Jameson's perfectly gelled head. All I could do was sit there with my heart pounding as Tara sashayed onto the bus.

Surprise! Tara, in a skirt that showed her knees (wait, she had knees?) and a cami that rode up to show a sliver of her flattish stomach. I'd never seen so much skin on the girl. She was all about jeans, be they school jeans or fancy jeans she wore to church. Someone let out a low whistle behind her.

If I weren't frozen, I'd have made a face. *Skinny bitch.*

The phrase whispered in my head, and I pushed it back. Tara wasn't one of *them*. She couldn't be. She was many things—smart, a kick-ass gamer, and a *Lord of the Rings* devotee. Skinny was not one of them.

"Hi," said her voice from above me.

Oh. Right.

I jerked my eyes away from Tara's stomach.

I opened my mouth to speak, but—I kid you not—I actually choked on my saliva. I sat there hacking like an eighty-year-old smoker while I tried to say something, anything. All I could do at that point was try to breathe.

"Damn, Tara." Benny Jameson's head was propped on the bus seat in front of us. "Summer was real good to you."

Tara smiled, all teeth and dimples. She slid onto the green vinyl seat next to me and pounded on my back until I managed to rasp that I was fine.

Her smile wavered a little at the corners. "Ta-da," she said weakly.

I straightened in my seat now that I was able to breathe better. This was where I was supposed to call her Tasty, because that's who we were: Tasty Delight, the awesome duo who loved all things sweet, even ice cream that wasn't quite ice cream. We'd gone to eat at Tasti D's so often that Tara had dubbed us with the name. Ten-year-old me had thought it was the coolest name of all time.

I was still Delight, but I wasn't so sure Tara was Tasty anymore.

Benny said, "What period do you have lunch? We can

sit together and catch up." The boys seemed to think she was tasty, if you counted Benny as one of them, which was questionable.

He used to tease Tara, and now he was flirting with her? I glared at him, at his freckled face and curly red hair. With his massive grin, he looked like Ronald McDonald. "Shut it, Ronald. We're busy."

Benny turned back around, muttering.

To Tara, I said, "So you're . . ." I trailed off, at a loss for words.

"Yeah, I know," Tara said.

"Why didn't you . . ."

"Tell you? I don't know." Tara took a deep breath, her chest moving up. Her boobs were still pretty big. If I lost a crapload of weight, I'd probably wind up as flat chested as a boy.

The bus stopped for another pickup, and more people filed in. Rashad Hart, the cutest boy in our class, did a double take when he saw Tara. Jeannie Mills, his girlfriend, swatted his head and glared at us.

"Sitting next to you is roomier," I whispered in Tara's ear. We used to basically be on top of each other, with me at the window and her spilling into the aisle. I kinda liked leaning on the old, fleshy Tara. This Tara, not so much.

She scooted closer, locking me in. I just might have had to go through the window to get some room. She leaned over and hugged me.

"I missed you," Tara said, pulling away quickly. Something passed over her eyes before they brightened up again.

"I feel like I saw you just yesterday. I can't believe it's been a whole summer."

"I sure can. We haven't seen each other in two months, one week, and three days."

Tara laughed. Geez, even her laugh was lighter. "Not that you're counting."

I stared at her face. The features were the same: same snub nose, same wide mouth. Only they were placed on a narrower, slightly longer face. It was her and it wasn't her.

"Did you get . . ." I lowered my voice as I said the forbidden L word, "lipo"?

"God, no. I just made changes. Diet, exercise, you know the drill."

I resisted the urge to roll my eyes. I did know the drill. And it was something I was never going to take part in ever again.

"So . . . what do you think?" Tara asked, gesturing at her body. "Of . . ."

I shrugged. "I just don't see the point."

"It's high school. I don't know. Maybe I felt like making a change."

I digested her words, cursing her mom internally. She had to be behind this, what with her "let's go on XYZ diet" pushes. "Really?"

Tara nodded. Her expression was tense, as if she were a little scared. Of what? Of me?

"And how do you feel now?" I asked.

"I feel great, I guess. How do you think I look? Really?"

"You look . . . good," I said, though I always thought she did.

Her smile began creeping up across her face again. "Really?"

Unable to repeat myself, I nodded jerkily.

"Thanks, Dee. People keep telling me I look nice, and I feel it, but it means more coming from you."

I got it, since that's how I felt with her, that I could trust her more than anyone. And even though I trusted her, I grabbed her hand. "You look nice either way. I'm on board if you feel good about yourself, I guess. I know all about the pressure to look a certain way, which is ridiculous, but if you're doing it for yourself and no one else, I'm here for you."

Tara's face closed down. "Of course. Who else would I do it for?" She tugged her hand away, laughing. "Hey, my hand is falling asleep."

I looked out the window. The spider was no longer there.

✦ ✦ ✦

I didn't see Tara again until lunch.

Coville High was massive, and the cafeteria was like the rest of the school—larger than junior high, but pretty much the same. Kind of a bummer. The food line snaked all over the place so that I could barely tell where it began and ended.

I felt my breath speed up as I navigated the crush, sucking in my stomach each time I squeezed past someone.

I was supposed to meet Tara around here somewhere, but I wasn't sure where the hell I was going. An upperclassman eventually let me cut through the line to get to the seating area with an eye roll. Normally, the sight of cafeteria pizza and fries grossed me out, but my growling stomach didn't seem to give a crap.

Free from the food line, I hustled with my tray toward the back end of the cafeteria where all the tables were. It was packed there too, but it actually looked almost open compared to the front end. I looked and looked but couldn't make out Tara in the crowd. I was planted in the middle of the room, people shoving past me left and right, and if I wasted any more time, I probably wouldn't even get a seat.

And there Tara was, three tables away, standing and waving her skinny arms to get my attention. Relief swept through me. I would have a seat, and I wouldn't be having lunch alone. All was right with the world.

Five steps later, I realized the world was a dirty backstabber. *Surprise!* Tara was sitting with people I didn't know and who I probably didn't want to know. Thin, preppy, perky. They could have been part of a college brochure, them and Tara, the pretty Dominican the advertisers stuck in for diversity.

I faltered a minute, but I wanted to talk to Tara. It's not like I wanted to hang with them. And if Tara was there, I was there.

She'd snagged an aisle seat and had saved the one across from her for me, bless her. There were four other people at that table, two guys and two girls. They all looked up as I approached. They all practically had question marks hovering over their heads.

"Hey," I said grimly. I did the quick smile and sat.

"This seat's saved," the girl next to me said. Sickly sweet smile. "Sorry."

"For me, actually," I said. *Surprise!* "Thanks ever so much."

"Everyone." Tara gestured at me in a flourish. She used to be a nail nibbler, but her nails were now polished red ovals. "This is Dee." She changed direction and swept her hand to encompass the group. "Dee, everyone. This is Candy, Mandy, Micky, Ricky."

Tara didn't recite those exact names per se, but I forgot as soon as she said them, so those names were as good as any.

At the end of the table, Micky and Ricky said hi and went back to talking about their awesome camping trip.

Candy asked Tara, "This is your . . . friend?"

"Best friend," Tara said. "We came from Jefferson."

"Cool," said the other girl. She had brown curly hair with golden-tipped ends and some seriously sharp-looking collarbones. I resisted the urge to rub my own.

Since she spoke first, I decided to talk to her. "Which school did you come from, Mandy?"

"It's Brandy," she said. What do you know? I wasn't too far off. "Lincoln. We all did. You're in my advanced bio section, right?"

I squinted at her. "You're in advanced bio?" I wouldn't have pegged her for an egghead.

Brandy nodded. "I hear it's a good class."

"Our teacher's supposed to be intense, though," I said.

"Seriously, right? I hope I make it out alive."

"I'm glad I didn't let you talk me into testing for advanced bio, Dee," Tara said. "I'd be freaking out. Earth science is more my speed."

"You could have handled it," I said, taking a bite of my pizza.

"How is it?" Tara asked, nodding at my food.

"Not bad for plasti-pizza. Want a bite?"

She shook her head, "I would, but I bought a turkey sub, thanks."

"Okay, but you do acknowledge that my pizza trumps your sandwich in the food hierarchy, right?"

Looking from her lunch to mine and back, Tara said, "I hate it when you're right."

"Just so we're clear." I took another bite.

Candy was watching me eat. All she had was a yogurt and an apple. "Um, want some pizza?" I asked.

Candy's eyes got big. "No way! If I ate like that, I'd get fat."

Tara paused midchew, and Brandy looked down at her tray as if she found something fascinating about it.

I sighed inwardly. "Fat like me? There's nothing wrong with being fat, you know."

"I didn't mean you," Candy said, her face reddening.

"So what did you mean?" Tara asked, giving her the stink eye.

Candy backtracked quicker than you could say fat-free. "I just can't gain weight is all." She fanned herself. "Anybody want some water? I'm getting some water." With that, she stood up and scurried off.

"Going, going, gone. Is she coming back?" I asked, watching her nearly sprint to the water fountain. I drank some of my own water, suddenly feeling thirsty myself.

"The odds are not good," Brandy said.

Tara swept her hand over Candy's lone yogurt and half-eaten apple. "She wouldn't leave such a spread behind."

Brandy laughed. "Don't take it personally. She's a good friend, once you get past her foot-in-mouth problem."

I shot Tara a look. Were we adopting Candy? Because if she and Brandy were applying for membership to our duo, I'd have to veto that fast. Tara put a hand over her mouth to stifle a laugh.

Brandy's phone chirped, and she looked down, sighing. "I swear, if my dad texts me one more time to see how my first day is going, I'll scream. He's so annoying." She rolled her eyes. "Parents, right?"

Tara's smile faded. "Yeah," she murmured, pushing her sandwich away. Her dad had vamoosed a few years ago. He just up and left to follow his dream of windsurfing in California or something. He called Tara once in a blue moon and visited even less often than that. She didn't like to talk about him, but I bet she'd kill to have her dad bugging her on a daily basis.

"Anyway," Brandy said, twisting her curls up into a bun and releasing it. "You guys should come by Il Trapezio after school. Have you been?"

I cleared my throat. "Uh, yeah. We've gone a couple times.

They have good gelato." To Tara, I said, "That's where you puked from eating a crapload of it, remember?"

Tara nodded, lips curving in a smile. "The good old days." If she were in a better mood, I'd have pointed out that it wouldn't be much fun going to a place where she probably couldn't even eat.

Brandy leaned in and lowered her voice. "This really cute guy told me that's where everyone goes to hang out after classes."

Everyone. The idea of meeting everyone. Brandy was nice and all, but I wasn't sure I had the energy to deal with everyone. Put me in a room with too many people and they tire me out, with all that forced smiling and chatting. Besides, this was catch-up day with Tara.

I put on an "aw, shucks" expression. "I'd be up for it another time, just not today. We're kinda busy."

"Can't you postpone your plans for tomorrow?" Brandy asked. "It being the first day of classes and all, it's the perfect time to get to know people."

Getting to know people was supposed to be a good thing? That may be their cute little philosophy, but it wasn't mine and Tara's. I opened my mouth to pass, but Tara beat me to it. Surprise! "Maybe we can. What do you say, Dee?"

My chin dropped. If I had glasses, I'd be looking over them at her. "I . . . don't know."

Brandy rubbed her hands together like a mad scientist. "I almost have Dee. Tara, what's the final word? Don't let me down."

I kept my eyes on Tara and noticed hers filling with regret. Something inside me eased, and I knew then she'd turn Brandy down.

"Can we hang tomorrow?" Tara asked.

I gave Brandy a consoling smile.

"Is that okay?"

My blood pressure rose as it slowly sank in that Tara—surprise—was talking to me. That she meant she and *I* could hang out tomorrow.

Tara's voice sounded far away as she said, "It'll be just us, promise."

"Just us," I repeated. I rubbed my left temple to soothe the pressure. Wasn't it always just us? When did "just us" no longer become implied?

✦ ✦ ✦

I slammed the back door shut and dropped my backpack, stretching my arms above my head. It was good to be home. Even if the TV was on full blast. Liv was watching *Teen Mom 2*. Again. This was one of her down days, then.

I sighed as I walked through the hallway that led into the living room. Liv was sprawled on the sofa, in the same leopard-print pajamas she'd worn to bed. So much for the job interview at Target, if there actually was an interview.

"Hey," she said, her mascara-smudged eyes still on the show.

"Can you keep it down so I don't get a headache?" I said.

"Hard day at the office, dear?" Liv yawned so widely I could almost hear her jaw crack.

"Not as hard as yours, apparently."

"I'll have you know that this couch isn't nearly as comfortable as it looks." She pointed her feet, then flexed them. "I think I have a charley horse. Massage me?"

"Don't make me hide the remote again."

Liv said something as I trudged up the stairs, but it was lost in the sounds of TV baby shrieks.

My head was starting to pound, so I popped some aspirin. Googled "how to deal with friends who change." Closed my Mac when the search came up with things like "Tulenda Forever?" and "How to Deal with Losing a Friend."

Gee, thanks, computer.

I logged onto Facebook and scrolled through my friends list. Nothing like watching people posting the things they did over the summer to numb the brain. I skipped the annoying selfies and found myself on Tara's profile. Her profile picture hadn't changed at least. It was the same, a picture of Robin beating the crap out of Batman. I smiled a little. She wasn't posing in a bikini just yet, so she hadn't gone to the other side completely. There was some comfort in that.

Tara stayed on my mind the rest of the afternoon. She stayed there when I changed into my sweats and danced to another song. She stayed there when I collapsed on my bed and passed out from exhaustion, dreaming of DC Comics sidekicks with powerful right hooks.

✦ ✦ ✦

Someone pounding on the door jerked me out of my nap.

"Dee!" Mom yelled. "If you don't come down, I'm feeding your dinner to Princesa!"

Right, like I'm sure Mr. Petrocelli would appreciate his dog eating anything other than pasta. I was way too groggy to function, even if it was just chewing food.

"I'm not hungry," I called out.

"I made tostones."

My stomach growled. The bites of pizza I'd had for lunch happened a year ago. "I had a snack."

Mom wasn't buying it. "If I have to cook, you have to eat. Get your butt downstairs before your food gets cold. Now." Her voice got lower as she walked away, chanclas smack-smacking her heels.

I exhaled loudly and closed my laptop. I rubbed my eyes and tried to focus them.

"Counting down now!" Mom yelled from downstairs. "Fifteen, fourteen, thirteen . . ."

Mom and her countdowns. She was notorious for them, and you never wanted to let her get to zero. She got down to zero once when I was a kid, when she tried to get me to pick up my Barbie dolls. Ken sure does miss them.

"Nine, eight, seven . . ."

I hurried down.

Mom was getting to one when I threw myself into the seat at the table. She was at the head, and I was at her left side, with Liv across from me on her right. Even Liv knew not to mess with Mom and her countdowns.

Mom smiled. "Kiss."

I leaned over and pecked her cheek. Her curly hair tickled my nose. "Thanks for the spread." Mom was an executive assistant at a law firm in the city and had a two-hour commute each way. She had all the local takeout places on speed dial, so her cooking was an event.

Mom passed me the chicken cutlet platter. "It's not every day you start high school."

"Maybe you'll actually finish and we'll get another feast," Liv said around a mouthful of arroz con gandules.

Mom's smile never wavered. "Or we'll have one when you test for the GED you've been studying for, Olivia."

If by studying, she meant hanging out all night and sleeping all day, then she'd pass that test, no sweat. Liv stuffed more food in her mouth and murmured noncommittally. I'll never know how someone so thin could eat so much. She eats more than I do, if you can believe it, which no one outside the family does.

"Tell me how it went," Mom said, turning back to me. "I'm on pins and needles."

"It was pretty unbelievable."

Mom's smile grew. "That's great, honey. In what way?"

"The, uh, lockers are bigger."

At Mom's quizzical expression, I added, "The boys are too." I lifted my hand above my head. "This big." I stuffed a piece of fried plantain in my mouth and offered her one as a distraction. "So how was your day?"

Mom took it. "Mr. Collier won that discrimination suit, so

he's in a good mood." Mom assisted a senior partner at the firm, and she never knew which way his mood would swing from one day to the next. With a recent win, though, his good mood should last the week. Mom bit into a tostón and chewed thoughtfully. "Anything else? Oh, like Tara, how's she doing?"

I so didn't want to talk about Tara, but I had to give her something. She'd never let up otherwise. I swallowed a spoonful of rice and gandules. "I don't think she ate much."

They were going to hear about it soon enough, so I added, "She lost weight."

"Oh yeah?" Mom said.

"Like, a lot. She's pretty thin now."

Mom's hand fluttered, touching the name necklace that spelled out Raquel in fancy script. "Well, then."

"Huh," Liv said. "Is Tara going to become a cheerleader or something?"

I glared at her.

"Oooh, maybe she'll date the quarterback of the football team," Liv continued with a smirk. "Then she'll become homecoming queen and ride the float, like in the movies."

I gritted my teeth. "Tara's not like that."

"Every girl's like that, given half a chance," Liv said. "I was."

"You didn't do any of those things," I pointed out. "Sleeping with the football team doesn't count as going with the quarterback."

Mom cleared her throat in that way she does when she's planning on changing the subject.

Liv shrugged and looked at her with a "What are we going to do with her?" expression.

"Anyway, that's not Tara." I wiped my mouth and started to get up from my chair.

Mom held out a hand to stop me from moving. "Oh no, you don't. We're not finished. How's school itself? Are you excited about the classes?"

I settled back in with a groan. "Mom."

Mom smiled, ever relentless. "Did you make new friends?"

Liv snorted.

I made a face. "It's the first day. There wasn't time to exchange friendship bracelets."

Mom frowned, so I threw her a bone. "I talked to a few people, not that we're going to be BFFs or anything."

"It's a start," Mom said.

"A start to a normal social life," Liv said.

This time it was Mom who gave her a look.

"What?" Liv asked.

"I'm pretty full," I said. "Mind if I go upstairs?"

Mom's eyebrows went up. "That's all I get?"

"Uh, and thanks for dinner?"

"You're welcome. But what I meant was, if that's all you're going to tell me about today." She pointed her fork at me. "Never mind, I'll get it out of you later. You go. Olivia will wash the dishes tonight."

Liv sagged in her chair and dropped her head back. "Seriously? I did them last night."

"No, I did," Mom said. "And Deirdre did them the night before."

"It felt like last night," Liv muttered as I got up.

"Have fun," I said, and escaped to my room.

✦ ✦ ✦

The next morning on the bus, Tara plopped down beside me and pinned me with a look. She looked pretty in a lacy yellow top that almost softened her stare. "Why didn't you come out with us last night?"

I started counting the rips in the fabric of the seat in front of me. "I'm surprised you noticed."

"Of course I did! What happened to you?"

"I wasn't feeling too well." The rips were almost constellation-like. I jabbed a fingernail at one of them.

"Liar." Tara flicked my hand, and I snatched it away from the now-larger hole I'd made. "Why won't you look at me?"

I dragged my eyes away from the seat back and made myself look somewhere near the vicinity of her ear. "Do you even eat gelato anymore?"

"I knew it." She shook her head, her dark hair falling over her shoulders, and pointed at me. "I *knew* it! You don't like that I look different."

I threw my hands up. "I don't know, I don't know. Why aren't you telling me why you lost weight?"

"What does that have to do with anything?" Tara's forehead wrinkled like she was confused, but come on.

"It has to do with everything!" I shifted my body toward her so I could really look at her. "You were so not into that diet BS. You mean, you just suddenly woke up and decided to lose weight? It's too random."

Now it was her turn to look away. "I told you why. I needed a change."

"That's such a cop-out."

She pressed her lips together and stayed quiet for the rest of the ride.

When we got off the bus, she walked briskly, as if she would try to shake me off. I trailed her all the way to her locker. Brandy passed us by, and Tara returned her wave with one of her own.

I leaned against the pea-green locker next to Tara's. "Is that what this is all about? New look, new friends?"

Tara took her time answering, opening her locker door and sticking her head inside before her muffled voice emerged. "Don't you think meeting people will be good for us?"

"We were doing fine," I said, addressing her locker door. "Who needs new people?"

"I do." A loud *thunk* came from inside. "We're in high school. I want to make a fresh start. I need to."

"Without me," I said. "A fresh start without me."

She blew out a breath as if talking to me wore her out. "I didn't say that."

"You didn't have to."

Tara straightened and slammed her locker door shut. "Not

everything is about you. Can't you think about someone other than yourself for once?"

I couldn't even respond to her accusation. How did she manage to twist this around? I was the victim here. I was the one being abandoned, not her.

"Can't you let me enjoy this?" Tara swept a hand over herself. "I'm feeling good and meeting new people for the first time ever. I worked hard to look this way, and you didn't even congratulate me."

"I did congratulate you," I said. *Didn't I?*

Tara gave me a get-real snort.

Fine, maybe not, but it was hard to congratulate someone who needed approval from other people to feel good. If that's what she wanted, fine. "Is that all you want? My congratulations?"

Her lips compressed.

"Congratulations, Tara. You're on your way to getting everything you want. New body, new friends, the whole deal."

Tara closed her eyes. She'd picked that up from some stupid magazine once, the idea of counting down to make herself calm.

"You've got to be kidding me." I kicked the bottom of the locker, the resulting clanging sound not nearly satisfying enough.

What felt like an hour later, Tara opened her eyes. Judging by her face, the countdown hadn't worked. "You forgot something."

"What?" I snapped.

Tara's mouth twisted. "To congratulate me about my dad. He's coming to visit."

The wind was knocked right out of me. Of all the things she could have said, that was not what I was expecting. "Wait, what?"

Tara's voice was as hard as her expression. "He's coming back. In a week."

The bell rang and she took off, leaving me there with my mouth trying to work. Watching her leave, I didn't recognize her. Tara was just another girl. I'd never have guessed she had been anything other than what she was now. Not a former fat girl. Just a girl, period.

And it scared me.

✦ ✦ ✦

The bus ride back home sucked as much as I thought it would. I held my breath when Tara boarded, messing with the zippers on my backpack so it seemed like I was looking for something. My fingers froze when Tara said, "Hey." By the time I looked up, she'd already proceeded down the aisle. Passed right on by. I caught sight of Brandy's confused expression as she followed Tara to the back.

I propped my backpack in Tara's spot.

The bus got more crowded as it made its stops.

"Can I sit down?" a tentative voice asked from the aisle.

I didn't bother looking up. "No." The girl didn't move away, hovering over me like she wasn't sure what to do next. I could have ignored her if she wasn't such a heavy breather. She exhaled through her mouth, sounding like a horse after a big race.

I lifted my head, and she wilted under my stare. "Seat's taken."

She sidled away.

✦ ✦ ✦

Liv clicked the radio buttons until she hit the right song. The rhythmic bass beats of reggaetón pounded through the car. The rapper's rough tones saturated the conversational void. I snuck a glance at Liv, her upper body moving to the music. I'd begged a ride from Liv after dinner and now I was trying not to regret it.

She glanced over at me, her chandelier earrings jingling. "Since you're interrupting my Korean face mask time, the least you can do is tell me what you did."

I scraped at my plum nail polish, making the chip on my thumbnail spread. Scrape, scrape.

"Hey," she said. "I'm the queen of screwups. How big a deal could it be?"

Bigger than she knew. "Let's just say I messed up and leave it at that."

Liv slowed for a stop sign.

"Does it have to do with Tara's extreme makeover?"

"Maybe," I said.

"Not clear, like, at all." Liv drummed her fingers on the steering wheel. "If you don't fess up, how can I help you?"

My head jerked up. "Help me? That'd be a first."

Liv's fingers paused midmotion. They resumed, and she said, "It's not a lost cause. With Tara."

"It might be."

"Nah. Say you're sorry and work your magic."

Liv thinks I've got magic to work. *What do you know?* "It's not that simple. I say sorry and then what? Everything's different."

She stayed quiet for a while, which was a first for her. "She's your best friend. It's a lot simpler than you think."

A few minutes later, we pulled up to Tara's white colonial. I tossed Liv a thanks and got out. All the way up the brick walkway, I wondered what the heck I was going to say. I was almost at her stoop when I realized Tara was sitting right on it. She was just a silhouette in the dim porch light, but I knew it was her. I paused in front of her, my hands jammed in my pockets.

She stared up at me, silent.

I said, "Congratulations, I guess?"

Tara's face crumpled, and I quickly dropped down beside her. I put my arm around her, and we just leaned into each other as she cried.

After some time had passed, I cleared my throat. "I think I did figure it out. You wanted to lose weight to look good for your dad?"

"He calls me his little princess, you know." Tara hiccuped. "I might have focused a bit much on the 'little' part of that."

"But you know that's ridiculous, right? Now, if you wanted

to be a princess, that I'd get. I know you were all about the castle in *Ever After*."

"The prince wasn't so bad either." She laughed weakly. "I kind of realized the reason for the makeover was messed up when I almost said it out loud. I don't know how to explain it. Mom was dieting, and it just made sense to do it too." Tara nudged me with her shoulder before I realized I'd straightened up in outrage. "And before you jump to conclusions, she didn't put me up to it."

I grunted, not fully believing her.

"Seriously. She even tried to feed me my favorite chocolate cake after dinner earlier. I haven't had sweets since forever."

"You should probably take her up on it. She might think you're wasting away."

"Maybe." Tara sighed. "I might have had a couple of slices. And they were amazing."

My mouth turned up. *There she was—my best friend, Tasty.* "I bet." I leaned forward and rested my chin in my hands, looking at her sideways. "So, your dad. He'll be here soon. That's big. Really big."

Tara nodded.

I resisted the urge to look away, focusing on her face and nothing else. "I'm sorry I made it about me."

Her hand crept over to mine, and I squeezed it.

We fell back into silence.

And then, "Dee, you'll make friends with Brandy and the others, right?"

"Let's not get too ahead of ourselves. How about I promise to be nice to them?"

Tara squeezed my hand back. "That's a start, at least."

And we didn't say anything more.

We didn't have to.

Surprise.

Liv was actually right. I guess it was that simple.

LETTING GO

Renée Watson

The ocean is big enough for my body.

Whenever I am in the Pacific my body feels fragile. And it never feels fragile, delicate. But in the ocean, it is easily knocked over by waves, pushed by the wind. This is why I love swimming, love being in water. I do not fit in most places, not comfortably, but in the ocean there is room and room.

It is only 60 degrees today, not exactly the sunny summer beach day I wanted. It was actually warmer in Portland when we left, but it's always cooler at the coast. The beach in June is unpredictable, but at least it's not raining and at least I'm with my cousins, Dionne, Bree, and Nicole.

We are opposite of everyone on this beach.

We are our mothers' daughters. Everything about us is big and brown.

Brown skin, brown eyes.

Big personalities, big bodies.

The four of us are celebrating our sixteenth birthdays at Seaside Beach.

We were all born in the same year so we celebrate together. This is tradition. Last year we celebrated Bree's birthday in April. She chose cosmic bowling even though she's not that good at it. She was much better at the arcade games, so we spent most of the night in a Pac-Man competition. The year before that, it was Dionne's choice and her birthday is in February so it was rainy and cold but we had a good time at a spa getting manicures and pedicures. For dinner we ate at the kind of restaurant where you have to dress up to get in and the portions are so small you leave just as hungry as you came. But that's what Dionne wanted. Next September, it will be Nicole's turn. She'll take forever to decide what we're going to do, like she always does, and then she'll ask her dad to grill and we'll have a party in her backyard, like we always do.

But this year it's my turn. Today is my actual birthday, and no one is surprised that I want a weekend at the beach. Even though it's my birthday, the day belongs to all of us. Today we walk through Seaside, making our way to the beach, like no one else is here, even though the boardwalk is full of families, of lovers, of loners, of locals. Today, we are in our swimsuits and sheer cover-ups, our big brown bodies not hidden, our polished toes on showcase in our flip-flops.

Nicole says, "Maybe we should have worn clothes over our swimsuits while we walk to the water. People are looking at us."

My swimsuit is the color of a freshly cut pineapple, Dionne's is fuchsia, and Bree's and Nicole's are a scramble of blues like the ocean we are walking to. We take up space, the four of us, as we walk the promenade. And Nicole is right, people notice us. It is a subtle noticing. It is the curious gaze, the looks of surprise. Sometimes there's a condescending question masked in friendliness—*"you need anything?" "can I help you?"*—when we are simply walking and minding our own business and not looking lost or suspicious at all. And sometimes there is the overly enthusiastic smile, an unspoken *you go girl* from strangers who think we are brave for walking out of the house without our bodies fully covered.

"Let them look," I say. "Wave and blow them a kiss if they stare too long."

We all laugh at that, but I know Nicole would never, ever do it. Truth is, neither would I. Not if it was just me. If I was here alone with everyone watching and whispering, I'd shrink a little bit, maybe walk faster, not want to be seen. But here with my family, it makes me rise, makes me laugh louder. Especially when Bree starts doing her impressions, asking, "Okay, so who walks like this?" and prances ahead of us switching her hips extra hard.

I immediately know she's teasing Dionne, and Dionne knows it too, so she yells, "That is not how I walk."

And we all just laugh because it is exactly how she walks.

We are laughing so loud, too loud maybe, because the two white women sitting in rocking chairs outside the candy store that sells saltwater taffy and pinwheel lollipops look at us with annoyance in their eyes.

"Let's get ice cream," Bree says.

And I always want ice cream but not right now. Right now, I just want to get to the water.

I am outnumbered so we go into the shop, buy ice cream cones, and eat them while walking the rest of our way. We are almost to the entrance of the beach when Dionne sees a store she wants to go into. "I won't take long. I promise," she says.

"Can we please just get to the beach?" I ask. That's all I want to do today.

Nicole agrees. "Yeah, Dionne, we can't go in there anyway. The sign says, No Food Allowed." When she says this, she licks her ice cream and the big strawberry scoop falls right off onto the cement.

We laugh even harder, even louder than the last time.

"Good," Dionne says, "now you can come inside with me." She is already biting her cone. She goes in while me and Bree speed eat.

I look at Nicole, who is lamenting over her fallen ice cream. "I would share with you but you're a germaphobe so I'm sure you don't want any of this," I tell her. For extra dramatics, I lick the ice cream again.

"I'll just buy another one on the way back," Nicole says.

We go into the store, and when Dionne sees us, she calls out, "I'm just scoping things out to see if I want to come back later to buy something."

My favorite part of coming to Seaside is the ocean. Dionne's is the shopping. Every time we come to the coast, we leave with extra bags and not enough room in the trunk for everyone's stuff. Our mommas are somewhere strolling the promenade too. Whenever we come to the beach, my mom and aunts never really come to the beach, never dip their toes in the water or trudge through the sand. They spend their days shopping, eating at their favorite seafood restaurants, and lounging in the rental house watching home makeover shows.

"There's nothing in this store but antiques," Bree says. "What are you going to do with an old clock?"

Dionne puts on her sophisticated voice. "I actually like mixing the old with the new, thank you very much." Dionne looks at me, says, "Tell them, Lynn."

I nod. "Have you been in her room lately? She did her own makeover upgrade. It's definitely an eclectic mix of modern and vintage."

Dionne continues with her fake classy voice. "Wanted to try something more *refined*, being sixteen and all." She curtsies and twirls to keep up her act, and as she finishes her twirl, she bumps into the display of necklaces, knocking a few down to the floor. None of our hips are made for these narrow aisles. Nicole bends over, picks them up, but not quick enough. The store owner is eyeing us now, walking our way.

She doesn't say anything, just watches.

"Why are you so clumsy?" Bree asks.

Dionne says, "I'm not clumsy," but then when she turns again she bumps into the shelf on her left and a frame wobbles. Nicole catches it just as the store owner clears her throat.

Now the four of us are laughing again and Bree says, "Dionne, you're going to get us kicked out of this store."

"Out of this town," I say. "Let's go."

We practically run out, and I can feel the store owner and a few of the shoppers watching us as we leave.

"Lynn, wait for me. You all are going too fast," Nicole calls.

Dionne and Bree are ahead of me, speed walking down the street. I don't stop for Nicole but I do slow down.

Nicole is always the one to say we are going too fast. We have been this way our whole lives. Nicole always last. The last one to wear a training bra, the last one to get her period, the last one to kiss a boy. She's even the last one to get dressed and be ready to go. Always.

But she is the first one I call when I need to talk, cry, rage. The first one I call when I am bored, when I have looked something up online and still can't find the answer. She is the only one who knows not just all my secrets but all my truths. I am the most honest when talking with Nicole.

To get to the sand, we have to walk down stone steps. It is crowded, and a large group of people are walking toward us, some of them wet from the waves, some clapping their sandals together, beating out the sand. The four of us weave through the people. Even though I am clearly walking down the right side, a man starts up the steps, directly in front of me. I do not move. Our shoulders knock against each other's; he keeps walking.

No one says excuse me or hello. They walk right past us like we are ghosts.

Here but not here.

But we keep walking because we are celebrating our

birthdays all weekend. And there is pound cake waiting for us back at the beach house, and tonight we will play board games and like always, I will lose at Monopoly but my team will win Taboo, and our mothers will fall asleep before us, and the four of us will stay up all night long, and when we see the sun rising from the depths of the ocean we will be in awe of it because no matter how many times we've seen the sun rise, it always feels like we are watching a miracle. And we will sleep through morning and our mothers won't understand, and we will find something else to tease Dionne about, and we will laugh more, and eat cake for breakfast, and at some point I will whisper to Nicole that she was right about *him*— and I won't have to say his name. She'll know. And she'll hug me and tell me I deserve better, anyway. And I do.

We get to the bottom of the stairs, my feet sinking in the sand, and already sand is on everything I am wearing, carrying. We find a spot to claim, drop our beach bags, and then Dionne looks at Bree and shouts, "Race you!" Dionne and Bree are wild butterflies soaring into the ocean, their laughter ricocheting off the waves.

I think it's a tie, but Bree is screaming, "I won, I won!"

I walk into the water, Nicole behind me, tiptoeing in because the ocean is so cold. The waves flirt with us, first coming close, then drawing back. We splash each other and run and let the ocean wash over us.

We leap and jump and tire ourselves out. We've been in the water so long, it doesn't feel as cold.

Now, we are just standing, catching our breath and

watching the boys on their surfboards trying and trying, the little children with their parents running in and out afraid but then brave enough to go again.

I turn to my cousins, say, "Remember when we used to play church and we baptized each other in the bathtub at Dionne's house?"

We all smile at the memory and retell the story of how our moms were so mad because we kept our clothes on when we dunked each other in the tub and so we had to go home wearing soggy wet clothes.

Nicole says, "Lynn, you should let us baptize you. It's your birthday."

"Uh, we are not little girls anymore," I say. "And this is the Pacific, not a bathtub."

"I know, that's why it will actually mean something. It'll be special," Nicole says. She starts walking deeper into the water. Bree and Dionne follow her. "Come on."

I walk toward them; they are farther into the water, enough so that I can go under but not so deep that we can't stand.

"Are we really doing this?" I ask. "What is the point?"

"It symbolizes your old self dying and a new self being born," Bree says.

"What does that even mean?" I look to Dionne because she is the oldest and is supposed to know everything or at least acts like it.

Dionne says, "It can mean whatever you want it to mean. Before you go under, make a wish or say a prayer or set a goal. It's just for fun."

"All right, all right," I say. "When I come back up I'm going to start shouting like the old churchwomen we used to make fun of."

"You ready?" Nicole asks. She is on my right side and Dionne is at my left.

Bree says, "Close your eyes."

"And don't forget to set a goal or say a prayer," Nicole shouts.

They count down from three, and then I am submerged. I am only underwater for seconds but with my eyes closed, I see *him* and the owner of the antique store, and the women swaying in rocking chairs, and the man who wouldn't move when he saw me coming. I see all the people who were whispering and gawking, see the people who point and stare every day, and I promise myself that I will never shrink again.

I am here.

I am here.

When I come up, the cold air revives me and I see my cousins being the sun on this gray beach day. And we are all big and brown and loud.

And we are here.

I leap out of the water and start pretending to catch the spirit and I wave my hands like something super spiritual just happened and while I am faking it, real tears start to fall and at first they think I am joking but then Nicole realizes I am serious and she starts crying too, and then Bree and then Dionne, and my face is soaked with salt water and tears and I say, "What is *happening?*"

And they all shrug their shoulders and Dionne says, "I don't know, I don't know," while wiping her tears. And then Bree starts laughing and then we are all laughing and crying and laughing and crying so, so loud under June's partly cloudy sky.

ABOUT THE CONTRIBUTORS

NAFIZA AZAD is a self-identified island girl. She has hurricanes in her blood and dreams of a time she can exist solely on mangoes and pineapple. Born in Lautoka, Fiji, she currently resides in British Columbia, Canada, where she reads too many books, watches too many K-dramas, and writes stories about girls taking over the world. Her debut YA fantasy, the Morris Award finalist *The Candle and the Flame*, was released by Scholastic in 2019. Her next book, *The Wild Ones: A Broken Anthem for a Girl Nation*, is out from Simon & Schuster in 2021.

Jamilah's story comes from Nafiza's own experiences trying to fit both physically and mentally in spaces that categorically refuse to include her. She hopes that Jamilah's story will let you, if you need it, know that you're your own kind of beautiful.

You can find Nafiza on Twitter at @Nafizaa.

CHRIS BARON is the author of the middle-grade novels in verse *All of Me* and *The Magical Imperfect*. He is a professor of English at San Diego City College and the director of the Writing Center. Chris has published numerous poems and articles in magazines and journals around the country, performed on radio programs, and participated in many readings, lectures, and panels. He grew up in New York City, but he completed his MFA in poetry at SDSU. Chris's first book of poetry, *Under the Broom Tree*, was released in 2012 by San Diego City Works Press as part of *Lantern Tree: Four Books of Poems*, which won the San Diego Book Award for best poetry anthology.

About "Food Is Love," Chris says, "This is a story from the heart, mixing together many long hours working in restaurants with my family life growing up. While we often expect issues like body image to come from outside forces and the culture around us (and it does), it is often those who love us most who have the greatest impact on how we feel. Well-meaning loved ones often applied pressure on me to change even when acceptance and empathy were really what I needed. Though there is still a long way to go, I am happy to see that more and more, those of us with large bodies are finding more acceptance in stories—we need more stories where the main characters have bodies of all kinds, including big bodies!"

Find more at chris-baron.com and on Twitter at @baronchrisbaron and Instagram at @christhebearbaron.

SHEENA BOEKWEG grew up reading books with tree branches peeking over her shoulder. Her novels *Glitch Kingdom* and *A Sisterhood of Secret Ambitions*, both from Feiwel and Friends/Macmillan, feature fat positive girls with ambitions, love stories, and sometimes battle axes. Sheena believes that beauty is intrinsic and worth is unquestionable, and thinks you can't solve all problems with food, but it will always help. She is a mentor, a teacher, and a leader. Sheena is well loved by a tall man with a great beard, her three kids, and the world's most spoiled puppy. Visit her online at boekwegbooks.com, or follow her on Twitter and Instagram at @SheenaBoekweg.

LINDA CAMACHO is a literary agent at Gallt & Zacker Literary Agency in New York City. She has her MFA in writing for children and young adults from the Vermont College of Fine Arts, where she did her thesis on fat characters. If you don't count the repurposed joke printed in *Highlights* when she was a kid in the early nineties, her short story in *Every Body Shines* is her first publication. "Unpleasant Surprises" was born of a need to see more fat characters in stories that are not all "Oh, woe is me," and especially, more fat characters of color. You can find Linda on Twitter at @LindaRandom.

Hippy Potter, a.k.a. **THADDEUS COATES**, was originally born in D.C. and is currently living in the heart of New York City. He is a quirky Black queer illustrator whose mission is redefining social stereotypes through vibrant, provocative images. That intention reverberates throughout his portfolio of beautiful black faces and body-positive art. He creates boundless imagery that promotes self-love, community acceptance, and of course #Black-Excellence. Find him online at @hippypotter (Instagram) and @itshippypotter (Twitter).

JIM DEVOS

Hi! I'm **KELLY DEVOS**! As a kid, I was one of the best kickball players in the third grade, but because I was fat, I was almost always picked last to play. After a while, I stopped trying to join the team. I sometimes wonder what might have happened if I had had the confidence to keep playing, and that's what inspired "Outside Pitch." I created Hayley Jean, a fast-pitching fat athlete, and put her in a story where my love of small towns, pie, and classic movies could intersect.

My work has been featured in the *New York Times* as well as on *Vulture*, *Salon*, *Bustle*, and *SheKnows*. My debut novel, *Fat Girl on a Plane*, was named one of the "50 Best Summer Reads of All Time" by *Reader's Digest* magazine. My next book, *Eat Your Heart Out*, features a squad of fat, butt-kicking zombie fighters.

Find me online at kellydevos.us and on Twitter at @Kde VosAuthor and Instagram at @kellydevos.

ALEX GINO is the author of middle-grade novels *Rick*; *You Don't Know Everything, Jilly P!*; and the Stonewall Award–winning *George*. They believe in the value and importance of do-it-yourself fashion, especially for fat, nonbinary, and other kids who can't find clothing to fit their body and style in most stores. They also now have a dream to own a rainbow crinoline like Sam's, and they're working on a full-length novel featuring Sam, TJ, and the early twentieth-century lesbian photographer Alice Austen. Find Alex online at alexgino.com and @lxgino.

AUBREY GORDON writes under the pseudonym Your Fat Friend, illuminating the experiences of fat people and urging greater compassion for people of all sizes. Her work has reached millions of readers and has been translated into nineteen languages. A columnist for *SELF* magazine and the author of *What We Don't Talk About When We Talk About Fat*, she lives in the Northwest, where she works as a writer and an organizer. Connect with her at yourfatfriend.com and at @YrFatFriend on Instagram, Twitter, and Facebook.

MONIQUE GRAY SMITH is an award-winning and best-selling author of books for children and youth, as well as adults. Her children's books include *My Heart Fills with Happiness*, *You Hold Me Up*, and *When We Are Kind*. Her YA/ adult books include *Tilly: A Story of Hope and Resilience*, *Tilly and the Crazy Eights*, and *Lucy and Lola*. She is a proud mom of teenage twins, and is of Cree, Lakota, and Scottish ancestry. Monique is well known for her storytelling, spirit of generosity, and belief that love is medicine. She and her family are blessed to live on the traditional territory of the WSÁNEC´ people, also known as Victoria, Canada.

Monique says, "I grew up in a house where sports were integral to our lives, and have continued this with my children. Being part of a team has taught me a great deal about how to navigate life, friendships, and relationships in general, as well as the importance of having goals and dreams and doing the hard work to achieve them. I wanted to write a story that reflected this and came from the perspective of a young

Indigenous girl. Jacqueline teaches us we may not always win, but showing up and giving one hundred percent is important. Not only in sports, but also in life."

Online, Monique can be found at moniquegraysmith .com, @ltldrum (Twitter), and @moniquegraysmithauthor (Instagram).

CLAIRE KANN is the author of *Let's Talk About Love* and *If It Makes You Happy* and is an award-winning online storyteller. "Guilt Trip" was inspired by her love of family drama and music, with Pumpkin Spice being a direct parallel to the band The Donnas. The main character, Mia, is a tribute to bassist Maya Ford—the first plus-sized musician Claire saw growing up who affected her in a significant way. Her next YA novel, *The Marvelous*, is scheduled for release in summer 2021. Find her online at claire kann.com.

AMANDA LOVELACE is the author of the celebrated "women are some kind of magic" series. she is also a two-time winner of the good-reads choice award for best poetry, as well as a *usa today & publishers weekly*

best-selling author. when she isn't reading, writing, or drinking a much-needed cup of coffee, you can find her casting spells from her home in a (very) small town on the jersey shore.
instagram: @ladybookmad
twitter: @ladybookmad

HILLARY MONAHAN is the *New York Times* bestselling author of *Mary: The Summoning* and the author of the critically acclaimed *The Awesome*, written under the name Eva Darrows. She likes spooky, funny, and soft in equal parts. She wrote a variant on "the Little Mermaid" as a rejection of the lovelorn girl dissolving into sea foam arc, à la Hans Christian Andersen, and minus Disney's victimhood narrative that relies so heavily on everyone else's bravery. This Little Mermaid is confident in herself and her body, driven, and most of all, *hungry*. Hillary's most accessible on Twitter at @HillaryMonahan.

I'm **CASSANDRA NEWBOULD**, creator and host of *Fat Like Me*, a podcast and community celebrating body diversity in life, in entertainment, and especially in literature. As a kid, I longed for stories that showed people of all sizes following their dreams, and spent so much time searching for books that told fat kids *they can*. Sadly, I found so many that said *they can't*

instead. So I, along with a fabulous group of contributors, created *Every Body Shines* because we wanted to celebrate fat bodies loving ourselves, experiencing flirtations and first loves, navigating friendships and families, pursuing goals, and following our dreams. To show the world we don't have to wait to enjoy our lives, but that *we can*, right now. I hope that *Every Body Shines* is a permission slip to love yourself in the moment, exactly as you are.

My story, "Shatter," is a tribute to those who still dance in the shadows. I found my confidence when I became a dancer. My only regret is that it took so long for me to let go of my fear. I hope that anyone who reads "Shatter" will also find a way to dance in the light. You deserve it! Like my main character, Brianna, I was hit as a pedestrian by a van. While that accident changed my life forever, I wanted to show in "Shatter" that we are so much more than our disabilities, that every person shines in their power and that all they need to do is have the courage to find it.

When I'm not writing or taping a show, you can find me somewhere in the woods or on the water, with the love of my life, my three amazing kiddos, and three derpy doggos. Readers, we get the happy endings too. Don't forget it!

You can find me on Twitter at @CassNwrites and @FatLikeMePod, and on Instagram at @cass_catalano_new bould, and hear *Fat Like Me* on Buzzsprout, SoundCloud, or any of your favorite listening platforms. I'm also a cohost of the *Better Than Brunch* videocast on YouTube.

FRANCINA SIMONE is a conscious being trying to uplift the world one conversation at a time. *Smash It!* is her debut about a curvy girl throwing caution to the wind to discover who she is and what it really means to love. Body positivity as a movement has had such an impact on her life, and she hopes to see the movement change the way we see bodies not only in life, but in all forms of media, and especially when we look in the mirror.

Find Francina online at francinasimone.com, on YouTube, or on Instagram at @francinasimone.

REBECCA SKY is a fat spoonie babe who lives on Vancouver Island with her rocker hubby, their quirky Boston terrier, Winston, and her leviathan book and plant collection (that she somehow managed to squeeze into their tiny home). Her debut series The Love Curse started on Wattpad before receiving over 10 million reads and going on to be picked up by Hachette's Hodder Children's Books. With a passion for intersectional body positivity (bopo) and a desire to see people like her represented in more books, Rebecca spends her time writing about fat and disabled babes in all kinds of situations, and she won't stop until every YA trope is filled with bopo protagonists. This is why she's extra excited about *Every Body Shines* and she can't wait for you to meet Maxine Cooper, the brave, talented, and badass teen volunteer firefighter, from her story "Liar, Liar, Pants on Fire." Maxine's story was inspired by that time an actual barn fell on one of Rebecca's friends (ouch!) and of course by the Australian firefighters, animal conservationists, and volunteers who risked their lives at the wildfires that claimed over 1 billion animals in early 2020.

Visit Rebecca online at rebeccasky.com, on Twitter at @RebeccaSky, or on Instagram or TikTok at @TheRebeccaSky.

© SHAWNTE SIMS

RENÉE WATSON is a *New York Times* bestselling author. Her novel *Piecing Me Together* received a Newbery Honor and Coretta Scott King Award. She says, "I am writing for the girls I know, the girl I was. To write realistic fiction and not include characters with big bodies is to erase our existence. They exist, I exist, and our stories deserve to take up space on the page." Renée's books include *Love Is a Revolution*; *Ways to Make Sunshine* and *Ways to Grow Love*; *Some Places More Than Others*; *This Side of Home*; *What Momma Left Me*; *Betty Before X*, cowritten with Ilyasah Shabazz; and *Watch Us Rise*, cowritten with Ellen Hagan, as well as two acclaimed picture books: *A Place Where Hurricanes Happen* and *Harlem's Little Blackbird*, which was nominated for an NAACP Image Award. Renée grew up in Portland, Oregon, and splits her time between Portland and New York City. Find Renée online at reneewatson.net and @reneewauthor.

CATHERINE ADEL WEST is an editor living and working in Chicago. She graduated with both her bachelor's and master of science in journalism from the University of Illinois, Urbana. Her work is published in *Black Fox*, *Five2One*, *Better Than Starbucks*, *Doors Ajar*, *805 Lit+Art*, the *Helix Literary Magazine*, *Lunch Ticket*, and *Gay Magazine*. *Saving Ruby King*, released in 2020, was her first novel. *Becoming Sara King*, Catherine's sophomore book, is slated for release in summer 2022.

Catherine wrote "Orion's Star" as a love letter to all the Black girls who have big dreams and long odds. The story serves as a testament that nothing is impossible, no matter your color or size or background.

Follow her on Twitter and Instagram at @cawest329 or visit her website, www.catherineadelwest.com.

JENNIFER YEN is a Taiwanese American author who tells stories about love, family, and the immigrant experience. Drawing inspiration from her own childhood, she highlights the struggles of growing up between two clashing cultures, and the pressure to conform to the expectations of both. She hopes her stories remind readers that what matters most is not the size of your clothes but that of your heart. Her debut novel, *A Taste for Love*, serves up food, fun, and flirtation during a baking competition that will leave you hungry for more. Find Jennifer online at jenyenwrites.com and @JenYen Writes. If you find Jennifer wandering around aimlessly, please return her to the nearest milk tea shop.

ACKNOWLEDGMENTS

When we tell our stories, we have the amazing gift of an opportunity to change the narrative, one conversation at a time. Because when we finally give ourselves permission to become ourselves, to take pride in ourselves, to allow ourselves the entire world, we can accomplish anything.

I can't deny that the journey is incredibly easier with a team behind you. I'm absolutely humbled by those who have come together to make this collection of dreams a reality.

✦ ✦ ✦

Thanks to my publishing team:

My greatest champion, my agent, Jordan Hamessley— You are truly an amplifier of underrepresented voices. Thank you for helping me breathe life into this book. It was a joy brainstorming with you about what I hoped to create and now it's REAL!

Joanna Volpe and Suzie Townsend—I am thankful to be a part of the amazing family at New Leaf Literary.

My editor extraordinaire, Sarah Shumway—I am forever grateful for the home you and Bloomsbury gave to me and *Every Body Shines*. I knew from the moment we first talked that you understood the heart of this collection and you've proven it over and over again.

The rest of the team at Bloomsbury—Erica Barmash, Ksenia Winnicki, Claire Stetzer, Oona Patrick, Donna Mark, John Candell, Alona Fryman, Teresa Sarmiento, Faye Bi, Jo Forshaw—I appreciate and thank you for all the work you do.

Thaddeus Coates—Thank you for bringing such a brilliant, shining cover to life!

Aubrey Gordon—Thank you for giving our book such an amazing and heartfelt foreword.

And the contributors—You are the magic that makes this collection shine. I am honored to have worked with each of you. I cannot even begin to express how much your stories mean to me.

✦ ✦ ✦

Thanks to my family:

Max—You'll always be my sweet baboo. Thank you for supporting my *occasional cafe* dreams over the last twenty-plus years while I discovered who I wanted to be when I grew up. You are my forever and I love growing old with you.

Niko, Keaton, Alexander—You are my heartbeat, my breath, my blood. I am honored to be your Mama. The three of you are the best parts of my journey. Love y'all to the moon and back.

Mom and Dad—Thank you for raising me with love to be strong, proud, and confident. Your story together is the fiber fairy tales are made of.

Jamey—I love that we're sisters. We will always thrive because we have each other.

My might-as-well-be-my-kids—Aaron, Kelsey, Maya: You're bright lights in my heart.

Gerry and Caroline—Thank you for loving me as a daughter.

All the powerful women who helped raise me—Beckey, Cindy, Wanda, Gretchen, Lynda, Kelly, Faith, and Leslie. And the women I grew up with—Heather, Tiana, Catie, Leah-Lani, MaryBeth, Anne, Whitney, Ashlyn, Jody, Kassie, Katherine, Leslie, Mickey, Britton, Rochelle, Monique, Latricia, Ginge, Hayley, Amy, Chrissy. You've all formed the backbone of my life's journey, thank you for lifting me up. Heather Cole—Near or far, we are family.

Sam, Rex, Annie, Scott—I always wanted a lot of siblings, now I have them. Extra love to all the littles—Bella, Lily, Rupert, Imogen, Spencer.

To Jimmy, Erik, Dov, Will, Noopy, John, the rest of my Runion, Catalano, Cove Point, Jupiter, Florida, Cali, Vegas, Pine Ridge Reservation, family and friends, and my mIRC-DOAEOTAD crew—This would have been a lonely adventure without you in it.

✦ ✦ ✦

A special thanks to my writing peers:

PCC for life crew—Aften Brook Szymanski, Kim Johnson, Sheena Boekweg, Shauna Barnes Holyoak, Maura Jortner, Danielle Doolittle, Brent Williamson, Laura Valin-Peñalba, Jamie Lane, Heather Dean Brewer, Jueneke Wong, Shelly Brown. Kim Johnson: Thanks for always being a shoulder.

Taj McCoy—You're the best part of my *Fat Like Me* podcast experience. A kickass producer, a wonderful human and a fantastic friend.

BTB FAM—Taj McCoy, Charish Reid, Denise Williams, I can't imagine what pandemic life would have been like without our Sunday sessions. You keep me sane!

Diana Pinguicha—You push me to be a better writer and you're a true confidante.

Ashley Hearn—Advice Queen, thanks for helping me hone my skills and for your friendship.

Diana and Ashley—I will forever be grateful that RT brought us together.That goes for you too, Monica Hoffman and Elly Blake!

Lori Lee—Thank you for your revision eye and uplifting chats.

The entire PNW crew—Cindy Baldwin, Joy McCullough, Shari Green, Gabby Byrne, Julie Artz, Rebecca Sky, Nafiza Azad, Erin Latimer, Roise Thor, Rachel Griffin, and Rebecca Schaeffer—I miss our weekend writing retreats.

To the guests of *Fat Like Me*—Thank you.

And to every reader—Thank you for being perfectly you. Dream BIG! Find the light. Become your shine, and may your path burn eternal.